International Praise for

Beneath the Bleeding

"McDermid's previous novels have set the bar vertiginously high, but the latest outing for criminal profiler Tony Hill and DCI Carol Jordan has all the craft, panache, and pace that we have come to expect from this outstanding writer. . . . Vintage stuff: unplug the phone, lock the door, and prepare to read in a sitting." —*The Guardian* (London)

"If Rankin is the king of British crime, Val McDermid is undoubtedly the queen. . . . Hill and Jordan are compelling creations and their encounters in *Beneath the Bleeding* fairly crackle. McDermid is a consummate plotter, so there are pleasing twists and turns in this first-rate story." —*The Observer* (London)

"This classy police procedural—[the] latest in a series featuring the criminal profiler Tony Hill—compels from start to finish. . . . A narrative of nerve-stretching immediacy. . . . Sharply written, suspenseful, and full of insight into the world of the criminal psychologist." —*The Times* (London)

"Tackled cleverly, with a well-concealed plot twist making a political point. . . . An accomplished performance. . . . This is Britain's most successful series featuring a woman police detective." —*The Sunday Times* (London)

"[McDermid is] the queen of serial killers. . . . As a former journalist, few can scoop Val on throat-clutching narrative, but at the same time she is marvelous on the subplot details."   —*Daily Mail* (London)

"Edgy and dark as always. . . . I love it."
                                        —*The Express* (London)

"This is a book that works on more than one level. It fulfills the criteria of a very good contemporary crime thriller in terms of excitement, topicality, and its sense of authenticity. But it delivers more than this: the complex and unpredictable relationship between Hill and Jordan lies at the heart of the series and is one of its greatest strengths. McDermid's writing gets better and better."
                                        —*The Spectator* (London)

"Val McDermid again proves herself one of Britain's top crime authors in *Beneath the Bleeding*, a sophisticated, complex, and gripping story. . . . It's a joy to follow along with Hill and Jordan. . . . Leave yourself lots of time for this one. I finished it at 3 a.m."
                                        —*The Globe and Mail* (Toronto)

About the Author

Scottish crime writer VAL MCDERMID is the author of twenty-two novels. Her books have won the Macallan Gold Dagger Award and a Los Angeles Times Book Prize, have been selected for the *New York Times Book Review*'s 100 Notable Books of the Year, and have been nominated for the Edgar Award. She lives in the north of England.

Beneath the Bleeding

A Novel

VAL McDERMID

HARPER

NEW YORK • LONDON • TORONTO • SYDNEY

HARPER

Lines from *Four Quartets*: "East Coker" by T. S. Eliot are reproduced by
permission of Faber and Faber Ltd.

Originally published in Great Britain in 2009 by HarperCollins
Publishers.

HarperCollins books may be purchased for educational, business, or
sales promotional use. For information please write: Special Markets
Department, HarperCollins Publishers, 10 East 53rd Street, New York,
NY 10022.

FIRST U.S. EDITION

Designed by Palimpsest Book Production Limited, Grangemouth, Stirlingshire

Library of Congress Cataloging-in-Publication Data has
been applied for.

ISBN 978-0-06-168897-3

09 10 11 12 13 ID/RRD 10 9 8 7 6 5 4 3 2 1

Acknowledgements

The music is what keeps me going through a book. It's the unacknowledged balm, the inspiration, the rhythm and delight. I work in a room alone so I can have it as loud or as soft as I want. I can listen to the same track as many times as I feel like without anybody accusing me of trying to drive them crazy. Every book is accompanied by old friends and new discoveries. So for this book, thank you to Richard Thompson, Sigur Rós, Deacon Blue, Roddy Woomble, Mary Gauthier, Ketil Bjornstad, Elvis Costello, Rob Dougan, Michael Marra, Rab Noakes, Karine Polwart, Wolfgang Amadeus Mozart and the Blue Nile. Thanks too to Radio Scotland's Iain Anderson, who has cost me a small fortune in CDs and downloads. And a particularly big hand for Sue Turnbull who came all the way from Australia to introduce me to Sigur Rós and Peter Temple.

I had two major orthopaedic surgeries between the previous book and this one, and I am very grateful to Mr David Weir and the nursing team at the Newcastle Nuffield Hospital for my magnificent new knees, and also for the inspiration for one element of this novel.

Some of the people who helped with this book have asked not to be named. I hope they don't feel their trust was misplaced. Harry and Louise assisted me with aspects of the medical stuff and the helpful staff at the Alnwick Garden unwittingly provided food for thought.

Finally, thanks to my loyal team at Gregory and Co, at HarperCollins and at Coastal Productions, particularly Jane, Julia, Anne, Sandra and Ken.

But most of all, thanks to Kelly, who makes everything better.

This one is for the members of the wedding,
who helped to create the best of memories.

Beneath the bleeding hands we feel
The sharp compassion of the healer's art

From *Four Quartets*: 'East Coker'
T S Eliot

Friday

The phases of the moon have an inexplicable but incontrovertible effect on the mentally ill. Ask any psychiatric nurse. For them, it's a truth universally acknowledged. None of them volunteers for overtime around the time of the full moon. Not unless they are absolutely desperate. It's also a truth that makes the behavioural scientists uneasy; it's not something that can be laid at the door of an abusive childhood or an inability to relate socially. It's an external rhythm that no amount of treatment can override. It drags the tides and it pulls the deranged out of their hampered orbits.

The internal dynamics of Bradfield Moor Secure Hospital were as susceptible to the undertow of the full moon as its name suggested. According to some of its staff, Bradfield Moor was a warehousing facility for those too dangerously crazy to walk free; to others, it was a haven for minds too fragile for the rough and tumble of life on the outside; and to the rest, it was a temporary refuge that offered the hope of a return to a loosely defined normality. The third group was, unsurprisingly, heavily outnumbered and heartily despised by the other two.

That night, it wasn't enough that the moon was full. It was also subject to a partial eclipse. The milky shadows of the lunar surface gradually metamorphosed through sickly yellow to dark orange as the earth moved between its satellite and the sun. For most of those observing the eclipse, it possessed a mysterious beauty, provoking awe and admiration. For Lloyd Allen, one of Bradfield Moor's less grounded inmates, it provided proof absolute of his conviction that the last days were at hand and thus his duty was to bring as many to his maker as he could. He had been hospitalized before he had achieved his goal of spilling as much blood as possible so that the souls of its owners might ascend more easily to heaven at the imminent second coming. His mission burned all the brighter within him for being thwarted.

Lloyd Allen was not a stupid man and this made the task of his keepers that much harder. The psychiatric nurses were well versed in low cunning and found it relatively easy to head off at the pass. It was much harder to spot the machinations of those who were deranged but smart. Recently, Allen had devised a method of avoiding taking his medication. The more experienced nurses were wise to tricks of this sort and knew how to subvert them, but the newly qualified, like Khalid Khan, still lacked the necessary canniness.

On the night of the full moon, Allen had managed to avoid taking both previous doses of the chemical cosh that Khan believed he had administered. By the time the eclipse began to be visible, Allen's head was filled with a low thrumming mantra. 'Bring them to me, bring them to me, bring them to me,' echoed continuously inside his brain. From his room, he could see a corner of the moon, the prophesied sea of blood occluding its face. It was time. It really was time. Agitated, he clenched his fists and jerked his lower arms up and down every couple of seconds like a demented boxer raising and lowering his guard.

He turned to face the door and stumbled awkwardly towards it. He had to get out so he could complete his mission. The nurse would be here soon with his final medication for the night. Then God would give him the strength he needed. God would get him out of this room. God would show him the way. God knew what he had to do. He would bring them to Him. The time was ripe, the moon was bursting with blood. The signs were beginning and he had a task to fulfil. He was chosen, he was the road to salvation for the sinners. He would bring them to God.

The pool of light illuminated a small area on the top of a low-grade institutional desk. A file lay open, a hand holding a pen resting on one side of the page. In the background, Moby yearned plaintively for the spiders. The CD had been a gift, something Dr Tony Hill would never have chosen for himself. But somehow it had become an integral part of the after-hours work ritual.

Tony went to rub his gritty eyes, forgetting about his new reading glasses. 'Ow,' he yelped as the nose-pieces bit into his flesh. His little finger caught the edge of the rimless glasses, sending them spinning off his face to land askew on the file he'd been studying. He could picture the look of indulgent amusement the moment would have provoked on the face of

Detective Chief Inspector Carol Jordan, the Moby donor. His distracted clumsiness had long been a standing joke between them.

The one thing she couldn't tease or taunt him about was that he was still at his desk at half past eight on a Friday night. When it came to reluctance to leave the office until everything possible had been dealt with, she was at least his equal. If she'd been around she would have understood why he was still here, going over the brief he'd so painstakingly prepared for the Parole Board. A brief they'd chosen blithely to ignore when they'd released Bernard Sharples into the care of the Probation Service. No longer a danger to the public, his lawyer had persuaded them. A model prisoner who had co-operated with everything the authorities had asked of him. The very exemplar of remorse.

Well, of course Sharples had been a model prisoner, Tony thought bitterly. It was easy to behave when the objects of your desire were so far beyond your reach that even the most obsessed fantasist would struggle to conjure up anything remotely like temptation. Sharples would offend again, he knew it in his bones. And it would be his fault in part because he had failed to make his case strongly enough.

He retrieved his glasses and marked a couple of paragraphs with his pen. He could have, should have stated his case more firmly, left no cracks for the defence to slither through. He would have had to assert as fact what he knew to be conjecture based on years of working with serial offenders plus the gut feeling that came from reading between the lines of his interviews with Sharples. But there was no place for shades of grey in the Parole Board's world of black and white. It seemed that Tony still had to learn that honesty was seldom the best policy when it came to the criminal justice system.

He pulled a pad of Post-It notes towards him but before he could scribble anything down, a noise from outside penetrated his office. He wasn't generally disturbed by the miscellaneous noises that made up the soundtrack to life inside Bradfield Moor; the soundproofing was surprisingly effective, and besides, the worst of the anguish was generally acted out far away from the offices where people with degrees and status worked.

More noise. It sounded like a football match or a sectarian riot. Certainly more than he could reasonably ignore. Sighing, Tony stood up, tossing his glasses on the desk as he made for the door. Anything had to be better than this.

Not many people regarded a job at Bradfield Moor as a dream come true. But for Jerzy Golabeck it represented more than he had ever imagined possible growing up in Płock. Nothing much had happened in Płock since the Polish kings decamped in 1138. The only work to be had these days was in the petrochemical refineries where wages were pitiful and industrial disease a way of life. Jerzy's narrow horizons had widened eye-poppingly when Poland had acceded to the European Union. He'd been one of the first to board a cheap flight from Krakow to Leeds/Bradford Airport and the prospect of a new life. From his perspective, minimum wage approximated a king's ransom. And working with the inmates of Bradfield

Moor wasn't so different from dealing with a senile grandfather who thought Lech Walesa might still be the coming man.

So Jerzy had bent the truth and manufactured a level of experience of dealing with the mentally ill that bore little relationship to the reality of his past as a production line worker in the pickle-canning factory. So far, it hadn't been an issue. The nurses and orderlies were more concerned with containment than treatment. They administered drugs and cleared up messes. Any attempts at cure or mitigation were left to doctors, psychiatrists, therapists of varying schools, and clinical psychologists. It appeared that nobody expected much more from Jerzy than that he turned up on time and didn't shy away from the physical unpleasantnesses that cropped up every shift. That much he could manage with ease.

Along the way, he'd developed a shrewd eye for what was going on around him. Nobody was more surprised at that than he was. But there was no denying that Jerzy seemed to have an instinct for spotting when patients shifted away from the equilibrium that made Bradfield Moor possible. He was one of the few workers in the hospital who would ever have noticed anything amiss with Lloyd Allen. The problem was that he was confident enough by then to believe he could deal with it himself. He wasn't the first twenty-four-year-old to have an inflated idea of his capabilities. Just one of the few who would die for it.

As soon as he entered Lloyd Allen's room, the hair on Jerzy's arms stood on end. Allen was standing in the middle of the cramped space, his big shoulders tensed. The fast flick of his eyes told Jerzy that either the medication had suffered a sudden and spectacular failure or Allen had somehow avoided taking it. Either way, it looked like the voices in his head were the only ones Allen was interested in listening to. 'Time for your meds, Lloyd,' Jerzy said, his voice deliberately offhand.

'Can't do that.' Allen's voice was a strained grunt. He rose slightly on the balls of his feet, his hands sliding over each other as if he were washing them. The muscles of his forearms danced and twitched.

'You know you need them.'

Allen shook his head.

Jerzy mirrored the movement. 'You don't take your meds, I have to report it. Then it gets hard on you, Lloyd. That's not how we want it to be, is it?'

Allen launched himself at Jerzy, his right elbow catching him under the breastbone and knocking the wind from him. As Jerzy doubled over, retching for air, Allen barged past, knocking him to the floor as he made for the door. In the doorway, Allen came to an abrupt halt then swung round. Jerzy tried to make himself look small and unthreatening, but Allen advanced all the same. He raised his foot and kicked Jerzy in the stomach, emptying his lungs in a dizzying explosion of pain. While Jerzy clawed at his gut, Allen calmly reached down and ripped his keycard from the clip at his waist. 'I have to bring them to Him,' he grunted, making for the door again.

Jerzy couldn't stop the terrible convulsive groans as his body struggled for oxygen. But his brain was still working properly. He knew he had to get to the panic button in the hallway. Armed with Jerzy's key,

Allen could roam almost anywhere in the hospital. He could open the rooms of other inmates. It wouldn't take long to free enough of his fellows to seriously outnumber the staff on duty at this time of the evening.

Coughing and gagging, strings of spittle trailing down his chin, Jerzy forced himself to his knees and shuffled closer to the bed. Clawing at the frame, he managed to drag himself to his feet. Clutching his guts, he stumbled into the hall. He could see Allen up ahead struggling to swipe the keycard through the reader mounted by the door that would release him into the main part of the building. You had to get the speed of the swipe just right. Jerzy knew that, but Allen, thankfully, did not. Allen thumped the reader and tried again. Swaying, Jerzy tried to cover the distance to the panic button as quietly as he could.

He wasn't quiet enough. Something alerted Allen and he swung round. 'Bring them to him,' he roared, charging. His weight alone was enough to bring Jerzy's weakened frame to the floor again. Jerzy wrapped his arms around his head. It was no defence. The last thing he felt was a terrible pressure behind his eyes as Allen stamped on his head with all his strength.

Opening his door brought Tony a sudden swell of volume. Voices shouting, swearing and screaming funnelled up the stairwell. The scariest thing about it was that nobody had pushed the emergency alarm. That suggested something so sudden and so violent that no one had had the chance to follow the procedures that were supposedly drummed into them from day one of their training. They were too busy trying to contain whatever was going on.

8

Tony hustled along the corridor towards the stairs, hitting the panic button as he went. A loud klaxon immediately blasted out. *Christ, if you were crazy already, what would this do to your head?* He was running by the time he reached the stairs but he slowed his pace enough to look down the stairwell to see what he could see.

Nothing, was the short answer. The raised voices seemed to be coming from the corridor off to the right, but they were distorted by the acoustics and the distance. Suddenly, there was the tinkle and crash of glass breaking. Then a shocking splinter of silence.

'Oh, fuck,' someone said clearly, disgust the apparent emotion behind the words. Then the shouting began again, the note of panic unmistakable. A scream, then the sound of scuffling. Without thinking about it, Tony had started down the stairs, trying to see what was going on.

As he rounded the final turn of the stairs, bodies spilled out of the corridor where the noise had come from. Two nurses were backing towards him, supporting a third man. An orderly, judging by the few areas of pale green scrubs left untouched by blood. They were leaving a smudged trail of scarlet behind as they scrambled backwards as fast as they could manage.

Carnage, Tony thought as a burly figure emerged from the corridor, swinging a fire axe in front of himself as if it were a scythe and he a grim reaper. His jeans and polo shirt were spattered with blood; the blade of the axe shed a fine spray with every swing. The burly man was intent on his prey, steadily pursuing them as they retreated. 'Bring them to him. Nowhere to hide,' he said in a low monotone. 'Bring them to him. Nowhere to hide.' He was gaining on them. Another couple of strides and the axe blade would be slicing through flesh again.

Even though the axeman wasn't a patient of his, Tony knew who he was. He'd made a point of familiarizing himself with the files of any inmates considered capable of violence. Partly because they interested him, but also because it felt like a kind of insurance policy. Tonight, it looked like he was about to lose his no-claims bonus.

Tony stopped a few steps from the bottom of the staircase. 'Lloyd,' he called softly.

Allen didn't break stride. He swung the axe again, in rhythm with his mantra. 'Bring them to him. Nowhere to hide,' he said, sweeping the blade inches from the nurses.

Tony took a deep breath and squared his shoulders. 'This is not the way to bring them to him,' he said loudly, with all the authority he could summon. 'This is not what he wants from you, Lloyd. You've got it wrong.'

Allen paused, turning his head towards Tony. He frowned, puzzled as a dog tormented by a wasp. 'It's time,' he snarled.

'You're right about that,' Tony said, moving down a step. 'It is time. But you're going about it the wrong way. Now, put down the axe and we'll figure out a better way of doing it.' He tried to keep his face stern, not to reveal the fear curdling his stomach. Where the hell was the back-up team? He had no illusions about what he could do here. He could maybe hold Allen up long enough for the nurses and the wounded orderly to get clear. But good as he was with the deranged and the demented, he knew he wasn't good enough to restore Lloyd Allen to anything like equilibrium. He doubted he could even get him to lower the weapon. He had to try, he knew that. But where the *fuck* was the cavalry?

Allen stopped swinging the axe through its long arc and raised it at an angle across his body like a baseball player preparing for the strike. 'It's time,' he said again. 'And you're not him.' And he launched himself across the gap between them.

He was so fast that all Tony could register was a slash of red and a glint of polished metal. Then a seam of pain exploded from the middle of his leg. Tony toppled like a felled tree, too shocked even to scream. Inside his head, a light bulb detonated. Then blackness.

List 2

Belladonna

Ricin

Oleander

Strychnine

Cocaine

Taxus Baccata

Sunday

Thomas Denby studied the chart again. He was puzzled. He'd diagnosed a severe chest infection when he'd first examined Robbie Bishop. He'd had no reason to doubt that diagnosis. He'd seen enough chest infections in the twenty years since he'd qualified and chosen to specialize in respiratory ailments. In the twelve hours since the footballer had been admitted, Denby's team had been administering antibiotics and steroids according to the directions he'd given them. But there had been no improvement in Bishop's condition. In fact, he had deteriorated to the point where the duty SHO had been prepared to risk wrath by summoning Denby from his bed. Mere House Officers didn't do that to consultants unless they were very, very nervous.

Denby replaced the chart and gave the young man lying on the bed his casually professional smile, all teeth and dimples. His eyes, however, were not smiling; they were scanning Bishop's face and his torso. The sweat of his fever had glued the hospital gown to his chest, revealing the outline of well-defined muscles currently straining to drag breath into his

13

lungs. When Denby had first examined him, Bishop had complained of weakness, nausea and pain in his joints as well as the obvious difficulty in breathing. Spasms of coughing had doubled him over, their intensity bringing colour back to his pale face. The X-rays had shown fluid on his lungs; the obvious conclusion was the one that Denby had drawn.

Now, it was beginning to look as if whatever ailed Robbie Bishop was no ordinary chest infection. His heart rate was all over the place. His temperature had climbed a further degree and a half. His lungs were incapable of keeping his blood oxygen levels stable, even with the assistance of the oxygen mask. Now, as Denby watched, his eyelids fluttered and stayed shut. Denby frowned. 'Has he lost consciousness before?' he asked the SHO.

She shook her head. 'He's been mildly delirious because of the fever – I'm not sure how aware he's been of where he is. But he's been responsive until now.'

An insistent beeping kicked in, the screen revealing a new low in Bishop's blood oxygen level. 'We need to intubate,' Denby said, sounding distracted. 'And more fluids. I think he's a little dehydrated.' *Not that that would explain the fever, or the cough.* The SHO, galvanized by the instruction, hurried out of the small room that was the best Bradfield Cross Hospital could provide for those who required their privacy even in extremis. Denby rubbed his chin, wondering. Robbie Bishop was in peak condition; fit, strong and, according to his club doctor, he had been perfectly well after Friday's training session. He'd missed Saturday's game, diagnosed initially by the same club doctor as having some sort of flu bug. Now here he was, eighteen hours later, visibly deteriorating. And Thomas Denby had no idea why, nor how to make it stop.

It wasn't a position he was accustomed to. He was, he knew, a bloody good doctor. A skilled diagnostician, a cunning and often inspired clinician, and a good enough politician to make sure his department's needs were seldom frustrated by the bureaucrats. He pretty much sailed through his professional life, rarely given pause by the ailments his patients presented. Robbie Bishop felt like an affront to his talent.

As the SHO returned with the intubation kit and a couple of nurses, Denby sighed. He glanced at the door. On the other side, he knew, was Robbie Bishop's team manager. Martin Flanagan had spent the night slumped in a chair next to his star player. His expensive suit was rumpled now, his craggy face rendered sinister by a scribble of stubble. They'd already gone head to head when Denby had insisted the pugnacious Ulsterman leave the room while the doctors consulted. 'Do you know what that lad's worth to Bradfield Victoria?' Flanagan had demanded.

Denby had eyed him coldly. 'He's worth exactly the same to me as every other patient I treat,' he'd said. 'I don't sit on the touchline telling you what tactics to employ. So let me do my job without interference. I need you to give my patient his privacy while I examine him.' The manager had left, grumbling, but Denby knew he'd still be waiting, his face pinched and anxious, desperate to hear something that would contradict the deterioration he'd already witnessed.

'When you're done with that, let's start him on

AZT,' he said to his SHO. There was nothing left to try but the powerful retroviral medication that might just give them pause enough to figure out what was wrong with Robbie Bishop.

Monday

'Remind me again why I let you open that third bottle,' Detective Chief Inspector Carol Jordan sighed, putting the car in gear and inching forward a few yards.

'Because it was the first time you've graced us with a visit since we moved to the Dales and because I have to be in Bradfield this morning and you don't have a proper spare room. So there was no point in driving back last night.' Her brother Michael leaned forward to fiddle with the radio. Carol slapped his hand away.

'Leave it be,' she said.

Michael groaned. 'Bradfield Sound. Who knew my life would come down to this? Local radio at its most parochial.'

'I need to hear what's happening on my patch.'

Michael looked sceptical. 'You run the Major Incident Team. You're affiliated to the British equivalent of the FBI. You don't need to know if there's a burst water main causing problems for traffic on Methley Way. Or that some footballer's been carted off to hospital with chest problems.'

'Hey, Mr IT. Wasn't it you who taught me the "micro becomes macro" mantra? I like to know what's happening at the bottom of the food chain because it sometimes provokes unexpected events at the other end. And he's not just "some footballer". He's Robbie Bishop. Midfield general of Bradfield Victoria. And a local lad to boot. His female fans will be staking out Bradfield Cross as we speak. Possible public order issues.'

Michael subsided with a pout. 'Whatever. Have it your own way, Sis. Thank god their reception doesn't stretch far from the city. I'd have lost my mind if you'd made me listen to this all the way in.' He rolled his head on his neck, wincing at the crackling it produced. 'Haven't you got one of those blue lights that you can slap on the car roof?'

'Yes,' Carol said, easing forward with the traffic flow, praying this time it would keep moving. She felt sweaty and faintly sick in spite of the shower she'd had less than an hour ago. 'But I'm only supposed to use it in emergencies. And before you go there, no. This is not an emergency. This is just the rush hour.'

As she spoke, the clotted traffic suddenly began to flow. Within a couple of hundred yards, it was hard to figure out quite why it had taken twenty minutes to travel half a mile when now they were moving relatively smoothly.

Michael frowned slightly, studying his sister, then said, 'So, Sis, how's it going with Tony?'

Carol tried not to let her exasperation show. She thought she'd got away with it. A whole weekend with her parents, her brother and his partner without any of them mentioning that name. 'It's working out

18

pretty well, actually. I like the flat. He's a very good landlord.'

Michael tutted. 'You know that's not what I meant.'

Carol sighed, edging in front of a Mercedes who blared his horn at her. 'We probably saw more of each other when we were living on opposite sides of the city,' she said.

'I thought . . .'

Hands tight on the wheel. 'You thought wrong. Michael, we're a pair of workaholics. He loves his nutters and I've had a new unit to get up to speed. Not to mention trying to put Paula back together again,' she added, her face tightening at the thought.

'That's a pity.' The glance he gave her was critical. 'Neither of you is getting any younger. If I've learned anything from being with Lucy it's that life's a lot easier when you share the nuts and bolts with somebody on the same wavelength. And I think you and Tony Hill are totally that.'

Carol risked a quick glance to check whether he was taking the piss. 'The man who once kind of, almost, sort of, maybe thought you might be a serial killer? This is the man you think is on the same wavelength as me?'

Michael rolled his eyes. 'Stop hiding behind the history.'

'It's not about hiding. History like ours, you need crampons and oxygen to get over it.' Carol found a space in the traffic and edged to the kerb, hazard lights flashing. 'This is the part where you run away,' she said in a bad imitation of Shrek.

'You're dropping me here?' Michael sounded mildly outraged.

'It'll take me ten minutes to get round to the front of the Institute,' Carol said, leaning past him to point out of the passenger window. 'If you cut through the new shopping arcade, you'll be at your client meeting in three.'

'God you're right. We've only been away from the city for three months and already I'm losing the mental map.' He put an arm across her shoulders, gave her cheek a dry kiss then climbed out of the car. 'Speak to you in the week.'

Ten minutes later, Carol walked into Bradfield Police headquarters. In the short gap between dropping Michael off and leaving the lift on the third floor, where the team she thought of as the ragged misfits was based, she had made the shift from sister to police officer. The only element the two personae shared was the mild hangover.

She carried on down a corridor whose lavender and off-white walls were broken up by doors of plate glass and steel. Their central sections were frosted so it was hard to see any detail of what was going on behind them unless it was happening on the floor or dangling from the ceiling. The tarted-up interiors still reminded her of an advertising agency. But then, modern policing often seemed to have as much to do with image as it did with catching villains. Happily, she'd managed to keep herself as close to the sharp end as was possible for an officer of her rank.

She pushed open the door of 316 and stepped into the land of the dead and the damaged. This early on a Monday morning, the living were thin on the ground. DC Stacey Chen, the team's IT wizard, barely glanced up from the pair of monitors on her desk, grunting something Carol took to be a greeting. 'Morning, Stacey,' Carol said. As she crossed to her office, Detective Sergeant Chris Devine stepped out from behind one of the long whiteboards that encircled their desks like covered wagons keeping the enemy at bay. Startled, Carol stopped in her tracks. Chris held her hands up in a placatory gesture.

'Sorry, guv. Didn't mean to freak you out.'

'No harm done.' Carol let her breath out in a sigh. 'We really do need to get those see-through incident boards.'

'What? Like they have on the telly?' Chris gave a small snort. 'Don't see the point, myself. I've always thought they're a proper bitch to read. All that background interference.' She fell into step beside Carol as her boss made for the glassed-off cubicle that served as her office. 'So what's the latest on Tony? How's he doing?'

It was, thought Carol, a funny way to put it. She gave a half-shrug and said, 'As far as I know, he's fine.' Her tone was calculated to close the subject.

Chris swung around so she was walking backwards in Carol's path, checking out her boss's expression. Her eyes widened. 'Oh my good god, you don't know, do you?'

'Don't know what?' Carol felt the clutch of panic in her stomach.

Chris put a hand on Carol's arm and indicated her office with a jerk of her head. 'I think we'd better sit down,' she said.

'Christ,' said Carol, allowing herself to be led inside. She made for her chair while Chris closed the door.

21

'I've only been in the Dales, not the North Pole. What the hell's been going on? What's happened to Tony?'

Chris responded to the urgency in her voice. 'He was attacked. By one of the inmates at Bradfield Moor.'

Carol's hands came up to her face, covering her cheeks and pushing her mouth into an O. She drew breath sharply. 'What happened?' Her voice was raised, almost a shout.

Chris ran a hand through her short salt-and pepper hair. 'There's no way to soften it, guv. He got in the way of a madman with a fire axe.'

Chris's voice sounded as if it was coming from a long way off. Never mind that Carol had inured herself to sights and sounds that would have made most people whimper and gibber. When it came to Tony Hill, she had a unique vulnerability. She might choose not to acknowledge it consciously, but at moments like this, it altered everything. 'What ...?' Her voice cracked. She cleared her throat. 'How bad is it?'

'From what I heard, his leg's pretty smashed up. He took it in the knee. Lost a lot of blood. It took a while for the paramedics to get to him, on account of there was a madman with an axe on the prowl,' Chris said.

Bad though this was, it was far less than her imagination had managed to conjure in a matter of seconds. Blood loss and a smashed knee were manageable. No big deal, really, in the great scheme of things. 'Jesus,' Carol said, relief in her released breath. 'What happened?'

'What I heard was that one of the inmates overpowered an orderly, got his key off him, trampled his head to a bloody pulp then got into the main part of the hospital where he broke the glass and got the axe.'

Carol shook her head. 'They have fire axes in Bradfield Moor? A secure mental hospital?'

'Apparently that's precisely why. It's secure. Lots of locked doors and wire-reinforced glass. Health and Safety says you have to be able to get the patients out in the event of fire and a failure of the electronic locking systems.' Chris shook her head. 'Bollocks, if you ask me.' She threw up her hands in the face of Carol's admonitory expression. 'Yeah, well. Better a few mad bastards burn than we get this kind of shit. One orderly dead, another one on the critical list whose internal organs are never going to be right again and Tony smashed up? I'd shed a few homicidal nutters to avoid that.' Somehow, the sentiment sounded even worse in Chris's strong Cockney accent.

'It's not an either/or, and you know it, Chris,' Carol said. Even though her own gut reaction matched that of her sergeant, she knew it was emotion and not common sense talking. But these days, only the reckless and the heedless casually spoke their mind in the workplace. Carol liked her mavericks. She didn't want to lose any of them because the wrong ears heard them sounding off, so she did her best to curb their excesses. 'So how did Tony get caught up in it?' she asked. 'Was it one of his patients?'

Chris shrugged. 'Dunno. Apparently he was the hero of the hour, though. Distracted the mad bastard enough for a couple of nurses to drag the injured orderly out of harm's way.'

But not enough to save himself. 'Why did nobody

contact me? Who was our duty officer this weekend? Sam, wasn't it?'

Chris shook her head. 'It was supposed to be Sam, but he swapped with Paula.'

Carol jumped up and opened the door. Scanning the room, she saw DC Paula McIntyre hanging her coat up. 'Paula? In here a minute,' she called. As the young detective crossed the room, Carol felt the familiar wash of guilt. Not so long ago, she had put Paula in harm's way and harm had come running. Never mind that it had been an officially sanctioned operation: Carol had been the one who had promised to protect Paula and had failed. The double whammy of that botched operation and the death of her closest colleague had set Paula teetering on the brink of abandoning her police career. Carol knew that place. She'd been there herself, and for scarily similar reasons. She'd offered what support she could to Paula, but it had been Tony who had talked her back from the edge. Carol had no idea what had passed between them, but it had made it possible for Paula to continue being a cop. And for that she was grateful, even if it meant having that constant reminder of her own inadequacy on her team.

Carol stepped aside to make way for Paula and returned to her chair. Paula leaned against the glass wall, arms folded as if that would disguise the weight she had lost. Her dark blonde hair looked as if she'd forgotten to comb it after towelling it dry and her charcoal trousers and sweater hung baggily on her. 'How's Tony?' she asked.

'I don't know, because I've only just found out

about the attack,' Carol said, careful not to make it sound like an accusation.

Paula looked stricken. 'Oh, shit,' she groaned. 'It never occurred to me that you wouldn't know.' She shook her head in frustration. 'They didn't even ring me, actually. The first I knew about it was when I turned on the TV on Saturday morning. I just assumed somebody would have called you . . .' her voice trailed off, dismayed.

'Nobody called me. I was having a family weekend in the Dales with my brother and my parents. So we didn't have the TV or the radio on. Do we know which hospital he's in?'

'Bradfield Cross,' Paula said. 'They operated on his knee on Saturday. I checked. They said he'd come out of surgery OK and he was comfortable.'

Carol got to her feet, grabbing her bag. 'Fine. That's where I'll be if you need me. I take it there's nothing fresh in the overnights that we need to concern ourselves with?'

Chris shook her head. 'Nothing new.'

'Just as well. There's plenty to be going on with.' She patted Paula's shoulder as she passed. 'I'd have made the same assumption,' she said on her way out. *But I'd still have called to make sure.*

Dry mouth. Too dry to swallow. That was just about the biggest thought that could make it through the cotton wadding filling his head. His eyelids flickered. Dimly, he knew there was a reason why opening them would be a bad idea, but he couldn't remember what it was. He wasn't even sure he could trust this fuzzy warning from his brain. What could be so bad about opening his eyes? People did it all the time and nothing bad happened to them.

The answer came with dizzying speed. 'About time,' the voice snapped from somewhere behind his left ear. Its critical edge was familiar but only historically so. It didn't seem to fit the ragged impression he retained of his current life.

Tony rolled his head to the side. The movement reawakened pain that was hard to locate specifically. It seemed to be a general ache throughout his body. He groaned and opened his eyes. Then he remembered why keeping them shut had been the better option.

'If I've got to be here, the least you could do is make conversation.' Her mouth clamped tight in the disapproving line he remembered so well. She closed her laptop, put it on the table beside her and crossed one trouser-clad leg over the other. She'd never liked her legs, Tony thought pointlessly.

'Sorry,' he croaked. 'I think it's the drugs.' He reached for the glass of water on his tray, but it was beyond his grasp. She didn't make a move. He tried to pull himself into a sitting position, idiotically forgetting why he was in the hospital bed. His left leg, weighed down in a heavy surgical splint, shifted infinitesimally but delivered a completely disproportionate blast of pain that made him gasp. With the pain came memory. Lloyd Allen bearing down on him, screaming something incomprehensible. The glint of light on blue steel. A moment of paralysing pain, then nothing. Since then, flickers of consciousness. Doctors talking about him, nurses talking over him, the TV talking at him. And her, emanating irritation and impatience.

'Water?' he managed, not sure whether she would oblige.

She gave the flouncing sigh of a woman much put upon and lifted the water glass, prodding the straw towards his dry lips so he could drink without having to sit up. He sucked at the water, taking it in small sips, enjoying the sensation as his mouth recovered moistness. Suck, savour, swallow. He repeated the process till he'd drunk half the glass, then let his head fall back on the pillow. 'You don't have to be here,' he said. 'I'm fine.'

She snorted. 'You don't think I'm here from choice, do you? Bradfield Cross is one of my client accounts.'

That she could still let him down so brutally was no surprise but it didn't stop it hurting. 'Keeping up appearances, eh?' he said, unable to keep the bitterness from his voice.

'When my income and my reputation are at stake? You bet.' She gave him a sour look, the eyes that were so like his narrowing in appraisal. 'Don't pretend you disapprove, Tony. When it comes to keeping up appearances, you could represent England at the Olympics. I bet none of your colleagues has a clue what goes on in your grubby little mind.'

'I had a good teacher.' He looked away, pretending to watch the morning magazine show on the TV.

'All right then, we don't have to talk. I've got work to do and I'm sure we can get someone to bring you some reading material. I'll stick around for a day or two, just till they get you on your feet. Then I'll be out of your way.' He heard her shift in her chair and the tap of fingers on keys.

'How did you find out?' he said.

'Apparently I'm on your personnel records as your next of kin. Either you haven't updated them for twenty years or you're still the Billy No Mates you always were. And some clever clogs senior nurse recognized me when I walked in. So I'm stuck here for as long as propriety demands.'

'I had no idea you had any connection to Bradfield.'

'Thought you were safe here, did you? Unlike you, Tony, I'm a success story. I have connections all over the country. Business is booming.' When she boasted, her face softened.

'You really don't have to be here,' he said. 'I'll tell them I sent you away.' He spoke quickly, his words tumbling over themselves in an attempt to minimize the effort of speech.

'And why exactly should I trust you to tell the truth about me? No thanks. I'll do my duty.'

Tony stared at the wall. Was there a more depressing sentence in the English language?

Elinor Blessing swirled the whipped cream into her mug of mocha with the wooden stirrer. Starbucks was a two-minute walk from the back entrance of Bradfield Cross, and she reckoned there was a groove in the pavement worn by the feet of junior doctors fixing themselves with caffeine to keep sleep at bay. But this morning she wasn't trying to stay awake, she was trying to stay out of the way.

A vertical line furrowed between her brows and her grey eyes stared into the middle distance. Thoughts tumbled over each other as she tried to figure out what she should do. She'd been Thomas Denby's SHO for long enough to have formed a pretty clear opinion of him. He was probably the best diagnostician she'd ever worked with, and he backed it up with solid clinical care. Unlike a lot of consultants she'd seen, he didn't seem to need to massage his ego by trampling junior doctors and students into the dirt. He encouraged them to take an active role in his ward rounds. When his students answered what was asked of them, he appeared gratified when they got it right and disappointed when they got it wrong. That disappointment was far more of an incentive to learn than the sarcasm and humiliation dealt out by many of his colleagues.

However, like a good barrister, Denby was generally asking questions whose answers he knew already. Would he be quite so generous if one of his underlings had the answer to a problem he had failed to solve? Would he thank the person who interrupted the smooth flow of his ward rounds with a suggestion he hadn't already considered? Especially if it turned out that they were right?

You could argue that he should be pleased, no matter who came up with the theory. Diagnosis was the first step on the journey of helping the patient. Except when it was a diagnosis of despair. Incurable, intractable, untreatable. Nobody wanted that sort of diagnosis.

Especially when your patient was Robbie Bishop.

There was, Carol thought, something dispiriting about knowing your way round a hospital so well. One way or another, her job had taken her to all the major departments of Bradfield Cross. The one advantage was that she knew which of the congested car parks to aim for.

The woman on duty at the nurses' station on the men's surgical ward recognized her. Their paths had crossed several times during the surgery and recovery of a rapist whose victim had miraculously managed to turn his knife against him. They'd both taken a certain amount of pleasure in his pain. 'It's Inspector Jordan, isn't it?' she said.

Carol didn't bother correcting her. 'That's right. I'm looking for a patient called Hill. Tony Hill?'

The nurse looked surprised. 'You're a bit high on the totem pole to be taking statements.'

Carol debated momentarily how to describe her relationship with Tony. 'Colleague' was insufficient, 'landlord' somehow misleading and 'friend' both more and less than the truth. She shrugged. 'He feeds my cat.'

The nurse giggled. 'We all need one of those.' She pointed down the hallway to her right. 'Past the four-bed wards, there's a door on the left right at the end. That's him.'

Anxiety worrying at her like a rat with a bone, Carol followed the directions. Outside the door, she paused. How was it going to be? What was she going to find? She had little experience of dealing with other people's physical incapacity. She knew from her own experience that when she was hurt the last people she wanted around her were the ones she cared about. Their obvious distress made her feel guilty and she didn't enjoy having her own vulnerability on display. She would have put money on Tony sharing similar feelings. She cast her mind back to a previous occasion when she'd visited him in hospital. They hadn't known each other well then, but she remembered it hadn't exactly been a comfortable encounter. Well, if it turned out that he wanted to be left alone, she wouldn't stick around. Just show her face so he'd know she was concerned, then bow out graciously, making sure he knew she'd be back if he wanted her.

Deep breath, then a knock. Then the familiar voice, blurred around the edges. 'Come in if you've got drugs.' Carol grinned. Not that bad, then. She pushed the door open and walked in.

She was immediately aware that there was someone else in the room, but at first she only had eyes for Tony. Three days' stubble emphasized the grey tinge to his skin. He looked as if he'd lost weight he could ill afford. But his eyes were bright and his smile seemed like the real thing. A contraption of pulleys and wires held his knee braced in its splint at an angle that looked scarcely comfortable. 'Carol,' he began before he was interrupted.

'You must be the girlfriend,' the woman sitting in the corner of the room said, the accent faint but recognizably local. 'What kept you?' Carol looked at her in surprise. She looked to be a well-preserved early sixties, doing a good job of keeping the years at bay. The hair was skilfully dyed golden brown, the make-up impeccable but understated. Her blue eyes held an air of calculation, and the lines that were visible did not speak of a kind and generous nature. On the thin side of slender, she was dressed in a business suit whose cut raised it above the average. Certainly well above what Carol could afford to pay for a suit.

'Sorry?' Carol said. She wasn't often caught on the back foot, but even villains were seldom quite so blunt.

'She's not my girlfriend,' Tony said, irritation

apparent. 'She's Detective Chief Inspector Carol Jordan.'

The woman's eyebrows rose. 'You could have fooled me.' A thin smile, entirely lacking in humour. 'I mean about the girlfriend part, not about you being a copper. After all, unless you're here to arrest him, what's a senior police officer doing sniffing around this useless article?'

'Mother.' It was a snarl through clenched teeth. Tony made a face at Carol, a mix of exasperation and plea. 'Carol, this is my mother. Carol Jordan, Vanessa Hill.'

Neither woman made a move to shake hands. Carol fought back her surprise. It was true that they'd never spoken much about their families, but she had formed the distinct impression that Tony's mother was dead. 'Pleased to meet you,' Carol said. She turned back to Tony. 'How are you?'

'Cram-jammed with drugs. But at least today I can stay awake for more than five minutes at a time.'

'And the leg? What are they saying about that?' As she spoke, she realized Vanessa Hill was packing her laptop away in a bright neoprene case.

'Apparently it was a clean, single break. They've done their best to stick it together ...' His voice tailed off. 'Mother, are you going?' he asked as Vanessa rounded the end of the bed, coat over her arm, laptop slung over her shoulder alongside her handbag.

'Bloody right, I'm going. You've got your girlfriend to look after you now. I'm off the hook.' She made for the door.

'She is not my girlfriend,' Tony shouted. 'She's my tenant, my colleague, my friend. And she's a woman, not a girl.'

'Whatever,' Vanessa said. 'I'm not abandoning you now. I'm leaving you in good hands. A difference that will be apparent to the nursing staff.' She sketched a wave as she left.

Carol stared open-mouthed at the disappearing woman. 'Bloody hell,' she said, turning back to Tony. 'Is she always like that?'

He let his head fall back on the pillow, avoiding her eyes. 'Probably not with other people,' he said wearily. 'She owns a very successful consultancy business in HR. Hard to believe, but she oversees personnel decisions and training in some of the country's top companies. I think I bring out the worst in her.'

'I'm beginning to understand why you've never talked about her.' Carol pulled the chair out of the corner and sat down next to the bed.

'I hardly ever see her. Not even Christmas and birthdays.' He sighed. 'I didn't see much of her while I was growing up either.'

'What about your dad? Was she that rude to him?'

'Good question. I have no idea who my father was. She's always refused to tell me anything about him. All I know is that they weren't married. Can you pass me the remote control for the bed?' He dredged up a proper smile. 'You saved me from another day of my mother. The least I can do is sit up for you.'

'I came as soon as I heard. I'm sorry, nobody called me.' She passed him the remote and he fiddled with the buttons till he was half-upright, wincing as he settled. 'Everybody assumed somebody else had told me. I wish you'd let me know.'

'I knew how much you needed a weekend off,' he said. 'Besides, there's only so many favours I can call in and I thought I'd rather save them for when I really needed them.' Suddenly his mouth fell open and his eyes widened. 'Oh shit,' he exclaimed. 'Have you been home or did you go straight to the office?'

It seemed an odd question, but his manner was urgent. 'Straight to the office. Why?'

He covered his face with his hands. 'I am so sorry. I forgot all about Nelson.'

Carol burst out laughing. 'A nutter smashes your leg with a fire axe, you spend the weekend in surgery and you're worried about not feeding my cat? He's got a cat flap, he can go and murder small animals if he gets desperate.' She reached for his hand and patted it. 'Never mind the cat. Tell me about your knee.'

'It's wired together but they can't put a proper pot cast on it because of the wound. The surgeon says they have to make sure that's healing properly, that it's not infected. Then they can put a cast on it and maybe I can try to move around with a walking frame by the end of the week. If I'm a good boy,' he added sarcastically.

'So how long are you going to be in hospital?'

'At least a week. It depends on how good I get at moving around. They won't let me out till I can get about with the walking frame.' He waggled his arm. 'And probably without the intravenous morphine too.'

Carol grimaced sympathetically. 'That'll teach you to play the hero.'

'There was nothing heroic about it,' Tony said. 'The guys who were trying to drag their mate out of there, they were the heroes. I was just the diversion.' His eyelids fluttered. 'That's the last time I work late.'

'Do you need anything from home?'

'Some T-shirts? That's got to be more comfortable than these hospital gowns. And some pairs of boxers. It'll be interesting to see if we can get them over the splint.'

'What about something to read?'

'Good thinking. There's a couple of books I'm supposed to be reviewing on my bedside table. You can tell which ones they are because they've got Post-It notes on the covers. Oh, and my laptop, please.'

Carol shook her head in amusement. 'You don't think this might be a good opportunity to chill? Maybe read something frivolous?'

He looked at her as if she was talking Icelandic. 'Why?'

'I don't think anybody's expecting you to be working, Tony. And I think you might find it's not as easy to concentrate as you imagine.'

He frowned. 'You think I don't know how to relax.' He was only half-joking.

'I don't think that. I know it. And I understand, because I have similar tendencies.'

'I can relax. I watch football. I play computer games.'

Carol laughed. 'I've seen you watch football. I've seen you play computer games and there is no sense of the word "relaxing" that applies to either activity where you are concerned.'

'I'm not even going to dignify that with a response. But if you are bringing the laptop, you might as well bring me Lara . . .' He gave her the full twinkle.

'You sad bastard. Where will I find her?'

'In my study. On the shelf that your left hand would

reach if you stretched out from the chair.' He stifled a yawn. 'And now it's time for you to go. I need to sleep and you've got a Major Incident Team to run.'

Carol stood up. 'A Major Incident Team with no major incidents to run. Not that I'm complaining,' she added hastily. 'I don't have a problem with a quiet day at the office.' She patted his hand again. 'I'll pop back this evening. If there's anything else you need, call me.'

She walked down the corridor, already pulling out her mobile phone so she could turn it back on as soon as she left the hospital building. As she passed the nurses' station, the woman she'd spoken to earlier gave her a wink. 'So much for feeding the cat.'

'What do you mean?' Carol asked, slowing.

'According to his mum, he does a bit more than that for you.' Her smile was arch, her eyes knowing.

'You shouldn't believe everything you hear. Does your mother know everything about you?'

The nurse shrugged. 'Point taken.'

Carol juggled bag and phone and pulled out a card. 'I'll be back later. That's my card. If there's anything he needs, let me know and I'll see what I can do.'

'No problem. Good cat feeders are hard to find, after all.'

Yousef Aziz glanced at the dashboard clock. He was doing well. Nobody expected him to make it back from a nine o'clock meeting in Blackburn much before lunchtime. Everybody knew what Monday morning trans-Pennine traffic was like. But what they didn't know was that he'd rearranged the meeting for eight. Sure, he'd had to leave Bradfield a bit earlier, but not

36

the whole hour, because he would avoid the worst of the rush hour this way. To cover himself, all he'd had to say to his mother was that he wanted to be sure he wouldn't be late for this important new client. He knew he should have felt uncomfortable when she'd used his supposed punctuality as a stick to beat his little brother with. But it was water off a duck's back with Raj. Their mother had spoiled him, the youngest son, and now she was reaping what she'd sown.

The main thing was that Yousef had created a little window of opportunity for himself. It was something he'd grown accustomed to doing over the previous few months. He had become adept at squeezing unmissed hours from the working day without raising suspicion. Ever since . . . He shook his head as if to dislodge the thought. Too distracting. He had to try to compartmentalize the warring elements of his life, otherwise he would be bound to give something away.

Yousef had kept the Blackburn meeting as tight as he could without appearing rude to the new client, and now he had an hour and a half for himself. He followed the instructions of his satellite navigation system. Down the motorway and into the heart of Cheetham Hill. He knew North Manchester pretty well, but this particular section of the red-brick warren was unfamiliar. He turned into a narrow street where a battered terrace of weary houses faced on to a small industrial estate. Halfway down, he spotted the signage for his destination. PRO-TECH SUPPLIES, in scarlet against a white background inside a border of black exclamation marks.

He parked the van outside and turned off the engine. He leaned on the steering wheel, breathing deeply, feeling his stomach wind itself into knots. He'd hardly eaten anything that morning, using his urgency to get to his meeting to defuse his mother's oppressive concern with his recent loss of appetite. Of course he'd lost his appetite, just as he'd lost the ability to sleep for more than a couple of hours at a time. What else could he expect? This was how it was when you embarked on something like this. But it was important not to arouse suspicion, so he tried to be away from the family table at mealtimes as much as he could.

Given how little he was eating and sleeping, he couldn't quite believe how energized he felt. A bit light-headed sometimes, but he thought that was more to do with imagining the effect of their plan than the lack of food and rest. Now, he pushed back from the steering wheel and climbed out of the van. He walked through the door marked RETAIL SALES. It led into a room ten feet square partitioned off from the warehouse behind. Behind a zinc-topped counter that bisected the room, a skinny man hunched over a computer. Everything about him was grey – his hair, his skin, his overalls. He looked up from his computer screen as Yousef entered. His eyes were grey too.

He stood up and leaned on the counter. The movement stirred the air enough to send the bitter after-smell of cheap tobacco across the gap between them. 'All right?' Yousef said.

'All right. What can I do you for?'

Yousef pulled out a list. 'I need some heavy-duty gloves, a face shield and ear protectors.'

The man sighed and pulled a dog-eared catalogue

along the counter. 'Best have a look in here. That shows you what we do.' He opened it, flicking through the creased pages till he reached the section on gloves. He pointed to a picture at random. 'See, there's a description. Gives you an idea of thickness and flexibility. Depends what you want them for, see?' He pushed the catalogue towards Yousef. 'You decide what you're after.'

Yousef nodded. He began to pore over the catalogue, a bit taken aback by the range of choices on offer. As he read the descriptions of the items, he couldn't help smiling. For some reason, Pro-Tech didn't list his project among their recommended uses for their protective gear. Mr Grey behind the counter would shit himself if he knew the truth. But he never would know the truth. Yousef had been careful. His tracks were clean. A scientific and chemical supplies warehouse in Wakefield. A specialist paint manufacturer in Oldham. A motorbike accessories shop in Leeds. A laboratory equipment supplier in Cleckheaton. Never, never, never in Bradfield, where there was an outside chance of being spotted by someone who knew him. Every time, he'd dressed the part. Painter's overalls. Biker's leathers. Neatly pressed shirt and chinos with a line of pens in a pocket protector in the shirt. Paid in cash. The invisible man.

Now, he made his decision and pointed out what he wanted, adding a protective chest shield for good measure. The warehouseman entered the details into the computer and told Yousef his goods would be along in a minute. He seemed nonplussed when Yousef offered to pay in cash. 'Have you not got a credit card?' he asked, sounding incredulous.

'Not a company one, no,' Yousef lied. 'Sorry, mate. Cash is all I've got.' He counted out the notes.

The warehouseman shook his head. 'That'll have to do, then. Your lot like cash, don't you?'

Yousef frowned. 'My lot? What do you mean, my lot?' He felt his fists clench in his pockets.

'You Muslims. I read it some place. It's against your religion. Paying interest and that.' The man's jaw took a stubborn set. 'I'm not being racist, you know. Just stating a fact.'

Yousef breathed deeply. As these things went, the man's attitude was pretty mild. He'd experienced much, much worse. But these days, he was hyper-sensitive to anything that had the faintest whiff of prejudice about it. It all served to reinforce his choice to stay on this road, to carry his plans through to the end. 'If you say so,' he said, not wanting to get into a ruck that would make him memorable, but equally reluctant to say nothing at all.

He was saved from further conversation by the arrival of his purchases. He picked them up and walked out without responding to the warehouseman's 'See ya.'

The motorway traffic was heavy and it took him the best part of an hour to make it back to Bradfield. He barely had enough time to take the protective gear to the bedsit, but he couldn't leave it lying round in the van. If Raj or Sanjar or his father saw it, it would provoke all sorts of questions he definitely didn't want to answer.

The bedsit was on the first floor of what had once been the town house of a railway baron. A sprawling pile of Gothic Revival, the stained stucco covering the gables and bays was scabby and crumbling, the window frames rotting and the gutters sprouting an assortment of weeds. It had once had a view; now all that could be seen from its front windows was the cantilevered slant of the west stand of Bradfield Victoria's vast stadium half a mile away. What had once been a quarter endowed with a certain grandeur had declined into a ghetto whose inhabitants were united only by their poverty. Skin tones ranged from the blue-black of sub-Saharan Africa to the skimmed-milk pallor of Eastern Europe. According to a survey carried out by Bradfield City Council, thirteen religions were practised and twenty-two native tongues spoken in the square mile to the west of the football ground.

Here, Yousef travelled under the radar of his own third-generation immigrant community. Here, nobody noticed or cared who else came and went from his first-floor hideaway. Here, Yousef Aziz was invisible.

The receptionist tried to hide her shock and failed. 'Good morning, Mrs Hill,' she gabbled on automatic. She glanced down at the calendar on her desk, as if she couldn't believe she'd got it so wrong. 'I thought you . . . we weren't . . .'

'Good, it keeps you on your toes, Bethany,' Vanessa said as she swept past on her way to her office. The faces she passed on the way looked startled and guilty as they stammered out their greetings. She didn't imagine for one moment they'd done anything to be guilty about. Her staff knew better than to try to put one over on her. But she liked that her unexpected arrival sent a ripple of anxiety through the office. It was a sign she was getting her money's worth. Vanessa Hill wasn't a touchy-feely employer. She had friends already; she didn't need to make her employees her buddies. She was tough, but she thought she was fair. It was a message she tried to hammer home to her clients. Keep your distance, win their respect, and your HR problems would be minimal.

Pity it wasn't that straightforward with kids, she thought as she dumped her laptop on the desk and hung up her jacket. When your staff didn't cut the mustard, you could sack them and recruit someone better suited to the job. Kids, you were stuck with. And right from the start, Tony had failed to live up to expectations. When she'd fallen pregnant to a man who had disappeared like snow off a dyke at the news, her mother had told her to put the baby up for adoption. Vanessa had refused point blank. Now, she looked back in bewilderment and wondered why she had been so adamant.

It hadn't been for sentimental reasons. She didn't have a sentimental bone in her body. Another position she recommended to her clients. Had she really gone that far out on a limb just to spite her demanding, controlling mother? There had to be more to it than that, but for the life of her she couldn't remember. It must have been the hormones, addling her brain. Whatever, she'd endured the neighbourhood spite and gossip that went with single parenthood back then. She'd changed jobs, moving right across town to where nobody knew her, and lied about her past, inventing a dead husband to avoid the stigma. And it wasn't as if she'd had any illusions about basking in a hazy glow of motherhood. With her father dead and no prospect of a husband now, she was the bread-winner. She'd always known she'd be back at work as soon as was humanly possible, like some bloody Chinese peasant dropping one in the ditch then getting back to the paddy field. And for what?

Her mother had taken reluctant charge of the boy. She didn't have much choice since it was her daughter's pay packet that kept them all afloat. Vanessa remembered enough of her own childhood to know the regime she was condemning her son to. She tried not to think about what Tony's days would have been like and she didn't encourage him to talk about it. She had enough to contend with, running a busy personnel department, then branching out to set up her own business. She relished the challenge of work, but she didn't have energy to spare for a whiny kid.

Credit to him, he got that pretty early. He learned to put up and shut up, and to do what he was told. When he forgot himself and bounced around her like a puppy, it only took a few sharp words to knock the stuffing out of him.

Even so, he'd held her back. No doubt about that. All those years ago, no bloke wanted to settle down with some other man's kid. He was a handicap professionally too. When she was getting her own business established, she'd had to keep the travel to a minimum because her mother kicked off if she was left overnight too often with the boy. Vanessa had missed chances, failed to build fast enough on the contacts she was making and played catch-up too bloody many times thanks to Tony.

And there had been no pay-off. Other women's

kids got married and provided grand-kids. Photos on the desk, anecdotes in the meeting breaks, family holidays in the sun. Ice-breakers, all of them. Confidence-builders. The bricks and mortar of professional relationships that generated business and earned money. Tony's continuing failures meant Vanessa had to work that much harder.

Well, it was payback time now and no mistake. Things couldn't have worked out better if she'd planned it. He was stuck in hospital, groggy with drugs and sleep. No hiding place. She could get access to him whenever she wanted and pick her moment. All she had to do was make sure she avoided the girlfriend.

Her PA slipped in and wordlessly delivered the coffee that always arrived within minutes of her settling behind her desk. Vanessa opened up her computer and allowed herself a grim little smile. Fancy Tony landing a woman with looks and brains. Carol Jordan wasn't the sort of catch Vanessa expected of her son. If she'd imagined him with anyone, it would have been some mousy slip of a girl who worshipped the ground he walked on. Well, girlfriend or no girlfriend, she was going to have her way.

Elinor raised her hand to knock then paused. Was she about to commit career suicide? You could argue that, if she was right, it didn't matter whether she spoke up or not. Because if she was right, Robbie Bishop was going to die anyway. Nothing could alter that. But if she was right and she didn't speak up, someone else could die. Whether accident or intent lay behind whatever had happened to him, it could happen to someone else.

The thought of having another death on her conscience swung it for Elinor. Better to make an arse of herself in a good cause than have to deal with that. She rapped on the door and waited for Denby's distracted, 'Yes, yes, come in.' He looked up impatiently from a stack of case notes. 'Dr Blessing,' he said. 'Any change?'

'In Robbie Bishop?'

Denby pulled a half-smile. 'Who else? We claim to treat all our patients equally, but it's not exactly easy when we have to run the gauntlet of football fans whenever we enter or leave the hospital.' He swung round in his chair and looked through the window to the car park below. 'Even more of them now than when I came back in after lunch.' He turned back as Elinor began to speak. 'Do you suppose they think being there can influence the outcome?' He sounded more bemused than cynical.

'I expect it depends whether they believe in the power of prayer. I did see a pair of them huddled in a doorway saying the rosary.' She shrugged. 'It doesn't appear to be helping Mr Bishop – he seems to be deteriorating steadily. The fluid on his lungs is building up. I'd say respiratory distress is getting worse. There's no question of him coming off the ventilator.'

Denby bit his lip. 'No response to the AZT, then?'

Elinor shook her head. 'Nothing discernible so far.'

Denby sighed and nodded. 'Damned if I know what's going on here. Oh, well. So it goes sometimes. Thanks for keeping me posted, Dr Blessing.' His eyes returned to the files on his desk in dismissal.

'There was one thing?'

45

He looked up, eyebrows raised. He appeared to be genuinely interested in what she had to say. 'To do with Mr Bishop?'

She nodded. 'I know it sounds crazy, but have you considered ricin poisoning?'

'Ricin?' Denby looked almost offended. 'How on earth would a premiership footballer be exposed to ricin?'

Elinor battled on. 'I've no idea. But you're a terrific diagnostician and when you couldn't come up with anything, I thought it must be something a bit off the wall. And I thought, maybe poisoning. So I checked it out on the online database and all his symptoms match ricin poisoning – weakness, fever, nausea, dyspnea, cough, pulmonary oedema and arthralgia. Add to that the fact that he's not responding to any of the medications we've tried him with . . . I don't know, it fits the way nothing else does.'

Denby looked bemused. 'I think you've been watching too many episodes of *Spooks*, Dr Blessing. Robbie Bishop is a footballer, not a KGB defector.'

Elinor stared at the floor. This was what she'd been afraid of. But the reason that had driven her through the door in the first place still existed. 'I know it sounds ridiculous,' she said. 'But none of us has been able to come up with an alternative diagnosis that makes sense of the symptoms and the fact that the patient is not responding to any of the drug regimes we've tried.' She looked up. His head was cocked to one side and although his mouth was a tight line, his eyes expressed interest in what she had to say. 'And I'm not saying this to flatter you into taking me seriously. But if you can't work out what is clinically

46

wrong with Robbie Bishop, I don't think there can be a straightforward explanation in terms of a viral or bacterial illness. Which only leaves poison. And the only poison that makes sense is ricin.'

Denby jumped to his feet. 'This is crazy. Terrorists use ricin. Spies use ricin. How the hell does a premiership footballer get ricin into his system?'

'With respect, I think that's somebody else's problem,' Elinor said.

Denby rubbed the palms of his hands over his face. She had never seen him flustered, never mind this agitated. 'First things first. We need to check whether or not you're right.' He looked expectantly at her.

'You can do an ELISA test for ricin. But even if they've got the right antigen in stock and they fast-track it, we still won't get the results of a sandwich ELISA till tomorrow.'

He took a deep breath and visibly pulled himself together. 'Set the wheels in motion. Take the bloods yourself, take them straight to the lab. I'll call ahead, make sure they know what's coming down the line. We can start treatment –' He stopped dead, his mouth hanging open. 'Oh fuck.' He squeezed his eyes shut momentarily. 'There is no bloody treatment, is there?'

Elinor shook her head. 'No. If I'm right, Robbie Bishop's a condemned man.'

Denby slumped back into his chair. 'Yes. Well, I don't think we need to share this possibility with anyone just yet. Not until we know for sure. Don't tell anyone else what you suspect.'

'But . . .' Elinor frowned.

'But what?'

'Shouldn't we tell the police?'

'The police? You were the one who said it was someone else's problem, determining how the ricin got into his system. We can't call the police in on a hunch.'

'But he's still having lucid spells. He can still communicate. If we wait till tomorrow, he could have lapsed into a coma and he won't be able to tell anyone how this happened. If it happened,' she added, seeing the ominous expression on Denby's face.

'And if you're wrong? If it turns out to be something quite other? This department will have lost all credibility within the hospital and the wider community. Let's face it, Dr Blessing, two minutes after we call the police in, the media will be screaming from the rooftops. I'm not prepared to put my reputation and that of my team on the line like that. I'm sorry. We don't tell anyone – not another living soul – until we get the ELISA results and we know for certain. Are you clear on that?'

Elinor sighed. 'I'm clear.' Then her face brightened. 'What if I was to ask him? When we're alone?'

Denby shook his head. 'Absolutely not,' he said firmly. 'I will not have you interrogate a patient like that.'

'It's kind of like taking a history.'

'It's nothing like taking a history. It's playing at Miss bloody Marple. Now please, let's not waste any more time. Get started on the ELISA protocol.' He managed a faint bloodless smile. 'Good thinking, Doctor Blessing. Let's just hope for once you're wrong. Apart from anything else, Bradfield Victoria have no chance of making it into Europe next season without Robbie Bishop.' Elinor's face must have revealed her shock for he rolled his eyes and said, 'I'm joking, for Christ's sake. I'm as worried about this as you are.'

Somehow, Elinor doubted that.

Tony started awake, eyes wide, mouth stretched back in a silent scream. The power of morphine dreams to recreate the gleam of the axe, the battle cry of his attacker, the smell of sweat and the taste of blood was terrifying. His breathing was fast and shallow and he could feel sweat curdling on his top lip. *Only a dream.* He deliberately controlled his breathing and gradually the panic subsided.

Once he'd calmed down, he tried to raise his wounded leg from the hip. He clenched his hands into tight fists, the nails biting into his palms. The veins on his neck corded up as he strained to move a limb that seemed to have been transmuted into lead. The futile seconds stretched out, then with a grunt of frustration, he gave up. It felt as if he'd never move his left leg again.

Tony reached for the bed control and eased himself upwards. He glanced at his watch. Half an hour till they would bring his evening meal. Not that he felt like eating, but it was a way of punctuating the day. He almost wished his mother had stayed. At least it gave him something to butt against. Tony shook his head, aghast at the thought. If his mother's company was the answer, he was asking the wrong question. Not that there weren't aspects of the history of their relationship that he ought to confront and deal with. But this wasn't the time or the place. He wasn't sure when or where would be appropriate for something so potentially painful, but he knew it wasn't here and now.

Still, it couldn't wait for ever. Carol had met her now, and she would have questions. He couldn't just blank her; Carol deserved more than that from him. The problem was where to start. His childhood memories lacked a narrative. They were fragmentary, a series of incidents loosely linked like dark beads on a tarnished chain. Not all of the memories were bad. But his mother featured in none of the good ones. He knew he wasn't the only person with such an experience. He had treated plenty of them, after all. Just one more aspect of his history he shared with the crazies.

He flapped his hand in front of his face as if swatting a fly and picked up the remote control. He began to flick through the limited range of channels. Nothing engaged his attention, but he was spared having to make a decision by a knock at the door.

The person on the other side didn't wait for an invitation. The woman who marched in looked like a peregrine falcon run to fat. Glossy brown hair swept back from her forehead in a wavy bob that stopped just short of her shoulders. Deep-set hazel eyes gleamed beneath perfectly shaped eyebrows and the hawk's nose jutted out from plump cheeks. The sight of Mrs Chakrabarti lifted Tony's spirits far more than any TV channel could have. Here was more interesting news than BBC24.

She was trailed by half a dozen acolytes in white coats who looked young enough to be doing sixth-form work experience. She gave Tony a swift, practised smile as she reached for his notes. 'So,' she said, looking at him from under her brows. 'How's it feeling?' Her accent bore a greater resemblance to that of the royal family than to the denizens of Bradfield. It made Tony feel as if he should doff a cap or tug a forelock.

'Like you replaced my leg with a lead pipe,' he said.

'No pain?'

He shook his head. 'Nothing the morphine can't take care of.'

'But you're not feeling any pain once the morphine kicks in?'

'No. Should I be?'

Mrs Chakrabarti smiled. 'It's not our preferred option. I'm going to take you off the morphine drip tomorrow morning, see if we can achieve the pain management by other means.'

Tony felt the clutch of apprehension. 'Are you sure that's a good idea?'

The smile grew positively predatory. 'Just as sure as you are about the advice you give your patients.'

Tony grinned. 'In that case, let's just stick with the morphine.'

'You'll be fine, Dr Hill.' She replaced the chart and studied his leg, angling her head round to see the twin drains carrying bloody fluid away from the wound in his knee. She turned to the students. 'You'll see there's not much coming off the wound site now.' Back to Tony. 'I think we might take the drains out tomorrow and get this splint off so we can get a sense of what you're going to need. Probably a nice cylinder cast.'

'When can I go home?'

Mrs Chakrabarti turned to her students with the perennial condescension of the surgeon. 'When can Dr Hill go home?'

'When he can bear weight on his leg.' The speaker looked as if he should be delivering newspapers, not clinical judgements.

'How much weight? His whole body weight?'

The students exchanged covert glances. 'When he can get around with a Zimmer frame,' another offered.

'When he can get around with a Zimmer frame, do a leg raise and climb stairs,' a third chipped in.

Tony could feel something inside his head stretch to its limit. 'Doctor,' he said forcibly. When he had her attention, he spoke very clearly. 'That was not an idle question. I need to not be here. None of the important things in my life can be accomplished from a hospital bed.'

Mrs Chakrabarti wasn't smiling now. This, Tony thought, must be what a mouse feels like eyeball to eyeball with a raptor. The only good thing about it is you know it's not going to last long. 'That's something you have in common with the vast majority of my patients, Dr Hill,' she said.

His blue eyes glittered with the strain of not showing his frustration. 'I'm perfectly aware of that. But unlike the vast majority of your patients, nobody else can do what I do. That's not arrogance. It's the way that it is. I don't need two functioning legs to do most of the things I do that matter. What I really need is for my head to function, and that's not happening very well in here.'

They glared at each other. None of the students fidgeted. They barely breathed. 'I appreciate your position, Dr Hill. And I understand your sense of failure.'

'My sense of failure?' Tony was genuinely puzzled.

'It was one of your patients who put you here, after all.'

He burst out laughing. 'Good God, no. Not one of my patients. Lloyd Allen wasn't one of mine. This isn't about guilt, it's about giving my patients what they need. Just like you want to do, Mrs Chakrabarti.' His smile lit up his face, infectious and compelling.

The corners of her lips twitched. 'In that case, Dr Hill, I'd say it's up to you. We can perhaps try a leg brace rather than a cast.' She eyed his shoulders critically. 'It's a pity you don't have better upper body strength, but we can try you on elbow crutches. The bottom line is that you have to be mobile, you have to be committed to your physiotherapy and you have to be off the intravenous morphine. Do you have someone at home to take care of you?'

He looked away. 'I share the house with a friend. She'll help.'

The surgeon nodded. 'I won't pretend the rehab isn't tough. Hard work and a lot of pain. But if you're determined to get out of here, we should be able to free up your bed early next week.'

'Early next week?' There was no hiding his dismay.

Mrs Chakrabarti shook her head, chuckling softly. 'Someone split your patella with a fire axe, Dr Hill. Just be grateful you live in a city whose hospital is a centre of excellence for orthopaedics. Some places, you'd be lying there wondering whether you'd ever walk properly again.' She dipped her head in farewell. 'One of this lot will be here tomorrow when they take the drains out and the splint off. We'll see where we go from there.'

She moved away from the bed with her entourage

in tight formation behind her. One of them scuttled in front of her to open the door and the surgeon nearly walked into Carol Jordan's raised fist. Startled, Mrs Chakrabarti recoiled slightly.

'Sorry,' Carol said. She looked at her hand and smiled sheepishly. 'I was just about to knock.' She stepped aside to let the doctors pass and raised her eyebrows at Tony as she walked in, loaded with cargo. 'That looked like a royal progress from the Middle Ages.'

'Close. That was Mrs Chakrabarti and her body slaves. She's in charge of my knee.'

'What news?' Carol asked, dumping assorted carrier bags and easing the laptop in its case on to Tony's bed table.

'I'm probably going to be stuck in here for another week,' he grumped.

'Only another week? God, she must be good. I thought it would take a lot longer than that.' She began to unpack the carrier bags. 'Ginger beer, dandelion and burdock, proper lemonade. Luxury roast nuts. Books as requested. All the Tomb Raider games Lara Croft ever starred in. Jelly beans. My iPod. Your laptop. And . . .' She produced a sheet of paper with a flourish. 'The access code for the hospital's wireless broadband.'

Tony mimed astonishment. 'I'm impressed. How did you manage that?'

'I know the senior nurse from way back. I told her how much easier her life would be if you were online. She seemed to think that a total breach of hospital regulations was a small price to pay. You've obviously made an impression already.' Carol shrugged off her coat and settled into the chair. 'And not in a good way.'

'Thanks for all of this. I really appreciate it. You're a lot earlier than I expected.'

'Privilege of rank. I suspect I'm going to have to show my warrant card next time I want to get in, though.'

'Why's that?' Tony handed her the power cord for his laptop. 'There's a socket behind you, I think.'

Carol got up and stretched behind the chair to plug it in. 'The Robbie Bishop fan club.'

'What are you talking about?'

'Have you not seen the news? Robbie Bishop's here, in Bradfield Cross.'

Tony frowned. 'Did he get injured in Saturday's match, then? I'm so out of touch in here, I don't even know if we won.'

'One–nil to the Vics. But Robbie wasn't playing. He supposedly had flu, but whatever it is, it got bad enough for him to be admitted here on Saturday. And I just heard on the radio that he's been moved to the ICU.'

Tony whistled. 'Well, it's obviously not flu, then. Are they saying what the problem is?'

'No. They're just calling it a chest infection. But the fans are out in force. You can't see the main entrance for a sea of canary yellow. Apparently they've had to bring in extra security to keep the more enterprising ones at bay. One woman even dressed up in a nurse's uniform in a bid to get to his bedside. I'm sure she won't be the last to try something like that. It's a big problem, because you can't close the hospital to the public. The patients and their families wouldn't stand for it.'

'I'm surprised he's not in one of the private hospitals.' Tony opened the bag of jelly beans and stirred them with his finger till he found his favourite buttered popcorn flavour.

'Neither of the private hospitals in Bradfield has the facilities to deal with acute respiratory problems, according to your friendly senior nurse. They're fine if you want a new hip or your tonsils out, but if you're seriously ill, Bradfield Cross is where you want to be.'

'Tell me about it,' Tony said wryly.

'You're not ill,' Carol said briskly. 'You're just a bit more damaged than usual.'

He pulled a half-smile. 'Whatever. I'd still bet that Robbie Bishop will be walking out of here ahead of me.'

Tuesday

Sometimes being right was no pleasure at all, Elinor thought as she stared at the lab report. This was definitely one of those times. The test results were incontrovertible. Robbie Bishop had enough ricin in his system to kill him several times over.

Elinor paged Denby, asking him to meet her at the ICU. As she crossed the covered walkway that linked the labs to the main hospital, she couldn't avoid the sight of Robbie Bishop's fans, their patient vigil rendered pointless by the piece of paper she held in her hand. According to one of the women in admin who had been holding forth in the staff canteen that morning, the hospital had been inundated with offers of blood, kidneys and anything else that might be donated to help Robbie. But there was nothing anyone could give Robbie now that would alter the fate in prospect.

As she approached the ICU, she folded the report in half and shoved it in her pocket. She didn't want any of the security staff to glimpse its contents as they checked her ID before allowing her into the unit. The tabloids had their spies everywhere; the least she could do was to ensure Robbie's last hours were as dignified as possible. She cleared security and crossed the reception area, spotting Martin Flanagan slumped against the end of a sofa. When he saw her, he jumped to his feet, eagerness and anxiety chasing the exhaustion temporarily from his face. 'Any news?' he asked, his flat Ulster accent lending the simple question an incidental air of aggression. 'Mr Denby's just gone in. Did he send for you?'

'I'm sorry, Mr Flanagan,' Elinor said automatically. 'There's really nothing I can tell you right now.'

His face collapsed in on itself again, hope disappearing with her words. He dragged his fingers through his silver-streaked hair, a beseeching look on his face. 'They won't let me sit with him, you know. His mum and dad are here, they get to be with him. But not me. Not now he's in there. I signed Robbie when he was just fourteen, you know. I brought him on. He's the best player I've ever worked with and he's got the heart of a lion.' He shook his head. 'I can't believe it, you know? Seeing him brought so low. He's been like a son to me.' He turned his face away from her.

'We're doing all we can,' Elinor said. He nodded and dropped back on to the sofa like a sack of potatoes. It didn't do to get emotionally involved, she knew that. But it was hard to see Flanagan's pain and not feel connected.

Being in the ICU was one of life's great levellers, she thought as she walked into the dim space with its bays crammed with equipment. Here, it didn't matter whether you were a household name or a nobody. You got the same total commitment from the staff, the same access to whatever means it took to keep you alive. And the same restrictions on visitors. Immediate family only, and they could and would be unceremoniously shunted to one side if necessary. Here, the needs of the patient were paramount, and here the medical staff ruled supreme, if only because the patients were in no fit state to question them.

Elinor headed straight for Robbie Bishop's cubicle. As she drew near, she could see the couple sitting on the left of the bed. A man and woman in their middle years, they were both clearly in the grip of the tension that comes with abject fear. Their focus was fierce and aimed exclusively at the figure wired to the machines. For all the notice they were taking of Thomas Denby standing at the end of the bed, he might as well be invisible. Elinor wondered if they had grown so accustomed to seeing their son from afar that they were somehow transfixed by his proximity as well as his infirmity.

She paused on the fringes of the group, the dim lighting creating a chiaroscuro effect that made her feel as if she were spying on a diorama in a gallery. At the heart of it, Robbie Bishop, a pale mockery of his former glossy self. Hard to imagine now, that mastery of the beautiful game, those fluid breaks down the wing and the curving crosses that had created so many opportunities for Bradfield Victoria's strikers. Impossible to equate the puffy, waxen face with the glowing good looks that had earned millions promoting everything from organic fruit and vegetables to deodorant. His familiar mop of light brown hair, expertly streaked to make him look like a surfer dude, was lank and dark now, grooming being lower on the priority list of

hospital staff than it was on that of premiership footballers. And Elinor was the one who was about to
wrench the last shreds of hope from this dramatic
tableau.

She took a step forward and cleared her throat tact-
fully. Only Denby registered her arrival; he turned,
gave her a half-nod and ushered her away from the
bedside towards the side office where the nurses were
stationed. Denby smiled at the two nurses sitting in
front of computer terminals and said, 'Can you give
us a minute, please?'

Neither looked particularly pleased at being shunted
out of their own space, but they were conditioned to
obey consultants. As the door closed behind them,
Elinor pulled the test results from her pocket and
handed them over. 'It's not good,' she said.

Denby read the report, his face impassive. 'No room
for doubt there,' he muttered.

'So what do we do now?'

'I tell his parents, you tell Mr Flanagan. And we
do everything we can to make sure that Mr Bishop
suffers as little as possible during his last hours.' Denby
was already turning, making for the door.

'What about the police?' Elinor said. 'Surely we
have to tell them now?'

Denby looked perplexed. 'I suppose so. Why don't
you do that while I talk to Mr and Mrs Bishop?' And
he was gone.

Elinor sat at the desk and stared at the phone.
Eventually she picked it up and asked the hospital
switchboard to connect her to Bradfield police. The
voice that answered sounded brisk and down-to-earth.
'My name is Elinor Blessing and I'm a Senior House

Officer at Bradfield Cross Hospital,' she began, heart sinking as she realized how improbable her news was going to sound.

'How can I help you?'

'I think I need to talk to a detective. I need to report a suspicious death. Well, when I say death, he's actually still alive. But he's going to be dead before too long.' Elinor winced. Surely she could have put it better than that?

'I'm sorry? Has something happened? An assault?'

'No, nothing like that. Well, I suppose technically, yes, but not in the way you're thinking. Look, I don't want to waste time explaining this over and over again. Can you just put me through to someone in CID? Someone who deals with murder?'

Tuesdays, Yousef Aziz made a point of dropping in on his main middleman. Knowing what he knew, it was hard to motivate himself, but for the sake of his parents and his brothers, he forced himself to do more than simply go through the motions. He owed them that, at least. His family's textile business had survived in the teeth of fierce competition because his father had understood the value of personal relationships in business. That had been the first thing he had taught his two elder sons when he had initiated them into First Fabrics. 'Always take care of your customers and suppliers,' he'd explained. 'If you make them your friends, it makes it hard for them to dump you when times get tough. Because the first rule of business is that times will always get tough sooner or later.'

He'd been right. He'd weathered the collapse of the textile business in the North when cheap imports from the Far East had all but obliterated British garment manufacturers. He'd hung on by the skin of his teeth, always keeping one step ahead, jacking up the quality of his merchandise when he couldn't pare his costs any further, carving out new markets at the higher end of the game. And now it was all happening again. This time, the customers were driving the changes. Clothes were going for a song, fall-apart fashions available in chain stores for peanuts. Buy it cheap, wear it once, sling it. The new philosophy had infected a whole generation regardless of class. Girls whose mothers would have taken poison rather than enter a cut-price fashion store rubbed shoulders with teenage mothers on benefit in Matalan and TK Maxx. So Yousef and Sanjar were sticking to the tried-and-tested formula for survival.

And he hated it. Back when his father had started the business, he'd been dealing mostly with other Asians. But as First Fabrics had stabilized and established itself, they had to deal with all sorts. Jews, Cypriots, Chinese, Brits. And the one thing they all had in common was that they acted like 9/11 and 7/7 had given them the right to treat any Muslim with contempt and suspicion. All the misapprehensions and downright deliberate misunderstandings of Islam operated as the perfect excuse for racism. They knew it wasn't acceptable to be openly racist any more, so they'd found another way to express their racism. All the stuff about women wearing the hijab. The complaints about them speaking Arabic or Urdu instead of English all the time. Fuck, had they never been to Wales? Go into a coffee bar there and suddenly it's like nobody ever learned English.

What pissed off Yousef more than almost anything else was the way he was treated by people he'd known for years. He'd go into a factory or a warehouse where he'd been buying or selling for the seven years since he'd started working for his dad. And now, instead of the locals greeting him by name and having a laugh with him about the football or the cricket or whatever, their eyes slid away from him like he was slick with oil. Either that or they did that false, bright thing that made him feel patronized, like they were only being nice so they could preface their remarks in the pub with, 'Of course, some of my best mates are Muslims . . .'

Today, though, he bit back his anger. It wasn't like this was going to be for ever. As if to confirm the thought, his mobile rang just as he was pulling in to the car park behind Howard Edelstein's factory. He recognized the ring tone and smiled, putting the phone to his ear. 'How's it going?' the voice on the other end said.

'All according to plan. It's great to hear from you, I wasn't expecting you to call this morning.'

'Cancelled meeting. I thought I'd give you a quick bell, just to make sure everything was on track.'

'You know you can rely on me,' Yousef said. 'When I say I'll do something, it's as good as done. Don't worry about me bottling out.'

'That's the one thing I'm not worried about. You know we're doing the right thing.'

'I do. And I tell you, days like these make me glad we decided to do it this way.'

'You having a bad one?' The voice was sympathetic, warm.

'The kind of arse-licking I hate. But I won't be doing this for much longer.'

A chuckle at the other end of the phone. 'That's for sure. This time next week, the world will feel like a very different place.'

Before Yousef could respond, the familiar figure of Howard Edelstein himself loomed up beside his driver's door, sketching a little wave and gesturing with his thumb towards the building. 'I gotta go,' Yousef said. 'I'll see you.'

'Count on it.'

Yousef thumbed the phone shut, jumping out of the car with a smile on his face. Edelstein nodded at him, unsmiling. 'Let's get sorted, then,' he said, leading the way indoors without waiting to see if Yousef was following.

This time next week, Yousef thought. *This time next week, you bastard.*

Carol stared at Thomas Denby, taking in the image. Prematurely silver hair swept back from his forehead, a single lock falling loose over one eyebrow. Greenish blue eyes, pink skin. A beautifully cut charcoal pinstripe suit, jacket thrown open to reveal a flamboyant scarlet lining. He could have sat for a portrait of the archetype of the successful young consultant. What he absolutely didn't look like was someone whose idea of a good time was to wind up a senior police officer. 'So let me get this straight. You're reporting a murder that hasn't happened yet?' She wasn't in the mood to be messed around, and keeping her waiting for the best part of fifteen minutes hadn't been the best way to get things started.

Denby shook his head. 'Murder is your word, not mine. What I am saying is that Robbie Bishop is going to die, probably within the next twenty-four hours. The reason he is going to die is that he has ricin in his system. There is no antidote. There's nothing we can do for him except to limit his pain as much as possible.'

'You're sure about this?'

'I know it sounds bizarre. Like some James Bond film. But yes, we're sure. We've done the tests. He's dying from ricin poisoning.'

'Could it be suicide?'

Denby looked bemused. 'I shouldn't think so for a moment.'

'But could it? In theory?'

He looked faintly annoyed. Carol thought he probably wasn't accustomed to having his views questioned. He lined up his pen with the edge of the file in front of him. 'I've been reading up on ricin since my SHO proposed it as the possible cause of Robbie Bishop's symptoms. Ricin works by invading the cells of a person's body and inhibiting the cells from synthesizing the proteins they need. Without the proteins, cells die. The respiratory system fails, the heart stops. I haven't seen any suggestion in the literature that it's ever been used for suicide. Against it, you'd have to say it's far from readily available. You'd have to have some skills as a chemist to manufacture it, even supposing you could get your hands on the raw material. Either that or you'd have to have connections to a terrorist organization – they allegedly found it stockpiled in the Al-Quaeda caves in Afghanistan. The other aspect militating against it is that it's a long-drawn-out and very painful way to go. I can't imagine why anyone would choose it as a means of suicide.' He spread his hands and raised his shoulders to emphasize his point.

Carol made a note on her pad. 'So we could also rule out accident, by the sounds of it?'

'Unless Mr Bishop was in the habit of hanging around castor oil factories, I would say so,' Denby said brusquely.

'So how did it get into his system?'

'He probably inhaled it. We've examined him thoroughly and we can't find any puncture wounds.' Denby leaned forward. 'I don't know if you remember the case of the Bulgarian defector Georgi Markov in the late seventies? He was assassinated with a pellet of ricin fired from a doctored umbrella. Once we knew ricin was involved here, I had our ICU team make a thorough examination of Mr Bishop's skin. No sign of any foreign body being injected.'

Carol felt bemused. 'It's hard to believe,' she said. 'It's not the sort of thing that happens in Bradfield.'

'No,' Denby said. 'That's why it took us a couple of days to figure it out. I suppose it was the same for the doctors at UCH who treated Alexander Litvinenko. The last thing they expected to confront was radiation poisoning. But it happened.'

'How could he be poisoned without realizing it?'

'Quite easily,' Denby said. 'The data we have on ricin tell us that, if injected, as little as 500 micrograms could be enough to kill an adult. There's animal research that indicates that inhaling or ingesting similar amounts could be lethal. A 500 microgram dose of ricin would be about the size of the head of a pin. Not hard to slip into a drink or into some food. In those quantities, it would be tasteless.'

'So we're looking for someone who had access to his food or drink?'

Denby nodded. 'That's the most likely route.' He fiddled with his pen. 'It might also be infiltrated into a recreational drug such as cocaine or amphetamine, something snorted. Again, one would not notice any taste or smell.'

'Do you have blood and urine samples that you can test for recreational drugs?'

Denby nodded. 'I'll see that it's done.'

'How did you figure it out?'

'My SHO, Dr Blessing. I think you or one of your colleagues spoke to her in the first instance?'

'Yes, I know Dr Blessing contacted us. But what alerted her?'

Denby gave a little smirk. Carol liked him even less. 'I don't want to sound vain, but Dr Blessing reckoned that if I couldn't work out what was wrong with Mr Bishop, then it must be something quite a long way out of the ordinary. She checked out the symptoms in our online database and ricin poisoning was the single thing that fit the bill. She brought her conclusions to me, and I ordered the standard test. It came back strongly positive. There really is no room for doubt, Chief Inspector.'

Carol closed her notebook. 'Thanks for explaining this so clearly,' she said. 'You said you'd been reading up on ricin – is there any chance you could put some sort of briefing together for me and my officers?'

'I'll get Dr Blessing on to it right away.' He stood, indicating that the interview was over as far as he was concerned.

'Can I see him?' Carol said.

Denby rubbed his thumb against his jaw. 'Nothing much to see,' he said. 'But yes, I'll take you through. His parents may have come back – they were in the relatives' room. I had to break the news to them, and they were understandably shocked and upset. I asked them to stay put until they were feeling a little calmer. It doesn't help the ICU team if people are in an emotional state around the patients.' He spoke dismissively, as if the smooth running of a hospital ward were infinitely more important than the anguish of parents about to lose a son.

Carol followed him to Robbie Bishop's bedside. The two chairs by the bed were empty. Carol stood at the foot of the bed, taking in the various monitors, the tubes and machines that were keeping Robbie Bishop as stable as possible on what was going to be a short journey to death. His skin was waxy, a sheen of sweat visible on his cheeks and forehead. She wanted to hold this image in her head. This was going to be a nightmare investigation for all sorts of reasons, and she wanted to make sure she didn't lose sight of the human being at the heart of it. The media would be clamouring for answers, the fans would be demanding someone's head on a platter and her bosses would be eager to cover themselves in whatever glory she could drag out of the situation.

Carol was determined to find out who had destroyed Robbie Bishop, and why. But for her own sake, she needed to be sure she was pursuing his killer for the right reasons. Now she'd seen him, she could be a lot more sure of that.

Detective Constable Paula McIntyre knew all about shock and grief. She'd seen countless examples and she was still recovering from experiencing the extremes of both at first hand. So she didn't read anything into Martin Flanagan's behaviour other than the obvious fact that he had been shattered to the core by the news Dr Blessing had delivered.

His was the active, agitated response. He couldn't keep still. It didn't surprise Paula; she'd seen it before, particularly with men whose livelihoods centred round physical activity, whether on a building site or a sports field. Flanagan paced restlessly, then threw himself into a chair where he fidgeted with fingers and feet till he could stand the confinement no longer. Then he was back on his feet, quartering the room. Paula simply sat, the still point of his whirling world.

'I can't believe it,' Flanagan said. He'd been saying it ever since Paula had arrived, the short sentence a punctuation between everything else he said. 'He's been like a son to me, you know. I can't believe it. This is not what happens to footballers. They break bones, they strain muscles, they snap ligaments, you know. They don't get poisoned. I can't believe it.'

Paula let him wind himself up, waiting till he began to wind down before starting with her questions. She was used to waiting. She had become very good at it. Nobody was better at the art of the interview than Paula, and that was due in no small part to her knack of knowing when to dive in and when to hold back. So she waited till Martin Flanagan ran out of steam and fell silent, his forehead leaning against the cool glass of the window, his hands on the wall on either side of the frame. She could see the reflection of his face, haggard with pain.

'When did Robbie first show signs of being ill?' she asked.

'Saturday breakfast. We always stay at the Victoria Grand the night before home games.' Flanagan shrugged one shoulder upwards. 'It's a way of keeping tabs on them, you know. Most of them, they're young and stupid. They'd be out on the town till all hours if we didn't keep them on a tight leash. I sometimes think we should have them electronically tagged, like they do with cats and dogs and paedophiles.'

'And Robbie said he was feeling ill?'

Flanagan sniffed. 'He came over to my table. I was with Jason Graham, my assistant, and Dave Kermode, the physio, and Robbie said he was feeling out of sorts. Tight chest, sweaty, feverish. And his joints were aching, like he was coming down with the flu, you know. I told him to finish his breakfast and go to his room. I said I'd get the team doctor to come and take a look at him. He said he wasn't hungry, so he'd just go upstairs and get his head down for a bit.' He shook his head. 'I can't believe it, so I can't.'

'So Friday night, he definitely wasn't out on the town?'

'No way. He shares with Pavel Aljinovic.' He turned to face Paula and slid down the wall into a crouch. 'The goalkeeper, you know. They've shared since Pavel came to Bradfield two seasons back. Robbie always says Pavel's a boring bastard, keeps him honest.' A sad smile tugged at his mouth. 'There's some I wouldn't trust as

70

far as I could throw them, you know, but Pavel's not one of them. Robbie's right, Pavel is a boring bastard. He'd never have tried to sneak out for a night on the randan. And he wouldn't have let Robbie do it either.'

'I'm a bit at sea here,' Paula said. 'I don't really have much of a sense of what Robbie's typical routine was. Maybe you could run me through it? Say, from Thursday morning?' Paula wasn't sure how long the symptoms of ricin poisoning took to develop, but she reckoned going back to Thursday would cover the moment of its administration.

'We had a UEFA cup match on Wednesday night, so they had Thursday morning off, you know. Robbie came in to see the physio, he'd taken a knock on the ankle and it was a bit swollen. Nothing serious, but they all take their physical condition seriously. It's their living, you know. Anyway, he was done by half past ten. I assume he went home. He's got a flat down in the Millennium Quarter, just off Bellwether Square. He turned up for training on Thursday afternoon. We just did a light session, you know. Concentrating on skills more than tactics. We were done by half past four. And I've no idea what he did after that.'

'You don't have any sense of how he spent his free time?' *Just like a son to you*, Paula thought ironically. Robbie Bishop might be twenty-six years old, but if he was anything like most footballers she'd read about in the tabloids, he probably had arrested development. The lifestyle of a sixteen-year-old granted unlimited pocket money and access to beautiful women. The last person who would know what he was up to was anyone in a parental role.

Flanagan shrugged. 'They're not children, you

know. And I'm not like some managers. I don't barge into their homes and turn off their stereos and kick their girlfriends out. There are rules about not going out the night before a game. But apart from that, they do their own thing.' He shook his head again. 'I can't believe it.'

'And what was Robbie's thing?'

'There's a fitness centre where he lives. They've got a full-sized pool down in the basement. He likes to swim, relax in the sauna, that kind of thing. He's good pals with Phil Campsie, he's got a bit of land up on the edge of the moors. They go fishing and shooting together.' Flanagan pushed himself upright and recommenced his restless pacing. 'That's about all I can tell you.'

'What about girlfriends? Was Robbie seeing anybody special?'

Flanagan shook his head. 'Not that I knew about. He was engaged for a while. Bindie Blyth, the Radio One DJ. But they called it a day about three months ago.'

Paula's interest quickened. 'Who called it a day? Robbie, or Bindie?'

'I don't know anything about that. But he didn't seem to be that bothered, you know.' He leaned his forehead against the window again. 'What's all this got to do with somebody poisoning Robbie, anyway? It's not his team-mates or his ex who'd be doing that kind of thing.'

'We have to look at all the possibilities, Mr Flanagan. So, since Bindie, he's been what? Playing the field?' Paula winced at her unintentional pun. *Please let him not think I'm taking the piss.*

'I suppose.' He turned back, rubbing his temples with his fingers. 'You'd have to ask the lads. Phil and Pavel, they'd likely know.' He looked longingly at the door that led to the ICU. 'I wish they'd let me see him, you know. To say goodbye, at least. I can't believe it.'

'What about Friday? Do you know what he did then?'

'We were at the training ground on Friday.' Flanagan paused for a moment. 'Come to think of it, he was a bit lacklustre. Head down, a bit slow off the ball. As if he was kind of dozy. I didn't think anything of it, you know. They all have their off days and, frankly, you'd rather they had them on a training session than a match. He wasn't off it enough for me to do anything about it, though. And then when he said he had the flu on Saturday, I put it down to that.'

Paula nodded. 'Anyone would have done the same. Now, I have to ask you this. Is there anyone you can think of who has a grudge against Robbie? Has he had any hate mail? Any problems with stalkers?'

Flanagan winced and shook his head. 'You don't get to where he is without pissing off one or two people along the way. You know? Like, there's always been a bit of needle between him and Nils Petersen, the Man United centre-back. But that's football. It's not real life. I mean, if he ran into Petersen in a bar, they'd likely indulge in a bit of argy-bargy, but that'd be the size of it. It wouldn't come to blows, never mind poisoning.' He threw his hands into the air. 'It's insane. It's like something in a bad film. There's nothing more I can tell you, because none of it makes sense.' He gestured towards the door with his thumb.

73

'That lad in there is dying and it's a tragedy. That's all I know.'

Paula sensed she'd reached the end of Flanagan's capacity for answers. They'd probably have to talk to him again, but for now she thought there wasn't likely to be much more he could tell her. She stood up. 'I hope you get to say goodbye, Mr Flanagan. Thank you for talking to me.'

He nodded, too distracted now to care what she had to say. Paula walked away, thinking about death and second chances. She'd been given her life back, complete with its load of survivor guilt. But thanks to Tony Hill, she was starting to understand that she had to make that gift mean something. Robbie Bishop was as good a place to start as any.

Not all of Robbie Bishop's fans were outside Bradfield Cross. Those who lived in Ratcliffe had decided against the cross-town journey and settled for bringing their bunches of supermarket flowers and their children's paintings to Bradfield Victoria's training ground. They were propped along the chain-link fence that kept the punters away from the stars. Detective Sergeant Kevin Matthews couldn't help a faint shudder of distaste as he waited for the gate security to call through and confirm their permission to enter the ground. He couldn't be doing with these public outpourings of synthetic emotion. He wouldn't mind betting that none of those who had made their pilgrimage to the Ratcliffe ground had ever exchanged more than a few words along the lines of, 'And who shall I sign it to?' with Robbie Bishop. It wasn't so long since Kevin had had to mourn for real, and he resented the cheapness of their gestures. In his view, if the pilgrims lavished those emotions on the living – their kids, partners and parents – the world would be a better place.

'Tacky,' Chris Devine said from the passenger seat as if reading his mind.

'This is nothing to what there'll be in a couple of days, after he's actually died,' Kevin said as the guard waved them through, pointing to the parking area near the long, low building that impeded the view of the field from the street. He slowed as they passed the Ferraris and Porsches of the players. 'Nice motors,' he said approvingly.

'You've got a Ferrari, haven't you?' Chris said, recalling something Paula had told her.

He sighed. 'Mondial QV cabriolet, Ferrari red. One of only twenty-four right-hand-drive cabs ever built. She's a dream machine, and she's going soon.'

'Oh no. Poor Kevin. Why are you getting rid?'

'She's really only a two-seater and the kids are getting too big to squeeze in. She's a single person's car, Chris. I don't suppose you're interested?'

'A bit rich for my blood, I think. I'd never hear the end of it from Sinead. She'd be telling me it was my mid-life crisis car.'

'Shame. I'd like to be sure she's going to a good home. At least I've managed to get a stay of execution for a bit.'

'How come?'

'There's this journalist, Justin Adams. He writes for the car magazines and he wants to do an article about ordinary blokes who drive extraordinary cars. Apparently a cop with a Ferrari is right up his street.

So I got Stella to agree that I get to keep the car till the magazine article comes out, so I don't get the piss taken out of me for having my name and my photo in a magazine when I don't own the car any more.'

Chris grinned. 'Sounds like a good deal to me.'

'Yeah, well, the countdown begins next week, when we do the interview.' Kevin sniffed as he got out of the car. 'Digestive day,' he said.

'What?'

He pointed to the west, where a two-storey brick building slumped along the boundary of the playing fields. 'The biscuit factory. When I was a kid, I trained for a season with the Vic juniors. When the wind's in the right direction, you can tell what biscuits they're baking. I always thought it was a refined form of torture for teenage lads trying to keep fit.'

'What happened?' Chris asked, following him round the end of the changing pavilion.

Kevin strode ahead of her so she couldn't see the regret on his face. 'I wasn't good enough,' he said. 'Many are called but few are chosen.'

'That must have been rough.'

Kevin gave a little snort of laughter. 'At the time, I thought it was the end of the world.'

'And now?'

'The money would have been better, that's for sure. And I'd have a fleet of Ferraris.'

'True,' Chris said, catching up with him as he paused, looking out across the grass where a couple of dozen young men were dribbling balls around traffic cones. 'But for most footballers, you're on the scrapheap by the time you're our age. And what's left? Sure, a handful make it into management, but a lot more end up behind the bar in some shitty pub trading on their glory days and bitching about the ex-wife that cleaned them out.'

Kevin grinned at her. 'And you think that would be worse than this?'

'You know it would.'

As they rounded the building, a man in shorts and a Bradfield Victoria sweatshirt headed their way. He looked to be in his middle forties, but he was in such good shape it was hard to be certain. If his dark hair had still been in a mullet, he'd have been instantly recognizable to football fans and indifferents alike. But now it was cut close to his head, it took Kevin a moment to realize he was face to face with one of the heroes of his youth.

'You're Terry Malcolm,' he blurted out, twelve again and besotted with the ball skills of the England and Bradfield midfielder.

Terry Malcolm turned to Chris with a smile and said, 'I'll be all right if I ever get Alzheimer's. You'd be amazed how often people feel the need to tell me who I am. You must be Sergeant Devine. I'm only guessing, mind. In a hopeful sort of way, on account of he's not my type and I can't see myself calling him Devine.' His expression said he was accustomed to people finding him funny and charming. Kevin, already disillusioned with his former hero, was pleased to see Chris Devine unmoved.

'Mr Flanagan told you why we're here?' Kevin said, his tone slightly incredulous. As if he couldn't quite believe anyone who worked for Bradfield Vic could be so flippant while their finest player lay dying.

Malcolm looked suitably chastened. 'He did. And

believe me, I'm gutted about Robbie. But I can't afford to let my feelings show. There's another twenty-one players on the squad who need to stay motivated. We've got Spurs in the premiership on Saturday and we can't afford to be dropping points at this stage in the season.' He gave Chris the benefit of his smile again. 'I hope that doesn't sound callous. Like I said, I'm gutted. But our boys need to be kept on their toes. On Saturday, we'll be winning it for Robbie. All the more reason not to chuck our routines in the bin.'

'Quite,' Chris said. 'And we need to check out Robbie's movements in the forty-eight hours before he started feeling ill on Saturday. We want to talk to his mates. The ones who are close enough to know what he was up to between the end of training on Thursday and breakfast on Saturday.'

Malcolm nodded. 'You want to talk to Pavel Aljinovic and Phil Campsie. Robbie bunks up with Pavel when we're in a hotel. And Phil's his best mate.' Malcolm made no move to summon the players.

'Now, Mr Malcolm,' Chris said.

Again the cheap and cheesy smile. 'It's Terry, love.'

It was Chris's turn to smile. 'I'm not your love, Mr Malcolm. I am a police officer investigating a very serious attack on one of your colleagues. And I want to talk to either Pavel Aljinovic or Phil Campsie right now.'

Malcolm shook his head. 'They're training. I can't interrupt that.'

Kevin flushed an unbecoming scarlet, his freckles darkening across his cheeks. 'Do you want me to arrest you for police obstruction? Because you're going the right way about it.'

Malcolm's lip lifted in a sneer. 'I don't think you'll be arresting me. Your boss likes his seat in the directors' box far too much for that.'

'That cuts both ways,' Chris said sweetly. 'It means we have a hotline to your boss, too. And I don't think he'd be very impressed to hear you've been impeding our inquiries into the attempted murder of his star player.'

Although Chris had spoken, it was Kevin who was on the receiving end of a glare of deep dislike. Malcolm was clearly one of those men who could only flirt with women and talk with men. 'I'll get Pavel.' He gestured with his thumb towards the pavilion. 'Wait inside there, I'll sort you out a room in a minute.'

Five minutes later, they were sitting in a weights room that smelled of stale sweat and muscle rub. The Croatian international goalkeeper was hot on their heels. As he walked in, his nose twitched and a look of distaste crossed his chiselled features. 'Stinks in here, sorry,' he said, pulling a plastic chair from a short stack against the wall and sitting down opposite the two detectives. 'I am Pavel Aljinovic.' He nodded formally to them both.

The word that came to Kevin's mind was 'dignified'. Aljinovic had shoulder-length dark hair, normally pulled back in a tight ponytail on match days, but flowing free this afternoon. His eyes were the colour of conkers baked in the oven then polished on a sleeve. High cheekbones over hollow cheeks, full lips and a narrow, straight nose made him look almost aristocratic. 'Coach says somebody tried to poison Robbie,' he said, his accent faint but unmistakably Slavic. 'How can this be?'

'That's what we're trying to find out,' Chris said, leaning forward, elbows on knees and hands clasped.

'And Robbie? How is he doing?'

'Not very well,' Kevin said.

'But he will be OK?'

'We're not doctors. We can't say.' Chris wanted to avoid making it clear that Robbie's death was inevitable. In her experience, there was a substantial brake on what people were willing to say once the stakes were raised to murder. 'It would help if we knew where Robbie was on Thursday and Friday.'

'Of course he was at training sessions. Thursday night, I don't know what he did.' Aljinovic spread his big goalkeeper's hands. 'I am goalkeeper, not Robbie's keeper. But on Friday night, we shared the hotel room. We all had dinner together, like usual. Steak and potatoes and salad and a glass of red wine. Fruit salad and ice cream. We always have the same thing, me and Robbie. Actually, most of the guys. We went upstairs about nine o'clock. Robbie took a bath and I called my wife. We watched the Sky football channel together until about ten, then we went to sleep.'

'Did Robbie have anything out of the mini-bar?' Kevin asked.

Aljinovic chuckled. 'You don't know much about football, do you? They don't give us keys for the mini-bar. We're supposed to stay pure. This is why we are in a hotel and not at home. They can control what we eat and drink and they can keep us away from women.'

Chris returned his smile. 'I thought that was a myth, keeping your strength up before a match by avoiding sex.'

'It's not the sex, it's the sleep,' Aljinovic said. 'They like us to have good sleep before a game.'

'Did Robbie have any food or drink with him? Bottled water, whatever?'

'No. There is always plenty of water in the room.' He frowned. 'You have reminded me. Friday evening, Robbie said he was very thirsty. He said he felt as if he was coming down with a cold or something. He didn't make a big deal out of it, just that he wasn't feeling great. And of course in the morning, he thought he had flu. I was worried in case I might catch it. This feeling like flu, is this the poison? Or is he sick too?'

'It's the poison.' Kevin looked directly into his eyes. 'Did Robbie take cocaine on Friday evening?'

Aljinovic reared backwards, an expression of affront on his face. 'Of course not. No. Who told you that? Robbie didn't use drugs. Why are you asking this?'

'It's possible he inhaled the poison. If it was mixed in with cocaine or amphetamine, Robbie might not have noticed,' Chris said.

'No. This is not possible. Not possible at all. I will not believe this about him.'

'You said earlier that you're a goalkeeper, not Robbie's keeper. How can you be so sure he never uses drugs?' Kevin said, his voice mild but his eyes intent.

'We have talked about it. About drugs in sports. And for fun. Robbie and me, we think the same. It's a fool's game. You cheat yourself, you cheat the fans, you cheat your club. We both know people who use drugs and we both despise them.' He spoke vehemently. 'Whoever poisoned Robbie, they didn't do it with drugs.'

By the time Carol arrived at Robbie Bishop's flat, Detective Constable Sam Evans had already made a start on the search. The footballer's home was a penthouse complete with roof terrace in the heart of the city. The building had been a department store; the main living area was bright with daylight that poured in through metal-framed Art Deco windows. Sam was going through the desk drawers, caught in a shaft of sunlight that made his coffee-coloured skin glow. He looked up as Carol walked in, giving her a rueful shake of the head. 'Nothing,' he said. 'Not so far.'

'What kind of nothing?' She snapped a pair of latex gloves over her hands.

'Neatly filed bills, bank statements, credit card statements. He pays his bills on time, he pays his credit cards off every month. He's got an account with a bookie, gambles a few hundred a month on the ponies. Nothing that stands out. I haven't looked at the computer yet, I thought I'd leave that for Stacey.'

'I'm sure she'll be thrilled. You think she knows what football is?' Carol said, crossing to look out of the window. A hawk's-eye view of the city centre; people going about their business, trams criss-crossing, fountains playing, *Big Issue* sellers cajoling, shoppers dawdling by windows full of promises. None of them thinking about poisoning a premiership footballer with ricin, not today. Tomorrow or the day after, when Robbie Bishop finally died, it would be different. But not today. Not yet. She turned back. 'What have you done so far?'

'Just the desk.'

82

Carol nodded. She looked around. Sam had been right to start at the desk. There weren't many other search options. The dining area, all glass and steel, had nothing to hide. There were a couple of groups of scarlet leather sofas, one centred on a huge plasma screen home cinema system complete with PlayStation, the other set around a low glass coffee table whose leading edge looked like a breaking wave. A wall of shelves housed a vast collection of DVDs and CDs. Someone would have to go through every one, but she'd leave that to the crime scene team. She walked over to the media collection. The CDs were mostly by people she'd never heard of. The names she did recognize were dance and hip-hop; she assumed the rest were similar in flavour.

The DVDs were roughly arranged – football on two shelves in the middle, popular action and comedy movies beneath them, TV comedy and drama above them. PlayStation and PC computer games filled the bottom shelf. The top one, appropriately, held the porn. Carol skimmed the titles, deciding Robbie's taste in porn was as unadventurous as his taste in film and drama. Unless there was a secret stash somewhere, it appeared that Robbie's sexual inclinations were not the sort to get him killed.

Carol wandered through to the bedroom, smiling wryly at the sight of a bed that must have been seven feet wide. The rumpled dark blue silk sheets were piled with fake furs, and a dozen pillows were scattered around. Another plasma TV dominated the wall opposite the bed, and the other walls displayed paintings of nudes that the vendor had almost certainly described as 'artistic'.

A walk-in wardrobe ran the whole length of one wall. There was an empty section. Carol wondered if that had been where his fiancée had hung her clothes, or if he'd just been having a clear-out. At the far end were two rectangular baskets, one labelled 'laundry', the other 'dry cleaning'. Both were almost full. Presumably, someone else took care of them. Luckily, they hadn't been in since Robbie had been taken ill.

The top layer of the laundry basket consisted of a pair of Armani jeans, Calvin Klein trunks and an extravagantly striped Paul Smith shirt. Carol picked up the jeans and went through the pockets. At first, she thought they were empty, but as her fingers probed, they encountered a screw of paper rammed right down into the seam of the front right-hand pocket. She pulled it out and gently teased the creases and folds apart.

It was the corner of a page of lined paper, apparently torn from a notebook. Written in black ink was, 'www.bestdays.co.uk'. Carol took it through to the living area and asked Sam for an evidence bag. 'What you got, boss?' he asked, handing one over.

Carol dropped the paper in the bag, sealing and dating it. 'A url. Probably nothing. Take it back for Stacey, please. You find anything?'

Sam shook his head. 'I tell you, he looks a pretty boring bastard to me.'

Carol went back through to the bedroom. Bedside tables held few surprises – condoms, breath mints, tissues, a blister pack of Nurofen, a pinkie-sized butt plug and a tube of KY. Carol was pretty sure that, these days, that counted as vanilla. Interestingly, the book tucked into the drawer on the left was Michael

Crick's critical biography of Manchester United's boss, Alex Ferguson. Though Carol was far from knowledgeable about football, even she knew that in a world of celebrity soccer hagiographies this was an interesting choice.

Nothing in the ensuite bathroom gave Carol a moment's pause. Sighing, she returned to Sam. 'It's almost spooky,' she said. 'There's so little personality here.'

Sam snorted. 'Probably because he hasn't got one. These football stars – they're all stuck in their adolescence. They get picked up by the big clubs before they've had their first kiss, and the management system takes over from their mums. If they make the grade, they're cash rich and common sense poor by the time they're out of their teens. They're wrapped in cotton wool and models' thighs. Way more money than sense or experience. Bunch of Peter Pans with added testosterone.'

Carol grinned. 'You sound bitter. Did you lose a girlfriend to one of them, or what?'

Sam returned her grin. 'The women I like are too smart for footballers. No, I'm just bitter because I can't afford a Bentley GTC Mulliner.' Sam waved an invoice at her. 'His new car. Delivery next month.'

Carol whistled. 'I know men who would kill for one of those. But probably not using ricin.' As she spoke, her phone rang. 'DCI Jordan,' she said.

'This is Dr Blessing. Mr Denby asked me to call you. Robbie Bishop's taken a turn for the worse. We don't think he's got long. I don't know if you want to be here?'

'I'm on my way,' Carol said. She closed her phone

and sighed. 'Looks like this is about to become a murder inquiry.'

They were waiting for Phil Campsie. Chris idly picked up a dumbbell and did a few forearm curls. 'He's the ugly one, isn't he?' she said. 'The one who looks like a cross between a monkey and Mr Potato Head?'

'Phil Campsie, you mean? Yeah, he's ugly.' Kevin stretched, yawning. His four-year-old daughter had recently lost the knack of sleeping through the night. His wife, not unreasonably, had pointed out that when Ruby had been breastfeeding, she had been the one who had had to deal with broken nights. Now it was Kevin's turn to soothe his daughter back to sleep. It didn't feel fair, not when he was going out to work and Stella was staying home. But it was hard to argue against without sounding like he didn't love his daughter. 'He's very ugly,' he said through the tail end of the yawn.

'So it's not just teenage girls who pair up according to looks.'

'What do you mean?'

'Pretty one, ugly one. Symbiosis. The pretty one gets to look even better next to the ugly one, and the ugly one gets the pretty one's cast-offs. Win-win.'

Kevin tutted. 'That's not very sisterly of you.'

Chris gave a derisive snort. 'See, Kevin, you keep conflating lesbian and feminist. Try lesbian and pragmatist next time.'

He grinned. 'I'll try and remember. So, you think that's what was going on with Robbie and Phil?'

'To some degree. Of course, Phil is also rich and famous, which trumps ugly every time. But I bet it didn't hurt, going out on the town with one of the most recognizable, handsome and eligible men in Europe. Not to mention sexy.'

'You think Robbie's sexy?'

'Sex appeal is gender blind, Kevin. Don't tell me you don't think Robbie is sexy, deep down.'

Kevin flushed. 'I've never thought about it.'

'But you like the way he looks. The way he moves. The way he dresses,' Chris persisted.

'I suppose.'

'It's all right, it doesn't mean you're a poof. All I'm trying to say is that Robbie's got sex appeal, charisma, call it what you will. David Beckham's got it, Gary Neville hasn't. John Lennon had it, Paul McCartney doesn't. Bill Clinton has it, Dubya definitely doesn't. And if you don't have it, the next best thing is to hang around with somebody who does.' Chris put down the dumbbell as the door opened. She turned on her best smile. 'Mr Campsie. Thanks for making the time to talk to us.'

Phil Campsie hooked his ankle round the chair and pulled it a couple of feet further away from them before he sat down. 'It's for Robbie, innit?' His London accent was almost as strong as Chris's own. 'Do anything for him. He's me mate.'

Kevin made the introductions. Close up, Phil Campsie was even more unattractive. He had pale, mottled skin like a scrubbed potato, a flat nose that looked as if it had been broken a couple of times. His small grey eyes were set wide on his cannonball head. His reddish hair was cut close and already the shape of male pattern baldness was etched into his hairline. But when he smiled, as well as uneven yellowing teeth he revealed a genuine spark of cheeky warmth. Kevin led off. 'We hear Robbie probably spends more time with you after work than any of his other team-mates.'

''S right. Me and Robbie, we're like that –' Phil crossed the first two fingers of his right hand.

'So, what kind of stuff do you guys get up to?' Chris raised her eyebrows, as if to suggest that nothing he said could shock her.

'This and that. I got a place outside the city. Bit of land, couple of miles of trout stream. Me and Robbie, we do a bit of rough shooting – rabbits, pigeons, that kind of thing. And we go fishing.' He grinned, looking like the small boy he must have been not so long ago. 'I've got this woman comes in from the village, cooks and cleans for me. She deals with the stuff we kill. Cooks it all up, sticks it in the freezer. There's something really cool about eating something you've killed yourself, know what I mean?'

'Impressive,' Chris said, before Kevin could put his foot in it. 'And what about a social life? What do you do for fun when you're not slaughtering the wildlife?'

'We go out in town,' Phil said. 'Nice bit of dinner somewhere smart, then on to a club.' He gave a curiously self-deprecating little shrug. 'The clubs like having us. Gives them a bit of a profile. So we get taken to the VIP areas, free champagne, very tasty girls.'

'We're interested in Robbie's movements on Thursday and Friday,' Kevin said.

Phil nodded, rolling his big shoulders as if squaring up to someone. 'Thursday after training, we went back to Robbie's flat. We played on the PlayStation for a bit. GT HD, you know? The new one, with the

Ferraris? Well cool. We had a couple of beers then we went out for dinner to Las Bravas. It's Spanish,' he added, apparently trying to be helpful.

'I hear it's very nice there. What did you have to eat?' Chris asked, mild as milk.

'We had a load of tapas between us. We kind of left it to the waiter and he brought us a right old mix of stuff. Most of it was lovely, but I couldn't be doing with some of the seafood.' He pulled a face. 'I mean, who wants to eat a baby squid? Yech.'

'Did you both eat the same things?' Kevin said.

Phil thought for a moment, his eyes turning up and to the left. 'Pretty much,' he said slowly. 'Robbie didn't have the garlic mushrooms, he doesn't like mushrooms. But apart from that, yeah, we both gave everything a whirl.'

'And drink?'

'We was on the rioja. We got as far as the second bottle, but we didn't finish it.'

'And afterwards?'

'We went on to Amatis. D'you know it? Dance club the far side of Temple Fields?'

Kevin nodded. 'We're police officers, Phil. We know Amatis.'

'It's a nice place,' Phil said defensively. 'Nice people. And great music.'

'You into music, then? You and Robbie?'

Phil blew out a big breath, making his lips flap. 'Me, I'm not bothered as long as it's got a decent beat. But Robbie, he's well into it, yeah. He used to be engaged to Bindie Blyth.' Seeing their looks of incomprehension, he gave them more. 'The Radio One late-night DJ. It was music what brought them together.' He shifted in his seat, sticking his legs out in front of him and crossing them at the ankles. 'Wasn't enough to keep them together, though. They split up a couple of months back.'

Chris could feel Kevin come alert beside her. She tried for nonchalant. 'How come?' she said.

'Why d'you wanna know about Bindie?'

Chris spread her hands. 'Me, I'm just interested in everything. Why did they split?'

Phil looked away. 'Just wasn't going anywhere.'

'Was he messing around behind her back?' Chris asked.

Phil gave her a cagey glance. 'This doesn't go no further, right?'

'Right. What happens in Vegas stays in Vegas,' Chris said.

'It's the world we live in,' Phil said. For an insane moment, Chris thought he was going to make some philosophical point about the human condition. 'Every time we go out the house, we're surrounded by people who want to make an impression. Women who want to shag us, blokes who either want to buy us a drink or fight us. And if your girlfriend's a couple of hundred miles away most of the time, you'd have to be a saint. And Robbie ain't no saint.'

'So Bindie got the hump and gave him the elbow?'

'Pretty much. But they didn't want the tabloids all over them, so they both agreed they'd just say it was a mutual thing, too hard to keep it going with them both having high-pressure careers. No hard feelings, that sort of thing.'

'And were there any hard feelings?' Kevin butted in. Chris wanted to slap him for breaking her flow.

Phil cocked his head. 'No.' It came out firm and defensive. Then a frown slowly furrowed his forehead. 'Wait a minute. You're not thinking Bindie had anything to do with this?' He gave a roar of laughter. 'Fucking hell, it's obvious you've never listened to her show. Bindie's got balls. If she was that pissed off, she'd have sent Robbie home with his nuts in a paper bag. Bindie's the kind of woman who lets you have it to your face. No way she'd be sneaking around with poison.' He shook his head. 'Mental.'

'Nobody's suggesting Bindie had anything to do with this, Phil. We're just trying to get a picture of Robbie's life. So, Thursday. Tell us about Amatis.'

Phil shifted in his chair, a man preparing to be less than candid. 'Not much to tell. We was in the VIP area mostly, drinking champagne. There was a couple of the lads from Yorkshire Cricket Club there, that geezer that presents the TV show about making a mint from what's in your attic, some twat that was on *Big Brother* a couple of series back. I didn't recognize any other blokes. And the usual sort of birds. Tasty but with a bit of class. That's the sort of bird you get at Amatis.'

'Was Robbie with anyone in particular?'

Phil thought for a moment. 'Not really. We was both up dancing, but he wasn't with the same bird for long. He kept chopping and changing, like he couldn't find one he really fancied.' He smirked. 'Not like me. I pulled practically right away. Jasmine, her name was. Legs up to heaven, tits out to here.' He mimed substantial breasts. 'So I wasn't paying too much attention to Robbie, if you catch my drift. He went down the vodka bar for a while after I clicked

91

with Jasmine. Me and her, we decided to go back to hers, so I went looking for Robbie. Found him on his way back from the toilet. I said I was going back to Jasmine's, he was cool with that. He said he'd run into somebody he was at school with and they was having a drink.' Phil shrugged. 'Next time I saw him was training on Friday and he looked rough as a badger's arse. I said he looked like he'd made a night of it. He went all sheepish, said he couldn't actually remember. Well, that's the way it goes sometimes, innit? You get so wellied, it's all just a black hole the next morning.'

Chris realized she was holding her breath. She let it out and said, 'This old school friend. Do they have a name?'

'He never said. He never even said if it was a bird or a bloke.' Phil looked upset. 'I should have asked him, shouldn't I? I should have taken better care of him.'

Chris hid her disappointment behind a smile. 'Nobody's blaming you, Phil. We don't know when Robbie was poisoned. But in my experience, when somebody is determined to attack another person, it's very hard to stop them succeeding.'

'He's going to be all right, isn't he? I mean, the doctors know what they're doing, right?' He bit his lower lip. 'He's strong as an ox, is Robbie. And he's a fighter.'

Kevin looked away, leaving it up to Chris to decide which way to go. 'They're doing their best,' she said. 'You guys'll be out on the town again before you know it.'

Phil pursed his lips and nodded. He looked close

to tears. 'You'll never walk alone, innit.' He got to his feet. 'Right then. I better get back.'

Chris stood up and put a hand on his upper arm. 'Thanks, Phil. You've been a big help.' She watched him go, broad shoulders bowed, all spring removed from his step. The door closed behind him and Kevin turned to her.

'I'm guessing you don't have him down as number one suspect?'

Chris shook her head. 'He probably thinks ricin is something horses and greyhounds do. At least he gave us something.'

'The old school mate?'

'The very same. Lots of potential motive there. Was the golden boy a bit of a bully? Did he seduce somebody else's girlfriend? Did he commit a dirty tackle that ruined somebody else's chances of stardom?'

Kevin headed for the door. 'Definitely a bone for the DCI to chew on.'

'Just what she needs. Something to take her mind off the fact that nobody told her Tony was in hospital.'

Kevin winced. 'Don't. I tell you, if it had been anybody except Paula on duty this weekend, there would have been blood and teeth on the floor.'

'What is it with Tony and the guv'nor? First time I met them, I was convinced they were an item. But everybody says no, nay, never. I don't get it.'

'Nobody gets it,' Kevin said. 'Least of all them, I suspect.'

If Sam Evans had a motto, it was that knowledge is power. His application of the aphorism was indiscriminate; he worked at acquiring information about and ahead of his colleagues as thoroughly as he did against criminals. So, after Carol had left Robbie Bishop's apartment, he decided to sneak a quick look at the footballer's computer ahead of Stacey. He knew there were good reasons why he should leave it alone, but from what he had gleaned of Robbie Bishop, Sam didn't expect his computer to be equipped with a logic bomb primed to destroy all data if a stranger attempted to access it.

He was right. It wasn't even password-protected. It was tempting to start opening files, but he knew that would leave the sort of traces Stacey couldn't fail to notice. But he reckoned he'd be safe enough copying files on to the blank CD-ROMs he'd found in one of the desk drawers.

It didn't take him long to realize there wasn't much worth copying, at least from an information point of view. There were thousands of music files; according to Robbie's iTunes software, it would take 7.3 days to listen to them all. A serious amount of music, but not likely to shed any light on Robbie's murder. Also unlikely to serve any useful purpose were a few dozen saved game files, further evidence of his recreational software habit. Instead, Sam concentrated on the emails, the photos and a handful of Word files. Even with such ruthless culling, it still took three CDs to download what he wanted for himself.

Then he closed down the machine, confident that he was bomb-proof. Let Stacey play with it as much as she wanted. He had the head start he needed to make sure he was right out in front of the rest of the team.

Satisfied, Sam turned off the computer and returned

to the desk. Now he had something solid to work with, he minded less that he was stuck here when he should be out on the front line interviewing the key players. Bloody Jordan. It didn't matter what he did, she refused to be impressed. He was going to have to figure out a way to go round her if he was going to make the headway he craved. Sill mildly pissed off, he reached for his cigarettes and lit up. It wasn't like Robbie Bishop would be back to complain.

Carol stood in the shadows, watching the final act of Robbie Bishop's tragedy play out before her. Not even the machines could keep him alive any longer. Denby had explained it to her when she'd arrived at the hospital. 'As I told you before, ricin stops the cells manufacturing the proteins they need, so they start to die. We can compensate for that to some degree with machines, but there comes a point where the blood pressure falls so low we simply can't get enough oxygen to the brain, and everything begins to shut down. That's the point we've reached now.'

He was, she knew, in no pain. There was morphine to take care of that. And prophanol to keep him asleep. Although he was still technically alive, there was nothing left of what had made Robbie Bishop himself. It was hard to believe that the man she was watching die had inspired his team-mates to a memorable victory only days before. He didn't look like an athlete any longer. His head was swollen to twice its normal size, his body bloated and distended. Under the thin bedclothes, his formerly beautiful legs looked like twin pillars. Robbie Bishop, sporting hero, idol of millions, looked utterly pitiful.

His mother sat by his side, both hands clutching limp fingers turned black from the lack of peripheral circulation brought on by the very drugs they'd given him in their attempts to raise his blood pressure. Silent tears coursed down her cheeks. She was only in her late forties, but the past couple of days had turned her into an old woman, hunched and bewildered. Behind her stood her husband, his hands tight on her shoulders. The resemblance between him and his son when healthy was striking. Brian Bishop was a living reminder of what Robbie would never become.

On the other side of the bed, Martin Flanagan stood, head bowed, hands clasped in front of him. Carol could see his face was screwed tight with the effort of not crying. After England's last dismal World Cup exit, Carol had thought it was acceptable for real men to shed tears. Perhaps not for those of Flanagan's generation, she thought.

As she watched, Robbie's chest seemed to seize, his body to spasm. All over in seconds. When it was done, the heart monitor's numbers were plummeting, the blood pressure sinking like a stone, the blood oxygen saturation falling in a blur of digital display. 'I'm very sorry,' Thomas Denby said. 'We need to switch off the life support now.'

Mrs Bishop wailed. Just one long keening cry, then she fell forward, her head against the side of her boy, her hand clawing at his bloated chest, as if she could somehow thrust life back into him. Her husband turned away, his hands over his face, his shoulders shaking. Flanagan was slumped against the wall in a crouch, his head on his knees.

It was too much. Carol stepped away. When she

96

emerged into the corridor, Denby was at her shoulder. 'We'll have to issue a statement, hold a press conference. I suggest we make it a joint one.' He looked at his watch. 'Half an hour enough for you to prepare?'

'I'm not sure we should . . .'

'Look, I'm going to have to tell them what we know, which is that Robbie Bishop died from ricin poisoning. They're going to want to know what you people are doing. All I'm trying to do is to make sure the whole story comes out at once, rather than have a raft of speculation floating around any announcement I make.' Denby sounded irritated, a man unaccustomed to being challenged.

Carol had never had any problem standing up to men like Denby, but she had learned to pick her battlegrounds. 'I suppose I've had more experience than you at trying to do my job in the midst of a hostile media rattling their sabres,' she said sweetly. 'If it makes it easier for you to have my support at the press conference, I'm sure it can be arranged. Where will we be meeting the press?'

Thoroughly wrong-footed, Denby said curtly, 'The boardroom on the second floor is probably the best place. I'll see you there in twenty minutes.' And he was gone, his white coat so starched it barely stirred in the wind of his passage.

'Bastard,' she muttered under her breath.

'Problems, chief?' Paula stood in the doorway of the family room where she'd earlier interviewed Flanagan.

'Mr Denby doesn't like hanging around. Pronounces death one minute, announces the press conference the next. I'd have liked a little more time to make sure I was up to speed, that's all.'

'You want me to ring round the team? Get the bullet points?'

Carol had trouble taking Paula's eagerness at face value. When she'd found herself in a similar position professionally, she'd felt rage, resentment and a burning desire for vengeance. She couldn't imagine any circumstances in which she could have worked for those who had let her down and betrayed her trust. Yet instead of hating her, Paula seemed to be even more driven to win her approval. Carol had asked Tony to explain it to her, but he'd been hampered by his own clinical involvement with Paula. All he'd felt able to say was, 'She genuinely doesn't blame you for what went wrong that night in Temple Fields. She understands that you didn't hang her out to dry. That you did everything you could to keep her safe. There's no hidden agenda here, Carol. You can trust that she's on your side.'

So now she tried. She smiled and put a hand on Paula's arm. 'That would be a big help. I'm going to put some notes together down in the café – I need the caffeine. I'll see you there in quarter of an hour.'

As she walked, Carol disregarded the hospital rule forbidding mobiles and called her boss. John Brandon, the Chief Constable of Bradfield Metropolitan Police, had been responsible for dragging her back into the world of policing when she'd desperately wanted to leave it for good. He'd created the Major Incident Team she headed up, and he was the one senior police officer she trusted without reservation.

She brought him up to date on the Robbie Bishop situation, explaining the need for a joint press conference.

'Go ahead,' Brandon said. 'You're the one on the ground. I trust your judgement.'

'There's only one thing I'm not sure of – I don't know whether to go public with murder or stick with suspicious death.'

'Do you think it's murder?'

'Hard to see how it could be anything else.'

'Then go with murder. High-profile case like this, they'll crucify us if they think we're covering our backs. Call it as you see it.'

'Thank you, sir.'

'And, Carol – keep me on the page with you on this one.'

Carol ended the call not a moment too soon. As she thrust her phone back into her bag, a TV reporter standing on the fringes of the press battalion recognized her. He broke away, calling her name, running towards her.

Carol smiled and waggled her fingers in a wave. She was deep in the warren of hospital corridors before he reached the main door. It was beginning.

Yousef walked into the living room just after the regional evening news programme began. He started to speak, but Raj and Sanjar both shushed him. 'What?' he protested, giving Raj a shove so he'd move up and let Yousef squeeze in on the end of the sofa.

'It's Robbie Bishop,' Sanjar said. 'He's dead.'

'No way,' Yousef protested.

'Shush,' Raj insisted. Of the three brothers, he was

the only real football fan. Sanjar loved cricket, but Yousef had never caught the sports bug. Still, given his plans for the weekend, this story was interesting.

On the screen, the newsreader looked solemn. 'And now we are going live to a press conference at Bradfield Cross Hospital where Robbie Bishop's doctor, Mr Thomas Denby, is making a statement.'

The picture changed. Some geezer in a serious suit and a sharp haircut was sitting at a table flanked by a good-looking blonde and a nothing brunette in a white coat. 'I'm sorry to have to tell you that Robbie Bishop died in the Intensive Care Unit here at Bradfield Cross half an hour ago. His parents and Martin Flanagan, the manager of Bradfield Victoria, were with him when he died.' Posh voice. Cleared his throat and went on. 'We have known for some hours that there was nothing further we could do for Robbie except to make sure his last hours were as comfortable as possible.' There was a buzz of voices in the background from reporters who didn't have the patience or the manners to wait for Denby to say what he had to say. Just like his baby brother, who kept repeating, 'So what did he die of?'

The posh geezer held up a hand, appealing for quiet. He gave it a few seconds then started again. 'This morning, we received the results of lab tests that proved conclusively that Robbie Bishop was not suffering from any kind of infection. What killed Robbie Bishop was a substantial dose of the poison ricin.' The room erupted.

'Fucking hell,' Sanjar breathed. 'Isn't that what they were arresting all them lads for making? Them so-called terrorists?'

'Yeah, but most of them got let go,' Yousef said. 'I think there was one bloke went on trial for it.'

'Then they'll blame us,' Raj said, his face solemn, his eyes bright. 'They'll say it was Muslim fundamentalists. I tell you, I've been supporting the Vics since I was a little kid, but that won't make no difference now.'

Yousef patted his shoulder awkwardly. He felt sorry for Raj, but he had to think of the bigger picture. Which was looking even better now. Recently, he'd been zoning out into a world of his own when he'd been planted in front of the TV, but for this, his mind was fully engaged. 'Let's see what they've got to say.'

They dragged their attention back to the TV set, where the geezer in the suit had given way to the blonde. 'My team have already begun our investigation into this tragic death,' she was saying. 'We are treating it as a murder inquiry.' So, a cop, then. 'We would like to talk to anyone who saw Robbie or spoke to him in the Amatis nightclub in Bradfield late on Thursday evening. We are also interested in his movements after he left the nightclub. We need to find the person who did this. If anyone has information, they should call this number.' She held up a piece of paper with a free phone number and read it out.

As soon as she finished speaking, the journalistic frenzy began again. 'Is there any question of terrorist involvement?' was the one that rose above the rest.

The blonde's lips pursed in a thin line. 'There is no reason to suspect terrorism in this case,' she said. 'Nor is there any suggestion that anyone else is at risk from the event that killed Robbie Bishop.'

'When did your investigation begin?'

'The hospital informed us this morning,' the cop said.

'We called the police as soon as the ricin diagnosis was confirmed,' the suit butted in.

'Covering his arse,' Sanjar said as the screen cut back to the studio, where the anchor promised any fresh information as soon as it was available. They moved on to a rapidly assembled montage of Robbie Bishop's greatest moments on the pitch. Raj stared avidly, soaking up the magic that would never be repeated.

'I was there,' he said, as they showed Robbie's spectacular shot from thirty yards out, the goal that had clinched the Vics' semi-final slot in the previous season's UEFA Cup. 'Oh man, we got no chance in the premiership now. Not without Robbie.'

Yousef shook his head. 'You should stay away from the games. Till they've caught whoever did this.'

'I've got a ticket for Saturday,' Raj protested. 'And the next European game.'

'Yousef's right,' Sanjar said. 'Till they find out who did this, there's going to be people looking for scapegoats. Even though that cop woman said it wasn't no terrorist thing, there's still going to be fuckwits out there who think it's an excuse to go paki-bashing. Feelings are going to run high, Raj. Better you stay clear.'

'I don't want to stay clear. Not from the matches, and not tonight either. Everybody's going to be down the stadium, paying tributes and that. I want to be part of it. It's my club too.' Raj was close to tears.

His elder brothers exchanged a look. 'Sanjar's probably right about the matches. Once it's sunk in, there'll be bad feeling, no doubt about it. But I'll come with you tonight if you're set on that,' Yousef said, understanding only too well the precariousness of the bridge between the two cultures that claimed his generation. 'We'll go together.'

Tony turned the TV off and leaned back on his pillows. The intravenous morphine had worn off and he could feel the beginning of a dull ache in his knee. The nurse had told him sternly that he didn't have to suffer, that he should summon a nurse and ask for pain relief. He tried moving his leg, testing the limits of his endurance. He reckoned he could wait a little longer. More drugs would just make him go to sleep, and he didn't want to be asleep now. Not when there was the prospect of a visit.

Carol was in the hospital. He'd just seen her on TV, doing a live press conference. She had a murder. And what a murder. Celebrity corpse and a creepy murder method. She'd want to talk to him about it. Of that he was certain. But he didn't know when she'd be able to get away.

He thought about Robbie Bishop and of the evenings he'd spent in the cosy cave that was his study, watching Bradfield Victoria on the satellite channel. He recalled a thoughtful player, seldom careless with his passes. In control of himself as much as he'd been in control of the ball. Tony couldn't remember ever seeing Robbie Bishop pick up a yellow card. But being mindful of what he was doing hadn't meant a lack of passion. Robbie in his number seven shirt would run himself into the ground. What had made Robbie special, though, were the gorgeous moves he'd created out of nothing, moments when there was no need to explain to unbelievers why football was the beautiful game.

And somebody had wiped that skill and grace from the map. They'd done it in the cruellest of ways, left him a dead man walking. Why would someone choose such a death for Robbie Bishop? Was it personal? Or was it a more general statement? Either was possible. Tony needed more detail. He needed Carol.

He didn't have long to wait. Within ten minutes of the end of her press conference, Carol was shutting his door behind her, leaning against it as if expecting pursuit. 'He doesn't like anybody else getting the limelight, does he?' Tony said, waving her towards the bedside chair.

'My way or the highway,' Carol said, abandoning her defence of the door and throwing herself into the chair. 'Like just about every consultant I've ever dealt with.'

'You should meet Mrs Chakrabarti. At least she lets you bask in the misapprehension that she's taking notice of what you say. So, you've got the poisoned chalice, have you?'

'Oh yes. CID took the call and as soon as they realized what they were looking at, they couldn't get rid of it fast enough. I'm not looking forward to the next few days. But enough of me and my troubles.' Carol made a visible effort to shrug off her problems. 'How are you?'

Tony smiled. 'It's me, Carol. You don't have to pretend you've got room in your head for anything other than Robbie Bishop. And as for me, if you really want to know, I'll feel a lot better as soon as you stop treating me like an invalid. It's my knee that's messed up, not my brain. You can run this past me, same as you would any other murder lacking an obvious motive.'

'Are you sure? You don't look like you're firing on all cylinders, to be honest.'

'I'm not, clearly. My concentration isn't great, which makes reading anything complex impossible.' He made a dismissive gesture towards the books he'd asked her to bring in. 'But I'm off the intravenous morphine and my brain is returning to what passes for normal. When I'm awake, I'd rather be puzzling over this than watching daytime TV. So, what can you tell me?'

'Depressingly little.' Carol ran through what she and her team had established so far.

'So, to sum up,' Tony said. 'We don't know of anybody who hated him enough to kill him, he was probably poisoned in a nightclub crammed with people and we don't know where the ricin came from.'

'That's about it, yeah. I did find a scrunched-up bit of paper in the pocket of the last pair of jeans he wore. It had a url on it that I've not had a chance to check out yet: www.bestdays. co.uk.'

'We could look at it now.' Tony offered, pressing the button to raise the bed and wincing as a fresh pain asserted itself. He flipped open the laptop and waited impatiently for it to emerge from hibernation.

'You in pain?' Carol asked.

'A bit,' he admitted.

'Can't they give you something for it?'

'I'm trying to keep the painkillers to a minimum,' Tony admitted. 'I don't like the way they make me feel. I'd rather have my wits about me.'

'That's just stupid,' Carol said firmly. 'There's nothing helpful about pain.' Without asking permission, she pressed the nurse call button.

'What are you doing?'

'Sorting you out.' She pulled her chair round so she could see the screen.

Tony typed in the url. It took them to a page with the banner heading, 'The Best Days of Our Lives.' For only £5 annual membership, the site promised it would provide the best service in the UK for reuniting old school friends and workmates. A brief exploration revealed that by registering with the site, people could check out their old contacts and get back in touch via emails which would be forwarded by the website administration. 'Why would Robbie Bishop be interested in contacting old school mates?' Tony said. 'I'd have thought they'd be falling over themselves to get back in touch with him.'

Carol shrugged. 'Maybe he wanted to look up an old flame who dumped him? He was footloose and fancy free after the end of his engagement.'

'I don't see it. He was good looking, rich and talented. Everywhere he went, women threw themselves at him. And apparently, he was quite happy to catch some of them. He was engaged to a very cool trophy babe. If he was still carrying a torch for somebody who dumped him when he was fifteen, he wouldn't be behaving like that. And he'd have done something about it before now.' He shook his head. 'No, the psychology's all wrong for that. Do we know for sure it's Robbie's handwriting?'

'We don't. It's with forensics now. You think somebody gave it to him?'

'He told Phil Campsie he was having a drink with someone from school. Maybe whoever he was drinking with suggested he should check out the site, look up some old mates. Robbie's not interested but he doesn't want to seem rude so he shoves it in his pocket and forgets all about it.'

'Could be. It makes sense.'

Tony opened a window and typed in, 'Harriestown High School, Bradfield.'

'You know where he went to school?' Carol sounded suspicious.

'I follow football, Carol. I know where he grew up. His mum and dad still live in the same house, in Harriestown. He offered to buy them a new place, but they wanted to stay where they belonged.'

'You don't learn stuff like that from following football.'

Tony had the grace to look shame-faced. 'So I surf the gossip from time to time. It doesn't make me a bad person. Look at that.' He pointed to the screen. There was a photograph of Harriestown High School, boxy sixties concrete and glass flanking the old Victorian brick core. Beneath a brief history of the school there was a section entitled 'Famous Alumni'. A couple of MPs, two rock bands who had made a small dent in the charts during the Britpop era, a mid-list crime writer, a minor soap star, a fashion designer and Robbie Bishop. A couple of clicks and he'd brought up the names of Harriestown High School former pupils who had overlapped Robbie Bishop's years in the school. 'Whoever gave him the url, chances are the name is here.'

Carol groaned. 'I suppose it does whittle down the

list a little. Rather than checking out every single person who was at school with Robbie, now we only have to go through the ones who are paid-up members of the Best Days of Our Lives.'

'At least now you're looking for a needle in a sewing box rather than a haystack.'

'You think that makes it easier? That's the trouble with not having an obvious motive. You don't know where to start.'

Tony winced. 'And that's what I'm for, right? The one who narrows things down when "Who benefits?" doesn't cut the mustard.'

Carol grinned. 'Something like that. And on that cheerful note, I'm going to leave you to it. I'm off to London to talk to Robbie's ex.'

'The lovely Bindie Blyth, would that be?'

'I see what you mean about surfing the gossip. You're absolutely right. And before I can take off, I need to sort out some bodies to acquire as much city-centre CCTV footage as we can get our hands on. And then the poor sods have to go through it all.'

'Rather them than me. What's the coverage like around Amatis?'

Carol rolled her eyes. 'It ranges from overkill to nothing at all. The front of the club is well covered, and so are the routes to the nearest multi-storeys. But there's a side exit near the VIP area. It opens on to an alley that runs down the side of the building. From there, you're into the warren of Temple Fields back streets. And in spite of our best efforts, far too much of that is still CCTV-free.' There was a moment's silence while they both remembered past cases that had revolved around Temple Fields, an area that managed to combine the red-light district, the gay village, designer apartments in converted warehouses and a honeycomb of small businesses. Temple Fields was the cusp of cool and crap, where edgy met enterprising for denizens who spanned the spectrum from criminal to righteous.

'It's still the only part of town where anything can happen,' Tony said, his voice almost dreamy. 'Good and bad.'

Carol snorted derisively. 'I'll have to take your word for the good.'

'We only ever see the worst. I suspect there's good magic there too.'

'Tell that to Paula.' Carol's voice was sour, remembering how Paula had almost died in a dingy room in Temple Fields.

Tony smiled. 'Carol, Paula understands much more about transgression than you or I ever will. She knows what tempers the down side of Temple Fields. For a long time, it was the only place where people like her could be safe. There were gays in Temple Fields long before the gay village became a cool destination.'

It was a gentle rebuke, but one that reminded Carol she couldn't lay her reactions over Paula's and expect an exact fit. 'You're right,' she admitted. Before she could say more, a nurse knocked and walked in.

'What can I do for you?' she said.

'He needs pain relief but he won't admit it,' Carol said, standing up and gathering her things together.

'Is that right?'

Tony nodded. 'I suppose so.'

The nurse consulted his chart and said, 'I told you, there's no medals for martyrs here. I'll bring you something.'

Carol followed her to the door. 'I'm not sure when I'll be back from London, but I'll try and come by tomorrow.'

'Good luck,' Tony said. He wasn't sorry to see her go; her visit had reminded him how little energy he had. It was a relief to know there would be no other visitors that evening. There were advantages to keeping the world at arm's length.

For a long time, he had mistrusted those few overtures of friendship that had come his way. He'd believed they were based on the misconception that the face he presented to the world had anything to do with what was going on inside him. He was aware how slender was the connection between the two. And that his own history placed him closer to those he hunted than those on whose behalf he hunted. He knew the extent of his damage and understood that its gift of empathy had to be paid for somehow. By the time he'd plucked up the emotional courage to lay some of the blame on his mother, he'd also acquired enough knowledge to understand that was too easy an option. He had spent years feeling like a child with its face pressed to the window behind which the happy family were celebrating the perfect Dickensian Christmas. It had taken him that long to understand that most of those apparently happy families hid as many dark places as his own. That he was not the only one doing what he called 'passing for human'. But by then he had built himself a life that willingly embraced solitude and spectatorship.

And then Carol Jordan had arrived. None of his psychology textbooks nor his thousands of hours of clinical practice had prepared him for someone who could walk straight through his defences as if they did not exist. It was both too simple and too complicated. If either of them had been different, they might have been able to fall in love and get it over with. But there had been too many snags and hitches at the start and now it seemed that every time they tentatively considered surrender, the world threw up mountains in their path.

Mostly, he wished it could be different. But sometimes, like now, he recognized that perhaps it was enough for each of them to know there was at least one relationship in their lives that was never going to be hamstrung by them acting out their needs. Whatever they did for each other meant itself alone. When she negotiated wireless access from a hospital bed for him, there was no ulterior motive. And now, he would trawl the world of information online and in his head to help her, just because he could.

When the nurse returned, he dutifully swallowed his medication and lay back, letting his mind wander free. Where there was no obvious motive, it was his talent to tease out meaning. What could Robbie Bishop's murderer have gained from the act of killing? To understand that would be a giant step on the journey to giving this stranger face and form. It was, thankfully, the sort of giant step he didn't need two functioning knees for. Just a brain that could possibly be helped on its way by the lovely, soothing chemicals infiltrating his bloodstream.

A twenty-four-hour news agenda is always hungry for headlines. Now that Robbie Bishop had died, the circus had moved from outside the hospital to the

111

Bradfield Victoria stadium. The story had moved so fast that most of the media were there ahead of the fans, having quicker access to their vehicles. To begin with, there were more journalists and camera crew than there were mourners. They milled around in the chilly evening air, cracking black jokes and waiting for the action they knew would arrive soon enough.

Within an hour, they got what they wanted. Hundreds of people drifted around in the shadow of the cantilevered Grayson Street stand, breath puffing in clouds around their heads. Already the iron railings that marked the boundary had become the literal props for bunches of supermarket flowers, beribboned teddies, mourning messages, sympathy cards and photos of Robbie himself. Distraught women wept, men in canary yellow home strips looked as gutted as if they'd just witnessed a five–nil home defeat. Children looked bewildered, youths betrayed. Reporters moved among them, mikes and tape recorders thrust towards the banalities of manufactured emotion. A discreet police presence patrolled the mourners, a precaution against any kind of excess.

Yousef and Raj were among the first to arrive. Yousef felt conspicuous and awkward. He thought he was probably the only person apart from cops and media not wearing a Vics shirt or scarf. He politely declined when a couple of TV reporters asked for his comments and dragged a protesting Raj away from their mikes and cameras. 'Why can't I say summat?' Raj said.

'You're supposed to be here because you're in mourning, not to get your gob all over the TV,' Yousef said. 'This isn't about you, remember?'

'It's not fair. I really loved Robbie. I love the Vics. Half the people that'll end up on the telly or the radio couldn't give a toss about the team from one week to the next. They just want to get in on the act.' Raj trailed behind his brother, scuffing his heels on the ground.

'So let them.'

Another reporter thrust a tape recorder at them. 'Some people are linking Robbie Bishop's death to Muslim terrorist production of ricin,' he gabbled. 'What's your view on that?'

'It's bollocks,' Yousef said, finally goaded into speech. 'Didn't you hear what that cop said earlier? No reason to link this to terrorism. You're just trying to stir up trouble. It's people like you that provoke race riots. My brother here, the only thing he's fanatical about is Bradfield Vics.' He spat on the ground. 'You've got no respect. Come on, Raj.' He grabbed his brother's sleeve and pulled him away.

'Great,' said Raj. 'I don't get to talk about Robbie, but you get to shout your mouth off, make us look like troublemakers.'

'Yeah, I know. It's not fair.' Yousef steered Raj away from the media and towards the tributes at the railings. 'But I'm so sick of that sort of shit. Why would terrorists kill Robbie Bishop, for fuck's sake?'

''Cos he's a symbol of the decadence of the West, dummy,' Raj said, imitating the stupid parrot tones of the big mouths he'd heard sounding off in the kebab shops and the mosque car park.

'That's true, actually. But not a good enough reason to kill him. Killing Robbie doesn't create terror, just outrage. For terrorism to work, you need to strike at ordinary people. But that's too sophisticated an argument for the likes of that wanker with the microphone,' Yousef said bitterly.

Without meaning to, they had reached the fringe of a growing crowd who had gathered round a cluster of night lights. The candles flickered in the light evening breeze, somehow more moving than all the other marks of respect piling up around them. Someone with a light tenor voice began singing the opening verse of 'You'll Never Walk Alone'. Others picked it up and, before they knew it, Yousef and Raj were caught up in the definitive football fans' anthem.

Yousef couldn't help smiling as his voice rose in the chorus. He knew how it felt, not to walk alone. He understood the strength that gave a man. Walking in company, that made anything possible. Anything at all.

The miles unfurled steadily behind them. By this time of night, the traffic that choked the motorway by day had diminished. The six lanes were still busy, but now the cars and lorries were moving in a rhythmic rumble through the bottlenecks and chokes of the Midlands. Carol reached for the radio controls and switched from the measured tones of Radio Four to the manic beats of Radio One. Since they were on their way to talk to Bindie Blyth, they might as well check out her show.

The ten o'clock news led with Robbie Bishop's death. At the wheel, Sam shook his head as the newsreader managed to spin it with dramatic breathlessness into a major crisis. 'They don't get it, do they? A story this big, all they need to do is lay out the facts. The last thing we need is them getting all hysterical, winding the punters up.'

'It's what they do best,' Carol said, weary at the excesses of the media. 'With a few rare exceptions. And everybody just plays along. What's the betting that the Prime Minister will have shoved his oar in by morning?'

Sam grinned. 'Robbie'll be "the people's player" by breakfast.'

'Only this time there's a real murderer on the loose, not just the phantoms conjured up by the conspiracy theorists.' She sighed. 'And it's our job to find him.'

The bulletin finished, segueing straight to a hectic dance track that seemed to go on for as long as the first act of an opera. Finally it subsided and a woman's voice, low and warm, said, 'Kicking off tonight's show, Kateesha featuring Junior Deff, with "Score Steady". This is Bindie Blyth, taking you through to midnight on Radio One, the beat nation's favourite station. You'll all have heard that Robbie Bishop died earlier this evening. Until a couple of months ago, me and Robbie were an item. He asked me to marry him and I said yes. We didn't make it to the altar, but he was still my best mate. One of the reasons we stayed so close was the music. We both loved the same sounds, the sounds you hear every night here on the show. Now, everybody has their own personal top tens, and Robbie was no exception. Me and Robbie used to lie in bed on a Sunday morning, running through our favourite tracks, making up our imaginary Desert Island Discs. "Score Steady" always made it to Robbie's hit list. Tonight, I'm sad. I've lost somebody that mattered a lot to me. So tonight's show is going to be a tribute to a man I loved.

115

A man who was really special. Don't worry, I'm not going to go all tragic on you. No tears, not for the next two hours. Instead, I'm going to play the sounds that Robbie loved. Dance and trance, hip-hop and trip hop and maybe even a bit of acoustic chill. So button back your ears and let your feet go their own way to "Stack My Beats" from the Rehab Boys.' The frantic beat started under her final words, building to a chest-vibrating drum and bass number.

Carol turned the volume down so they could hear themselves again. 'Sounds like she's got a better handle on things than the news reporters. What's with her name? Bindie? Is that a nickname? Short for something?'

'Short for Belinda, according to her website.'

Carol smiled. Of course Sam would have checked her out online. Sam never missed a trick when it came to acquiring information. Channelled properly, it could be a huge advantage to the team. But Sam wasn't a team player by instinct. She always had to make sure he remembered to share. 'Right. I bet her mum still calls her Belinda and it drives her crazy. So where is she from? I'm hearing something in her accent that isn't standard Estuary, but I can't make it out.'

'She's from East Anglia somewhere,' Sam said, one finger beating a silent tattoo on the steering wheel. 'Near Norwich, I think. She's good.'

'I think I'm a bit too old for this kind of thing.'

'I dunno. I think it's more about taste than age. Me, I think people fall into two camps where music's concerned. You either listen for the rhythm because you like to feel that dance inside you, or you listen for

116

the way the words and the music fit together. There's not much crossover, really. The beats or the lyrics. I'd have you pegged as somebody who appreciates the lyrics.'

'I suppose. Not that I get much time for music these days.' They fell silent, letting the music wash over them.

When it ended, Bindie back-announced the track. 'What we're all hearing tonight is that somebody poisoned Robbie. Me, I can't get my head round that. You gotta be a twisted individual to dose somebody up with a poison that takes days to kill them. That takes a lot of hate. And I don't see how anybody could have hated Robbie enough to do that to him. How could you hate a man who loved this next track?' She was right. There was an infectious bounce to the music that had Carol's feet tapping in spite of herself. She checked the clock. They would be in London about half an hour before the end of Bindie's show. Hopefully she'd still be wired with performance adrenaline and willing to talk. Carol needed Bindie to open up about Robbie. Making that happen tonight would help her keep the momentum of the investigation going. That was much more important than Bindie Blyth's beauty sleep. Or, come to that, her own.

Eleven o'clock and Amatis was just starting to warm up. The lighting was subtle, the volume crushing and the air heavy with the stale smell of alcohol, cigarettes, perfume and hot bodies. Paula and Kevin had left Chris in the manager's scruffy little office, ploughing through interviews with the bar staff and the door crew. She hadn't held out much hope of getting anything from them. 'By the time Robbie was hanging out with his old mate, it would have been Karno's behind the bar,' she'd said. 'Too many punters trying to catch their eye. I doubt they'll have even noticed who he was with. If any of them saw something hooky going on with his drink, it would have been pure chance and they'd have been on the bell to us or the red-tops by now. No, if anybody's going to get lucky tonight, it'll be you two.'

Somehow, Paula doubted it. For most of the people who came to Amatis, the idea of a good night out involved consuming sufficient drink and drugs to diminish to vanishing point the possibility of any detailed memory of the outing. Those were the ones who looked bemused when Paula asked if they had been there the previous Thursday. Once Paula had managed to convey who she was and what she wanted by a mixture of gesture, the display of her warrant card and a photo of Robbie, most of them mimed a yes or no, followed by a shrug that conveyed forgetfulness or indifference. The only variation on the theme came from those who had a mission beyond getting legless and/or laid – to spot someone whose name they could drop casually into conversation at work the next day. 'Oh yeah, like I said to Shelley last night . . . You know Shelley, Shelley Christie, off *Northerners* . . . Course I know her, look, here's her photo on my mobile, right?' What slender hopes Paula had rested on them.

After an hour, she had to concede that luck wasn't going her way. The stargazers she'd spoken to were either crestfallen that they'd missed the last chance for a happy snap with Robbie Bishop or bitter that they'd seen him but failed to record the fact. The nearest she'd got to a witness was one lad who'd admitted to seeing Robbie at the bar, drinking in company. 'Was it a man or a woman he was drinking with?' Paula had asked eagerly.

'Some bloke. I didn't recognize him, so I didn't pay him any attention, like. I would've asked him to take a pic of me and Robbie, but I'd forgot to charge my phone and it was dead, so I never bothered.'

'You ever seen him before, this bloke?' Paula wasn't prepared to let it go just yet.

'I told you. I never paid him any mind. I dunno if I've seen him before. Maybe, maybe not. I didn't notice anything about him.'

'Tall? Short? Fair? Dark?' Paula tried not to let her exasperation show.

The witness shook his head. 'Tell you the truth, I'd had a few. I never took much of a look at him. That's the thing about running into somebody like Robbie. You're so busy checking them out, you don't notice who they're with. Unless it's somebody else famous. Or some cracking bird. You're just like, "Fucking hell, I'm standing next to Robbie Bishop."' He looked momentarily rueful. 'Poor bastard.'

Dispirited, Paula pushed her way through to the corner of the bar and tried to catch the eye of one of the bar staff. She was sweating like a pig, needed to get some water into her system. Finally, one of the black-clad staff took her order. As she waited for her change, Paula gazed absently down the bar.

And drew her breath in sharply when she spotted the tiny video camera nestling among the spotlights that shone down on the sticky granite bar top. 'Oh, you beauty,' she said softly.

When the barman returned with a handful of coins, he was surprised to see his customer had disappeared.

The heavy door that shut off the studio from the production booth opened and Bindie Blyth emerged, a half-empty bottle of mineral water dangling from one hand. With her other hand, she pulled off a headband in the colours of the ANC then shook her dark corkscrew curls free. They must have made a striking couple, Carol thought. Handsome Robbie with his traditional clean-cut Englishness and olive-skinned Bindie, small features resembling a pixie from an illustrated children's fairy tale, framed in a riotous mass of ringlets. The volume of hair and the black jeans and clinging black top she wore empha-sized the slightness of her frame. Carol reckoned she could probably get away with wearing kids' clothes. 'All right, Dixie?' she said to the plump woman at the controls.

'Spot on. Nice one, Bindie. You've got visitors,' Dixie said, jerking her head towards Carol and Sam perched on the other two chairs.

Bindie glanced at them, her shoulders slumping. 'Do we have to do this now? I've just finished work.'

'And we're still working,' Carol said, producing her warrant card and introducing herself. 'It's our job to find out who's responsible for Robbie Bishop's death.'

'Yeah, well, he's dead, isn't he? What difference does it make who did it? All that matters is that Robbie's gone. There's nothing you can do to alter that.' This was a very different Bindie from the one who had spent two hours playing music to celebrate and honour her dead friend. Now, she simply sounded bitter and angry. Dixie, the producer, was transfixed, her eyes swivelling between Bindie and Carol.

'I'm sorry about Robbie,' Carol said. 'But in my experience, people who commit cold-blooded crimes like this generally don't stop at one. I want to stop whoever killed Robbie from taking someone else's life.'

'Fair enough. So why are you here? Why aren't you out there doing whatever it is you're supposed to do?' Bindie moved to a rack of coathooks and grabbed a dark green fleece.

'I have a colleague, a psychologist. One of the things he's taught me is to pay attention to the point where a victim and his killer intersect. The more I find out about the victim, the more chance I have of getting closer to that point of intersection. And when it comes to knowing Robbie Bishop, you're one of the experts. That's why I need to talk to you, and why it needs to be now.'

Bindie rolled her eyes. 'You sound like that wanker in *Law and Order: Criminal Intent*. All right, you win. But let's get out of here. I need a fag and a drink.' She turned and said, 'See you tomorrow, Dixie.' Dixie looked disgruntled as she nodded goodbye.

Out in the corridor, Bindie said, 'Meet me back at mine. It's only a ten-minute drive.' She looked at Sam for the first time. 'Got a bit of paper and a pen?'

She scribbled down an address and directions. 'If you like milk in your tea, you'll need to stop at the all-night garage.' And she was off, her short legs whisking her down the corridor far more quickly than seemed possible.

Fifteen minutes later, Sam drifted slowly down one

121

of Notting Hill's grand crescents, searching in vain for a parking place. 'Sod this,' Carol said. 'We could be here all night. Just double park. Leave a note with your mobile in case anybody needs you to move.'

Sam pulled up outside the number Bindie had given them. A security light came on as they mounted the steps under the white pillared porch, allowing them to read the names attached to the four intercom buttons. 'Blyth' was third from the top. Sam pressed it and waited, gently banging the litre of milk against his thigh. Carol stared grimly into the lens of a security camera.

Within seconds, a distorted voice said, 'First floor,' and the door buzzed. Their footsteps clattered on the black-and-white terrazzo tiles covering the narrow hallway before the sound was swallowed by the thick carpeting on the stairs. 'Nice gaff,' Sam muttered.

Bindie was waiting for them, leaning in the single doorway at the first-floor level, arms folded, legs crossed at the ankles. At some point in the past quarter of an hour, she'd managed to apply a skim of make-up that seemed to put a little distance between them. She stepped back without a word and gestured for them to enter. The hall was big enough to accommodate a pool table, the balls racked and ready, four cues clipped to the wall behind it. Between the doors that led off in all directions, moody black-and-white photographs of pool halls and their familiars were spotlit by a rig suspended from the high ceiling. 'Straight ahead,' she said, shooing them forwards.

They walked into a splendid room that ran the whole width of the house. Squashy leather sofas and beanbags sprawled seemingly at random, with low wooden tables scattered among them, their surfaces cluttered with magazines, newspapers and clean ashtrays. Three walls were lined with shelves of CDs and vinyl, the only gaps filled by an impressive sound system and a plasma screen; the fourth was taken up by the closed wooden shutters that covered the tall windows. Their panels were decorated with posters for gigs and new album releases. Most of the posters were signed. The room smelled of cinnamon and smoke. Carol recognized the sweet smell of marijuana mingling with the more acrid notes of Marlboro Gold. Light came from a handful of paper-shaded pillars placed strategically round the room. It felt curiously intimate.

'Make yourselves at home,' Bindie said. 'I see you brought milk.' She nodded at Sam. 'Kitchen's out there, door to the right of the front door. Tea, coffee in the cupboard above the kettle. Diet Coke, juice and water in the fridge.'

Sam looked momentarily flustered. 'I'll have a coffee, Sam. White, no sugar,' Carol said, sharing a swift glance of complicity with Bindie. *Come on, Sam, catch on.* Sam caught on, realizing his boss was allying herself with Bindie for the benefit of the interview. She wasn't really belittling him.

'Can I get you something, Ms Blyth?'

'No thanks, sweetie, I'm sorted.' She pointed to a tall glass that was already sweating condensation. It could have been straight Diet Coke; Carol doubted it, though. Bindie folded herself into a beanbag next to the table with her drink and cigarettes.

'Nice flat,' Carol said.

'Not quite the rock-and-roll lifestyle you were

expecting, eh? It's not the BBC salary that pays the mortgage,' Bindie said. 'It's club work. I'm not a bimbo, DCI Jordan. I've got a degree in economics which I also paid for with spinning and scratching. I know I've probably got a limited shelf-life up among the high earners, so I'm making the most of it while I can.'

'Makes sense.'

'I've always been sensible.' She pulled a face. 'Some might say boring. One of the things Robbie liked about me, he said. He knew I wasn't going to tempt him into the things that would wreck his career. So, is it right, what they're saying in the newsroom? Ricin? He was poisoned with ricin?'

'The hospital ran tests while he was ill. We still have to confirm that. But yes, it looks as if he was poisoned with ricin.'

Bindie gave an impatient shake of the head. 'It's crazy. It's like, does not compute. Robbie, ricin. What's the connection?'

If I knew the answer to that, we could all go home. 'Right now, I don't know either. That's one of many things I'm trying to find out.'

'Fair enough. So, what do you want to ask me?' Bindie reached for the Marlboros, flipped the pack open with her thumbnail and pulled one out.

'What was he like?'

Bindie lit her cigarette and exhaled the first drag, squinting at Carol through the smoke. 'You have no idea how many times I've been asked that. Usually a bit more breathlessly, though.' Carol opened her mouth to assert herself, but before she could speak, Bindie waved her hands in a calming motion. 'I'm not being funny with you, I know you've got to ask.' She sighed and smiled, her face softening. 'What was Robbie like? He was a nice boy. And I use the word "boy" advisedly. He still had a lot of growing up to work his way through. He was talented and he knew it. Not arrogant, but aware, if you know what I mean? He knew his worth and he was proud of what he'd achieved. What else?' She paused to inhale. 'He adored music and football. If he hadn't been a footballer, I think he would have been a DJ. He knew his stuff and he loved it. That was the glue between us.' She swallowed a mouthful of smoke. 'That and the sex, I suppose. He was good at that too.' Now the smile was wistful. 'At the start, I was so in love with him. But the whole being in love thing, it doesn't last.' She looked away, studying the burn of her cigarette.

'If you're lucky, it grows into something deeper,' Carol said.

'That only works if you're both grown-ups. The trouble with Robbie, he had all the emotional maturity of *National Lampoon's Animal House*. He always started out with good intentions, but they were easily derailed, especially when blondes and champagne collided in his vicinity.' She stubbed out the cigarette and leaned back. 'I just got fed up of the photos in *Heat* and the snide little sneers in the gossip columns. Gave him his ring back and told him we could maybe have another crack at it once he'd finished running around like a kid in a sweetie shop.'

'So it was you who ended it?'

The click of balls followed by the soft clunk of one dropping drifted through the partly open door. Bindie smiled, gesturing towards the hall with her thumb.

125

'Mr Tact and Diplomacy, eh? Yes, it was me that called it off.'

'How did Robbie take it?'

Bindie reached for another cigarette. 'He was upset at first. Hurt pride, mostly. That and worry that he wasn't going to get invited to the coolest gigs any more. Then when he realized I meant it when I said I wanted us to stay friends, he brightened up. The last few weeks, we've been sweet. Talked on the phone most days, file-swapped some sounds, had dinner when the lads were down in London the other week for the match with the Arsenal.'

'So you'd say it was amicable between you?'

Bindie frowned. 'Wait a minute, you don't think this is anything to do with me?' She glared at Carol, fierce and forceful, tears suddenly sparkling on her lashes.

'I'm trying to get a picture of Robbie's life, that's all,' Carol said gently.

'Yeah, well, check his phone records. Check mine. You'll see how often we spoke, and how long for.'

'When was the last time you spoke?'

'I called him on Saturday morning,' she said, her voice a little shaky now. 'We always spoke before a game. He said he couldn't talk, he thought he was coming down with flu and he was waiting for the team doctor.' She blinked furiously. 'He was already poisoned by then, right?'

Carol nodded. 'We think so. Before Saturday morning, when did you last talk?'

Bindie thought for a moment. 'Thursday. Early evening. He was going out with Phil.'

Bugger. 'When you spoke on Saturday, did he say

126

anything about running into an old school friend on Thursday, when he was at Amatis?'

'No. Like I said, he didn't have time for a chat. I just wished him luck and told him to call me when he was feeling better.' Comprehension sprang into her eyes. 'You think this old school friend was the one who poisoned him?'

'We're keeping an open mind. But he mentioned to Phil that he'd run into someone he was at school with. They might be able to give us a clearer picture of Robbie's evening. That's all. Tell me, Bindie, did Robbie ever do drugs?'

'Are you kidding? He wouldn't even sit in the same room with anybody smoking a spliff. He loved a drink, but he would never touch drugs. He always said you knew exactly what effect alcohol was going to have on you. But when it came to drugs, you had no way of knowing what they were going to do to you. If you're thinking someone got this drug into his system by pretending it was coke or whatever, you're barking up the wrong tree.'

Maybe it was a whitewash, maybe it was the truth. Either way, the post mortem would show whether Robbie's posse were painting a plaster saint whiter than white. 'And there was nothing in your last conversation to suggest that had changed?'

'No way. Like I said, we just exchanged a few sentences.'

'At least you parted on good terms,' Carol said.

'There's that . . .' She tried a brave little laugh. 'You know, if I'd have been going to kill Robbie, I'd have done it to his face, not behind his back. He'd have been in no doubt what was happening to him and why. Only . . .' Her face crumpled and she coughed on the smoke. 'I never wanted to kill him. The blondes, maybe. But Robbie? No way.'

'So who might have wanted to kill him? Who hated him enough to do this to him?'

Bindie ran a hand through her curls. 'I have no fucking idea. He wasn't the sort of guy who provoked that kind of reaction. Like I said, he was a nice boy. Some footballers, they go through life looking for a fight. They need to see themselves as hard men. Robbie wasn't like that. He was polite, well brought up. More David Beckham than Roy Keane. Guys tried to mix it with him off the field, he'd just walk away. The only thing I can think of . . .' Her voice trailed off and she shook her head.

'What?'

'It's stupid, forget it.'

Carol leaned forward. 'I'm clutching at straws here, Bindie. I'm open to any suggestions, no matter how stupid you think they are.'

She shook her head again, taking an angry toke on her cigarette. 'It's just . . . Gambling. I know there's shitloads of money swilling around in gambling. You read about these syndicates, millions of pounds up for grabs. Australia, Hong Kong, Korea, the Philippines. A lot of the betting goes on football. There's been exposés on Five Live and in the papers. I was just wondering . . . the Vics are doing better than everybody expected this season. They're up there in contention. They're giving the big boys headaches. What if . . .' She reached for her glass and took a swig of her drink.

'Would taking out one player make enough of a difference?' Carol asked, thinking out loud.

Sam's voice came from the doorway. 'It would if it was Robbie. Think of all the goals that got scored because Robbie laid them on. Think of all the goals that didn't get scored because Robbie got the crucial tackle in. Some players, they can lift a whole team. Robbie was like that.'

There was a long silence as they all considered Sam's words. Then Bindie spoke. 'I can't tell you how much the thought of that pisses me off. Taking that much beauty out of the world just for money.' Bindie made a spitting sound. She covered her mouth with her hand as she drew breath.

'It's an interesting suggestion,' Carol said.

Bindie looked up at her, eyes swimming with tears. 'My poor sweet boy,' she said. She sniffed hard and fought her way out of the beanbag. 'I think it's time you left. I can't think of anything else that would help you, and I've got music I need to listen to. If I think of anything else, I will call you. But right now, I need to be on my own.'

Out on the street, they leaned against the bonnet of the car, contemplating the dirty orange reflection from the clouds. 'Interesting idea, the gambling syndicate,' Sam said.

'It's the first thing I've heard that makes any sense,' Carol said. 'Hell of a way to do it, though. I'd have thought the last thing they'd want would be to draw attention to themselves. Wouldn't they try to make it look like an accident?'

Sam yawned. 'Maybe that's what they thought they were doing.'

'What do you mean?' Carol pushed herself upright and held her hand out. 'I'll do the first hour's driving.'

'From what I can gather, most doctors wouldn't have picked up that this was ricin poisoning,' Sam said, walking round to the passenger side. 'If it hadn't been for Elinor Blessing's little hunch, they'd probably have put it down to some sort of virus. That's what they were treating him for before she had her brainwave.'

Carol started the car and eased it forward. 'Good point, Sam. Maybe you're right. Maybe we were never supposed to suss out that it was murder.'

Wednesday

4:27, according to the clock in the bottom right corner
of the laptop screen. Sound sleep had never been one
of Tony's accomplishments, but general anaesthesia
seemed to have buggered it up completely. He'd
slipped easily enough into slumber around ten, but
it hadn't lasted. Sleep seemed to be coming in fifty-
minute chunks, punctuated with varying intervals of
wakefulness. While the fifty-minute hours did seem
ironically apposite for a clinical psychologist, he could
have wished for more therapeutic effects.

He'd last shimmered into consciousness just after
four. This time, he knew instinctively that there was
no going back in the immediate future. At first, he
lay still, his thoughts circling the re-emergence of his
mother in his life in spite of his best intentions to
move on to something else. It didn't matter that there
was nothing there but frustration and regret, a tightening gyre of pain and bitterness that kept him from
sleep. It seemed impossible to ignore.

With an effort of will, he wrenched his thoughts
round to the death of Robbie Bishop. He'd moved on
from his memories of Robbie's grace and glories to

those elements that had more to do with his own expertise.

'You're not a novice,' Tony said, his voice soft but distinct. 'Even with beginner's luck, you'd never have got away with this if it was your first outing. Not with someone as high-profile as Robbie. Whether you did this for personal reasons or because somebody paid you, you've done it before.'

He rolled his head against the pillows, trying to ease the stiffness in his neck. 'Let's call you Stalky. It's as good a name as any, and you know I always like to make it a little bit personal. The question is, were you really an old school friend, Stalky? Maybe you were just pretending. Maybe Robbie was too polite to say he didn't remember you. Or maybe he was conscious of the fact that his fame made him memorable compared to the other kids who were at school with him. Maybe he didn't want to seem like an arsehole, acting like he'd never seen you before. Even so, even with Robbie's reputation for being a nice guy, you'd still be taking a hell of a risk.

'But if you were genuinely an old school friend, you were taking an even bigger risk. This is Bradfield, after all. Chances are that a fair chunk of the people in Amatis that night had also been at Harriestown High. They'd have recognized Robbie, for sure. But they might also have recognized you, unless you've changed a lot since schooldays. Very high-risk strategy.'

He found the bed controls and raised himself to a sitting position, wincing as his joints shifted. He pulled the bed-table across and flipped the laptop open, hitting the power switch. 'You took a lot of risks, either way. And you took them with confidence. You got right alongside Robbie and nobody noticed you. You have definitely done this before. So let's find your previous victims, Stalky.'

The light from the screen morphed in colour and intensity as Tony began his search, casting light and shade on his features, creating movement where none existed. 'Come on,' he muttered. 'Show yourself. You know you want to.'

Carol opened the blinds that cut her off from the rest of the team. She'd called the case conference for nine, but although it was only ten past eight, they were all there. Even Sam, who hadn't dropped her off till five to four. She wondered whether his sleep had been more refreshing than hers. She'd been conscious of him watching and waiting till she was safe inside the basement flat she rented from Tony. Then it had been her turn to watch and wait. As Carol fed the complaining Nelson, she kept an eye out until Sam's lights swept across her kitchen window and the hedge that demarcated next door's drive from theirs. Once she was sure he was really gone, she'd poured herself a resort-sized brandy and headed upstairs.

Picking up the mail from the doormat was a reasonable thing to do and it provided a pretext for her to climb the stairs to Tony's first-floor office. She laid the letters on the desk, then subsided into the armchair opposite the one he habitually chose. She loved this chair – its depth, its width, its enveloping cushions that seemed to hold her close. In scale, it felt like a cave, as adult armchairs feel to children. In this seat, she'd discussed her cases, talked through her feelings about her team members, explored the need for justice that drove her to do this job in the teeth of all the dangers and disappointments. He'd talked about his theories of offender behaviour, his frustrations with the mental health system, his burning desire to make people better. She couldn't even hazard a guess at the number of hours they'd spent at ease with each other in this room.

Carol curled her legs under her and snuggled, glugging half of the brandy without a shudder. Five minutes, then she'd head back downstairs. 'I wish you were here,' she said out loud. 'I feel like we're getting nowhere. Normally, nobody would be expecting much progress at this stage in a case like this. But this is Robbie Bishop and the eyes of the world are watching. So getting nowhere isn't going to be an option.' She yawned, then finished the drink.

'You scared me, you know,' she said, burrowing more deeply into the squashy cushions. 'When Chris told me you'd run into the mad axeman, I felt like my heart stopped, like the world went into slow motion. Don't you ever do that to me again, you bastard.' She shifted her head, butting a cushion into a more comfortable shape, closing her eyes and feeling her body unwind as the alcohol hit. 'Wish you'd warned me about your mother, though. She's something else. No wonder you're as weird as you are.'

The next thing Carol had known was the blare of the radio alarm from the bedroom across the hallway. Stiff and disorientated, she'd stumbled to her feet and checked her watch. Seven o'clock. Less than three hours' kip. Time to start all over again.

And here she was, showered, in fresh clothes,

caffeine levels already jitterbug high. Carol combed her thick blonde hair with her fingers and started skimming the pile of Robbie Bishop news stories Paula had already clipped for her. Focusing hard, because the last thing she wanted to do was examine how she had spent her night. She only looked up when Chris Devine knocked and entered, a brown paper bag in her hand. 'Bacon and egg roll,' she said succinctly, dropping it on the desk. 'We're ready when you are.' Carol smiled at her retreating back. Chris had a knack for the gesture of solidarity, the little touches that made her colleagues feel supported. Carol wondered how they had managed before she'd joined them. The plan had been for Chris to be there from the off, but her mother's terminal cancer had kept her in her old job with the Met for three months longer than she'd anticipated. Carol sighed. Maybe if Chris had been around from the get-go, Detective Inspector Don Merrick would still be among them.

'Pointless,' she chided herself, reaching for the bag and tucking in without really registering what she was eating. Hardly a day went by without her wondering whether this or that detail might have made a difference to Don. In her heart, she knew she was only trying to find a way to blame herself instead of him. Tony had told her more than once that it was OK to be angry with Don for what he'd done. But it still didn't feel possible, never mind right.

As she ate, Carol made a few notes, sketching a rough agenda for the case conference. By quarter to nine, she was ready. There was no reason to wait for the prearranged time, so she emerged from her office and assembled the team around her. Carol stood in front of one of the whiteboards that contained a digest of all the information they had amassed so far on Robbie Bishop.

On her word, Sam kicked off the proceedings with a recap of their interview with Bindie Blyth. He finished up with Bindie's vague theory about gambling. 'Anybody have any comment?' Carol asked.

Stacey, their computer and ICT specialist, waggled her pen. 'She's right that there's a huge amount of gambling money swilling around in the Far East. And a lot of it is staked on football. The Australians in particular have done a lot of investigative work into the way they use computer networks to rake the money in. And yes, there's a lot of associated crime and corruption. But the point is, the gambling syndicates don't have to resort to assassination to skew the odds in their favour. They can buy what they need.'

'You're saying that even with the amount of money we pay our footballers, they've still got their hands out for more?' Paula feigned shock.

'There's more than one way to fix a game,' Stacey said. 'Arguably, the match officials have more influence over outcome. And they don't earn mega salaries.'

Sam snorted derisively. 'And they're so crap, nobody would notice them doing it on purpose. If a referee can give one player three yellow cards in the same game when he's supposed to send him off after the second one, imagine what he could do if he was taking backhanders. So you're saying that while these gambling syndicates might cross the line to make sure the sums come out in their favour, you don't think they'd go as far as murder?'

Stacey nodded. 'That's exactly what I'm saying. It doesn't match the way they go about things.'

Kevin looked up from the gun he was doodling on his pad. 'Yeah, but that's what you might call the traditional end of dodgy gambling. See, this ricin thing, that spells Russian mafia to me. A lot of those guys, they're ex-KGB and FSB. It was the KGB that helped the Bulgarians assassinate Georgi Markov using ricin. What if the Russians have decided they want a slice of the international betting cash? It would be just like them to be so bloody heavy-handed.'

Stacey shrugged. 'It makes a kind of sense, I suppose. But I've not heard anything about the Russians getting into this sort of thing. Maybe we should ask Six?'

Carol shuddered. The last thing she wanted was to allow the intelligence services anywhere near her operation. Their reputation slithered before them, in particular their reluctance to go away empty-handed once they'd been invited in. Carol didn't want to have her murder inquiry transformed into some sinister conspiracy until she was certain it wasn't a straight-forward murder for one of the customary motives. 'Until we've got something more solid connecting the Russians to this, I'm not going near the spooks,' she said firmly. 'At this point, we have nothing to suggest Robbie Bishop's murder was anything to do with gambling or the Russian mafia. Let's wait till we have some evidence before we get over-excited about theories like Bindie's. We'll keep it in mind, but I don't think it's worth spending investigative resources on it right now. Stacey, what have you got for us?'

Never at her best when dealing with humans, Stacey shifted in her seat and studiously avoided eye contact. 'So far, I've found nothing of interest on Bishop's computer. No emails sent after his night out on Thursday, except one to his agent agreeing to an interview for a Spanish men's magazine. Also, he never visited the bestdays.co.uk website. Not from his home computer, at any rate. His history list iş almost exclusively related to football or music. He bought some new speakers online just last week. Which kind of knocks the suicide idea on the head, if that was in anybody's mind.'

'I don't know. If I was depressed, I might spend a few bob to cheer myself up,' Sam said. Catching Carol rolling her eyes, he hastily added, 'Not that we're thinking suicide.'

'Not with ricin. Too obscure, too painful, too slow,' Carol said, echoing what Denby had said to her. 'As for the Best Days website, given that Robbie did have the url on him, I think we can assume that whoever he was drinking with that night was familiar with the site. Stacey, do you think there's any way they can help us?'

'Depends on their attitude,' she began.

'And on whether they're football fans,' Kevin said.

Stacey looked dubious. 'Maybe. What I thought we could ask for in the first instance is for them to send an email to all their Harriestown High subscribers asking them to contact us with a recent photo and an account of their movements on Thursday night. That way, we set things in motion without having to wait for a warrant.'

'Isn't that sending out a big fat warning to our killer?' Kevin asked. 'Tipping them off to our interest? I went to Harriestown High, you know. We weren't the most authority-friendly bunch. Harriestown wasn't yuppified back then, it was pretty rough. Even in Robbie's day, it wasn't the sort of place where they fall over themselves to help the police. You're dealing with the kind of people who could easily send a photo of someone completely different just to wind us up, never mind throwing us off the trail. I say we ask the site for the names and addresses of their subscribers and if they won't come across, we go for the warrant.'

Carol saw the momentary flash of irritation in Stacey's eyes. She normally kept her opinions on her colleagues' lack of understanding of the world of information technology to herself; it was rare to catch a glimpse of her true feelings.

Assuming an air of weary patience, Stacey said, 'The only address the website will have stored for their subscribers is the email address. It's possible they may have credit card billing addresses, but even if they do, that's covered by the data protection legislation and we definitely would need a warrant to get that. The important thing here is that, however we get in touch with these people, there's no way to keep it secret. The first person we talk to will be online before we're back in our cars, posting our line of inquiry. We might as well be upfront from the start. The online community is much more inclined to co-operate when they're included in the process. We take them with us, we get their help. We treat them as potentially hostile and they'll make our life twice as difficult.' It was a major speech for Stacey. A measure, Carol thought, of how seriously she was taking this case.

'OK. Give it a whirl, Stacey. See if you can get the

Best Days people to co-operate. If you hit a wall, come back to me. And, Kevin? You can cast an eye over the pics from your era, see if your old classmates are confounding your expectations and telling the truth. Chris?' Carol turned to the sergeant. 'How did you guys get on at Amatis?'

Chris shook her head. 'The bar staff who were on duty on Thursday remember seeing Robbie in the vodka bar, but they were too busy to pay attention to the company he was keeping. Same with the punters. I think we can probably rule out a stunning blonde. They would have noticed that, I suspect. Paula did notice one thing . . .' Chris tipped a nod to Paula and took a sheet of paper out of a folder. 'There's CCTV covering the bar area. Unfortunately for our purposes, it's there to keep an eye on the staff, not the punters. It's the management's way of making sure all the cash ends up in the till and that nobody is dealing drugs from behind the bar. So it's not pointed at the customers. However, we did get this.' She moved to the whiteboard and pinned up a grainy enlargement. 'This is Robbie,' she said, pointing to a hand on the very edge of the photo. 'We know it's him because of the Celtic ring tattoo on his middle finger. And next to him, we can see someone else.' A couple of inches from Robbie's fingertips was half a hand, a wrist and a section of forearm. 'Male,' she said, her expression a mixture of disgust and triumph. 'A few more degrees of angle on the camera and we'd have him. As it is, all we know is that it is a him and that he doesn't have a tattoo on the right half of his right hand, wrist or lower arm.' She stepped away from the board and sat down again. 'So at least Stacey

140

can tell the website people we're only interested in the blokes.'

'Can we, though? Can we be sure this is the person he was referring to?' Sam butted in.

'Sure as we can be. We've been through all the footage and we've not been able to put anybody else alongside Robbie. Someone talking to him from behind wouldn't have been able to get at his drink. See, it's too close to Robbie for anyone to tamper with it except the person facing him at the bar.'

'OK.' Sam subsided. 'Point taken.'

'Thanks, Chris. Anybody else got anything?'

'I've got the results from the street CCTV,' Paula said. 'I got the graveyard-shift CID to work it through the night. Robbie definitely didn't leave by the front door, which is a massive pain in the arse because that area's saturated with cameras. He must have left by the side door, the so-called VIP exit. There's no coverage there – the club wants to keep on the good side of its so-called celebrity patrons. This way, there's no temptation for the club's security staff to flog stuff to the gossip mags. If there are no pix of C-list TV reality-show arseholes shagging some drunken fan up against the wall, they're not going to be exposed in print. So goes the theory.

'The back lane behind the club opens out into Goss Street, the effective border of Temple Fields . . .' Paula paused for a moment, lips pursed, eyes narrowed. 'And of course, Temple Fields has pretty sketchy coverage. Too many of the businesses there are reliant on the streetlife for them to want CCTV, so they always oppose the council when they want to put more cameras up. So we don't have any footage of

Robbie entering Goss Street. What we do have, however, is a very brief clip from one of the cameras on Campion Way. I've just put it up on the network, you'll all be able to see it on your screens. But here it is for now.' She pulled a laptop towards her and tapped the mouse pad. The interactive whiteboard to the side of Carol immediately sprang to life, an obscure picture appearing, an abstract chiaroscuro of dark and light created by the streetlights on Campion Way. 'This is pretty raw,' Paula said. 'We should be able to get it cleaned up a bit. But I don't know how helpful it's going to be.'

The camera was looking down the street, angled to pick up car number plates as kerb crawlers idled down Campion Way. At first, nothing moved. Then two figures emerged from a cross street, paused at the kerb, waiting for a night bus to pass, then walked briskly across the road and disappeared down the other arm of the side street. Knowing Robbie Bishop was the target made it possible to distinguish the walker closest to the camera as the footballer. But the person beyond him was nothing but a darker smudge, except for one brief moment at the kerbside when a blur of white appeared at Robbie's shoulder.

'And the killer is Caspar the friendly fucking ghost,' Kevin said. 'At least we know he's white. Almost makes you think he knew the camera was there.'

'I think he did know,' Paula said. 'I think it's very instructive that this is the only CCTV camera shot we have of Robbie and his probable killer. Even with the scant coverage there is in Temple Fields, it's impossible to get from one side to the other without being picked up at least once on camera.' She tapped again

142

on the mouse pad. This time, a map of Temple Fields appeared, with Amatis and the CCTV cameras highlighted. Paula tapped again. This time, a scarlet line zigzagged through the streets, avoiding all but the Campion Way camera. 'By taking this route, they were only picked up from the side. And for less than a minute. Any other route and they'd have been filmed head-on. Look at the way they must have come. You don't make all those twists and turns by chance. And I don't think it was Robbie who was avoiding the cameras.'

They all stared at the map for a long moment. 'Well spotted, Paula,' Carol said. 'I think we can safely say that we are looking for somebody local. Somebody who attended Harriestown High School and who has intimate knowledge of Temple Fields. With all respect, Kevin, this is looking more like one of your fellow former pupils than the Russian mafia. Unless of course they're using local talent. So let's keep our minds open. Paula, do we know how they left Temple Fields?'

'It's a blank, chief. There are plenty of smart flats in that part of town these days. Or they might have got into a car. We've no way of knowing. All we can say for sure is that they don't show up on foot on any of the main drags on that side of Temple Fields.'

'OK. Let's see if we can get any more commercial CCTV footage of the area. Are we any further forward on where he might have got the ricin?'

Kevin consulted his notebook. 'I spoke to a lecturer in the pharmacology department at the university. He says it's easy to make. All you need are some castor beans, lye and acetone and a few basic bits of kitchen equipment – a glass jar, coffee filter, tweezers, that level of stuff.'

'Where do you get castor beans?' Chris asked.

'They're common anywhere south of the Alps. You can buy them online without any trouble. Basically, if any of us wanted to make enough ricin to wipe out the people in this building, we could do it by a week on Wednesday. I don't think there's any mileage in trying to trace the components,' Kevin said wearily.

It was hard not to let despondency seep into the briefing. Carol told herself they had made some progress, even if it did feel insignificant. Every investigation had stages where it felt bogged down. Soon the forensic and pathology results would begin to trickle in. Please God, that might give them a crack they could lever open into a break.

Red-hot worms covered in barbed hooks tore through his flesh. Stoicism abandoned, Tony screamed. The pain subsided into a pulsing stab, an electric eel inside his thigh. The breath escaped from him in tight little groans. 'Everybody says having the drains out is the worst,' the middle-aged nurse said cosily.

'Ungh,' Tony grunted. 'Not wrong.' Sweat beaded his face and neck. His whole body stiffened as he felt the twinge of a movement in the second drain. 'Just a minute. Gimme a minute,' he gasped.

'Better out than in,' the nurse said and carried on regardless.

Knowing what was coming didn't make the second one any easier to endure. He clenched his hands and eyes shut and took a deep breath. As the scream died away, a familiar voice grated in his ears. 'He's always been a big girl's blouse,' his mother said conversationally to the nurse.

'I've seen strong men cry, having their drains out,' the nurse said. 'He's done better than many.'

Vanessa Hill patted the nurse on the shoulder. 'I love the way you girls stick up for them. I hope he's not giving you any trouble.'

The nurse smiled. 'Oh no, he's being very well behaved. He's a credit to you, really, Mrs Hill.' And she was gone.

His mother's bonhomie left with her. 'I had a meeting with the Bradfield Cross Trust. I thought I'd better show my face. What are they saying?'

'They're going to try me in a leg brace, see if I can get out of bed today or tomorrow. I'm pushing to be out of here by next week.' He recognized the dismay on her face and considered winding her up. But the small boy in him kicked in, warning him that the consequences would probably not be worth the moment of pleasure. 'Don't worry, I'm not going to let them discharge me into your care. Even if I tell them that's where I'm going, all you'll have to do is turn up when they're sending me home. Then you can deliver me to my own house.'

Vanessa smirked. 'The girlfriend going to take care of you, is she?'

'For the last time, she is not my girlfriend.'

'No, I suppose that would be too much to hope for. Pretty girl like that. Smart too, I don't doubt. She could do better for herself, I expect.' Her lips compressed into a thin line of disapproval. 'You've never had my talent for attracting interesting people.

Apart from your father, of course. But then, we're all entitled to one mistake.'

'I couldn't possibly comment, could I? Since you've never told me anything about him.' Tony heard the bitterness in his voice and wished it gone.

'He thought he was better off without us. In my book, that makes us better off without him.' She turned away, looking out of the window at a flat grey sky. 'Listen, I need you to sign something.' She faced him, leaning her shoulder bag on the bed and taking out a folder of papers. 'Bloody government, they try to screw us for every penny. Your gran's house, it's in both our names. She did it that way to save me paying inheritance tax. It's been rented out all these years. But with the property market the way –'

'Wait a minute. What do you mean, Gran's house is in both our names? This is the first I've heard of it.' Tony pushed himself up on one elbow, wincing but determined.

'Of course it's the first you've heard of it. If I'd left it up to you, you'd have had it running as a probation hostel or a halfway house for some of your precious nutters,' Vanessa said without a trace of indulgent affection. 'Look, I just need you to sign the instructions to the solicitor and the transfer deed.' She produced a couple of sheets of paper and placed them on the bed-table, grabbing the bed control and fiddling with the buttons.

Tony found himself being shunted up and down as Vanessa tried to figure out how to get him to sit up. 'Why am I only hearing about this now? What about all the rent money?'

Satisfied with the bed position, Vanessa flipped her

146

wrist dismissively. 'Would have been wasted on you. What would you have done with it? Bought more bloody books? Anyway, you'll get your share when you sign up for the sale.' She raked in her bag and came up with a pen. 'Here, sign these.'

'I need to read them,' Tony protested as she pushed the pen between his fingers.

'What for? You'll be none the wiser once you're done. Just sign, Tony.'

It was, he thought, impossible to know whether she was trying to con him. Her manner would have been the same either way. Impatience, irritation, the unmistakable conviction that he, like the rest of the world, was trying to throw any available obstacle in her path. He could try standing up to her, demand the opportunity to read the papers in full and the time to think over what she wanted. But right now, he didn't care. His leg hurt, his head hurt, and he knew she could take nothing from him that mattered. Yes, she might be keeping from him things that were his. But he'd got along fine without them so far and he probably would continue to do so. Getting her off his case and out of his room was much more important. 'OK,' he sighed. But before he could use the pen, the door swung open and Mrs Chakrabarti entered like a predatory schooner, her fleet round her in battle order.

In a single move, Vanessa spirited the papers away and into her bag. Under the cover of a pat on the hand, she removed the pen, all the while giving Mrs Chakrabarti the benefit of her finest corporate smile.

'You must be the famous Mrs Hill,' the surgeon said. Tony thought he imagined a dryness in her tone that he couldn't quite believe.

147

'I owe you a debt of gratitude for making such a good job of my son's knee,' Vanessa replied sweetly. 'The idea of being crippled for life is one he'd struggle to come to terms with.'

'I think most people would.' The surgeon turned to Tony. 'I hear they managed to get your drains out without killing you.'

His smile felt ancient and tired. 'Just about. I think it hurt more than being hit in the first place.'

Mrs Chakrabarti raised her eyebrows. 'You men are such babies. It's as well you don't have to give birth or the human race would have died out a long time ago. So, what we are going to do now is to remove that big heavy splint and see what happens. It's going to hurt like blazes, but if this pain is too much, then attempting to stand is certainly going to be beyond you.'

'I'll be off, then,' Vanessa cut in. 'I never could stand to see him suffer.'

Tony let the lie pass. It was worth it to see the back of her. 'Do your worst, then,' he said as the door closed behind Vanessa. 'I'm tougher than I look.'

Stacey Chen was also tougher than she looked. She'd had to be. In spite of a phenomenal talent for programming and systems analysis, little had come easily to her. The silicon-based world should have been blind to her gender and her status as the child of immigrant parents, but it had turned out to be just as biased as everywhere else. That was one reason why she'd turned her back on a brilliant academic career and opted for the police. She'd made her first million while she was still an undergraduate with a clever bit of code she'd sold to a US software giant which secured their operating system against potential software conflicts. But success had come with a larding of condescension and she knew she didn't want to be part of that world.

In the police, however, you knew exactly where you were. Nobody apart from the bosses in offices far removed from the sharp end pretended your gender and ethnicity didn't matter. It was prejudiced, but it was honest. She could put up with that because what Stacey loved more than anything was the opportunity the police service gave her to fiddle around inside other people's computer lives. She could nose around in people's emails, wriggle her way through their perversions and dig up the secrets they thought they'd buried. And it was all legal.

The other thing about police work was that there was no possible conflict between her salaried life and her freelance work. Her monthly pay packet barely covered the overheads of her city-centre penthouse, never mind the made-to-measure suits and shirts she wore to the office. The rest of the cash – and there was a lot of it – came from the code she wrote in her home office on her own machines. That was one kind of satisfaction. Poking her nose into other people's privacy was the other. These days, she had what she wanted, but by God, she'd earned it.

The only downside was that from time to time, she had to deal with people face to face. For some reason, the police still believed that you got better results when you were breathing the same air as the people you were questioning. Very twentieth century, Stacey thought as her GPS system announced, 'Destination road reached.'

The headquarters of Best Days of Our Lives didn't look like any software company Stacey had ever visited. It was a suburban semi on the outskirts of Preston, a short but traffic-choked distance from the M6. It seemed odd that a company which had been the subject of a multi-million dollar buyout attempt only months before was based in a 1970s box that couldn't with the best will in the world have been worth much more than a couple of hundred thousand. But it was the address registered at Companies House and the one they'd given her via email.

The front door opened as Stacey climbed out of the car and a woman in her late twenties dressed in fashionably ripped jeans and a Commonwealth Games rugby shirt smiled cheerfully. 'You must be DC Chen,' she said in a West Country accent. 'Come on in.'

Stacey, who had dressed carefully in geek chic Gap chinos and hoodie, smiled back. 'Gail?'

The woman pushed her streaked blonde hair back and held out a hand. 'Pleased to meet you, come on in.' She ushered Stacey into a living room crammed with sofas and chairs. Children's toys were piled in a random heap in the corner by the TV set. A coffee table was strewn with magazines and print-outs of lists. 'Sorry about the mess. We've been trying to move for about a year now but we never seem to have the time to look at houses.'

The idea of not having children ever was fine with Stacey. She loved the clean lines of her loft, its space and its harmony. Living here would drive her nuts. No two ways about it. 'It's OK,' she lied.

'Can I get you a drink? Tea, coffee, herbal tea, Red Bull, Diet Coke ... Milk?'

'I'm fine, thanks.' Stacey smiled, her dark almond eyes turning up at the corners. 'I didn't realize you guys ran the business from home. Cracking idea, by the way.'

'Thanks.' Gail dropped on to one of the sofas and pulled a face. 'It started as a hobby. Then it took over our lives. We have big corporations contacting us pretty much every day, wanting to buy us up. But we don't want it to change and become all about making money. We want it to stay about people, about lives reconnecting. We've had people come together after a lifetime apart. We've been to weddings. We've got a whole cork board of photos of Best Days babies.' Gail grinned. 'I feel like a fairy godmother.'

Stacey recognized the quote. She'd read it in a couple of online interviews Gail had given about the business and its impact on people's lives. 'It's not all sunshine, though, is it? I've heard marriages have broken up as well.'

Gail fiddled with the frayed cloth on the sofa arm. 'Can't make an omelette without breaking eggs.'

'Not good publicity, though, is it?'

Gail looked slightly baffled, as if she was wondering how this conversation had derailed itself so quickly from the sunny and warm. 'Well, no. To be honest, we try to avoid talking about that side of things.' She grinned again, but less certainly this time. 'No need to harp on about it, I say.'

'Quite. And I'm sure the last thing you want is to be associated in a negative way with a murder inquiry,' Stacey said.

Gail looked as if she'd been slapped. 'Murder? That can't be right.'

'I'm investigating the murder of Robbie Bishop.'

'He's not one of our members,' Gail said sharply. 'I'd have remembered if he was.'

'We have reason to believe that he was drinking with somebody who is one of your members on the night he was poisoned. It's possible ...'

'Are you trying to tell me one of our members *murdered* Robbie Bishop?' Gail reared back into the sofa, as if she was trying to get away from Stacey.

'Please, Gail, just listen.' Stacey's patience was wearing thin. 'We believe the person he was drinking with may have seen something, or Robbie may have said something to them. We need to trace that person and we think they were a member of Best Days of Our Lives.'

'But why?' Gail looked frantic. 'Why do you think that?'

'Because Robbie told another friend he was having a drink with someone from school. And we found a scrap of paper with the website url in the pocket of the trousers he was wearing.'

'That doesn't mean ...' Gail kept shaking her head, as if the movement could make Stacey disappear.

'What we want you to do is to send a message to all of your male subscribers who were at Harriestown High with Robbie, asking them if they were the person who was drinking with him on Thursday. And because they might be nervous about admitting it, we also want them to send you a recent photograph and an account of their movements between ten in the evening on Thursday and four in the morning on Friday. Do you think you can do that for us?' Stacey smiled again. It was as well the children were not at home, for her expression would surely have reduced them to terrified tears.

'I don't think . . .' Gail's voice trailed off. 'I mean . . . It's not what people sign up for, is it?'

Stacey shrugged. 'The web is, by and large, a positive place. I think people will respond well to being asked for help. Robbie was a popular guy.' She pulled out a phone with email capacity. 'I can email you the message we'd like you to send out.'

'I don't know. I need to talk to Simon. My husband.' Gail leaned forward, reaching for the mobile on the coffee table.

Stacey shook her head, miming regret. 'The thing is, we don't have time to waste here. Either we do this the nice way, where you stay in control of your addresses and your system, or we do it the other way, where I get a warrant and we cart your computers out of here and I do whatever it takes to get your subscribers to come across. It may not be pretty and I doubt you'll have much of a business left to attract the corporate sharks once somebody leaks to the press that you tried to obstruct the investigation into Robbie Bishop's murder.' Stacey spread her hands. 'But, hey, it's up to you.' Chris Devine would have been proud of her, she thought, monstering the poor woman so thoroughly.

Gail looked at her with hatred. 'I thought you were one of us,' she said bitterly.

'You're not the first one to make that mistake,' Stacey said. 'Let's go and send some emails.'

Vanessa drew her reading glasses from her face and dropped them by her pad. 'I think that's us,' she said.

The plump woman opposite her settled back in her

chair. 'I'll get everything under way,' she said. Melissa Riley had been Vanessa Hill's second-in-command for four years. In spite of all the evidence to the contrary, she persisted in her belief that Vanessa's steely professionalism disguised a heart of gold. Nobody who was that shrewd or swift in her assessments of human behaviour and personality could really be as hardboiled as Vanessa seemed to be. And today, finally, there was proof of that. Vanessa had cancelled all her appointments to be at the bedside of her injured son. OK, she'd reappeared mid-morning and had been working like a Trojan ever since, but still. She'd only come away because her son's partner had insisted on relieving her. 'How are you feeling?' she asked, her smooth face shining with concern.

'Feeling?' Vanessa frowned. 'I'm fine. It's not me that's in the hospital.'

'It must have been a terrible shock, all the same. And to see your son laid up like that . . . I mean, as a mother, you want what's best for them, you want to take their pain away . . .'

'You do,' Vanessa said, her tone indicating the conversation was at an end. She could see Melissa was gagging for something more intimate. Her social work training had left her avid for other people's disasters. There were times when Vanessa wondered if Melissa's brilliant organizational skills were sufficient to outweigh her desire to insinuate her fat little fingers into every crevice of any passing psyche. Today, it was a close call.

'And of course, you're absolutely riven with anxiety about his recovery,' Melissa said. 'Have they said whether he'll walk properly again?'

'He might have a limp. He'll probably have to have another surgery.' It killed Vanessa to reveal this much, but she understood that sometimes she had to give a little to maintain the respect of her team. As Melissa wittered on, she wondered what it felt like to be consumed with maternal concern. Mothers talked about bonding with their kids, but she'd never felt that burning intimacy they spoke of. She'd felt protective towards her baby, but it didn't seem much different from the way she'd felt about her first puppy, the runt of the litter who'd had to be bottle-fed. In a way, she was relieved. She didn't want to be chained to this child, to feel a physical absence when they were apart as she'd heard other women describe. But she had known right from the start that her lack of response was not the sort of thing it was acceptable to admit to. For all she knew, there were millions of women who felt as disengaged as she did.

But as long as there were Melissas out there laying claim to the moral high ground, Vanessa and her multitudes would have to pretend. Well, that wasn't such a big deal. She'd spent most of her life pretending one thing or another. Sometimes she wondered if she really knew any more what was real and what was constructed.

Not that it mattered. She would do as she had always done. Look after number one. She didn't owe Tony a damn thing. She'd fed and clothed him and put a roof over his head till he'd left for university. If there was any debt owed, it was in the other direction.

Running a unit like hers meant there was no hiding place, Carol thought bitterly as some sixth sense kicked in and she looked up to see the main office door open on John Brandon. The time it took her Chief Constable to cross the office to her cubicle was enough for Carol to compose herself mentally, to review what little there was to share.

She stood up as he walked into her small domain. She was conscious that Brandon and his wife were her friends, a consciousness that made her stand on ceremony whenever they met in the semi-public arena of the police HQ. 'Sir,' she said with a tight smile, waving him to a chair.

Brandon, his lugubrious bloodhound face reflecting her own low spirits, eased into the chair with the care of a man suffering back pain. 'The world has its eye on us today, Carol.'

'Robbie Bishop will get the same commitment from my team as every other victim, sir.'

'I know that. But our investigations don't usually attract quite this much attention.'

Carol picked up a pen and rolled it between her fingers. 'We've had our moments,' she said. 'I don't have a problem with being the focus of the media's attention.'

'Other people do, though. I have bosses and they want a quick result. Bradfield Victoria's board want this brought to a successful conclusion ASAP. It's unsettling their players, apparently.' Brandon was enough of a diplomat to hide his feelings generally, but today, his irritation was just visible beneath the surface. 'And it seems that every citizen of Bradfield was Robbie Bishop's number one fan.' He sighed. 'So where are we up to?'

Carol weighed up her choices. Should she make the

little she had sound more or less than it was? More
would put pressure on her to deliver on it; less would
put pressure on her to find something to chase. She
settled for laying it out exactly as it was. At the end of
her short recital, John Brandon looked even more miserable. 'I don't envy you,' he said. 'But that doesn't mean
I don't want a result. Anything you need in terms of
bodies and resources, let me know.' He got up.

'It's not a matter of resources now, sir. It's a matter
of information.'

'I know.' He turned to go. His hand was on the
door handle when he looked back. 'Do you need me
to sort out another profiler? With Tony out of action?'

Carol felt a flash of panic. She didn't want to have
to forge a working relationship with somebody whose
judgements would be based on a scant knowledge of
her and her team. She didn't want to have to worry
about how to mitigate another psychologist's conclusions. 'It's his leg that's busted, not his brain,' she said
hastily. 'It'll be fine. When there's something for a
profiler to get his teeth into, Dr Hill will be there for
us.'

Brandon raised his eyebrows. 'Don't let me down,
Carol.' Then he was gone, walking across the office
with a word of encouragement.

Carol stared at his back, fizzing with anger. The
implied criticism in his words was out of order. No
other officer under John Brandon's command had
done more to demonstrate commitment to the job,
or to the abstract principles of justice that drove her.
No other officer had a better track record when it
came to dealing with the kind of destructive high-
profile cases that fucked up lives and made Bradfield's

citizens look over their shoulders in fear. And he knew that. Somebody somewhere must have given him one hell of a kicking to make him act as if he didn't.

DC Sam Evans was supposed to be canvassing residents of the converted warehouse where Robbie Bishop had lived. The boss had had this idea that Robbie might have said something to a fellow resident in the sauna or the steam room after his night out at Amatis, something that might lead them to the poisoner. Sam thought the idea was crap. If there was one thing that people like Robbie Bishop learned, it was to keep your mouth shut in front of anybody who might be tempted to grass you up to *Heat* or the *Bradfield Evening Sentinel* diary. He knew that Carol Jordan thought he needed to mend his maverick ways, especially after Don Merrick's decision to follow a hot lead without waiting for back-up had ended so disastrously. She had indicated there was no room now for anything other than team spirit, but he knew she hadn't got where she was today by putting her own interests second. She couldn't blame him for doing his own thing as long as he got results.

So instead of pointless door-knocking, he was holed up in his own living room, laptop on his knees, Robbie Bishop's emails on his screen. Stacey had said there was nothing there, but he didn't think she'd had time to go through them one by one. Not when she'd been doing all the techie stuff with his hard drive as well. She might have skimmed the emails, but he'd bet this month's salary that she hadn't scrutinized them in detail.

After an hour, he couldn't find it in his heart to

find fault with Stacey for her presumed dereliction. It was bad enough that Robbie cleaved to the text message style of prose, making it less than straightforward to read. Even worse was the banality of his messages. If there was a duller correspondent than Robbie Bishop, Sam hoped earnestly he'd never have to wade through his mail. He supposed the ones about music might contain something worth reading if you had a consuming passion for the minutiae of obscure trip-hop tracks. Maybe Robbie's fascination for bpm made Bindie's heart race. All it did for Sam was provoke a strong desire for sleep.

The love stuff was almost as boring as the music. And since Bindie was his principal correspondent, love and music was most of what there was. But Sam wasn't about to give up. He understood that the most interesting information was often the stuff that was most deeply buried. And so he persevered.

The clue came halfway through the third hour of excruciating assertions of love and analyses of music. He almost missed it, so casually was it buried among the other stuff. Robbie had written, 'Maybe u shd report this fuckwit. U say he means u no harm, bt wot abt me? Peple like him do al kinds of shit with guns & stuff. Let's talk about it l8r.'

It didn't make much sense on its own. Sam went back to the email filing cabinet and called up the saved incoming mail folder. When he clicked to open it, the message read, 'You have 9743 messages in this folder. It may take some time to sort these messages. Do you want to go ahead?' He clicked <yes> and while he waited, checked the date on Robbie's outgoing message.

It took only a few seconds to find the message from Bindie that had prompted Robbie's reply. 'I'm starting to get a bit weirded out by this geezer who keeps turning up at gigs,' Sam read.

'He's been sending me letters for a while now – beautiful fancy handwriting, looks like it's written with a fountain pen – all telling me how we're meant to be together and how the BBC are conspiring to keep us apart. None of it very sensible, but whatever, he seemed harmless enough. Anyway, he's finally figured out that I do live club gigs too and he's started showing up there. Thankfully most of them won't let him in becoz he fails the dress code, but then he just hangs around outside. He's taken to parading up and down with a placard saying there's a plot to keep him from me. So one of the doormen took it on himself the other week to show him that spread we did for the Sunday Mirror for Valentine's Day. And apparently he was very put out. Ever since, he's been telling all the door crews that you've hypnotized me and made me your sex slave. And that he's going to put it to rights. I don't imagine for a moment that he will do anything except crawl back in his burrow eventually, but it is a BIT freaky.'

Sam drew his breath in slowly. He'd been sure there was something to be found on Robbie's computer. Something that would finally give them a solid lead. And here it was. Twenty-four carat freak. Just the sort who would come up with some complicated plot involving a rare poison and a slow, horrible death.

He smiled at the screen. A couple of phone calls to nail it down, then he'd show Carol Jordan how wrong she was to sideline Sam Evans.

Tony refined the search parameters again and set his metacrawler to work once more. Google was fine for broad-brush searches, but when it came to fine-tooth comb work, it was hard to beat the search engine an FBI profiler colleague had given him with a nod and a wink. 'It takes a little longer, but you can see the hair in their ears and nostrils,' he'd said. Tony suspected a lot of what it did was in breach of European data protection laws, but he didn't think the cops would be coming after him any time soon.

The big advantage he had over his American counterparts was that the sample he was looking at was much smaller than theirs. If an FBI profiler wanted to look at suspicious deaths of white males between the ages of twenty and thirty over the previous two years, he'd have something like 11,000 cases to consider. But in the UK, the total number of murders committed over two years scarcely reached 1600. When suspicious deaths were added, the numbers rose a little, but not by much. The difficulty Tony faced was actually to identify the target group he was interested in. With relatively few murders committed, there was less impetus to break them down into neat categories of age, gender and race. He'd wasted much of the day acquiring information that had turned out to be completely irrelevant. The process was slowed even further because his concentration span had been temporarily shrunk by drugs and anaesthesia. Tony was embarrassed at the number of times he'd started into consciousness, laptop in hibernation and drool running down his chin.

He had, however, narrowed his search to nine cases by the time Carol arrived in the early evening. He'd wanted to do better, to have something to show her, to prove he was still in the game. But clearly he wasn't, not yet. So he decided to say nothing about his trawl.

She looked frayed round the edges, he thought, watching her slip out of her coat and pull the chair up to the bedside. Eyes heavy-lidded, recent lines showing the strain at the corners. Mouth a despondent line. He knew her well enough to read the process as she pulled herself together and smiled for him. 'So, how did it go today?' she asked. 'Looks pretty different from here.' She nodded at the shape under the covers.

'It's been quite a day. I got my drains out, which was frankly the most painful experience of my life to date. After that, getting the splint off was a piece of piss.' He gave a wry little smile. 'Actually, I'm exaggerating. The splint coming off was no picnic either. But it's all relative. And now I have a leg brace that holds the joint in place.' He gestured at the lump under the covers. 'Apparently the wound is healing well. They took me down for an X-ray, and the bone is also looking in pretty good shape. So tomorrow the sadists from physiotherapy are let loose on me to see if I can get out of bed.'

'That's great,' Carol said. 'Who knew you'd be back on your feet so soon?'

'Hey, let's not get carried away here. Out of bed means a short stagger on a walking frame, not the

162

Great North Run. It's going to be a long road back to anything like I was before.'

Carol snorted. 'You make it sound like you were Paula Radcliffe. Come on, Tony, you were hardly the Rambling Boy of Bradfield.'

'Maybe not. But I had a great action,' he said, his upper body miming an athletic movement.

'And you will have again,' Carol said indulgently. 'Pretty good day, then.'

'More or less. My mother stopped by, which does take the shine off any given twenty-four hour period. Apparently, I own half of my grandmother's house.'

'You've got a granny as well as a mother that I don't know about?'

'No, no. My grandmother died twenty-three years ago. When I was still at university. Half a house would have come in quite handy then. I was always skint,' he said vaguely.

'I'm not sure I'm following this,' Carol said.

'I'm not sure I did either, not entirely. I think I'm still a little less than morphine-free. But what I under-stood my mother to say is that her mother left me half of her house when she died. It seems to have slipped my mother's mind. It's been rented out for the last twenty-three years, but my mother thinks it's time to sell it and she needs my signature on the documents. Of course, whether I'll ever see a penny of the proceeds is another matter.'

Carol stared at him in disbelief. 'That's theft, you know. Technically speaking.'

'Oh, I know. But she is my mother.' Tony wriggled himself more comfortable. 'And she's right. What do I need money for? I have everything I need.'

'That's one way of looking at it.' She dumped a carrier bag on the bed-table. 'All the same, I can't say I approve.'

'My mother is a force of nature. Approval's irrelevant, really.'

'I thought your mother was dead. You've never spoken about her, you know.'

Tony looked away. 'We never had what you'd call a close relationship. My gran did most of the hands-on child rearing.'

'That must have been strange. How was it for you?'

He squeezed out a dry little laugh. 'The Yorkshire translation of *The Gulag Archipelago*. Without the snow.' *Please God, let the flippancy divert her.*

Carol harrumphed. 'You men are such wimps. I bet you never went to bed cold or hungry.' Tony said nothing, unwilling to invite either anger or pity. Carol pulled a wooden box from the bag, opening it up to reveal a chess set. Tony frowned, bemused. 'Why are you setting up a chess board?' he said.

'It's what intelligent people are supposed to do when one of them is in hospital.' Carol's tone was firm.

'Have you been secretly watching Ingmar Bergman films, or what?'

'How hard can it be? I know the moves, I'm sure you do too. We're both smart. It's a way of exercising our brains without working.' Carol continued to lay out the pieces without pause.

'How long have we known each other?' Tony was laughing now.

'Six, seven years?'

'And how often have we played any kind of game, never mind chess?'

164

Now Carol paused. 'Didn't we once . . . No, that was John and Maggie Brandon.' She shrugged. 'Never, I guess. That doesn't mean we shouldn't.'

'You're wrong, Carol. There are very good reasons why we shouldn't.'

She leaned back. 'You're afraid I'll beat you.'

He rolled his eyes. 'We both like winning too much. That's just one of the reasons.' He pulled his notepad and pen towards him and started scribbling.

'What are you doing?'

'I'm going to humour you,' he said absently as he wrote. 'I'm going to play a game of chess with you. But first, I'm going to write down why it will be a disaster.' He carried on writing for a couple of minutes, tore off the page and folded it in half. 'Let's do it, then.'

Now it was Carol's turn to laugh. 'You're joking, right?'

'Never more serious.' He picked up a white and a black pawn, muddled them in his hands and offered her his fists. Carol chose white, and they were off.

Twenty minutes later, they were down to three pieces each and a long tedium of strategy beckoned. Carol let out a huge breath. 'I can't take it. I resign.' Tony smiled and handed her the piece of paper. She opened it and read aloud. 'I take far too long to make a move because I'm exploring all the possibilities four moves ahead. Carol plays kamikaze, trying to get as many pieces off the board as possible. When there are hardly any pieces left and it's clear it's going to take for ever, Carol gets bored and cross and resigns.' She dropped the paper and gently punched his arm. 'You bastard.'

'Chess is a very clear mirror of how individuals think,' Tony said.

'But I'm not a quitter,' Carol protested.

'Not in real life, no. Not when there's something meaningful at stake. But when it's just a game, you can't see the point of expending all that energy with no guarantee of a result.'

Ruefully, Carol scrambled the pieces together and closed the box on them. 'You know me too well.'

'It's mutual. So, given you've studiously avoided it so far tonight, dare I ask how the Robbie Bishop investigation's going?'

Carol snapped the chess set open again. 'How about another game?'

Tony gave her a sympathetic look. 'That bad, eh?'

Five minutes later, having listened to Carol's thorough resumé of what had happened since last they'd met, he was forced to agree. It was indeed that bad. Later, when she tiptoed out as his eyes were closing, the faintest of smiles lifted one corner of his mouth. Maybe tomorrow he would have something better than a game of bad chess for her.

Thursday

The sequence of events that had practically buried Paula McIntyre had also reintroduced her to the balm of nicotine. She hated the smell of stale smoke in the house; it reminded her too much of when Don Merrick had been camping out in her spare room. He'd been her mentor, teaching her so many of the skills she now took for granted. And then he'd become her friend. She'd been the one he turned to when his marriage had imploded and, after his death, she'd been the one who'd had to pack up his personal possessions and return them to the wife who'd pushed him into feeling he had something to prove. Now Paula missed his friendship enough without creating occasions for memory. So she'd spent time, money and energy building a deck on the back of her house with a covered area where she could huddle in the morning with her coffee and cigarettes, trying to pull enough of herself together to make it into the shower and then the office. She was under no illusions about her relationship with the job. She still loved it enough almost to forgive it for what it had done to her: And the time she had spent talking to Tony Hill had helped her to understand that only by staying with Bradfield Police would she ever come anywhere near healing the scars. Some people recovered from trauma by putting as much distance between themselves and their past as was humanly possible. She wasn't one of those.

She dragged on her Marlboro Red, loving the feeling but hating the need. Every morning she berated herself for starting again. And every morning, she reached for the packet before her first mouthful of coffee had made it as far as her stomach. To begin with, she'd told herself it was only a temporary crutch. First case she helped to crack, she'd be able to walk away from it. She'd never been more wrong. Cases had come and gone, but the fags were still with her.

Today was a typically brutal Bradfield morning; low sky, air bitter with pollution, a swirl of damp wind that cheated its way through clothes to the very bones. Paula shivered and smoked and started out of her seat when her phone rang. She grabbed it from her pocket and frowned. Nobody but work would dare call at this time of the morning. But she didn't recognize the number. She froze for a moment, swore out loud at herself and pressed a key. 'Hello?' she said cautiously.

'Is that DC McIntyre?' Ulster accent, dark growl of a voice.

'Who is this?'

'It's Martin Flanagan. From Bradfield Victoria.'

Recognition dawned a split second ahead of the name. 'Mr Flanagan, of course. I'm sorry, there's no ...'

'No, no, it's me that's got something for you. With all the worry about Robbie, like, it completely slipped my mind. Until I came in this morning and there it was.'

Paula sucked smoke and tried to stay calm. She hadn't got to be the queen of the interrogation suite by letting her impatience show. 'Totally understandable,' she said. 'Just take your time, Martin.'

An audible breath. 'Sorry, I'm getting way ahead of myself. Sorry. One of the things we do at the Vics, we do random drug testing on the lads. It's in our interests to keep them clean. Any road, I totally forgot that we tested on Friday morning. And of course, that meant Robbie.'

Paula dropped her cigarette and ground it out with her heel. 'And you got the results this morning?' she said, trying to keep the excitement from her voice.

'That's right. That's why I'm calling you. Ah Jesus ...' Flanagan's voice cracked and he coughed to cover it. 'I don't even know if I should be telling you this. I mean, it was days before he died.'

'There was something on Robbie's test?'

'You could say that. According to the lab ... Christ, I can't bring myself to say it.' Flanagan sounded close to tears.

Paula was already through the kitchen door and moving towards the stairs. 'I'm coming round right now, Martin,' she said. 'Just sit tight. Don't say anything to anyone. I'll be with you inside the half hour. OK?'

'That sounds fine,' he said. 'I'll be in my office. I'll tell them you're coming.'

To her surprise, Paula felt tears pricking her eyes. 'It'll be all right,' she said, knowing it was a lie and knowing it didn't matter.

The pathology suite at Bradfield Cross Hospital was the home ground for Carol Jordan's specialist team.

169

This was where the bodies that interested them ended up, under the careful knife and watchful eyes of Dr Grisha Shatalov. Shatalov's great-grandparents had emigrated from Russia to Vancouver eighty-five years before; Grisha had been born in Toronto and liked to claim his move to the UK was part of the family's slow migration back east. Carol liked his soft accent and his self-deprecating humour. She also liked the way he treated the dead with the same respect she felt he'd give his own family. For Carol, the morgue helped to reaffirm her personal commitment to finding justice. Faced with the victims, the desire to bring the villains to justice always burned that little bit brighter inside her. Grisha's consideration for those victims had resonated with her and built a bridge between them.

Today, she was here for Robbie Bishop. The post mortem should have been done the day before, but Grisha had been in Reykjavik at a conference and Carol hadn't wanted anyone else working on this particular body. Grisha had started work early and by the time Carol arrived, he was almost finished. He looked up as she walked in, acknowledging her presence with a curt nod. 'Ten minutes and we'll be done, DCI Jordan.' His formality was for the benefit of the digital recording which might one day be produced in court. Off-mike, she was Carol to him.

She leaned against the wall. Impossible not to feel sadness seeping through her at the thought of what Robbie had been. Lover, son, friend, athlete. Someone whose grace had been beamed round the world, whose talent had made people happy. All that gone now, gone because some bastard's need not to have him in the world outweighed all the positives. It was her job to find who that bastard was and to make sure they never got the chance to repeat their act of destruction. She'd never relished the job nor hated its difficulties more than she did that day.

At last, Grisha was done. The body approximated wholeness again; the samples were taken, the organs weighed and the incision stitched. Grisha peeled off gloves and mask, stripped off his apron and stepped out of his lab boots. In stocking soles, he padded down the corridor to his office, Carol in his wake.

The office was a defiant gesture against the concept of the paperless workplace. Crammed folders, loose sheets, bound stacks of paper covered every surface except for the chair behind the desk and a lab stool against the wall. Carol took up her customary perch and said, 'So what have you got for me?'

Grisha dropped into his chair like a stone. His perfectly oval face was grey from lack of sleep and daylight, a combination of the job and a baby who had yet to discover the delight of unbroken sleep. His grey eyes, shaped like long, low pyramids, had matching shadows underneath them and his full lips seemed to have become bloodless. He looked more like a prisoner than a pathologist. He scratched a stubbled cheek and said, 'Not much that you don't know already. Cause of death, multiple organ failure as a result of ricin poisoning.' He held up one finger. 'I should qualify that by saying my conclusion is based on the information supplied by the doctors treating him at the time of his death. We'll have to wait for our own tox screening before we can confirm that officially, let's be clear about that, eh?'

'Nothing else?'

Grisha smiled. 'I could tell you all about his physical condition, but I don't think that would take you any further. There is one thing that may or may not have some bearing on how he died. There's some ano-rectal trauma – nothing much, just some internal bruising in the anal area. And also some faint irritation of the tissue just above the anal sphincter.'

'Provoked by what?' Carol asked.

'The bruising is consistent with sexual activity. I'd say the rough side of consensual. Not rape. Well, not rape in the sense of him being held down and forcibly penetrated. But quite forceful. No semen traces, so I couldn't hazard an opinion as to whether he was penetrated by a penis or something else. A dildo, a bottle, a carrot. Could have been anything of a reasonable size, really.' He smiled. 'As we both know from this line of work, it takes all sorts.'

'Does it look like this sort of sexual activity was something he did regularly?'

Grisha stroked his chin, a hangover from a recently departed goatee. 'I'd say not. There's no evidence of Robbie indulging in regular anal sex. He might have gone for a neat little butt plug, but nothing the size of a penis.'

'And the tissue irritation? What about that? What does that tell us?'

Grisha shrugged. 'Hard to say. Given where it is, whatever caused it, any trace is going to be long gone. It's the sort of thing you might get if some foreign substance was inserted into the anus.'

'Like ricin? Would that produce a reaction like this?'

Grisha leaned back and stared at the ceiling.

'Theoretically, I suppose.' He returned to the vertical abruptly. 'I thought he was presumed to have inhaled it?'

Carol shook her head. 'We assumed his drink or food had been spiked.'

'No way. Not if Dr Blessing's account of the process of his dying is correct. What it is, Carol... the symptoms manifest in a different way if you ingest ricin rather than inhale it. But if you absorbed it through a sensitive mucous membrane like the rectum, then your symptoms would be more like inhalation than ingestion. Now, until I did the PM, I would have gone for the inhalation theory.'

Carol shook her head. 'Everybody we've spoken to is adamant he didn't do drugs. I don't think they're trying to protect his memory. I think they're telling the truth. Besides, the hospital labs tested their samples and found no traces of recreational drugs.'

Grisha raised his eyebrows, obviously mildly sceptical. 'Depending on what he was given and when he took it, there might not have been traces by the time they took their samples. But if he genuinely didn't snort drugs, I'd say this is maybe how the ricin got into his system. It would have had a vehicle – a Hard Fat NF suppository, a gel capsule, something like that. But again, we're not going to find any traces, not this long after the event. I've taken samples, obviously. We might just get lucky, but don't hold your breath.'

Carol sighed. 'Great. This is shaping up to be the case from hell. I've got the brass and the media jackals all over me, looking for a quick resolution. Which frankly is about as likely as Bradfield Vics signing me as Robbie's replacement.'

Grisha leaned forward and clicked his mouse. 'I'll do what I can to help, but you're right, it's a tough one.' He flashed her a sympathetic smile. 'But while I've got you here, it's been too long since we had you over for dinner. I know Iris would love to see you.' He peered at the screen. 'How would Saturday be for you?'

Carol thought for a moment. 'Sounds good to me.'

'Seven?'

'Make it eight. I have some hospital visiting to do first.'

'Hospital visiting?'

'Tony.'

'Oh, of course, I heard about that. How is he?' Before Carol could answer, there was a tap at the door. 'Come in,' Grisha called.

Paula stuck her head round the door. 'Hi, Doc. I'm looking for . . .'

'You found her,' Grisha said.

Paula grinned and walked in. 'It doesn't hurt that you're here too, Doc.' She waved an envelope at them. 'I think we're finally cooking with gas, chief. I've just come from a meeting with Martin Flanagan. He really didn't want to come clean –'

'But you'd already worked the McIntyre charm on him,' Carol said. She'd seen enough of Paula's killer interview technique not to be surprised.

'I think it's that he cares more about us catching Robbie's killer than the reputation of the club, to be honest. Anyway, according to Mr Flanagan, it totally slipped his mind that the club did a routine drug sweep on Friday. Like all the rest of them, Robbie peed into a bottle. Unlike the rest of them, in his case,

174

out came roofies.' She pulled a sheet of paper out of the envelope and proffered it to Grisha.

'Positive for rohypnol,' Grisha read. 'I've heard of this lab, they're supposed to be pretty thorough. But you should contact them, ask if they've got any of Robbie's sample left. I'm not seeing enough detail here to get any accurate sense of how much and when.' He handed the paper to Carol.

'I think we know when. Thursday night in Amatis,' Carol said sourly.

Grisha frowned. 'Probably not, actually.' He tapped keys, clicked his mouse. 'That's what I thought. The forget-me pill. It starts to take effect between twenty minutes and half an hour of being ingested. So if Robbie had been given it in the nightclub, by the time he left he'd have been acting like he was totally off his face.'

'Nobody's even suggested he was drunk,' Paula said. 'And he was moving OK on that CCTV footage.'

'So he must have trusted whoever he was with enough to go somewhere else with him. Somewhere he was given a drink spiked with rohypnol,' Carol said, thinking aloud.

'Its effects are aggravated by alcohol, so given that he'd been drinking earlier, he'd likely be out of it within an hour of taking it,' Grisha said. 'He'd go along with whatever was happening to him. He wouldn't resist anal penetration. He wouldn't mind having a suppository inserted rectally. And he wouldn't remember anything about it afterwards. It's the perfect murder, really. By the time your victim dies, his connection to you is a long way away.'

Carol handed the paper back to Paula. 'Well done,'

she said. 'But this is a bitch of a case. Every scrap of information we get seems to make things harder.'

Half an hour later, they were harder still. Carol sat in her office, door closed, blinds drawn to avoid distraction. Elbows on the desk, one hand held the phone to her ear, the other clutched a chunk of her hair. 'I hope I didn't wake you,' she said.

'Actually, you did. But it's just as well, there's shit I need to get sorted,' Bindie Blyth said, her voice rusty from sleep. She coughed, cleared her throat then sniffed. Carol could hear her moving.

'There's something I need to ask you. It's a bit personal.'

The unmistakable snap of a lighter, then the inhalation of smoke. 'Isn't this where I'm supposed to say, "It's all right, nothing's personal in a murder investigation"?' Bindie said in a passable American accent.

There was, Carol thought, no easy answer to that one. 'I think it's more that nothing's private in a murder investigation. We need to find out everything we can about our victims, even if it turns out to be completely irrelevant. We're not being prurient. Just prudent.' She tutted at herself. 'I'm sorry, that sounded glib. It wasn't meant to be. I mentioned my colleague, the psychologist. He always reminds me that you can never know too much about the victim of a murder. So I hope you'll forgive me for what might feel like prying.'

'It's OK, I'm kind of hiding behind flippancy. Fire away with your questions, I'm not going to take offence.'

Carol took a breath. There was no point in coyness here. 'Did Robbie like anal sex?' she asked.

176

A surprised snort of laughter exploded down the phone. 'Robbie? Robbie take it up the arse? You have got to be joking. I tried to talk him into it, but he was totally convinced that any straight man who liked pegging was a secret gay.'

'Pegging?' Carol felt ancient and out of touch beside Bindie.

'You know. *Bend Over Boyfriend* stuff. Shagging your bloke with a dildo. It's called pegging.'

'I'd not heard the term before.'

'That'll be living up North,' Bindie said. Her tone said she was teasing, but Carol felt hopelessly provincial nonetheless. 'My ex, the guy I was with before Robbie, he was really into it. I still have the harness and the dildos and all the gear. I tried to get Robbie to go for it, but honestly, you'd think I was suggesting we went out and found some stray dogs to shag. He didn't even like having a finger in his arse when we were fucking.'

'We found a butt plug in his bedside table drawer,' Carol said neutrally.

A moment's silence. 'That would be mine,' Bindie said. 'It's all right, I don't want it back.'

'Right,' Carol said. 'Thanks for being so frank with me.'

'No problem. Now, what was the personal question?' Bindie gave a bitter little laugh. 'Sorry. I told you I was being flippant. Why do you want to know what Robbie liked to do in bed?'

'I'm sorry, I can't tell you details of an ongoing investigation,' Carol said, aware she wanted to give Bindie something in return. 'We're pursuing several lines of inquiry. But I'll be honest, it's a slow process.'

'Time's not the issue, Chief Inspector,' said Bindie, never more serious than now. 'The issue is catching the fucker who did this.'

Imran opened and closed the drawers in his bedroom once again. That made five times, Yousef reckoned. 'You gotta have everything you need by now, man,' he said. 'You checked a million times already.'

'Easy for you to say. I don't want to get to the airport and bang, no iPod. Or get to Ibiza and find my number one Nikes are still under the bed here, know what I mean?' Imran dropped to the floor and raked an arm under the bed.

'You're not going to get to the airport at all if you don't get your arse in gear,' Yousef said. 'That's a clapped-out Vauxhall van you've got, not the Batmobile.'

'And it's not like you're Jeremy Clarkson, cousin.' Imran bounced back on his feet again. 'OK, I'm sorted.' He zipped up his holdall, still looking mildly uncertain, patted his pockets. 'Passport, money, tickets. Let's get gone.'

Yousef followed Imran downstairs and waited patiently while he said goodbye to his mother. Anyone would think he was going for a three-month trek in the Antarctic, not a three-night freebie to Ibiza. Eventually, they managed to get out of the house. Imran tossed the van keys to Yousef. 'You might as well get used to it while I'm there to sort out any problems,' he said. 'Sometimes the clutch sticks a bit, know what I mean?'

Yousef didn't care about the clutch. What he cared about was taking possession of a van that had 'A1 Electricals' emblazoned along the side. 'Whatever,' he muttered, starting the van and slamming it into first. The stereo cut in, blasting out some Tigerstyle drum and bass remix so loud it made Yousef flinch. He reached for the volume control and turned it right down. 'Cut it out, Imran,' he complained. 'My ears.'

'Sorry, man. Them Scottish soldiers know how to hit it.' Imran punched him gently on the shoulder. 'Man, I'm gonna hear some great sounds in Ibiza. I really appreciate this, cuz.'

'Hey, it's cool. I mean, clubbing's never been my thing,' Yousef said. As soon as he'd realized their plan would be made much easier if he could lay hands on a proper tradesman's van, he'd known his cousin Imran was the answer. The question then became how to separate Imran and his vehicle for two or three unsuspecting days. They'd talked it over a few times, trying to come up with a plan that would work, then Yousef had his brainwave. It wasn't uncommon for customers and suppliers to hand out freebies, supposedly to encourage loyalty. Neither Yousef nor Sanjar was big into the club scene, but Imran loved to dance the night away. Yousef could pretend that he'd been given a three-day clubbing break in Ibiza then pass it on to Imran as a gesture of goodwill. Imran would be in Ibiza, and Yousef would have access to the van. It had worked like a dream. Imran had been so chuffed that he hadn't even thought to question why they were going to the airport in his van rather than Yousef's. Now, 'You're welcome, man,' Yousef said. And he meant it.

'Yeah, but, I mean, you could have sold it on to somebody, made some readies.' Imran rubbed fingers and thumb together.

'Hey, you're family.' Yousef half-shrugged one shoulder. 'We should be there for each other.' He felt a twinge of guilt. What he was planning would drive a stake through the heart of his family. It would twist the kaleidoscope and create a completely different picture of his actions. He didn't think any of his relatives would be praising his family spirit any time soon.

'Yeah, that's what everybody says, but when it comes to putting money in their pockets, it's a different story,' Imran said cynically. 'So yeah, I'm totally impressed with you, cuz.'

'Yeah, well, you take it easy out there.'

'I'll be cool.' Imran's fingers crept towards the volume knob. 'Just a little bit, yeah?'

Yousef nodded. 'Sure.' The music filled the van. Even at low volume, the bass reverberated in his bones. There were only two years between him and Imran, but he felt like his cousin was still a kid. He'd been like that himself not so long ago, but he'd changed. Things had happened to him, things that had made him grow up and take responsibility. Now, when he looked at Imran, he felt like they were from different generations. Different planets, even. It was amazing how someone else's interpretation of the world could lead you to question what you'd taken for granted all your life. Recently, Yousef had come to understand the way the world really worked and it made a nonsense of pretty much everything he'd been encouraged to believe in.

'Only thing I feel bad about is missing the match on Saturday, innit? It's gonna be a big deal, saying goodbye to Robbie. Is Raj going?'

Yousef nodded. 'Wild horses, man. You'd think it was me or Sanjar had died, not some football player.'

Imran reared back in his seat. 'Whoa, that's heresy, cuz. Robbie wasn't just "some football player".' He signed the inverted commas in the air with his fingers. 'He was *the* football player. Home-town boy turned hero. We loved Robbie, I tell you. Loved him. So you tell Raj, say goodbye to Robbie from me.'

Yousef rolled his eyes. Had the world gone mad? Hysterical grief over Robbie Bishop, and not a hair turned over the daily death tolls in Iraq and Palestine and Afghanistan. Something had gone badly wrong with their values. He couldn't pretend that he'd been the world's most perfect Muslim, but at least his thinking had never been as twisted as Imran's.

Imran fell silent, his fingers beating time on his denim-clad thighs, his Nikes tapping on the rubber floor mat. It kept him occupied the rest of the way to Manchester Airport. Yousef pulled up in the drop-off zone outside Terminal One, keeping the engine running while Imran grabbed his bag and got out. He stuck his head in the door. 'Be cool, Yousef. See you Monday.'

Yousef smiled. He wouldn't be seeing Imran on Monday. But there was no need to tell his cousin that.

Tony drifted up from a delicious sleep. Delicious because it came from genuine exhaustion, not a drug-induced escape. Who knew it could take so much energy to get out of bed, move three metres into a bathroom clutching a walking frame, pee and then get back to bed? When he'd slumped back on the pillows, he felt as if he'd climbed a small mountain. The physio had been happy with his progress; he'd been delirious. She'd promised him elbow crutches tomorrow. The excitement was almost too much for him.

He sat up, rubbing sleep from his eyes, and woke the laptop from its hibernation. Before sliding into sleep, he'd set up a final array of searches but he'd been out for the count before it finished. He hadn't been optimistic; he'd even begun to accept that he might not find what he was looking for. That didn't mean it wasn't there, just that it was too well hidden.

The screen cleared and to his surprise, a little box in the middle of the display read, '(1) match found'. The brackets meant that the match wasn't perfect but that it was over 90 per cent congruent with the terms of his search. Wide awake now, Tony summoned the search results.

It was a story from a free newspaper covering the west side of Sheffield. There wasn't much detail, but there was enough to give Tony pause for thought as well as material for further detailed searches.

Eagerly, he typed in a new set of parameters. This was going to be interesting. It looked as if he might just have something to show Carol after all.

Sam Evans left his jacket hanging on his chair and strolled out of the office as if he had nothing more pressing on his mind than a trip to the toilet. Once the door closed behind him, however, he picked up speed and headed for the lifts. He descended to the car park and got into his car. Out came the mobile and he dialled Bindie Blyth's number.

She answered on the second ring. When he identified himself, she groaned. 'Not more questions. I've already had your DCI on this morning.'

Sweat popped out on Sam's forehead. What if he'd called earlier, before Carol Jordan? How would he have explained himself to the woman who already had him marked down as too much of a maverick? Shit, he had to be careful with this stuff. 'I'm sorry you've been bothered twice. We each have our own lines of inquiry,' he said, hoping to Christ he wasn't about to cover the same ground as his boss.

'Well, that's a relief. I didn't fancy a second excursion into the wilder reaches of my sex life. So, how can I help you, Detective?'

'Back in February, you wrote an email to Robbie about some guy that was bothering you. Turning up to gigs. Minor stalker stuff. Do you remember?'

Bindie groaned. 'Do I remember? It would be hard to forget.'

'Can you tell me a bit more about what happened?'

'You can't think this has anything to do with Robbie's death? This was a pathetic little no-mark, not some criminal mastermind.'

'I wouldn't be doing my job properly if I didn't check out every possibility,' Sam said. 'So tell me all about this guy.'

'It started off with letters, cards, flowers, that sort of thing. And then he began to turn up when I was DJ'ing at clubs. Mostly, they wouldn't let him in because he looked too geeky or freaky or whatever. But sometimes he would get in and he'd hang around the stage or the booth, trying to talk to me, or have his picture taken with me. It was irritating, but it felt pretty harmless. Then Robbie and I had a bit of a bust-up in public one night. You know how it is. A few drinks, things get a little out of hand? We ended up having a screaming match outside a club. The paparazzi picked it up, it was all over the papers and the mags. I mean, we'd made up by the time the pictures hit the streets, but it's breaking up, not making up that gets the headlines.' He heard her light a cigarette and waited for her to continue. Waiting. A trick he'd learned from Paula.

'So this geezer takes it upon himself to defend my honour against this evil boyfriend who is not treating me as he should. He confronts Robbie as he's leaving the team hotel in Birmingham. Starts reading the riot act. Nothing violent, just loud and a bit embarrassing, according to Robbie. Though of course, Robbie was the last man alive to admit to being scared. Anyway, the police were called, the geezer got carted off to the cells. Turns out that was just the wake-up call he needed. According to the cop I spoke to, once the potential consequences of his behaviour were explained to him, he saw the light. Desperately sorry, realized he'd got things out of proportion. And of course he would leave me and Robbie alone in future. So they let him off with a caution. And in fairness, I haven't heard anything from him since. And that's all I can tell you.'

Somehow, it all sounded too pat to Sam. From what he knew about stalkers, they didn't just pack up and go home when somebody rattled their cage. If they were stupid, they kept on doing the same kind of thing only more so till they eventually got locked up for it. And by that stage, there was often blood and teeth on the carpet. If they were smart, they either found another object for their warped affections or they became more subtle. And the smart ones often ended up causing even more blood and teeth on the carpet. Ask Yoko Ono about that. 'You've really not heard from him since?'

'Nope. Not even a sympathy card about Robbie.'

'Have you had many of those?' Sam asked.

'Forty-seven delivered by hand yesterday at the BBC. I expect there'll be more in the post today.'

'We might want to have a look at those.'

Bindie made an exasperated noise. 'She was right, your boss. Nothing's private in a murder investigation. What do you want me to do? Bag them up and post them to you?'

'If you could bag them up, I'll have somebody collect them. At your convenience, obviously. If we could just backtrack ...'

'His name was Rhys Butler. He lived in Birmingham. That's all I can tell you. I gave all the letters and cards to the Brummie cops. Just in case he went off on one again.'

'Thank you. You read my mind.'

Bindie snorted. 'Hardly a Booker prize-winner, Detective.'

Sam hated witnesses who thought they were cleverer than the cops. 'The name of the officer who dealt with you would also be helpful,' he said, working at keeping the sarcasm out of his voice.

'Hang on a minute, I've got his details some-where ...' The sound of movement, a drawer being opened, another cigarette lit. At last, she came up with the information. 'DC Jonty Singh. God, it's so beautiful, what's happened to names in this country. Jonty Singh. What a fab name. I love that cricket, the most English thing in the world, has Ramprakash and Panesar alongside Trescothick and Strauss. I adore the way we went from empire to multi-culti in the space of fifty years. Doesn't that bring a smile to your face, Sam?'

He didn't much care, All that mattered was that Jonty Singh was the sort of name it wouldn't be hard to track down in a big force like the West Midlands Police. He also noticed she had gone from 'detective' to 'Sam' and wondered if she was flirting. It was hard to tell, given her on-air personality. And even if she was, it wasn't something he wanted to pursue. Didn't want to be her next bit of rough. 'Thanks for your time,' he said.

'I don't mind,' she said, suddenly serious again. 'It's all I can do for him now. I really cared about him, you know.'

'I know,' Sam said, desperate now to get off the phone and get cracking on his lead. 'We'll be in touch.' He ended the call abruptly. Now, if only he had a computer in his car like the uniformed patrol guys. He'd be well away, fingers flying, carrying him on the next step of his journey. Instead, he'd have to go back to his desk and hope that Stacey wasn't watching his every keystroke. He was on to something and he was damned if he was going to give anyone else a look in.

He was on tenterhooks waiting for her arrival, but still Tony didn't announce his discovery the moment Carol walked in. He wanted to savour the anticipation. Besides, he had to admit there was something

186

gratifying about her concern for his welfare. All the ebb and flow of pain and danger that had infiltrated their relationship had left little room for something as simple as sitting around being kind to each other. He knew she'd experienced that – still experienced it, for all he knew – with her family, but it had never been something he'd known. Kindness had always been viewed as weakness in his family. So even though he didn't entirely know what to do with it, he wasn't about to sacrifice a moment of their closeness to the demands of work. They'd get to that soon enough.

It was, he recognized, a reordering of his priorities. The part of himself that viewed his own reactions as a perpetual experiment was intrigued to see whether it would last and what it would mean. But to his surprise, there was another part that was happy just to go with the flow.

So Carol asked about his day and he told her. They had a conversation that he thought must be what ordinary friends and even lovers might weave together routinely. But of course, it couldn't last. There had to come a point where equilibrium demanded that he ask about her day. And she told him.

At the end of the recital, she leaned an elbow on the arm of the chair and ran her fingers through her thick hair. 'This is unlike any other case I've ever worked on. When murder happens, two or more people come face to face. An act takes place and somebody dies. You can connect the dots. You've got forensics, witnesses, evidence. A precise point in time. But there's nothing like that here. There's a huge gap between the act that killed Robbie Bishop and the death itself. And we don't know when or where or with whom that fatal act took place.' She scuffed the carpet with the toe of her shoe. 'The more we find out, the more obscure it gets. Kevin was right, this killer is Caspar the fucking friendly ghost.'

Tony waited for a second, to make sure she'd got her frustration out. 'It's not quite as bad as you make out. We do know some things about him. I mean, apart from the Harriestown High connection and that he knows Temple Fields as well as a hooker.'

Carol gave him a sceptical look. 'Like what?'

'We know he's a planner. He's thought this through and decided what level of risk he can safely assume, so we know he's not reckless. He doesn't feel the need to see his victim's pain. He's happy for it to happen offstage. So whoever he was at school, he wasn't the class bully. Do we know if Robbie was a bully at school?'

Carol shook her head. 'Apparently not. He was a charmer, by all accounts. Though we've still got to plough through everybody on the Best Days website who knew him.'

'Right. So this is not about revenge for adolescent humiliation. Unless the revenge element is about success . . .' Tony's voice tailed off and he frowned. 'I need to think about that some more. But we do know he must know something about chemistry or pharmacology. I mean, he's not just making ricin, he's making ricin suppositories. I wouldn't know where to start.'

Carol leaned into the carrier bag she'd brought with her and produced a screw-top bottle of Australian shiraz. 'I'd start with the internet. That's where we learn everything new these days, isn't it? Are you allowed some of this?'

'Probably not, but don't let that stop you. There's a couple of plastic tumblers in the bathroom.'

When Carol returned with two substantial doses of red wine, he said, 'And speaking of the internet ...'

'Mmm?' Carol savoured her drink. She'd sneaked a couple of glasses after the post mortem, but apart from that, this was her first of the day, a small achievement in itself.

'I don't think this is the first time he's done this. There's too much assurance here for a beginner.'

He could see the scepticism on her face. 'You see serial killers everywhere, Tony. What possible evidence do you have for saying that? Apart from not liking the fact that this killer is either very good or very lucky.'

'I don't believe in lucky. Lucky is what we call it when our intuition leads us in the right direction. And intuition is a product of observation and experience. Did you know there's been some recent research that suggests we make better decisions when we trust our gut reactions than when we weigh up the pros and cons of a situation?'

Carol grinned. 'I see Captain Tangent is reasserting himself. You didn't answer the question, Tony. What evidence do you have for saying he's done this before?'

'Like I said, Carol: the internet. Source of all bollocks and a bit of wisdom too. Since we spoke last night, I've been on the prowl. And I found something very interesting.' He reached for his laptop, tapped the mouse pad and turned the machine to face Carol. As she skimmed the short local paper story on screen, he said, 'Danny Wade. Twenty-seven years old. He died two weeks ago at his luxury home on the outskirts of Sheffield. He was poisoned by deadly nightshade. Belladonna, the beautiful lady. Supposedly in a fruit pie prepared by his Polish housekeeper. The fruit pie works, you see, because belladonna berries are notoriously sweet. And there's a belladonna bush by the patio. You need to find out if that was container-grown, by the way. It's possible the killer brought it with him. The housekeeper denies making any fruit pie even though the remains of a pie containing deadly nightshade berries was found in the fridge. And the night he died was her night off. She was staying with her boyfriend in Rotherham, like she did every Wednesday and Saturday. They opened the inquest then adjourned it pending further inquiries.'

'I don't understand why you think this –' pointing at the screen '– is anything to do with Robbie Bishop,' Carol said. 'It seems to be straightforward. The housekeeper made a mistake with the berries, and now she's lying about it. Tragic accident. That's what the story says.'

'But what if she's not lying? If she's telling the truth, it's the second instance of a man in his twenties being the victim of a very bizarre poisoning.' Tony tried to turn so he could face Carol more directly, but it wasn't possible. 'Move that chair so I can see you properly,' he said impatiently. 'Please.'

Slightly surprised, Carol did as he asked. 'OK, now you can see me. This is just supposition, Tony.'

'It's always supposition till the evidence is nailed down. Supposition is what I do. We call it profiling.

People other than me speak of it as if it's a science, but it's supposition based on experience and probability and instinct. More art than science a lot of the time, if we're honest. Even the algorithms that the geographic profilers use, they're based around probabilities, not certainties.'

'So show me something that outweighs the probability of an immigrant housekeeper lying about accidentally killing her boss,' Carol said. He could see she was humouring him, that she thought his sharp edge blunted by pain and drugs and strange sleep patterns.

'Danny Wade wasn't local to where he was killed. He moved to Dore on the western edge of Sheffield a couple of years ago because he was sick and tired of being pestered where he was living. In Bradfield. The reason he couldn't get any peace and quiet there was that three years ago, he won the lottery. Big time. He got just over five million. He'd worked for Virgin Trains as a conductor. He was unmarried. The two things he cared about were model railways and his dogs, a pair of Lakeland terriers. He was a bit of a loner. Until he won the money. Then suddenly they all came out of the woodwork. Old school friends after a handout. Former workmates acting like he owed them. Distant relatives suddenly remembering that blood's supposed to be thicker than water. And it all got a bit too much for Danny.'

'Still, at least he had the money,' Carol said. 'It can buy you a lot of peace and quiet, five million.'

'So Danny found out. He upped sticks and bought himself a lovely house on the edge of the moors. High walls, electric gates. Lots of space for model railway layouts. Didn't tell anyone where he'd gone, not even his mum and dad. Nobody to bother him except for Jana Jankowicz who is by all accounts a very nice young woman with a fiancé who is working as an electrician on a building site in Rotherham.'

Carol shook her head in disbelief. 'Where did you dig all this up? This is tons more background than there is in the local paper.'

Tony looked pleased with himself. 'I spoke to the reporter. Stories like this, they've always got more in their notebook than they get on the page. She gave me Jana's mobile number. So I called her. And, according to the lovely Jana, Danny was happy as a pig with his dogs and his railways and his three meals a day. But here's the thing. I already found out Danny was a pupil at Harriestown High. Two years ahead of Robbie Bishop. And although Jana's English wasn't up to deep and meaningful conversations, she did understand enough to tell me that Danny had come back from the local pub a few nights before his death, saying he'd met somebody he was at school with.' He grinned, a dog with two tails. 'What do you think of that?'

Carol shook her head. 'I think you're stir crazy.'

He threw his arms out in a gesture of frustration. 'There are connections, Carol. Murder at arm's length by weird poisons. Both victims went to the same school. Both rich men. And both met up with an old school friend before they died.'

Carol filled up her glass and took a swig of her wine. Her body language was as combative as her words. 'Come on, Tony. Danny's death wasn't murder. As far as I can see, nobody except you thinks it was anything other than a tragic accident. I don't know much about poisons, but I do know that if you slip somebody deadly

192

nightshade in the pub, they're going to be dead that night, not a few days later. And Danny wasn't in the same year as Robbie. Think back to your schooldays. You hang with the kids in your own year. Older kids don't want to have anything to do with you, and only losers hang out with kids younger than them. So anybody who was a school friend of Robbie's probably wasn't going to be a friend of Danny's. I mean, it doesn't sound like they had much in common.' Carol let her hands fall open as if she were weighing two items against each other. 'Let's see. Ace footballer. Model railway geek. Hmm. Let me think.' She pointed at the newspaper story on the laptop screen. 'Look at Danny. He's not good looking. He's not athletic. What could he have in common with Robbie Bishop?'

Tony looked crestfallen. 'They both became very rich from humble beginnings,' he tried.

'And much good it did them. Better to be lucky than rich when rich ends up dead before you're out of your twenties.' Carol slugged back the rest of her wine. 'Nice thought, Tony. Very interesting. But I think you're snatching at ghosts. And I need to go home and try to get a decent night's sleep.' She stood up and pulled her coat on, then leaned across to give him an awkward hug and a kiss on the cheek. 'I'll try to come in tomorrow. See what else you can come up with to entertain me, OK?'

'I'll do my best,' he said. He'd learned a long time ago that disappointment was often the spur to his best work.

Jonty Singh looked like a big rumpled bear propped up in the corner of the balti restaurant in the centre of Dudley, incongruous against the traditionally kitsch decor. When Sam had tracked him down, DC Singh had suggested they meet for a meal in his local. Since he was doing Sam the favour, there really was no argument. 'I'll be the big bugger up the back in a brown pinstripe suit and no turban,' he'd said. Sam didn't anticipate any problem recognizing him and he was right. As soon as he walked into the Shishya Balti, he spotted Singh, talking animatedly to a waiter. He hadn't lied about his size; he was crammed into the corner chair at a table for four and even sitting, he towered over the table. He had a thick mop of shiny black hair, big brown eyes, a fleshy nose and a prominent chin. It wasn't a face you'd forget in a hurry.

Sam weaved through the crowded restaurant. Half a dozen steps in, the big man broke off his conversation and homed in on the stranger in town. The waiter slipped away and Sam approached. As he drew near, Singh pushed himself to his feet. A couple of inches over six feet, he was an imposing sight. 'Sam Evans?' he said, his voice a much lighter tenor than his frame implied. He reached out and shook Sam's hand in a two-handed grip. 'I'm Jonty Singh, pleased to meet you. How're you doing?' Even in those few words, the unmistakable Black Country accent grated on Sam's ear.

'Good, thanks.'

'Park yourself.' Singh gestured at the chair opposite him and waved to the waiter. 'Two large Cobras, soon as you like.' His grin was open and friendly. 'Now, do you trust me to order for both of us or what?'

Sam was in no doubt what the correct answer was. 'Go ahead,' he said, resigning himself to some gargantuan selection of over-sauced meat, unidentifiable vegetables and clumpy rice. He didn't have to drive all the way to Dudley for that, but if that was what it took to find out what he needed to know about Rhys Butler, he'd swallow manfully and stop on the motorway for antacids.

'I love this place,' Singh confided. 'Two of my uncles own it, but that's just a bonus. I'd eat here every bloody night if I could.'

Sam tried to keep his eyes away from Singh's sizeable belly and held back the obvious retort. 'You can't beat a good curry,' he lied. Singh summoned the waiter and rattled off a stream of what Sam presumed to be Punjabi.

Singh turned his attention back to Sam. 'So, you're interested in Rhys Butler. Well, a nod's as good as a wink round here, Sammy. It doesn't take Brainiac to figure out that you're on the Robbie Bishop case. Funny, I was talking about giving you lads a bell about our Rhys, but my sarge thought it was far too long a shot. And then you turn up on my voicemail, looking for a briefing.' He gave a rolling laugh that turned heads three tables away. 'Nice to be right.'

'To be honest, Jonty, we've got fuck all to go at. This is me clutching at straws,' Sam said. The waiter scurried up with a stack of spiced poppadoms and a plate of mixed pickles. Jonty fell on them like an attack dog on a kitten. Sam waited for his initial onslaught to pass, then delicately broke a piece off one. At least they were crisp and fresh, he thought as the smoky bite of black pepper tickled his soft palate.

'So when the lovely Bindie told you about Rhys Butler, you thought you'd have a sniff around? Quite right, Sammy, just what I'd have done in your shoes.'

Sam didn't bother to correct the misapprehension as to how Butler's name had entered the investigation. 'So what can you tell me about Rhys Butler?'

A foot-high mound of bhajis and pakoras arrived at the table and Singh set about it. In between mouthfuls, and sometimes alarmingly during them, he told the story of Rhys Butler. 'Normally, it would be a uniform matter, a brawl outside a nightclub. But we got dragged in because of who was involved.' He grinned. 'Course, there are them as think we should have just let young Rhys kick the shit out of Robbie, on account of Robbie set up the winning goal for the Vics against Villa in the cup quarter-final last year. But despite what you might have heard about West Midlands, we don't stand for that kind of nonsense no more round here.'

Sam bit into a perfect fish pakora – crisp on the outside, meltingly moist inside – and began to revise his initial impression of the Shishya as just another identikit curry house. 'Great food,' he said, correctly estimating the way to Singh's heart.

The big man lit up. 'Fan-bloody-tastic, innit? Anyway, by the time we arrive, it's all over. According to the witnesses, Robbie came out of the club with a couple of mates, and Rhys Butler threw himself at him, fists and feet flying. Lucky for Robbie, our Mr Butler's not much cop when it comes to fighting. He lands a couple of kicks and punches, but Robbie's mates soon drag him off and hang on to him till my colleagues in uniform get there. Once we arrive, we decide to take everybody down the nick and sort it out there, away from prying eyes and cameras.'

Nothing remained of the appetizers but a scatter of crumbs. Before Sam could draw breath, the plate was whisked away and replaced by half a dozen bowls of various main dishes. A platter of mushroom biryani appeared, flanked by stacks of assorted Indian breads. The varied aromas tickled Sam's nose, kindling a hunger he hadn't anticipated. Singh piled his plate high, gesturing to Sam to do the same. He didn't need a second invitation.

'At first, Robbie's all for letting it go. He's not really hurt, people get carried away, no harm done, blah, blah, blah. Then I mention Butler's name and suddenly it's all, "Throw the book at the bastard, bang him up, danger to society." I don't get it, frankly. I leave him ranting at my oppo, and I head back down to the interview room to see if Butler wants to talk about it. And then it all comes out. How Bindie Blyth is the love of his life, only Robbie's come between them, and he's not treating her like he should. So Butler decided to teach him a lesson.'

Singh pointed with his fork at a dark brown stew. 'You've got to get yourself outside that. Lamb and spinach and aubergine and nobody but my auntie knows what spices. I tell you, you'd sell your granny for a bowl of that.' He tore off a chunk of paratha and scooped up the lamb stew, dextrously getting the loaded bread into his mouth without spilling a drop.

'So I lay it out for him. How, if he carries on like this, he's going to end up behind bars. And how that will destroy a nice middle-class lad like him. How he'll lose his home, his job . . . And that's when he really loses it. Tears and snotters, the lot. Turns out he's already lost his job. That's what's tipped him over the edge. So we have a little chat and by the end of it, he's seen the error of his ways.' He paused to shovel more food down.

'Great grub,' said Sam. 'I really appreciate this after the week I've had. So what happened then?'

'Well, I go back to have another word with Robbie. I point out he's not going to be doing any favours to his girlfriend or himself if he drags this poor pathetic bastard through the courts. I tell him how Butler is promising never to contact Bindie again, to leave her alone from this day forward, and how I think the best thing for everybody is to give Butler a caution and let the whole thing drop. Robbie's not thrilled with that, but he does see the sense of keeping it all out of the papers. Eventually, I promise I'll keep a personal eye on Butler, and Robbie caves in. And we agree that if Bindie hears from Butler again, I'll have him for harassment.' He looked expectantly at Sam.

'And?' Sam dutifully said.

'I kept my word. Every couple of weeks for the next few months, I dropped in unannounced on Butler. First time, the place was papered with photos of Bindie and articles about her. I told him he should get rid of the stuff. That if he was planning on getting over her and getting a life, he needed to not be seeing her face every minute of the day. Next time I went, the place was clean. You'd not have known he'd ever heard of her. And so it went on. I never heard a dickie bird from her or from Robbie, so I guess he kept his word. Then, about six weeks ago, he finally managed to get another job. Moved away to Newcastle and that's all she wrote.' He turned his attention away from the food briefly and hunted through his pockets. He drew a folded piece of paper from his pocket and handed it to Sam. 'Forwarding address in Geordieland.'

Sam pocketed it without looking. 'This new job . . . What is it that Butler actually does for a living?'

Jonty Singh gave a slow, wicked grin, revealing a slick of spinach filling the gap between his front teeth. 'I thought you'd never ask,' he said. 'He works as a lab assistant. In the pharmacology industry.'

Carol was right. He was snatching at ghosts. But not the ones she imagined. Tony rolled his head from side to side on the pillow. He needed to talk, but there was no possible listener for him. He couldn't involve Carol in this because there were things about himself he did not want her to know. The only psychiatrist he trusted enough to unburden himself to was on a sabbatical in Peru. And he couldn't imagine explaining these ills to one of Mrs Chakrabarti's acolytes.

He sighed and pressed the nurse call button. There was someone he could trust to keep his secrets. The only question was whether they would let Tony pay him a visit.

It took twenty minutes, a call to Grisha Shatalov, a wheelchair and a porter, but finally Tony found himself alone with the chilled corpse of Robbie Bishop. Tony's chair was backed against the rack of mortuary drawers, Robbie pulled out next to him. 'I wouldn't have recognized you,' Tony said as the door closed behind the porter. 'I promise I'm going to do all I can to help Carol find the person who did this to you. In return, you can listen to me for a while.

'There are some things you can never say to another living soul. Not when you do what I do. Nothing could prepare you for the horror and disgust you'd see on their faces. And that would just be the start of it. They wouldn't be able to let it go. They'd have to do something about it. Something about me.

'And I really don't want them to do something about me. Not because I'm happy, pain-free and well adjusted. Because obviously I'm none of those things. How could I be, doing what I do?

'But what I am is well-balanced. What is it that W.B. Yeats says? "In balance with this life, this death." That's me. In perfect equilibrium on the tipping point between life and death, sanity and madness, pleasure and pain.

'You mess with that at your peril.

'So, this isn't about me wanting to change. Because I don't see any need for change. I can live with myself very well, thank you. But when you do what I do, it's impossible to deny it has an impact. I'm subject to the opinions of others, after all. People who are not like me – and that accounts for about ninety-nine per cent of the population, I'd say – constantly make judgements about me that are based more on their needs than on my truth. That's why I don't want anyone to hear what I have to say about my mother. Especially Carol.

'I passed the local primary on my way to buy milk the other morning and there they were, the kids and the parents, every expression from delight to despair on both sets of faces. It made me wonder about my own childhood memories. There are lots of fragments – an image of a living room whose owner I can't now put a name to, the taste of dandelion and burdock tied eternally to the sound of rain on the scullery roof, the smell of my grandmother's dog, the feel of damp grass on my knees, the shocking intensity of wild strawberries on the tongue. Fragments, but not many fully formed incidents.' He ran a hand over his face and sighed.

'I've sat in group therapy sessions and listened to other people talking at length and in remarkable detail about things that happened to them as children. I can't be sure whether they were remembering for real, making it up, or constructing a story that fit the few key elements they really could dredge up from the sludge of memory. All I know is that it doesn't match the way my memory works. Not that I'd want their memories. They veer from the banal to the truly horrendous. None of them talks about childhood the way writers and poets and film-makers do. These are not histories you would feel any nostalgia for.

'That's the one thing I do have in common with those non-fragmentary narrators. I have no nostalgia for my childhood. I am not the person at the dinner party who waxes lyrical about the endless summers of childhood, the golden light on skinned knees and the delicious pleasures of gang huts and tree houses. On the rare occasions when I get invited, I am the one who sits mute on the subject of their youth. Trust me, nobody wants to hear the few joined-up bits I can remember.

'An example. I'm playing on the rug in front of the fire at my gran's house. My gran collects ship ha'pennies for reasons too obscure to have stuck in my mind. There's a whole biscuit tin full of them, almost too heavy for me to lift. I'm allowed to play with the ha'pennies, and I like to build castle walls with them. The best part is pretending to be the enemy after they're finished; they collapse in a very satisfying way. So I'm on the rug with the ha'pennies, minding my own business. Gran is watching the telly but it's a grown-up programme so I'm not interested.

'The door opens and my mum comes in, damp with rain from the walk from the bus stop. She smells of smoke and fog and stale perfume. She takes her coat off like she's fighting it. She flumps down in the armchair, scrabbling in her bag for her cigarettes and sighing. Gran's mouth tightens and she gets up to make some tea. While she's gone, Mum ignores me, tilting her head back to blow smoke at the ceiling. Picturing her face now, I see it as petulant and put-upon. I didn't have the words as a child, but I knew even then to keep my distance.

'Gran brought the tea through and handed a mug to Mum. She took a sip, pulled a face because it was too hot, then put it down on the broad arm of the chair. Her sleeve must have caught it as she moved her hand away, for it tipped into her lap. She jumped up, scalded, doing a funny little dance, kicking the ha'pennies all over the floor.

'And I laughed.

'I wasn't laughing at her. God knows, I understood only too well by then that pain was never comical. My laughter was nervous, a release of anxiety and surprise. But, beside herself with hurt and shock, my mum understood nothing of that. She yanked me to

202

my feet by the hair and slapped me so hard my hearing stopped functioning. I could see her mouth moving, but I couldn't hear a thing. My scalp was a shivering sheath of agony and my face stung like I'd been swiped with a bundle of nettles.

'Next thing was, Gran pushed Mum back into the chair. Mum let go my hair as she dropped down, then Gran grabbed me by the shoulder, marched me into the hall and threw me into the cupboard so hard I bounced off the back wall. It was morning before the door opened again.

'I know this wasn't an isolated incident. I know that because I have so many different fragments of sojourns in the cupboard. What I don't have, by and large, are whole incidents. Various professionals have offered to help me fill in the blanks, as if that would somehow be desirable. As if it would be a treat for me to have access to more lovely memories like that one.

'They're more crazy than I am.' He sighed. 'And now she's back. She's been out of my life for so long I could kid myself that I was over her. Like a bad love affair. But I'm not.' He rolled himself forward and pushed the drawer close. 'Thanks for listening. I owe you one.'

Blinking the tears from his eyes, Tony manoeuvred the wheelchair over to the phone. He didn't quite understand why, but something inside him had shifted, leaving him indefinably easier. He dialled the porters' extension. 'Hi,' he said. 'I'm done.'

The Mother of Satan. That's what they called the end product Yousef was aiming for. Triacetone triperoxide.

TATP. Supposedly given its nickname because of its instability. And that's why he was being more careful than he'd ever been in his life. Careful made it possible to do extraordinary things. The London tube bombers had carted it about in backpacks. On and off trains. Walking from train to tube. So if he got it right, it would be safe. Until he wanted it not to be, of course.

He read the instructions one more time. He'd already committed them to memory, but he'd also printed them out in a large font. Now, he stuck the sheets up on the wall above his makeshift lab bench. He put on his protective gear then took his chemicals from the fridge one by one, placing the three containers on the bench. Eighteen per cent hydrogen peroxide bought from a chemical supplier for wood bleaching. Pure acetone from the specialist paint company. Sulphuric acid for batteries from the motor bike supply shop. He set a beaker, a measuring tube, a thermometer, a stirring rod and an eyedropper, all made of glass, and a sealable Kilner jar alongside them. It felt very weird. He'd never done anything so grown-up in his life, yet it felt like being back at school in the chemistry lab. The mad scientist in short trousers.

He walked away from the bench and took off his gloves and ear protectors. He needed something to help calm his nerves. He took his iPod from his backpack, plugged the little buds into his ears and set random shuffle on his personal chilling playlist. Some slow beats from Talvin Singh filled his head. Imran would laugh at his choice of music, but he didn't care. Yousef replaced his ear protectors and gloves and set to work.

First, he filled the sink basin with ice, pouring in a little cold water to make it more effective as a chiller.

He put the empty beaker in the ice bath and took a deep breath. This was the point of no return. From here on, he was a bomber. However beautiful his reasons, in the eyes of the world he was crossing a line that nothing could redeem. Lucky, then, that he didn't give a shit what the world thought of him. Where it mattered, he would be forever regarded as a hero, a man who did what had to be done, and in a way that also made a statement.

He measured out the hydrogen peroxide, then poured it into the beaker. Swallowed hard, then did the same with the acetone. Gently placed the thermometer in the beaker and waited for the temperature to drop to the correct level. Stood humming softly along to Nitin Sawhney's *Migration*. Anything rather than think about what was going to happen beyond this process.

Now the tricky part. He sucked up a precise amount of sulphuric acid with the eyedropper. Drop by slow drop, he added it to the mix, keeping a careful eye on the temperature. Above ten degrees, it would explode. This was the point where most amateur bomb makers got too enthusiastic, added too much too fast and ended up in bits against the nearest surfaces. Yousef was absolutely clear that wasn't going to happen to him. His fingers were trembling, but he was careful to move the eyedropper away from the beaker every time he added a drop.

Once the recipe was complete, he began stirring with the glass rod. Fifteen minutes, the recipe said. He timed himself. Then, infinitely slowly, he eased the beaker out of its bath and put it in the fridge, making sure that the temperature setting was at its lowest.

Tomorrow evening, he would return and carry out the next stage. But for now, he'd done all he could.

Yousef closed the fridge and felt his shoulders drop with relief, He'd trusted the recipe; he was no fool and he'd checked it against others he'd managed to track down on the internet. But he knew that things could and did go wrong in the preparation of explosives. What a pointless waste that would have been. He stripped off his protective gear and tossed it on the lumpy bed.

Time to go home and be the dutiful son and brother. Two more nights, then no more of that. He loved his family. He knew that would be cast into doubt by what he was going to do, but it was incontrovertible for Yousef himself. He loved them and he hated that he was going to lose them. But some things were stronger than family bonds. Recently, he'd found out just how strong.

Friday

The dirty grey city sky was starting to pale on the far side of town when Carol pulled up in the shadow of the Grayson Street stand. Before she had even turned off her engine, a uniformed officer, rendered squat by the weight of equipment on her belt, was heading in her direction. Carol got out, fully expecting what she heard. 'I'm sorry, you can't park here,' the officer said, weary tolerance in her voice.

Carol produced her warrant card from the pocket of her leather jacket and said, 'I'm not going to be long.'

The young female officer was blotchy with embarrassment. 'Sorry, ma'am, I didn't recognize you . . .'

'No reason why you should,' Carol said. 'I'm out of uniform.' She gestured to her jeans and construction boots. 'I didn't want to look like a cop.'

The uniform gave an uncertain smile. 'Then maybe you shouldn't be parked there?' she said, clearly knowing she was chancing her arm.

Carol laughed. 'Good point. And if my time wasn't so tight, I'd move it.' She walked on towards the railings where the flowers, cards and soft toys swamped the pavement, so deep in places there was barely enough room for one person to pass without stepping into the road.

There was no doubt that it provoked a complicated emotional response. Her work had conditioned Carol against knee-jerk sentiment. You couldn't indulge in that and do her sort of job. Cops, firefighters, ambulance crews – they all had to learn early on not to be sucked into the genuine, personal grief of those they came into contact with. They had a level of inoculation against the seas of public emotion that greeted events like the death of Diana and the Soham murders. Theoretically she knew that each life snuffed out prematurely was equally valuable. But when it came to the murder of someone like Robbie Bishop – someone young, someone talented, someone who gave pleasure to millions – it was hard not to feel more anger, more sorrow, more determination to put things as right as she could.

She'd seen glimpses of sections of it behind TV reporters, but Carol had had no idea of the scale of the display outside the football ground. It moved her, but not because of its sentimental appropriation of grief. It moved her because of its pathos. The soft toys and cards were spattered with specks of dirty water sprayed by the tyres of passing cars, sodden with the overnight rain. Strewn with wilted flowers, the pavement had started to resemble a fly-tipping site.

This early in the morning, she was the only worshipper at the shrine. A few cars dawdled by, their drivers paying little attention to the road. Slowly, she walked the length of the railings. At the far end she stopped and pulled out her phone. She was about to press the 'call' button when she thought better of it. Given he was in an NHS hospital, Tony was probably already awake. But if he was asleep, she didn't want to wake him. That was how she rationalized it, shoving her phone back in her pocket impatiently.

The truth was, she didn't want to have to get into it with him again about the slender connections between Robbie Bishop and Danny Wade. Being stuck in hospital was boring him so much that he was inventing phantoms to stimulate his brain. He wanted something to occupy him, and so he'd allowed himself to be carried away with a level of coincidence he'd have laughed at in other circumstances. Instead of dismissing it, he was seeing serial killers where none existed. It was, she supposed, only to be expected. It was what he did best and probably what he missed most. Carol wondered how long it would be before he could get back to work, even if it was only part time. At least the insane of Bradfield Moor might keep his own demons at bay.

She could live in hope. And in the meantime, she could trust her own instincts. Instincts, she reminded herself, that had been honed by the experience of working as closely with Tony as she had. She didn't always have to run her ideas past him for validation. She pulled the phone out again and dialled. 'Kevin,' she said. 'Sorry to bother you at home. On your way in, I want you swing by uniform and organize some bodies to come down to Victoria Park and take photos of the stuff here. I want every card and letter and drawing photographed and anything that seems at all dodgy collected and brought back for our team to take a look at. See you later.' She closed her phone and walked back to the car. Time to go home and change into the plain-clothes uniform. Time to prove to herself that she could still work the hard ones without Tony when she had to.

Stacey Chen was invariably first into the office. She liked to commune with her machines in peace and quiet. When she walked into the office that Friday to find Sam Evans already there, the kettle boiled and an Earl Grey teabag ready in her mug, she was instantly on her guard. It was true that it didn't happen often on this team, but everywhere else she had been assigned, colleagues were always lining up to ask favours. Everybody needed what the electronics could do for them, but none of them could be bothered to figure out how to make the computers really work for them. They just used her as a short cut. And it pissed her off more than she ever showed.

She accepted the cup of tea with chilly gratitude, then set up in hiding behind her twin monitors, pausing only to hang the jacket of her severe Prada suit on a hanger. Sam seemed to be working quite happily in front of his own machine, so Stacey let her guard drop and instead focused on her deep analysis of the inner secrets of Robbie Bishop's hard drive. There were some photographs he'd recently deleted, and she was determined to make sense of the fragments remaining. Probably nothing, but Stacey never liked admitting defeat.

So absorbed was she that she didn't even notice Sam get up and come over to her workstation until he was right next to her, leaning over her, smelling of citrus and spice and maleness. Stacey felt her muscles tensing, as if she was steeling herself against a blow. *Don't be stupid,* she told herself. *It's Sam, for God's sake. It's not like he's going to ask you out or anything.* Much as she would have liked that, if she could have got past the idea that he was after something in virtuality rather than reality. 'What is it?' she said, nothing welcoming in her tone.

'I just wondered if you wanted a hand, sifting through all Robbie's emails and stuff.'

Stacey's eyebrows shot up. She couldn't remember Sam ever offering to do any sort of electronic scut work. 'I know what I'm doing, thanks,' she said, stiff as a clerical collar.

Sam held his hands up in what she took to be a placatory gesture. 'I know that,' he said. 'All I meant was I could help with actually reading stuff. I totally defer to you when it comes to anything complicated. But I thought maybe you could use some help with the bits that any old plod could access.'

'I'm fine, thanks. Everything's under control. It's not like Robbie Bishop was a master of his machine,' Stacey said, not hiding her contempt for those less computer-literate. Maybe if telling him directly she didn't need or want his help didn't work, she'd have more luck with the indirect insults.

Sam shrugged. 'Please yourself. It's just that I can't get any further with what I'm working on till somebody gets back to me with more info. And let's face it . . .' He did have a good smile, she thought. Very beguiling, if you were the sort who was willing to be beguiled.

'Face what?' Stacey had to ask.

'Well, you're wasted on that sort of shit, frankly.

211

Like I said, any old plod could do it. But the other stuff, the stuff that idiots like me are clueless about – that's what we need you for. The bread and butter? You should be shovelling it towards the likes of me.'

'The ones who like the credit without the work, you mean?' Stacey smiled to soften her words.

Sam looked offended. She couldn't believe his cheek. Everyone knew he was a glory hound. He clutched his chest, miming heart-broken. 'I can't believe you said that.'

'Sam, what's the use pretending? I wasn't born yesterday. I remember the Creeper investigation, when you tried to make an end run round the boss. You'd have to be totally blinded by ambition to try something as mental as that.'

He looked sheepish. 'That was then. Trust me, Stace, I learned my lesson from that little débâcle. Come on, let me help. I'm bored.'

'You'd be a lot more bored if I handed off the collected wittering of Robbie Bishop. I know that much already.'

The door opened and they both looked up as Chris Devine walked in, looking ready for a country walk in her waxed jacket, cords and green wellies. She saw their expressions and pulled a face. 'I know, I know. I slept in, the dog needed a run, Sinead's in Edinburgh on business, what can you do?' She kicked off her wellies and slipped into a pair of shoes she produced from a Tesco bag. Under the jacket she wore a perfectly respectable cashmere sweater.

'Quite the transformation,' Sam said.

'Yeah, I clean up nice for an old slapper,' Chris said. 'What are you two up to?' She headed for the kettle and the cafetière she had added to their brewing equipment.

'I'm offering to help Stacey but she won't let me,' Sam said. Stacey pursed her lips. He made it sound like she was the problem here.

'I'm not surprised,' Chris said. 'You and computers? From what I've seen ...'

'He's a lot more competent than he lets on,' Stacey said, surprising herself with her candour. The look Sam turned on her held no warmth, only cold speculation. She saw Chris weighing up the situation. From what she had seen of Chris, the only thing on her mind would be how best to use this tension between her and Sam in a creative way. One that worked for the benefit of the unit. Stacey dreaded what was coming.

'What is it you want to do, Sam?' Chris said, eyeing them both.

'I thought it would free Stacey up for the complicated stuff if I read through the emails,' Sam said, eyes wide.

Chris looked at Stacey. 'And this is a problem ... how?'

Because if he finds anything, he'll make sure I look bad and he gets the credit. Because I don't trust him. Because I think I might like him too much and I don't want him in my space. 'Security, Sarge. We don't want this stuff flying round the system. In a case like this, if background info gets into the wrong hands, before we know it, it's all over the tabloids.'

'I see your point, but Sam's one of us, Stacey. He understands the importance of confidentiality. I don't understand what the issue is. If Sam's got nothing else to work on, he might as well do your shit work.'

'No problem, Sarge.' Stacey looked back at her monitors, not wanting to show Chris how pissed off she was. 'I'll print out all the relevant files,' she said in a last-ditch attempt to prevent him from having direct access.

'No need for that,' Sam said. 'Just burn me a CD, or send them to my mailbox. I'm happy reading on screen.'

Stacey knew when she was beaten. Honestly, what was the point in having lesbians on the team when they sided with the men? 'Fine,' she muttered.

By the time Carol arrived an hour later, Stacey had much more to worry about than who was reading Robbie Bishop's emails.

Carol stared at the screen with a look of incredulity. The temporary mailbox Stacey had set up for responses from the Best Days of Our Lives subscribers already contained over two hundred responses. She gave Stacey a bemused look. 'I guess that proves your point about getting the online community on our side,' she said dryly. 'What exactly did you ask them for?'

Stacey looked bored. 'The obvious stuff. When they were at school, whether they knew Robbie, anything they can tell us first hand about Robbie at school or since. Recent photos of themselves and anyone they were at school with. What they were doing on Thursday night. Who can corroborate that. And whether they have any bright ideas about who might want Robbie dead or why.' She cracked a smile. 'I think you might get quite a few people suggesting those fat cats who own Chelsea and Man United.'

214

Carol couldn't fault Stacey's logic. 'OK. Chris and Paula, I want you to split them between you. Weed out any possibles. Print out photos. And tonight, it's back to Amatis with the photos. Let's see if any of our revellers or bar staff pick out any faces.'

Chris leaned over to study the screen. 'That's a big ask. There's four more come in just while we've been talking. We might need some more bodies.'

'Point taken. See how you get on this morning. If it's taking too long, we'll hijack some help.' Carol looked around the room. 'Sam, what are you working on?' she asked.

'Robbie's emails,' he said without looking up.

'OK. If Chris and Paula need a hand, you can put that on the back burner and weigh in with them.' Carol checked through her mental list of things to do. Kevin was busy making sure the shrine down at the Victoria Park stadium was properly recorded and assessed; he'd be coming back at some point with more potential evidence to be collated. There was a lot of activity going on. But the question was, did it have a point? Were they moving in the right direction? And how would they know when they were?

At times like this, Carol missed being able to rely on Tony's insights, however off the wall they sometimes seemed. She wasn't afraid to think outside the box herself, but it was always more comfortable to go out on a limb when there was someone shouting encouragement from the safety net below.

At least she could rely on this team to dig beneath the surface. If there was anything to be found, they'd find it. The hard bit was figuring out what it meant and where it led. But for now, all she could do was wait.

Learning from the mistakes of others was always preferable to the pain of making your own, Yousef thought. Like the London bombers. They'd met up together and travelled down to London by train mob-handed. When the security services started examining CCTV footage, they stuck out. They were easy to spot, easy to trace, and from there, easy to blame. Easy to backtrack to their homes, easy to unravel their networks of support and friendship.

All of that would have been slowed right down if they'd each made their own ways to the target. Diverting the security forces altogether was the best option in the aftermath, but failing that, slowing them down was far better than making it easy for them. What made most sense was to have as little contact with each other in the time leading up to the bombing itself. Given that Brits were the most surveilled people in the world, and given that most CCTV footage wasn't stored for more than a couple of weeks, they'd agreed they wouldn't meet during that time unless there was some sort of emergency. Contact would be kept to a minimum and, if it became necessary, they would use text messages with agreed codes. The target would be referred to as 'the house', the bomb as 'dinner', and so on. Each knew what had to be done, and they were prepared to do it.

And so Yousef was sitting in the rooftop café of the Bradfield City Art Gallery, third table on the left-hand wall, inconspicuous among the late-morning coffee drinkers, back to the self-service array and the till.

216

In front of him, a Coke and a wedge of the café's notoriously calorific lemon drizzle cake. He'd only managed a couple of forkfuls; it stuck in his throat like a lump of sweet sandstone. It wasn't just at home that he was having trouble eating. He had that morning's *Guardian* strewn across the table, minus the sports section. He was pretending to read the G2 supplement, his left hand positioned so that he could read his watch. His right leg jiggled in nervous expectancy.

As the minute hand crept towards ten past, his face grew hot and a slither of sweat spread across his neck and shoulders. Anticipation made his bowels clench.

It was over in seconds. A woman in a swaggering raincoat passed close to his table. He only saw her from behind as she made her way through the doors and out on to the roof terrace, where she sat down with her back to him, a bottle of mineral water beside her. A dark headscarf covered her head. He wished he could go and sit with her to ease the loneliness he felt.

On the table in front of Yousef was the sports section. He forced down the rest of the cake, swilling his mouth with Coke to get through it. Then, casually, trying not to show how sick he felt at the sudden accession of sugar, he gathered his newspaper together and strolled towards the exit.

He couldn't wait till he got back to the van. He slipped into the gents' toilet outside the café and locked himself into the cubicle. With fingers made clumsy by nerves and sweat, he rustled through the sports pages. There, ironically enough between a two-page spread about Bradfield Victoria's premiership

217

chances without Robbie Bishop, nestled inside a plastic folder, was the paperwork that would take him where he needed to be tomorrow. A fax, supposedly from Bradfield Victoria's general manager, to their usual electrical contractors, complaining of an urgent problem with a junction box under the Albert Vestey stand. And a second fax from their contractors to A1 Electricals, subcontracting the emergency work.

Yousef breathed deeply, letting himself relax a fraction. It was going to work. It was going to be amazing. Tomorrow, the world would be a different place. *Insha'Allah*.

Tony summoned up all his nerve and swung the leg that was whole on to the floor. That was enough to send a jagged line of pain through the other leg in spite of the brace holding its damage firm. He clenched his teeth and used his hands to help drag the braced limb through an arc. As it reached the edge of the mattress, he let go and almost fell forward, letting gravity bring him into a more or less upright position. Sweat popped out across his forehead and he wiped it away with the back of his hand. He had to master this before they would let him out of here.

He paused, his weight distributed between his buttocks on the bed and his right foot. Once his chest stopped heaving, he reached for the elbow crutches he'd learned to use earlier that day. Carefully, he gripped them, making sure his forearms were inside the plastic cuffs. Rubber ferrules on the floor. Deep breath.

Tony pushed himself upright, amazing himself by his steadiness. Crutches forward, swing with the good leg, let the bad leg follow, toes touching the floor, tiniest fraction of weight on the damaged knee. Jolt of pain. Not unbearable, though. Manageable with clenched teeth and buttocks.

Five minutes later, he'd made it as far as the toilet. Going back took eight minutes, but even in that short time, he felt his movements were smoother, more assured; he'd have something to show Carol when she came next. He'd need her help if he was going to go home. It would be hard to ask for it, but he suspected it would be even harder to wait for her to offer it.

Getting back in bed and making himself comfortable took another few minutes. He swore he would never again take for granted the simple act of getting up for a piss. He didn't care if people laughed, he'd happily stand there going, 'Look at me. I just got up and walked over there. Did you see that? Amazing.'

Once settled, he had no excuse to avoid thinking about Robbie Bishop and Danny Wade. Or rather, Danny Wade and Robbie Bishop. It was possible that Danny Wade was not Stalky's first victim, but after exhaustive trawling of the internet, Tony couldn't find an earlier example of what might be considered his handiwork.

'You love the planning and the outcome, but you don't much care for the act,' he said. 'Technically you're not a serial yet, but I think you're going that way. And what makes you unusual is that, mostly, serial is about sex. It might not always look that way, but that's what's at the heart of it, time after time. Twisted circuits that need twisted scenarios to achieve what comes relatively naturally to most people. But that's not what you're about, is it? You're not inter-ested in them as bodies, as objects of desire. At least, not sexual desire.

'So what are you getting out of it? Is it political? A kind of "eat the rich" message? Are you some neo-Marxist warrior intent on punishing the ones who achieve riches and don't share them with the people who are still stuck where our heroes came from? It makes a kind of sense . . .' He stared at the ceiling, turning the idea around in his head, examining it from different angles.

'The problem is, if that's who you are, why aren't you shouting about it? You can't deliver a political message if it's written in a language nobody under-stands. No. You're not doing this out of the need to make some abstract political point. This is personal, somehow.'

He scratched his head. God, how he longed for a proper shower, a long soak under a torrent of water, cleaning his hair and clearing his head. Tomorrow, maybe, the nurse had said. Wrap his brace in cling-film, tape it to his leg and see what happens.

'So if it's not sexual and it's not political, what's the point? What are you getting out of it? If it was just Robbie, I could believe in revenge for something that happened at school – he took something from you, he made you feel small, he hurt you in some way he probably didn't even know about. But it's inconceivable that Danny Wade could have done any of those things. Danny was geek boy – model rail-ways, for Christ's sake. That's so far down the food chain, the only thing lower was the ones who escaped from Special Needs.' He sighed. 'It doesn't make sense.'

What did make sense, however, was that the killer must have left tracks. Given that the locals had written it up as a tragic accident, there wouldn't have been anything more than desultory inquiries on the ground at the time, especially since it was already established that Jana gained nothing from Danny's death. But even now, if the right questions were asked, there might be answers. Someone may have seen Danny meeting up with his killer in the pub. Someone may have seen him arrive at Danny's on the night of the murder. If only he wasn't stuck in this hospital bed, it wouldn't matter that Carol was dismissing his intuitions. He could go to Dore himself and talk to the locals. Though on balance that wasn't always the best way.

For every person he could connect with, there was usually at least one other who picked up on the weirdness in him and freaked out. All his life, Tony had felt he was passing for human. It was a masquerade that didn't fool all of the people all of the time. And the leg brace wouldn't help, that was for sure.

None of which mattered, of course, because he wasn't going to be able to go to Dore and sniff around on his own account. Tony gave a frustrated sigh. Then suddenly, his eyes widened. There was someone who could charm information from a Trappist. Someone who owed him a favour.

Smiling now, Tony reached for the phone.

Carol looked out at her team. Everybody was either staring at a screen or deep in a phone conversation. She slipped a miniature of vodka out of her drawer, uncapped it below desk level, then discreetly tipped it into her coffee. She'd learned from her own traumas in the job that alcohol was a good friend and a bad master. It had come close to making her its servant, but she'd clawed her way back from that and now she could readily convince herself that she was in charge. Her truth was that in times of stress and frustration, times like this, it was her refuge and her strength. Especially when Tony wasn't there.

Not that he would rebuke her. Nothing so blatant. No, it was more that his presence was a reproach to her, a reminder that there were other options for escape. Options they had come close to pursuing several times before. But always, whenever they drew close, something intervened. Usually something related to work. It was, she thought, the ultimate irony. That which brought them together invariably threw obstacles in their way. And neither of them could ever figure out how to overcome the obstacles until the moment of possibility had passed.

She sipped the drink, loving the way she could feel it spread through her. God, but they needed something to break on this case.

As if in answer to her fervent request, Sam Evans stuck his head round the door. Carol nodded him in. She always felt a certain ambivalence towards Sam. She knew he was ambitious, and because she had once shared that trait, she understood both how valuable and how dangerous that was for a cop. She also recognized his maverick instincts as being close to her own. He was no team player. But then, she hadn't been much of one either when she'd been at his rank. She'd only become a team player once she'd found a team worth playing for. There was enough of her in Sam for her to understand him

222

and thus to forgive. What she couldn't forgive was his sneakiness. She knew he spied on his colleagues, though he did it well enough for them not to have worked it out. He'd once dropped her in the shit with Brandon to make his own achievements seem even better than they were. The bottom line was that she couldn't trust him, which felt more of a liability the longer the unit was up and running.

'I think I might have something, guv,' he said, almost preening as he sat. He tugged the knees of his trousers to preserve the crease and squared his shoulders inside the well-ironed shirt.

She hardly dared hope. 'What sort of something?'

He tossed the original email on to the desk and gave her a moment to read it. 'I spoke to Bindie. This stalker, Rhys Butler, he jumped Robbie outside the team hotel in Birmingham. The cops lifted him, let him off with a caution. I spoke to the arresting officer. They went easy on Butler because Robbie and Bindie didn't want the publicity. Anyway, this DC Singh kept an eye on Butler. Dropped round his place, made sure he took down his wank wall and stayed well away from them both. Butler swore he was over it. He'd lost his job and that had tipped him over the edge, he claimed. He played the good boy for a few months then he got a new job and moved to Newcastle. But here's the kicker, guv.' He gave it the dramatic pause. 'He's a lab rat in a pharmacology company.'

Experience had taught Carol that there were more false dawns in murder investigations than decent meals in a police canteen. But in the absence of anything stronger to chase, she was more than willing to pursue this lead. 'Great work, Sam. I want you to get on to Northumbria and see if they can help us with an address.'

Sam's smile reminded her of Nelson faced with a bowl of chicken livers. He laid a second piece of paper in front of her. 'Work and home,' he said.

Now she let herself return his smile. The only question was whether to let Northumbria bring him in. It didn't take long to make the decision. Carol told herself she wanted to see Rhys Butler's home for herself. She didn't want to delegate it to some uniform who didn't know what he was supposed to be looking for. She pushed her chair back and stood up. 'So, what are we waiting for?'

Yousef opened the fridge. The glass beaker sat on the shelf, clear liquid filling most of it. But the bottom layer was the crystalline powder he needed. Carefully, he took the beaker out and placed it on the worktop. He'd already set up a glass funnel lined with filter paper. He closed his eyes and muttered his way through a prayer asking the prophet to intercede and help his plan to fruition. Then he lifted the beaker and poured the liquid through the filter.

It took less time than he'd expected. He peered through the window in his face protector at the heap of white crystals. It didn't look enough to cause the mayhem he'd been told it would. But what did he know? Fabric and the rag trade, that was what he knew about. He had to rely on what he had been told. Nothing made sense otherwise. Not the sleepless nights, not the transformation of his spirit, not the pain he was going to cause his family. He couldn't be the only one of them feeling this way.

He just had to get past his weaknesses and focus on the goal.

Gently, he lifted the filter paper out of the funnel and tipped the contents into a bowl of iced water. He swilled the crystals around, washing them clean of the liquid they'd been precipitated from. Then he distributed the explosive among a couple of dozen paper plates so it could dry with the least chance of an accidental explosion.

He pushed up his face protector and shook his head in amazement. He'd done it. He'd made enough TATP to blow a hole in the main stand of Victoria Park. All that remained was for him to assemble the rest of the components in the morning.

Then he could transport it to the place where it would demonstrate that the war on terror was definitely not being won. Yousef allowed himself a crooked smile. He'd show them what shock and awe really was.

'You're crazy,' Paula said firmly. She'd thought it often enough, but there had never really been an appropriate or opportune moment to say it.

'Which part is the crazy bit?' Tony asked sweetly.

'Which part isn't?' She looked around. 'Have you got a wheelchair? Can we get out of here?'

'No and no. You don't need a cigarette to have a conversation.'

'I do when it's this crazy,' she said.

'You keep saying that. But just because Carol Jordan doesn't want to pursue it doesn't make it a crazy idea. She's not infallible.' *Which you know better than anyone* hung in the air between them.

Paula pointed at his leg. 'And neither are you.'

'I never said I was. The point is, Paula, this needs to be checked out. If I could do it myself, I would. But I can't. Look at it this way. If I'm wrong, no harm done. But if I'm right, the investigation into Robbie's death changes completely.'

Paula could feel herself wavering. She had to defend herself against his logic and against the debt she owed him for helping her back to dry land when she was drowning in her own misery and self-pity. 'It's easy for you to say, "no harm done". It's not your career on the line. I can't go storming all over some other force's ground and hope it won't get back to the chief.'

'Why should it get back to her? In the first instance, all I'm asking you to do is to talk to people. The local pub, the local dog walkers, Jana Jankowicz. I'm not saying, "Go down the nick in Sheffield and tell them they fucked up, can you see the paperwork on the murder they didn't recognize."'

'Just as well,' Paula grumbled. 'Now that would be career suicide.'

'See? I'm not asking you to do that. Just a few questions, Paula. You have to admit, it's worth a look.'

And that was where he had her on the hook. She revered Carol Jordan. She knew she was maybe a little bit in love with her boss, But as he had implied, she knew better than anyone that the DCI sometimes got it wrong. Unconsciously, Paula rubbed her wrist. The wounds had long since healed, but there was still a network of fine scars barely visible across the base of her palm and her wrist. 'It's pretty thin,' she said, trying to find a form of words to show she thought he might have something but which didn't say flat out that Carol Jordan was wrong.

'From what Carol tells me, thin is better than what you've got.'

Paula moved restlessly round the room. 'Maybe not. Her and Sam, they're off to Newcastle on a hot lead. Some stalker of Bindie Blyth's who took a pop at Robbie outside the team hotel.'

Tony tutted. 'Waste of time. I told her that when she called to say she wouldn't be round tonight. When stalkers lose it, they want the world to know what they're prepared to do for love. It's John Hinckley trying to assassinate Reagan to make Jodie Foster love him. These are not secret squirrels, they're shout it from the rooftop guys. Whoever killed Robbie, he wasn't doing it to impress Bindie.'

'And when exactly am I supposed to go and do these interviews?' Paula said, realizing as soon as she'd spoken that she had capitulated.

Tony spread his hands, the picture of bewildered innocence. 'Tonight? Now you're off duty.'

'I am not off duty,' Paula said, teeth clenched and lips bared. 'I am not even supposed to be here. I am supposed to be helping Chris deal with the avalanche of emails from the Best Days website so we can go back out tonight to Amatis with a pile of photos to see if we can ID any of them.'

Tony didn't even flinch. 'Well, maybe tomorrow, then?'

Paula kicked the end of his bed, hoping it hurt. 'Stop playing the fool, Tony. You know the way we work. When there's something big on, we work every hour God sends. There's no such thing as overtime on the MIT. We sleep when it's over.'

Tony shook his head. 'Great speech, Paula. It might even work on somebody who doesn't know how this MIT works. You talk a lot about teamwork. You fetishize the concept of a team. But I've seen you lot operate at close quarters. You're like Real Madrid. A bunch of *galacticos* who ride your own hobby horses into the sunset. Sometimes you're all riding in the same direction and it looks like you're a team. But that's more by accident than design.'

Paula stopped in her tracks, shocked to hear Tony speak that way about Carol Jordan's pride and joy. She didn't think he had it in him to be so blunt about them. 'You're wrong,' she said. It wasn't even defiance, just an automatic denial.

'I'm not wrong. Every one of you, you're desperately trying to prove something. You live the job. And you all want to be the best, so you all go off on your own little missions.' He sounded angry now. 'When it works, it's great. And when it doesn't . . .'

'Don Merrick.' Paula fought to keep her voice cold and emotionless.

Tony smacked his fist into the mattress. 'Damn it, Paula, let it go. It wasn't your fault.'

'He wanted to show us all that he deserved his promotion. That he deserved to be one of our elite little band.' Paula looked away. There were some things she still didn't like Tony to see. 'You're right. We are a law unto ourselves.'

'So help me here.'

He was, she thought, utterly implacable. It made him a great clinician, that refusal to take no for an

answer. But it made him a right pain in the arse sometimes too. She wondered how Carol dealt with it. 'If
I can,' she said. 'No promises.'

'No demands,' he said. 'I wouldn't ask if I didn't
think it was important, Paula.'

She nodded, conscript and unwillingly complicit.
'And if it all comes on top, I am blaming you.'

Tony laughed. 'Of course you are. After all, if she
tries to sack me, I can always evict her.'

Friday teatime on the A1 was an experience guar-
anteed to fray the nerves of the most patient driver.
It had been a long time since anyone had accused
Sam Evans of patience and Carol Jordan was no
better. Like most passengers, she was convinced she
could get them there faster than the person behind
the wheel. As they approached the Washington services, the traffic slowed to a halt. Lorries, vans and
cars formed a frustrated clot of traffic, made worse
by the opportunists who kept trying to peel off into
another lane that seemed to be moving more quickly.
Silver, white and black in the gathering gloom of
the late afternoon, they formed a monochrome blot
on the landscape. 'This makes the decision for us,'
Carol said, waving at the wall of vehicles around
them.

'Sorry?' Sam sounded as if she'd dragged him back
reluctantly from a faraway place.

'Whether to hit him at work or at home. It's taken
so long to get here, there's no point in considering
anything other than home.' She flipped through the
map sheets she'd printed out before they left. 'We
should have brought my car, it's got GPS,' she

muttered as she tried to make sense of where they were in relation to where they wanted to be.

It took them the best part of an hour to find Rhys Butler's address, a red-brick two-up, two-down in the middle of a terrace in one of a dozen identical streets leading down to the Town Moor. The house had an air of depressed dilapidation, as if it were only held up by the sheer willpower of its neighbours on either side. There were no lights visible and no car parked outside. Carol checked her watch. 'He's probably on his way home now. Let's give it half an hour.'

They found a pub a few streets away. Busy and friendly, the atmosphere made up for the length of time since it had last had a makeover. It was packed with three distinct groups – young men drinking pints of lager and wearing short-sleeved shirts with the tails hanging over their jeans and chinos; older men in sweatshirts and jeans, beanie hats crammed in their back pockets, hands rough from manual labour, drinking pints of bitter and Newcastle Brown Ale; and young women in outfits that would have looked opti-mistically skimpy in midsummer, their make-up inexpertly applied, necking Bacardi Breezers and vodka shots like they hoped to hell there would be no tomorrow. Everyone who noticed Carol and Sam stared, but not in a hostile way. It felt more like the look a naturalist would give a previously uncatalogued oryx – a bit exotic, but nothing to get too excited about, we've seen the likes of this before.

Carol pointed Sam at a table in the far corner and returned with a large vodka and tonic for herself and a mineral water for Sam. He looked at it in disgust. 'You're driving,' she said.

'So? I could still have had a lager shandy,' Sam complained.

'You don't deserve it.' Carol took a drink and gave him the hard stare. 'I had time to think while we were driving up here. You've been up to your old tricks, haven't you?'

His look of injured innocence was so on the money she nearly gave him the benefit of the doubt. 'What do you mean?'

'You didn't dig this up this morning. You got too much too fast. You sneaked a peek when you were searching Robbie's flat, didn't you?' She was guessing, but the shift of his eyes to the side told her she was right.

'Does it matter?' he said, stroppy as he could be with his boss. Which wasn't really very belligerent at all. 'I didn't try and keep it to myself. I brought it to you once there was something to go at.'

'Fair enough. But why wait? Why keep it to yourself at all? The only reason I can see is that you wanted more than just the credit for finding the lead. You wanted to show Stacey up at the same time. Because this was her part of the inquiry. So, her miss. Is that what it was about?' Carol spoke so softly he had to lean forward to hear her. She thought she saw a blush colour his coffee skin but it could have been the warmth of the pub.

Sam looked away, apparently fascinated by the navel piercing of a woman at the next table. 'I knew she was over-stretched. I wanted to make sure we didn't miss anything.'

'That's bollocks, Sam. We've had inquiries with IT elements five times the size of this, and Stacey's coped.

231

Stacey would have caught this. Maybe a day or two later than you, but she would have caught it. You wanted to be the hero and at Stacey's expense. We've been over this ground before.' Carol shook her head. 'I don't want to lose you, Sam. You're bright and you're a grafter. But what I need more is to be able to trust everyone in the team to work together. I once saw a cheesy greetings card that said true love wasn't about gazing into each other's eyes. It was about standing shoulder to shoulder, facing in the same direction. Well, that's what being in MIT is supposed to be like too. This is truly your final warning. If I catch you at this kind of thing again, you'll be reassigned.' She downed the rest of her drink in one without taking her eyes off him. 'And now I'll have a vodka and tonic, please.'

Carol watched him go. The anger was clear in his movements. She hoped there was something beyond the anger, something that would make him pause and consider his future. She wished there was a way of reaching out to him, to explain why she was being so tough on him. But she also knew that he would read it wrong, coming from her.

When he came back with her drink, he'd buried the anger. There was nothing in his demeanour to suggest he was anything other than the dutiful subordinate. 'I was out of order,' he said, not looking her in the eye. 'At school, I was a runner, not a footballer. I never got the hang of it. Know what I mean?'

'Oddly enough, I do.' She sipped her drink. The single measure was so weak, it hardly seemed worth the bother. 'What do you think? Time for another look?'

Ten minutes later, they were back outside Rhys Butler's house. It was fully dark by now. And still no sign of life. 'You think we should take a walk round the back?' Sam said.

'Why not?' They walked down the street, almost to the corner. A break in the houses led them into the alley that ran the length of the back yards. Sam counted the houses as they went, stopping at last outside the back of Butler's home. He tried the handle of the door in the wall and shook his head. Carol put her fingers behind her ear. 'Did you hear that, Constable?'

Sam smiled. 'Would that be the scream or the sound of breaking glass?'

'Probably the scream,' Carol said, stepping back to let Sam have a clear run at it. To hell with equality when the alternative meant you could escape the aching shoulder. He rammed the door, simultaneously turning the handle. The soft wood around the lock splintered and the door fell open.

The back yard seemed even darker than the alley because of the shadows cast by its high walls. No light came from the house. Carol reached into her bag and took out a rectangle of plasticized cardboard the size of a credit card. She flexed it and a narrow beam of light spread out from it. 'Nifty,' Sam said.

'Christmas stocking.'

'You've obviously got an in with Santa. I got socks.'

Carol moved the light around. The yard was more or less empty. An outside toilet occupied one corner, its door half-open. 'He's not been here long enough to accumulate much crap,' she said. The back of the house had an L-shape, the kitchen jutting out towards them. Windows from the kitchen and the back room both looked on to the empty yard. Carol crossed to the kitchen window and angled the beam inside.

The kitchen was fitted with the dark wooden units popular in the seventies. It looked untouched since then. Carol could see an electric kettle, a toaster and a breadbin on the worktop opposite. In the sink, she could make out a bowl, a mug and a tumbler. On the draining board, a noodle bowl and a wine glass. Looking over her shoulder, Sam said, 'Looks like he still hasn't found Ms Right.'

Looks like home to me. Carol thought with a pang of recognition. She turned away and did her best to illuminate the other window. It looked as if the walls were a giant collage stretching right round the room.

'Fuck,' Sam said. 'Looks like we hit the mother-lode.'

Before Carol could reply, she heard a noise behind her. The ticking of an idling bike wheel stood out against the steady thrum of traffic noise. She whirled round in time to see a man and a bike silhouetted in the doorway. 'What the fuck?' he shouted.

Sam charged, but he was too slow. The door slammed shut in front of him. Carol ran across to help him pull the door open but there wasn't enough room for them both to gain purchase. 'You're too late,' the voice from the other side yelled. 'I've chained my bike to the door. You won't be able to get it open. I'm calling the police, you dirty thieving bastards.'

'We ...' Carol clamped her hand over Sam's mouth before he could come up with the hackneyed line so beloved of comedy writers.

'Shut up,' she hissed. 'If we tell him who we are

and he's guilty, he'll be off into the night and we'll have a hell of a job trying to find him. Let's just chill until the local boys get here and sort it out then.'

'But . . .'

'No buts.'

They could hear the faint chirp of mobile phone keys being pressed. 'Hello, police please . . .' This was a nightmare, she thought.

'You could give me a leg-up on to the toilet roof. It's lower than the wall,' Sam murmured. 'At least I can keep an eye out, make sure he stays put.'

'Bloody Keystone Cops,' Carol muttered.

'Yes, I've just caught two people trying to break into my house. I've got them trapped in my back yard . . . Butler. Rhys Butler.' He gave them the address. 'Like I said, they can't get out, I've got them trapped . . . No, I won't do anything silly, just wait till you get here.' A pause then the voice shouted, 'See? The police are on their way so don't try anything stupid.'

'We are never going to live this down,' Carol sighed.

'Help me to get up on the roof,' Sam urged.

'You just want to get a new suit on the firm,' Carol said, following him round to the end of the toilet furthest from the gate. Nevertheless, she braced herself and made a cradle of her hands. She bent so Sam could get his foot anchored. 'One, two, three,' she breathed, straightening as he pushed himself off the ground.

Sam hit the roof at chest height, using the strength of his shoulders and upper arms to lever himself higher and on to the roof as Carol shouted, 'You're bang out of order, mate, you're going to be so sorry,' to cover the scrabbling of his body against the tiles.

'You shut up,' Butler shouted back. 'The cops will be here soon and then you'll be sorry you messed with me.'

It was, Carol thought, the bantam cock bravado of the small man with something to prove. Even in that short glimpse, she'd seen how slight Rhys Butler was. Taking on Robbie Bishop in a fist fight had been madness. All the more reason to take him on at arm's length. 'We'll see who's sorry,' Carol shouted. 'Little big man.'

She leaned against the toilet, pissed off and cold. She wasn't given to standing on her dignity, but an episode like this would rocket round her own force and likely end up on somebody's blog. Carol Jordan, captured by the villain she'd gone out to arrest.

It didn't take long for the local bobbies to show up. Two of them, by the sounds of it. Butler, sounding over-excited as a birthday child, told them what he believed had happened. 'I came home and there they were, breaking into my back room. They already broke the gate down, look, you can see where it's all splintered, I had to chain my bike to the handle.'

Butler kept repeating himself. One of the cops evidently decided he'd had enough. 'This is the police,' he shouted. 'We're going to open the door now. I advise you to remain calm and stay where you are.'

Sam stuck his head over the edge of the roof. 'Up or down, ma'am?'

'Stay where you are,' she grunted. 'This is going to be very embarrassing.' She took out her warrant card and held it in front of her. Various metallic noises came from the other side of the wall, then the door inched open. A very large man filled most of the doorway, his torch held at shoulder height and blinding her.

'What's going on here, then?' he asked.

'Detective Chief Inspector Jordan from Bradfield Police,' she said. 'And that –' she gestured up to the roof; the torch beam followed her arm, '– is Detective Constable Evans. And he –' she pointed over the PC's shoulder to where Butler was frowning next to the other uniformed officer, '– is Rhys Butler, whom I am about to invite to return to Bradfield with me to answer questions relating to the murder of Robbie Bishop.'

Butler's mouth fell open and he took a step backwards. 'You're kidding,' he said. Then, seeing the look on her face, he said, 'You're not, are you?' And, predictably, he took to his heels.

He'd taken two steps when Sam landed on top of him, knocking the breath out of his lungs and two teeth out of his mouth.

It was going to be a very long, very farcical evening, Carol thought wearily.

Paula ran her thumb and index finger down the glass, making a path in the condensation. 'So you see, I don't know what to do for the best,' she said. 'On the one hand, I owe Tony for the help he gave me after . . . after I got hurt. On the other hand, I don't want to go behind the chief's back.'

Chris had a pile of photographs they'd printed from the emails Stacey had solicited. All of the subjects had been at school with Robbie and none of them had alibis other than partners or spouses for the previous Thursday. She sorted through them again, rearranging them according to some set of criteria known only to her. 'You could always run it past her,' she said.

'According to Tony, she's already blown it out of the water.' Paula reached for the photos and looked through them critically. Most of them had printed up pretty well. They looked like people, as opposed to police mug shots.

Chris shrugged. 'What you do on your own time is your own business. So long as you don't do anything to jeopardize an existing investigation.'

'But should I be doing it at all?' As the evening had worn on, Paula had grown less convinced of the appropriateness of what Tony was asking.

Chris put her hands flat on the small bar table, thumbs underneath, as if she was going to tip it over in one swift movement. She looked down at her neatly manicured fingernails. 'Once upon a time, there was somebody I thought I owed a favour to. Kind of like you with Tony, but for different reasons. She asked me for something. Just a phone number, that was all. A number I could get easily and she couldn't, not without questions being asked. Anyway, I did the needful. And that was the first step on a journey that got her killed.' Chris sniffed hard, then looked Paula straight in the eye. 'I do not blame myself for what happened. If I hadn't done her that favour, she would have found another way of getting what she wanted. What's important to me is that when she called on me for help, I was there. When I think of her now, I know I didn't let her down.' Chris let go of the table and gave Paula a rueful smile. 'It's up to you. You know what it is to live with consequences. You have to think about where you might be with this six months, a year down the road.'

Paula was touched. Chris didn't often share personal stuff, not even with her. She knew everybody else thought there was a special bond between the two of them because they were both lesbians, but they were wrong. Chris treated Paula exactly as she treated everyone else. No special favours. No secret intimacy. Just a sergeant and a constable who respected each other professionally and liked what they knew of each other. Paula was comfortable with that. She had friends enough outside work and the one time she had succumbed to a close friendship at work it had ended up causing her more grief than she cared to think about. But tonight's revelation was a reminder that she still had a lot to learn about her sergeant. She nodded. 'Point taken. The only question is when I'm going to be able to follow it up. It's not like this is going to ease up any time soon.'

Chris glanced at her watch. 'You could be in Sheffield by nine if you left now. That would give you time to talk to people in the pub. And if you check into a cheap motel, you could talk to the house-keeper first thing.'

Paula looked surprised. 'But I'm supposed to ...'

'Kevin and I can manage Amatis. It's probably a waste of time anyway. I'll cover for you in the morning. If Carol gets lucky in Newcastle, she won't even notice you're not around.'

'If she's doing interviews, she might. She likes to pull me in on those if they get sticky.'

'Good point.' Chris smiled. 'I'll buy you a couple of hours. I can tell her you were exhausted and I told

239

you to take your time coming in. But you need to do your bit. You need to make sure you catch up with the housekeeper bright and early. You think they do breakfast meetings in Rotherham?'

Paula grinned. 'She's Polish. They work all the hours God sends. She'll totally get an early meeting.'

Chris shoved the pile of photos towards her. 'You better take these. If it's the same killer, he might be among this lot.'

'What about you and Kevin?'

'I'll go back and print out another set. It won't take long, not now Stacey's got the file set up. If I call her now, she'll have them done by the time I finish my drink and get back.' She reached for her glass. 'And you need to get your arse in gear, Constable.'

Paula didn't need telling a second time. She scooped up the pictures and headed for the door, a bounce in her step. She didn't want to think about how awkward it would be to prove Carol Jordan wrong. What she was focused on was proving Tony Hill right.

Paula had never done the lottery. A mug's game, she'd thought. But as she walked into the Blacksmith's Arms on the outskirts of Dore, she wondered if maybe she'd been wrong. Danny Wade's house was only quarter of a mile away from the pub, and she'd swung past it on her way there. What she'd been able to see through the gates had made her whistle. She could think of lots of ways to fill a mansion like that without once having to resort to 00 gauge. She made a mental note to check out who was going to inherit. It never hurt to eliminate the obvious. Or not, as it often turned out.

The pub matched its environment. Paula reckoned

it was a lot more modern than it looked. The ceilings were too high, for a start. She guessed the beams might be polystyrene, but it didn't matter. They looked authentic. The bar was decked out with wood panelling and chintz, tables and chairs grouped so that it imitated a drawing room rather than a saloon bar. At one end of the room, old church pews flanked an inglenook fireplace where logs blazed on substantial iron fire dogs.

Paula guessed they had a lively lunchtime and weekend trade. But at quarter past nine on a Friday evening, it was much quieter than a city-centre bar would be. Half a dozen tables were occupied by couples and foursomes. They all looked like accountants and building society managers to her. Smartly dressed, nicely turned out, scarily interchangeable. Stepford couples. In her leather jacket, black jeans and solitude, she stuck out like a hoodie at a Tory fête. As she walked to the bar, she was aware of conversations pausing and heads turning. A middle-class version of *Straw Dogs*.

There were a couple of blokes sitting on high stools at the bar. Pringle sweaters and dark slacks. They could have wandered straight off the nearby golf course. As she drew nearer, she realized they were probably a couple of years younger than her. Barely in their mid-twenties, she guessed. She thought her dad probably had more sense of adventure. Probably right up Danny Wade's street.

Paula smiled at the barman, who looked as if he'd be more at home in a Spanish karaoke bar than here. 'What can I get you?' he said in an accent that matched her preconception.

God, how weary she got of soft drinks when she was working. 'Orange juice and lemonade, please,' she said. As he prepared her drink, Paula pulled out the bundle of photos. There was no point beating about the bush in here. Nobody was going to become her friend. Not the Spanish barman, not the Nick Faldo clones, not the cosy couples. She had her ID ready when the drink was placed in front of her, precisely centred on the beermat. 'Thanks. I'm a police officer.'

The barman looked bored. 'It's on the house,' he said.

'Thanks, but no thanks. I'll pay for it.'

'Up to you.' He took the money and brought her change back. The Pringle twins were openly staring at her.

'I'm investigating the death of Danny Wade. He lived up the road?'

'He the one who got poisoned?' The barman's interest was barely awakened.

'That's what happens when you use cheap foreign labour,' the Pringle nearest her said. He was either incredibly stupid, incredibly insensitive or incredibly offensive. Paula couldn't be sure which. She'd have to wait for his next utterance to be sure.

'Mr Wade was poisoned, yes,' she said coolly.

'I thought that was all sorted out,' the other Pringle said. 'The housekeeper made a tragic mistake, isn't that what happened?'

'We just need to clear up one or two details,' Paula said.

'Bloody hell, are you saying she did it on purpose?' Pringle One said, turning round properly and giving her an avid look.

'Did you know Mr Wade, sir?' she said.

'Knew him to speak to.' He turned to his friend. 'We knew him to say hello, didn't we, Geoff?'

Geoff nodded. 'Just to chat at the bar, you know. He had a lovely pair of Lakeland Terriers, very well-behaved dogs. In the summer, he'd bring them down with him and sit out in the beer garden. What happened to the dogs? Carlos, do you know what happened to the dogs?' He looked at the barman expectantly.

'I have no idea.' Carlos carried on polishing glasses.

'Was he always on his own?' Paula asked. 'Or did he come in with friends.'

Pringle One snorted. 'Friends? Do me a favour.'

'I was told that he ran into an old school friend in here recently. You don't remember that?'

'I remember,' said Carlos. 'You two know the guy. He came in a few times on his own, then one night Danny came in and he recognized him, this other guy. They had a couple of drinks together over by the fire.' He pointed across the room. 'Vodka and Coke, that's what he drank.'

'Do you remember anything else about him?' Paula asked, deliberately casual. Never make them think it's important; then they want to please you, so their imagination fills in the blanks.

The Pringles shook their heads. 'He always had a book with him,' Carlos said. 'A big book, not like usual.' With his hands, he described something about eight inches by ten. 'With pictures. Flowers, gardens I think.'

'Not enough to do with your time, that's your trouble,' Pringle One pronounced.

243

Paula spread the pictures across the bar. 'Do you see him here?'

All three crowded round. Geoff shook his head dubiously. 'Could be any one of these,' he said, pointing to three dark-haired, blue-eyed men with thin faces.

The barman frowned, picking up a couple of the pictures to study them more closely. 'No,' he said firmly. 'Is not them. Is this one.' He put his index finger on a fourth shot and pushed it towards Paula. This image had dark hair and blue eyes. His face was long, like the other three, but much broader across the eyes, narrowing to a blunt chin. 'His hair is shorter now, combed to the side. But it's him.'

Geoff stared at the chosen photo. 'I wouldn't have picked that one, but now I look at it. . . you could be right.'

'I spend all my time looking at faces, matching them to drinks,' Carlos said. 'I'm pretty sure this is him.'

'Thank you. That's very helpful. Did you happen to hear any of their conversation?' Paula asked, gathering the photos together with the identified shot on top.

'No,' Carlos said. 'My English is not good enough for this kind of talk.' He spread his hands in so foreign a gesture that Paula instinctively knew he was lying. 'All I do is take orders for drinks and food.'

Yeah, right. She'd be talking to him again, she suspected. 'Never mind,' she said, her smile reassuring. 'You've been very helpful. I might have to come back and talk to you again, Carlos.' She produced her notebook. 'Maybe you could write down your full name and contact details?'

244

While he wrote, she turned her attention back to the Pringles. 'Have you seen that bloke in here again, after the night he met up with Danny?'

They exchanged glances. Geoff shook his head. 'Haven't seen hide nor hair of him, have we?'

As if he'd accomplished his mission and didn't have to come back. Paula gathered up her notebook and made her escape. Back at the car, she stared at the photo Carlos had identified. Number 14. According to Stacey's key, this was Jack Anderson. He hadn't sent in his own photo. He'd been one of a group of three in someone else's picture. But he'd been to Harriestown High, and he'd overlapped with Robbie Bishop.

Paula looked at the clock on the dashboard. Only quarter to ten. She was due to meet Jana Jankowicz at eight. She could either find a cheap motel in Sheffield and sleep badly or head back to Bradfield for a few comfortable hours in her own bed. And that way she'd be able to show her face at Amatis. Maybe they'd get lucky and pick up a second ID on the photo. For sure, she would pay back some of the favour Chris Devine had granted her. For Paula, who always preferred debtors to debts, it was no contest.

Midnight

Would he know she'd been spending so much time here? Would her presence leave a stain? Would he turn to her, like one of the three bears, saying, 'Who's been sitting in my chair?' She might be blonde, but Carol was no Goldilocks. She swallowed the last mouthful of wine in her glass and reached for the bottle, conveniently placed within reach on the floor. There was something comforting about being here. Even though she'd just arrested a suspect who ran counter to Tony's convictions about Robbie Bishop's murder, Carol felt confident in her professional judgement.

It was her private emotions that gave her more trouble. It was easy to be sure of her feelings when he wasn't here – she missed him, she could create a conversation between them on any subject under the sun, she could picture the shifting expressions on his face. She could almost dare to think the l-word. But when they were in the same space, all her certainties shifted. She needed him too much and her anxiety over doing or saying something that would drive a wedge between them became her overriding consideration. And so the things unsaid and undone loomed large in everything they said and did. She had no idea how to resolve it. And for all his professional expertise, she suspected Tony was no wiser than her in this crucial respect.

In his hospital room, Tony lay with the lights off and the curtains open. The thick clouds reflected the city's glow, taking the edge off the darkness. He'd dropped off to sleep earlier, but it hadn't lasted long. He wanted to be home in his own bed. Or at least on his own sofa, given how impossible the thought of stairs seemed right now. Nobody waking him at six with a cup of tea he didn't want. Nobody making judgements about him based on his choice of boxer shorts. Nobody treating him like he was five years old and incapable of making his own decisions. Above all, nobody to let his mother in.

He sighed, a long, deep exhalation that left him hollow. Who was he kidding? He'd be just as restless and miserable at home as he was here. What he needed was work. That was what made him tick, what made his mind inhabitable. Without work, without direction, his thoughts were like a hamster on a wheel, circling and dancing with no destination and no possibility of arrival. With work, he could avoid anything but the most superficial consideration of Carol Jordan and his feelings for her. Once, there might have been a faint hope of them building a future. But circumstances and his reactions to them had blown that. If there had ever been a real possibility of her loving him, that was history.

And probably best that it was, for all concerned. Especially now his mother was back on the scene.

The insistent bass seemed to have taken up residence in Chris's thighs. With every beat, her muscles contracted a fraction and her bones seemed to vibrate. She was sweating in places she didn't know could sweat and her heart rate seemed to have shifted up a gear. Funny, when she was out clubbing for fun, she never noticed these reactions. She was too absorbed in the beats, too fixated on having fun with Sinead or whoever, too alive to the possibility of the night to feel the anxiety the music was creating in her tonight.

She was moving through the dancers, working round the fringe of the dance floor, leading with her ID, then fanning out the photos, making them stop and look. A few times, she'd had to grab T-shirts and go nose to nose with those either too recalcitrant or too high to want to co-operate. Every now and again, she would catch a glimpse of Kevin or Paula going through the same routine.

Kudos to Paula for coming back. Chris had been surprised when she'd seen the young detective moving through the crowd at the bar, but she'd been bloody delighted to learn about her success in Dore. Earlier, she'd heard about Carol and Sam picking up Rhys Butler. So now they had two avenues to pursue. One way or another, the search for Robbie Bishop's killer was picking up the momentum it needed.

Sinead might as well have stayed on with her friends in Edinburgh for the weekend, Chris thought. The way things were going, it didn't look like she was going to have a whole lot of free time in the immediate future. But hey, that was the way this job went. And the flexibility Carol Jordan had built into MIT meant she had more down time than she'd ever had since she joined the police.

Only one regret in all of this. She didn't know a senior detective she respected who didn't carry a similar weight. Talking to Paula earlier had brought it all back. Chris had once worked with a young detective who would have been stellar if she'd lived long enough to make it as far as MIT. A cop who was just beginning to fly when some bastard clipped her wings for good. A woman that Chris had failed to avoid loving more than she should have. A death that she couldn't help shouldering some of the responsibility for. A gap that would always be there. A gap she tried to fill by doing the job as well as she possibly could.

'You sentimental cow,' Chris muttered under her breath. She pulled her shoulders back and moved into the eye line of the next dancer. It didn't matter who you did it for. What mattered was doing it.

Garbled chunks of code scrolled down the screen. Algorithms were constantly battering them, unravelling the clues and making the strings of numbers carry meaning again. Stacey leaned back, yawning. She had done as much as was humanly possible with Robbie Bishop's hard drive. Now it was up to the machines.

She got up from her ergonomically designed chair and stretched her arms over her head, feeling the creaks and crackles in her neck and shoulders. She crab-walked over to the window, moving muscles and joints cramped in one position for too long, then gazed down on the city below. So many people on the streets so late at night. Out there, trying to meet their needs. Hoping, searching, desperate.

Stacey turned away. That's what you got for being needy. Friday night in Temple Fields, sad bastards craving something that would get them through the night. If they got unlucky, they might even get sucked into one of those greedy relationships that used up so much energy and resources.

She'd seen too many swallowed up that way. Good people with something out of the ordinary to give. But those needy emotional co-dependencies had fucked them up every time. If she did get it together with Sam Evans, it would never be that sort of cannibalistic, draining thing. Because the one thing she knew was that she was not going that way. Nobody was going to come between her and the mysteries she wanted to unpick, the solutions she was going to find.

Her parents wanted her to marry and have children. They had this strange notion that first Stacey, then her husband and their children were going to take over the family chain of Chinese supermarkets and food wholesalers. They'd never understood how different her destiny was from that. No marriage to come between her and her machines. If her biological clock demanded children, well, there were ways to deal with that and enough money to make it as convenient as she wanted.

Meet your own needs, that was what it was about. Sam would be nice to play with, but she could manage perfectly well without him. Barefoot, she padded across the loft, stripping off her clothes as she went. On to the big bed, hand reaching automatically for the remotes. The home cinema screen sprang to life, the DVD player kicked in. On the screen, a woman thrust a dildo into a man who in turn was fucking another woman's mouth. Their grunts and moans spilled out into the antiseptic air of Stacey's flat. She rummaged among the covers till she found her vibrator. She spread her legs.

She was ready to roll.

The strobe lights pulsed and the music thundered. It was like being in the middle of a storm, Sam thought, his feet skittering to keep the beat. He moved well, dance the only language that allowed him to express everything he normally held in close check. And tonight was one of those times when he truly wanted to get the previous day out of his system. The shitty drive, the unfairness of the bollocking from Jordan, the mortification of being taken prisoner by their suspect, the drudgery of hanging around while Butler had emergency dental treatment – today had not been one to cut out and keep.

Driving back from Newcastle with Jordan and Butler, he'd been praying that she wouldn't want to go straight into interrogation. Thankfully, Butler had known his rights and demanded a duty solicitor. And the first thing his brief had insisted on was an eight-hour sleep break. Jordan had liberated him and within an hour, he'd been on the dance floor, dressed for action and ready to strut like a peacock.

For the longest time while he'd been growing up, the dance was enough. He couldn't remember when music hadn't made him want to move. Toe tap, knee bounce, hip swivel, shoulder sway, finger click. It had bemused his parents, neither of whom were anything other than special occasion dancers. His primary teacher had suggested dance classes, but his dad had vetoed it on the grounds of cissiness. Sam didn't care either way – he danced regardless, whenever he had the chance.

In his teens, he'd discovered the big deal. Girls loved a boy who loved to dance. Any lad who rescued them from the handbag circle was halfway to paradise after any given ballroom blitz. It had been his teenage one-way ticket to the moon.

These days, it still worked the old magic and it had the added advantage of keeping him fit. He couldn't get on the floor as often as he would like, but that just meant he had even more energy pent up. It was his only relaxation and he loved it.

As the clock turned midnight, Sam was playing to the girl gallery. He drank half a bottle of mineral water and poured the rest over his head. Knowledge was the power. But dance was the glory.

Across town, Yousef Aziz lay on his back, fingers locked between his head and the pillow he'd had since childhood, a pillow that smelled comfortingly of himself. Tonight, its familiarity held none of its customary subliminal reassurance. Tonight, all Yousef could think of was what lay ahead of him. It was his last chance for sound sleep, but he knew that wasn't going to happen. It didn't matter. The last few weeks had taught him that there were other sources of energy.

In the other bed, Raj snored softly, his duvet rising and falling with each breath. Not even the death of his idol could disturb his rest. Every night, he was spark out by the time Yousef came to bed, and nothing seemed to rouse him. Not the overhead light, not the insistent beep of a Gameboy, not the jangle of bhangra nor the rustle of sweet wrappers. The boy slept as if innocence was his own personal invention.

Innocence. No question that Yousef had lost that. He'd learned to look at the world in a different way, and tomorrow the world would learn to do the same with him. He almost wished he'd be around to see what they all had to say. He didn't like having to leave his parents and his brothers to face the music on his behalf. But there was no other way.

All over Bradfield, people were sleeping together for the last time. Some loved each other, some barely tolerated each other, some were indifferent to each other. What they had in common was that they had no idea that their lives were about to be sundered. As far as they were concerned, it was just another Friday night. Some had particular rituals – a Chinese takeaway, a DVD rental and perfunctory sex; a swim and a sauna at the health club; or a game of Monopoly or Cranium or Risk with the kids. Others played Friday night by ear – a few drinks then a curry; dinner on their knees in front of the TV; last-minute tickets for a rock gig at the BEST arena; or a joint wander round the aisles of Tesco. No matter what, it would be the last time they'd do these things together. The events of that evening would take on a kind of hallowed significance because of what was about to happen.

All over Bradfield, couples were sleeping together for the last time. And there was nothing they could do to change that.

List 1

1. Be a millionaire by the time I'm thirty

2. Play professional football in the premiership

3. Own a house on Dunelm Drive

4. Drive my own Ferrari

5. Cut a CD that makes the charts

6. Date a top model

Saturday

It was getting easier. Tony wasn't dreaming it. He'd woken up just after six, needing to pee. It had taken less effort and less time to get on to his crutches, and he was sure he was managing to put more weight on his shattered knee. Maybe he could persuade the physio to let him try the stairs today.

He got back into bed and luxuriated in the relief of being horizontal again. Time to get back in touch with the world. He pulled the table over and booted up the laptop. Among the new emails, the one from Paula leapt out at him. Written at 2.13 a.m., it said, **Looks like you were right. Positive ID in the pub in Dore. More later. Well done, Doc, good to see you've not lost your touch.**

Tony made a fist and gave the air a tiny punch. It might not seem much, but from where he was sitting right now, it was a big deal. Profiling was like walking out on the tightrope. Confidence was a crucial part of the performance. If you didn't believe in yourself, if you didn't trust your instincts and your judgement, you ended up hedging your bets so much that your profile was worthless. It was an incremental process.

If you got something right, it made you feel better about doing it next time, and that increased your chance of being useful. Conversely, you only needed to fuck up once and you started from ground zero next time.

So, given that he was recovering from major surgery and feeling slow as a storyline in *The Archers*, and given that Carol had already rubbished the idea, getting it right about Danny Wade made him feel pretty damn good about himself. If the same person had killed Danny and Robbie, he should be thinking about what connected the victims to each other and to their killer. Maybe he could be useful from a hospital bed after all.

The flat Jana Jankowicz shared with her boyfriend was spotless. It smelled of polish and air freshener. It had obviously come furnished. Nobody that neat and clean would have chosen such scruffy, unmatched and flimsy items. What made it feel like a home were the hand-quilted throws on the sofa and the photos on the walls – printed on a colour printer and laminated, a cheap and cheerful alternative to professional prints and expensive frames. Jana, a round-faced, dark haired woman with an elusive prettiness, faced Paula over a scrubbed Formica-topped table, its edges chipped and scarred. Between them, an enamel pot of strong coffee and an ashtray. The presence of the ashtray explained the strong chemical smell of synthetic fragrances, Paula thought. Her sinuses would go on a protest strike if she had to live here.

Jana had asked no questions about Paula's reason for being there. She had agreed to the interview with genial resignation and had greeted her politely. It was as if she had decided the safest way to cope with the police in a foreign country was to be meekly co-operative. Paula had a sneaking feeling it wasn't Jana's normal style.

Jana thumbed her way through the photos for a second time. She shook her head. 'I have never seen any of these men with Mr Wade,' she said, her English only faintly accented. She was, she told Paula, a qualified teacher of English and French back in Poland. Skills her country couldn't afford too well right now. She and her fiancé were here to make enough money to buy a house back in Poland. Then they'd go home. They could manage to make ends meet if they didn't have rent to pay, Jana reckoned.

She paused at the shot of Jack Anderson. 'This man, though. I think I've seen him, but I don't know where or when.'

'Maybe he came to the house?' Paula offered her cigarettes to Jana. She took one and they both lit up while Jana frowned at the photo.

'I think he came to the house but not to see Mr Wade,' she said slowly, exhaling a thin stream of smoke. 'He was selling something. I don't remember. He had a van.' She closed her eyes, her brow furrowed. 'No, it's no use. I can't remember. It was a while ago.' She shook her head, apologetic. 'I can't be certain.'

'Never mind,' Paula said. 'Did you ever hear Mr Wade mention a man called Jack Anderson?'

Jana drew on her cigarette and shook her head. 'You have to understand, Mr Wade didn't talk about anything personal. I didn't even know he came from Bradfield.'

'What about football? Did he ever mention a footballer called Robbie Bishop?'

Jana looked confused. 'Football? No, model railways. That was what Mr Wade was interested in.' She spread her hands. 'He never watched football.'

'That's fine. Did anybody come to the house to visit Mr Wade?' Paula inhaled. Even if the interview wasn't very productive, at least she could smoke. That wasn't something you could say about many interviews these days. Even police interview rooms were non-smoking, which some prisoners claimed was a breach of their human rights. Paula tended to agree with them.

Jana didn't even have to think. 'Nobody,' she said. 'But I don't think that was a reason to pity him. Some people are happier on their own. I think he was like that. He liked that I was there to cook and clean, but he didn't want me to be his friend.'

'Don't take this the wrong way . . .' Paula gave a helpless little shrug, the kind that says, *I have to ask this and I wish I didn't.* 'Do you know what he did for sex? I mean, he was a young man, presumably he had sexual desires . . .'

Jana didn't seem in the least offended. 'I have no idea,' she said. 'He was never improper with me. I don't think he was gay, though.' Paula raised an eyebrow. Jana grinned. 'No gay porn. But sometimes, those magazines you can get at the newsagents. Nothing very bad. But girls, not boys. Sometimes he would go out in the car without the dogs for a couple of hours. When he came back, he seemed to be a bit embarrassed and he would usually take a bath. Maybe he went to prostitutes, I don't know.' She gave Paula a shrewd look. 'Why are you asking these questions?

Are you maybe starting to believe I am telling the truth about not making the pie?'

'It's possible Mr Wade's death is connected to a murder in Bradfield. If that's the case then yes, it would appear that you've been telling the truth,' Paula said.

'It would be good if that happened,' Jana said. A wry smile twisted her plump lips. 'Getting a job as a housekeeper when the newspapers print that you poisoned your last boss is a bit hard.'

'I can see that.' Paula shared Jana's smile. 'But if we're right about the connection, you can bet there will be even more publicity about you not making the pie than there ever was when we thought you had. Maybe that'll act as a reference.' She drew the pictures together and put them back in their envelope. 'You've been a big help,' she said.

'I wish I knew more,' Jana said. 'For his sake as well as mine. He was a good employer, you know. Not demanding, very grateful. I do not think he was accustomed to having someone to do things for him. It would be good if you found the person who killed him.'

Rhys Butler sat with his left arm across his narrow chest, hand cupping his right elbow, right hand covering his mouth and chin. His shoulders hunched, he glared at Carol Jordan from under his gingery brows. His red hair stood up in spikes and clumps, a classic night-in-the-cells hairdo. 'My client will be pursuing a claim against Bradfield Metropolitan Police for the assault against him,' his solicitor said sweetly, pushing a strand of her long black hair behind her ear with a perfectly shaped and painted fingernail.

Bloody Bronwen Scott, Carol thought. *Proof that the devil wears Prada.* Just her luck that the duty solicitor from the night before had been one of the baby lawyers in Scott's high-profile criminal law firm. And of course, since the case had the potent combination of Robbie Bishop, Carol Jordan and a possibly lucrative civil action against the police, Bronwen herself had grabbed it with both hands. In her immaculately tailored suit and full make-up, she was clearly prepared for the 'spontaneous' press interviews she'd doubtless be conducting later that morning. And so the old adversaries faced off across the table again. 'Good to know he's come to a decision,' Carol said. 'Me, I'm still pondering whether to pursue an action against your client for false imprisonment.'

Sam leaned forward. 'Not to mention he shouldn't have legged it the minute he found out we were police officers. Verging on resisting arrest, that is.'

Bronwen gave them both a pitying look and shook her head, as if to say she'd expected better from them. 'My client is still experiencing some pain as a result of your actions. Nevertheless, he is willing to answer your questions.' She spoke as if this were an extraordinary favour granted from a great height.

Carol's confidence took another knock. In her experience, Bronwen Scott's clients tended to go 'no comment', which translated in Carol's mind to, 'I did it.' That she was allowing Rhys Butler to talk to them told Carol that the chances were good she was wasting her time. Still, this might be the one time when a stupid client had managed to overrule the feisty Ms

Scott. She pulled her thoughts together and smiled at Butler. 'Sorry to spoil what must have been a good week for you,' she said pleasantly.

His forehead wrinkled like skin on rice pudding. 'What d'you mean?' he mumbled through his hand.

'Robbie Bishop dying, of course. That must have cheered you up.' Butler looked away and said nothing. 'You probably think that he deserved it,' she continued. 'I mean, we know you didn't think much to the way he treated Bindie.'

Butler glared at her. He let his hand fall from his face and spoke with venom. 'Bindie chucked him ages ago. Why would I care what happened to him?'

'Well, I would think you wouldn't want them to get back together again.'

Butler shook his head. 'No way. She wouldn't lower herself. She's just waiting for the right time so we can be together.'

'And now Robbie's dead, that time can't be far away.'

'Don't say anything, Rhys,' his solicitor butted in. 'Don't let her wind you up. Just answer the questions.'

'You want a question? OK. Where were you between ten p.m. the Thursday before last and four o'clock on the Friday morning?' Carol fixed him with an unblinking stare.

'At home. On my own, before you ask. But I was at work until six and back at work on Friday at eight. And I don't have a car. Just a bike. I'm fast but I'm not that fast,' Butler said, his attempt at an insolent leer turned into a wince by the pain in his mouth.

'There's trains,' Sam said. 'Two and a half to three hours, Newcastle to Bradfield. Depending on whether it's non-stop or change at York. You could have borrowed a car. Or nicked one. Whatever, it's do-able.'

'Except that I didn't do it. I was in Newcastle all night.'

They'd have to canvass the stations and train staff, Carol thought. She'd have liked to have done that before they'd arrested Butler, but it had been clear as soon as they'd picked him up off the ground behind his house that he was not going to accompany them voluntarily. She'd had to arrest him to be sure he didn't do a runner. And now the clock was ticking and she had no evidence. 'Did you think you were doing Bindie a favour, getting rid of Robbie?'

'Whoever got rid of him did her a favour, but it wasn't me,' he said stubbornly.

'Are you sure about that? Because I reckon poison would be right up your street,' Sam came in, as agreed in advance. 'Let's face it, when you tried to take him on like a man, Robbie gave you a proper coating. There was no way you could take him in a fair fight. Poison, now that's more like it. A man can't fight back against poison.'

Butler flushed, the colour ugly on his pale, freckled skin. 'I made my point. I made Bindie see that people who really cared about her were prepared to stand up for her. And she got rid of him. I never killed him.'

'My client has made himself clear, Chief Inspector. I suggest you confine yourselves to questions rather than insinuation and innuendo.' Scott made a note on her pad.

'Pharmacology, that's the line of work you're in,

262

right?' Carol said, hoping the tangent would unsettle him.

'That's right,' Butler said.

'So you'll know all about ricin?'

'You probably know more about ricin than I do. I'm a lab technician in a company that makes cough medicine. I wouldn't know a castor bean if it arrived on toast.'

There was a moment's grisly silence. Carol could have sworn she saw Bronwen Scott momentarily roll her eyes. 'So you do know where it comes from,' Carol said.

'So does half the country,' Butler said, his voice rising. 'All that stuff in the papers about terrorists making ricin? And now Bishop dying from it? We all know where it bloody comes from.'

Carol shook her head. 'I didn't remember. I had to look it up after Robbie was diagnosed. I bet most people did. But you remember.'

Butler turned to his lawyer. 'Are you going to put a stop to this? They've got nothing on me.'

Scott gave a smile that showed little sharp teeth. Carol thought she'd probably learned it from a piranha. 'My client's right. This is a fishing expedition. Unless you've got anything that you have not disclosed this far, you've got no grounds for keeping us here. I want you to release my client without charge right now. Because we are done here. He's not saying another word, and you have nothing.'

The worst of it was, she was right. 'Police bail,' Carol said, getting to her feet. 'We'll be back round this table again, Ms Scott.'

Bronwen Scott smiled again. 'Not until you get

your act together, Chief Inspector Jordan. You'll be hearing from us about the assault suit.'

Carol watched them leave, then gave a rueful shrug. 'That'll teach me to be impatient,' she said. 'They're going to be laughing about us from John O'Groats to Land's End.' She gave herself a shake. 'Next time you try to blindside one of your colleagues, Sam, see if you can make it worth our while, eh?'

When Carol got back to the MIT room, Chris and Paula were waiting for her. They both looked as if they could have used a few more hours' sleep, and Paula was looking distinctly shifty. 'Any luck with Butler?' Chris asked.

'We've got nothing and he's got bloody Bronwen Scott.' There was no need to say more. She stifled a yawn, told herself she did not need a drink and settled into her chair. 'What about you two? Any joy last night at Amatis?'

The other two exchanged a look. 'Some joy, but not at Amatis,' Chris said, shifting in her seat. 'I agreed to let Paula pursue another line of inquiry –'

'That's not how it was, chief,' Paula interrupted. 'It wasn't Sergeant Devine's responsibility. I talked her into it. It's down to me. If there's going to be any trouble, it's all down to me.'

'What are you two on about?' Carol said, amused at their earnestness. 'If we're making progress, I don't much care who's responsible. Spit it out, Paula. What was your other line of inquiry?'

Paula stared at her feet. 'I don't know if you know, but Dr Hill's been . . . helping me get myself back together,' she said, obviously struggling. 'I was going to quit. But he got me to see things a different way.'

'I know how good he is at that,' Carol said gently. She too had needed his talent for repair, though she suspected Paula had gained more from the process because of the lack of intimacy between them.

Paula looked up and met Carol's eyes, defiance in the line of her jaw. 'I owe him. So when he asked me to go and see him yesterday, I didn't hesitate. He told me about another case he believed to be connected to Robbie Bishop. He told me you had already dismissed the idea, and I have to say I wasn't surprised when he explained how thin it was.'

Carol managed to keep her face still, but inside her composure had evaporated. What the hell was he playing at? At the very least, this felt like lack of faith. At the worst, it felt like betrayal. How could he pluck out one of her own team and use that detective to try to show her how the job should be done? 'Are you about to tell me you've been making inquiries into the death of Daniel Wade?' she said, her voice dangerously precise.

Paula tensed in her chair but didn't flinch. 'Yes, chief.'

Carol tilted her head to one side, considering Paula with the same disdain she gave prisoners in the interview room. 'And remind me, Detective Constable McIntyre, when exactly you resigned from MIT and commenced your employment with Dr Hill?'

'It's not like that,' Paula began. 'I owe him.'

'You had a task assigned to you in a murder inquiry, and you chose to abandon that because a civilian who occasionally works with this unit told you to go and do something else?' Carol's voice would have stilled a storm. She could see her words cut into Paula and she was petty enough at that moment to be glad.

To her surprise, Chris took up the cudgels. 'I think what's important here is what Paula found out, guv. You can see she's not proud of what she's done, but there's no question that she has got a result. She's a good copper and she doesn't deserve a caning for going out on a limb. We all do that from time to time.' Her eyes challenged Carol. They'd had over-lapping service in the Met. Carol knew that Chris Devine was bound to know more about her than anybody else on her squad.

'There'll be time to deal with the disciplinary side of this after the investigation's over and done with,' she said coldly, not wanting to admit the fear Chris's words had provoked in her. Paula had got a result. Which meant Carol had been wrong to disregard Tony's opinion. Was she losing it? Was she cutting her nose off to spite her face because he'd seen things she should have but hadn't? Was the drink taking its toll on her judgement? God only knew she'd seen that happen with plenty of others. 'What did Dr Hill have you do?'

Looking shaken, Paula told Carol about her trip to the pub and her interview with Jana Jankowicz. She placed the photo of Jack Anderson on the desk. 'This is the man Carlos identified. Jana thinks he came to the house when Danny was out, but she can't remember why or when.'

'We didn't get any positive IDs on Anderson at Amatis, but one of the barmen thinks he could have been the bloke with Robbie that Thursday night,' Chris added. 'All a bit vague, but we thought it might be worth getting Carlos in to work with Stacey to see if we can turn that pic into a better likeness. Different hair, a bit of computer enhancement, that sort of thing.'

Carol felt the rip of conflicting emotions. Part of her wanted to nurse her anger and let them feel the rough edge of her tongue. And the other part of her wanted to congratulate them and set the wheels in motion to find Jack Anderson and bring him in. Even as she recognized the split, the cop in her was battering the angry child into submission. At the same moment, she saw Paula recognize her shift and relax a fraction. 'Fuck it,' Carol said, a wry smile creeping out in spite of herself. 'You have no idea how much I hate being wrong. But next time, Paula – if there is a next time – bring it to me before you go off on one of Tony's hunches. He's not always right, you know. And I will always listen.' As she spoke, she saw Paula's shoulders drop. There was still a hot coal of anger in Carol's heart, but she was reserving that for the person who really deserved it. 'So. Who is Jack Anderson and where do we find him?'

'That,' said Chris with a sigh, 'is where we run into a bit of a problem. According to Stacey, he doesn't exist.'

'Meaning what?' Carol was still prickly, in no mood for guessing games. 'We have his photo. That must have come from somewhere.'

'We've spoken to the person who sent it to us. And to the third person in the original photo. They both say the same thing. They were at school with Jack Anderson and he used to turn up at the same pub quiz as them. Tuesday nights at the Red Lion in

Downton. He was in a team that called themselves The Funhouse. About three years ago, he stopped coming. Our lads asked The Funhouse why Anderson had dropped out and they said he'd moved to Stockport. And that's where that bit of the trail goes cold,' Paula said.

'Because, according to Stacey, he didn't go to Stockport,' Chris continued. 'Or if he did, he's not registered to vote. He doesn't pay council tax, he's not in the phone book, he's not registered for VAT and he hasn't filed a tax return for four years. He hasn't filed for bankruptcy and he doesn't have a current credit card. Doesn't it scare you what that girl can find out on a Saturday morning?'

Carol shivered theatrically. 'I try not to think about it. What about family? Old school friends?'

'We're working on it,' Paula said. 'According to the bloke who gave us the photo in the first place, Anderson's dad was in the army. Apparently he was killed in the first Gulf War, not long after Anderson started at Harriestown High. Our source isn't sure he's remembering it right, but he thinks it was a friendly-fire incident.'

'That's gotta hurt,' Carol said. 'What about his mum?'

Chris looked at her notebook. 'I'm still trying to get detail on this, but we're being told she committed suicide the summer after Anderson's first year at university. Sounds like she waited till he was sort of settled then did what she had to do. We're not sure which university. One guy thought Leeds, the other Manchester. And we're not sure what he studied either. Might have been biology, might have been zoology. Might have been fucking needlework, frankly. I think the pair of them were making it up as they went along by that point.' She shook her head in disgust. 'Why do they try so hard to please us?'

'Probably because we have the power to throw their arses in jail, Chris,' Paula said pointedly.

'All right, all right, enough of the stand-up routine. Piss off, the pair of you. And don't come back till you've got everything there is to know about Jack Anderson. Including his current address.' She got up and grabbed her jacket from the coat stand. 'I'm going to swing by Robbie's mum and dad's house. Maybe they remember Jack Anderson. You never know. And then I'm going to talk to a man about officer deployment. Just as well he's already in hospital, he won't have far to go to get fixed.'

Ex-Detective Superintendent Tom Cross owned one of the most expensive houses in Bradfield, thanks to a spectacular win on the football pools some years before his enforced retirement. His pension was adequate to support him and his wife comfortably. But nothing could have convinced him he was lucky. There are some people who are incapable of contentment, and Tom Cross was one of them.

He stared moodily out of the bathroom window at a perfectly groomed lawn sloping gently down to the River Brade, where a neat day boat was moored to a concrete jetty. Miserable bloody day for the game, he thought. No matter how well wrapped up he was, his nose would be a bulb of ice by half-time.

Cross turned back to the mirror, switching on his

electric shaver and applying it to his heavy jowls. His pale green eyes were prominent, responsible for his old nickname of Popeye. Like his cartoon namesake, Cross still had the massive muscular shoulders and upper arms of the rugby prop forward he'd once been. The mirror didn't reveal the massive gut that years of fast food and beer had created; Cross had always tended to avoid the truth whenever it made him uncomfortable. Some would say that had been the source of his professional downfall. Cross himself would have laid it at the door of that sanctimonious bitch Carol Jordan.

He shaved swiftly, then ran a deep basin of warm water. He immersed his whole head, running his fingers over the grey bristle that surrounded his bald crown. He rose gasping from the water, his little cupid's bow mouth spraying droplets over the marble sink surround. Bloody Jordan and bloody John Brandon. Pair of prigs. Jordan had stepped into his shoes and Brandon had put the word out that Tom Cross was a cheat and a liar. It had made it bloody hard to get his mitts on the sort of security work he deserved. At least today, before he froze his arse off watching the Vics struggle to make headway without Robbie Bishop, he'd be working with somebody who recognized his worth.

The letter from Harriestown High had come out of the blue. He'd not been back there since his sixteenth birthday, when he'd buggered off and got himself a job on a building site till he could get taken on as a police cadet. But according to the letter from the head, the school now had a policy of employing former pupils wherever possible. When it came to planning security for a major fundraising event, Tom Cross's name had been the first to come up.

As invited, he'd called the number on the letterhead. To his surprise, it was an answering machine which simply said, 'You have reached Harriestown High School. Please leave your name and number and we will call you back as soon as possible.' The call back came within five minutes, from the head himself. 'Sorry about the answering machine,' he'd said. 'You wouldn't believe how many threatening and abusive phone calls we get from parents.'

Cross snorted. 'I'd believe you all right. In my day, if the school or the police got in touch with your parents, you were in for the high jump. Now, the parents take the kids' part and we're the ones getting the kicking.'

'Quite so. Thank you for getting back to me. If you're interested in this project, I think the best thing is for you and Jake Andrews to have a meeting. Jake's organizing the whole thing. He has all the details at his fingertips. It's going to be quite the do. Robbie Bishop's already pledged to support it with his presence, and he's persuaded his former fiancée to DJ a session. She works for Radio One, you know,' he added conspiratorially. 'I'll have Jake call you.'

And later that day, Jake had indeed called. They'd had a preliminary meeting over lunch in a very fine French restaurant in town. The sort of place Cross wouldn't normally have chosen, but he would admit they knew how to cook steak and chips. Now, they were going to look at the detailed plans, including the layout of the venue, the stately home of Lord and Lady Pannal. Though God alone knew who they were going to get to headline the event now that Robbie Bishop had popped his clogs.

Cross slapped aftershave on his cheeks, never flinching at the sting. He glanced at his watch, hanging up by the mirror. He'd better get a move on. He was meeting Jake at a pub on the far side of Temple Fields. They'd have a swift half, then go to Jake's flat for lunch. The lad had been apologetic. 'Sorry about having to meet in the pub. It's just that my place is a nightmare to find. Everybody gets lost. I've learned it's just easier to meet in the pub first. All the stuff we need is back at the flat, so I'll do us some lunch and we can work while we eat. I'm a vegetarian, but don't worry, I do cook meat for my visitors,' he'd added with a smile.

Cross walked through to his dressing room and pulled a pair of thermal long johns from his underwear drawer. Thermals on the outside, a good lunch on the inside. He'd survive an afternoon at the football no trouble.

Yousef slammed the door of the bedsit and leaned against it, eyelids pressed tight together, the lump in his throat set to choke him. He'd worked so hard to keep his aim true. He'd silently recited his motivation like a mantra, morning noon and night. He'd held fast to his conviction that his heart and mind were as one. That what he was doing was not only for the best, but also the only possible way forward.

It wasn't as if he'd tried to kid himself that there would be no consequences. He'd allowed himself to think of how it would be for his family. Intellectually, he'd known they would be shocked and distraught, unable to believe him capable of this. But they'd get over it, he'd told himself. They would get past it, write him out of their lives. The community would sustain them. They'd be all right. Not everyone would agree with what he'd done, but they wouldn't cast out the whole Aziz family as a result.

But this morning, the enormity of it all had hit him like a train. Not that anything special had happened. They'd all done their usual Saturday-morning stuff. His mother to the local Asian mini-market to buy halal meat, vegetables and fruit for the weekend. His father to the mosque for prayers and conversation with his friends. Raj to the madrassa for an hour of Koranic studies. Sanjar in bed, sleeping off the week. And Yousef to the warehouse to make sure everything was running as it should. It had been strange, knowing he was doing it for the last time. Strange, but not emotional. It was hard to be emotional about an old factory and a bunch of workers who could never become his friends.

The killer had been Saturday lunch. Traditionally, they ate together. His mother always prepared some slow-cooked miracle of spicy lamb and vegetables, with a pile of chapattis to soak it up. It was a brief interlude of family time in a life where everyone was busy with their own concerns. The knowledge that he was never going to experience it again had made it almost impossible for Yousef to eat. And that in turn had provoked his mother to wonder what was wrong with him. She'd only let up when Raj had started whingeing because Sanjar had to make an emergency delivery in Wakefield so he wouldn't be able to drop Raj off to meet his friends for the football.

'Don't worry, Raj, Yousef will take you,' his mother had said.

'I can't,' he said. 'I arranged to go over to Brighouse, to meet some guy about a new contract. I haven't got time.'

'What do you mean, you haven't got time? It won't take you far out of your way to take the boy to meet his friends,' his mother insisted.

'What new contract?' his father demanded.

'Nobody ever bothers about me,' Raj wailed.

Sanjar looked at him and winked. He clearly didn't believe in the new contract either, but whatever he thought Yousef was up to, there was no chance he'd be anywhere near the truth.

And that's when he'd nearly lost it. His last meal with his family, and it was turning into a bickering match. When they all looked back, there would be no warm memory of a happy family meal, when they still held fast to their illusion of who he was. There would only be the bitter taste of bad feeling.

He'd had to get out then, before he broke down in front of them. Tears had blurred his vision on the drive over to the bedsit. He loved them, and he was never going to see them again.

Yousef shook his head as if to shake off his painful thoughts. There was no going back. He had to look forward. He had to think about a glorious future, when his dreams would come true. He pushed himself away from the door. The last phase still had to be carried out.

Carefully, he packed a catering-sized ghee tin with the TATP, placing the gunpowder engine from a model rocket kit in the middle. He fastened thin plastic-coated wires to the engine with little alligator clips then attached them to an electronic ignition device wired up to an electronic timer in a small bundle held together with packing tape. He hadn't made this part of the bomb; he had no skills in this area. But it had been explained to him. He was to be ready with the bomb in place at 3.30, two-thirds of the way through the first half. He was to set the timer for forty minutes, so it would go off in the middle of the second half, leaving time enough for him to make his escape. It was simple. Kept simple to minimize what could possibly go wrong.

Concentrating on the assembly of the bomb calmed him down. By the time he'd finished and packed it in the bottom of Imran's toolbox, he was steady again.

Yousef carried the toolbox down to Imran's van with great care. He knew how volatile the TATP was, how easily the friction of movement could trigger the chain reaction that would blow him and the rest of the house sky high. He placed it gently on the ground while he opened the back of the van, then laid it on the foam pad he'd already prepared. He closed the doors carefully then stepped away from the van. He wished he smoked.

He checked his watch. Almost time to set off. He wanted to arrive at the staff and players' entrance about five minutes before kick-off, when the security crew were too busy to pay too much attention to him. Allowing for traffic, he should leave in about five minutes.

Yousef got into the van and fumbled the keys into the ignition. His hands were clammy with sweat. 'Calm,' he told himself. No reason to panic. No reason to be afraid. Nothing could go wrong.

He didn't know about the third component, taped between the ignition and the timer. A component that would change all Yousef's carefully laid plans.

Tony was feeling very pleased with himself. Today, he was the man who had climbed half a flight of stairs. OK, he'd had a certain amount of difficulty getting back down, but he had made it to the landing. Nine steps up and nine steps down. And not a single fall. He'd been so exhausted afterwards he'd wanted to lie down and weep, but he would leave that bit out when he told the tale.

Tony fired up the laptop and went to Bradfield Victoria's site. Because he wasn't good at remembering to keep office hours, he'd subscribed to their private TV channel at the start of the season. So wherever he was, as long as he had broadband access, he could watch the Vics' games live. He logged on and turned the volume down low. He didn't need to hear pre-match chat from a couple of second-rate retired footballers and a commentator who had fallen from grace with the networks. All they'd be talking about would be Robbie, and Tony didn't imagine for a moment they would have any useful insights to offer.

Thinking of Robbie reminded him that he ought to be trying to come up with something that would get Carol past the embarrassment of refusing to follow up his suggestion now it had turned out he'd been right. She was going to be pissed off with herself and the chances were that she would get it out of her system by being pissed off with him. Best to have something ready to head her off at the pass. The only trouble was what.

'What makes them right for you, Stalky? Is Harriestown High the important connection? What happened there to make you care so much?' He considered the options, but couldn't come up with something that could have linked Robbie Bishop and Danny Wade in their schooldays. 'But that changed,' he mused. 'By the time they died, they did have something in common. Rich men, both of them. And the rich are different. So they'd become different. They'd left the rest of Harriestown High in the dirt. They were lucky, you could say. Danny definitely. No skill in the lottery. Just blind luck. But Robbie was lucky too. Right club, right manager. We've all seen it go the other way – great talent pissed up against the wall.' He was struggling and he knew it. Two cases just didn't yield enough data. It was the hardest thing about his job. The more people who died, the easier it was for him.

So, nothing much to link the victims. What about the murder method? Plant poisons. It was like Dorothy L. Sayers or Agatha Christie. Some village murder mystery. 'Historically, poisoners were assassins or family members. But now we've got guns for the assassins, and forensic toxicology knocked family poisoning on the head a long time ago ... So why use it? It's hard to get your hands on, and getting hold of it leaves a trail. Its only advantage is if you don't get your kicks out of killing.' He nodded to himself. 'That's it, isn't it? What you like is not killing, it's having killed. You like the sense of power but you've not got a taste for the dirty work. It's almost as if you're keeping your distance. Your innocence. When you left them, they were fine. You don't have to see yourself as some low-life killer.' He paused for a moment, lost in thought. 'You can almost convince yourself you're giving them a chance. Maybe they'll be able to beat it, or maybe they won't. Maybe they'll get lucky. Or maybe their luck's just run out ... And speaking of running out, there are my boys.' On the screen, the familiar canary yellow shirts were emerging from the tunnel, black bands circling the upper arms of all the players. The Tottenham Hotspur players followed, also wearing black armbands, heads bowed.

The two teams lined up facing each other and Tony edged the volume up in time to hear the commentator say, '. . . for a minute's silence in memory of Robbie Bishop, who died tragically this week.'

Tony bowed his head and joined the silence. It seemed to pass almost too quickly. Then the crowd roared, the players shuffled their feet and moved into position. Robbie had been formally consigned to memory. Now it was showtime.

The streets around Victoria Park were choked with fans promenading towards the stadium. No cars allowed, held back and diverted by police officers in yellow fluorescent jackets. Just pedestrians and horses, the mounted division relishing home games for the peaceful exercise they almost invariably offered. Through the middle of the yellow streams of home fans was a demarcated ribbon of white, where Spurs supporters strutted their defiance in the enemy's territory.

There was another, smaller patch of white among the yellow. The A1 Electricals' van eased forward through a crowd reluctant to part for anything or anyone. Behind the wheel, Yousef prayed steadily, his lips barely moving, his mind racing. If he concentrated on the details, he didn't have to confront the horror of what he was about to do. The paperwork had got him past the first checkpoint. A policeman stopping traffic heading for the stadium had glanced over the two fake faxes and Yousef's equally false ID and waved him through without comment. Next came the acid test.

He checked the time. He was right on schedule. The Grayson Street stand loomed ahead of him, the tall wrought-iron gates with the club crest clearly visible. The entrance to the car park for staff and players was a dozen yards past the gates, the way blocked by a barrier and a cordon of security men. He pulled his baseball cap further down so it better obscured his features from above.

Yousef passed the gates, tapping his horn to clear a way through the supporters. The road was even more clogged than usual because the pavement was entirely occupied by the shrine to Robbie Bishop. His photo smiled out at Yousef again and again, the confident grin of a man who sees the world turning his way. He'd been so wrong, Yousef thought.

He swung the wheel round, pointing the van at the barrier. As he drew close, he was surrounded by security men. They looked identically menacing with their black-and-yellow Vics bomber jackets, black jeans and shaved heads. He lowered his window and smiled. 'Emergency electrical repair,' he said. 'There's a problem with the mains supply under the Vestey stand.' He produced the faxes. 'If it blows, there'll be no power to corporate hospitality.'

The nearest security guard sneered. 'Poor bastards won't be able to find their prawn sandwiches in the dark. Gimme a minute, let me show these to the guy on the barrier.' He took the paperwork and went over to the small cabin by the guard barrier. Yousef could see him showing the faxes to the man inside. He felt the sweat in his armpits and the small of his back.

'That's quite a display, innit?' he said to the guard who had stepped up to take the first one's place. 'Poor sod.'

'No kidding,' the guard said. 'What kind of evil bastard would do a thing like that?' He did a double take, as if only just realizing he was speaking to a young Asian male, the tabloid archetype of a contemporary bogeyman. 'Sorry, mate, I didn't mean … You know?'

'I know. We're not all like that,' Yousef said, his toes literally curling with discomfort. Not because he was lying, but because he was lying so cravenly. Before they could get into it any further, the first guard came back with the paperwork.

'You'll need to let me take a look in the back of the van,' he said.

Yousef turned off the engine, took out the keys and walked to the back of the van. He could feel his hands trembling, so he tried to put his body between the lock and the security man. He told himself that he had nothing to worry about, that it was all going to be OK. He swung the door open. The van was lined with cable holders and plastic boxes full of clips, fuses, screws and switches. Reels of various gauges of cable were piled together behind a fence of bungee cord, and Imran's toolbox sat to one side, a long squat metal box covered in chipped blue paint.

'You want to open the toolbox?' the security guard said.

'Sure.' Yousef swallowed hard and unclipped the lid. He spread the first layer open to reveal an array of pliers, wire strippers and screwdrivers. 'OK?' He laid his hand on the tray, as if he was going to open it further. His bowels were clenching, his bladder bursting. If the bastard guard didn't back off, the next thing he was going to see was a bomb.

The guard glanced over the tools. 'Looks like an electrician's kit to me. OK, mate,' he said. 'Park over at the far end.' He pointed to the extreme edge of the parking area. 'You'll see a gate over there. The security bloke there knows you're on your way. He'll let you in. You follow the walkway round the corner and it'll bring you to the staff entrance. They'll show you where you need to be.' He winked. 'They might even let you see a bit of the game if you get the job done quick.'

Yousef did as he was told, hardly able to believe it was all so easy. Once past that first barrier, it was clear that he was accepted as someone with a valid reason to be there. Ten minutes later, head down to avoid the CCTV cameras, he was carrying Imran's toolbox with its deadly cargo down a narrow service corridor under the middle tier of the giant cantilevered Vestey Stand. The stand, named after Albert Vestey, England and Bradfield Vics' legendary striker of the inter-war years, contained the media centre up on the top tier as well as the corporate hospitality boxes. As they walked, the ebb and flow of the fans' chanting and cheering accompanied their steps. Yousef was surprised by how loud it was. He'd thought it would be much quieter inside the stand, insulated by concrete and bodies. But here it was almost as strident as being one of the shouting spectators.

Yousef's destination was a small room off the service corridor where the electricity junction boxes were housed. From here, the electrical supply to the media centre and the corporate boxes was controlled. Immediately above, separated by a tracery of girders and poured concrete, was the partition wall between two boxes, each of which held a maximum of a dozen spectators. Both of those were flanked by identical boxes. All four boxes, like the others that stretched out on either side of them, were full of people enjoying food and drink at someone else's expense. The football, it often seemed, was incidental. What mattered was being there.

The guard who had accompanied Yousef from the staff entrance stopped in front of a grey door which featured a yellow plaque with a black lightning bolt on it. 'Here we go, mate,' he said, unlocking the door and opening up. He pointed to a house phone on the corridor wall a few feet away. 'Call down on that when you're done and I'll come and lock up behind you.' He pushed the door open, reached for the light switch then stood back, waving Yousef into the small space. 'And if you're done before full time, we'll find you somewhere to perch for the rest of the match.'

Yousef felt sick, but he managed to smile and nod. The door closed behind him with a soft click. The room was dim and cramped. It smelled of dust and oil. The junction boxes covered the far wall. Cables festooned the walls, their surfaces silted with greasy dust. He didn't think anyone was going to bother him here, not when there was a match going on a few hundred feet away. But to be on the safe side, he jammed the end of the toolbox against the door. If anyone tried to get in, he'd know about it.

Without warning, Yousef felt his throat tighten as tears welled up in his eyes. This was a terrible thing to be doing. It was the right thing, no doubt about that. The best way to achieve their goal. But he hated that he had to live in a world where things like this were necessary. Where violence became the only language that people listened to. Where violence was the only language available to those who were frustrated at every turn by the way the world was run. George Bush had been right, it was a crusade. Just not the one that bastard in the White House thought it was.

He rubbed his eyes with the back of his hand. This wasn't the time or the place for grief or for second thoughts. Yousef opened the toolbox and lifted out the top shelf. Underneath, wrapped in layers of bubble wrap, was the bomb. It didn't look much. Somehow, Yousef felt it should be grander. More of a statement than could be made by a ghee tin and a kitchen timer.

He checked his watch. He was doing just fine. Twelve minutes past three. He took out a roll of duct tape and fastened the bomb to a bunch of cables halfway up the wall. Then, his mouth dry and his stomach churning, he started to set the timer.

Two minutes in, and Phil Campsie had made a blinding run down the left side, only to be brought low by in a bruising but fair tackle. 'Oh no,' Tony cried.

'Oh no is right,' Carol said, marching in, all flags flying indignation. 'What the hell do you think you're doing?'

Tony gave her the bemused look of a man who has only been doing what men are supposed to do, not taking in her body language at all. 'I'm watching the footie,' he said. 'The Vics and Spurs. It's only just started, pull up a chair.'

Carol slapped the screen of his laptop shut. Tony looked outraged. 'What did you do that for?'

'How dare you suborn my staff to run around the countryside in pursuit of your little fantasies,' she shouted.

'Ah.' Tony grimaced. 'That would be Paula, then.'

'How could you? Especially after I said I didn't think there was any point?' Carol paced agitatedly to and fro.

'Well, that's precisely why I had to.' Tony eased his laptop open again. 'If I could have done it myself, I would have. But as it is, you're saved the embarrassment of having to admit you passed on the best lead you've got so far.'

'Bullshit. We have a suspect who is nothing to do with Danny Wade.'

Tony tapped the mouse pad to bring the match up again. 'And I have no doubt that you will also find he's nothing to do with Robbie Bishop. At least, not as far as his murder's concerned.' He gave her a brilliant smile. 'And now Paula has given you another lovely lead. I mean, she must have. Because if she'd drawn a blank, you'd never have been any the wiser.'

Carol stabbed her index finger at him. 'You are bloody impossible. You are bang out of order. Paula works for me, not for you.'

Tony gave a self-deprecating smile. 'I could say she helped me out in her own time,' he said. 'Because she likes me so much.'

Now it was Carol's turn to smirk. 'But that would be a lie. She did it on Bradfield Police's time, when she was supposed to be working for MIT.'

Tony shook his head, his blue eyes darkening as he prepared to play hardball. He looked at the game on his screen but his words were directed at Carol. 'You can't have people working completely undefined hours and then claim all of their waking time is dedicated to your service. Paula's entitled to breaks. You can't really complain if she rolls them up into one big slice of time off. I bet she didn't get eight hours clear between coming off duty last night and starting again this morning. Even your prisoners are entitled to that.'

Carol glared at him. 'I hate it when you twist things to suit yourself. You were out of order, and you know it. And Paula of all people. You know she's vulnerable.'

'I think when it comes to Paula's mental state, I'm probably a better judge than you.' He scrutinized her, trying to gauge how angry she still was. 'Come on, come and sit down and watch a bit of the football with me. The lads are playing their hearts out for Robbie. It'd bring tears to a glass eye, I promise you.'

'You can't just deflect this, pretend it didn't happen,' Carol said. But he could see she was softening.

'I'm not. I agree, I was out of order. All I can say is that normally, I would have done it myself. And I thought it was too important to a murder investigation to leave it undone. I will apologize to Paula for putting her in an awkward position, but I'm not going to apologize to you for putting your investigation on the right track.' He patted the arm of the chair next to the bed. 'Now, will you sit down and watch the bloody game?'

With obvious ill grace, Carol threw herself into the chair. 'You know I hate football,' she grumbled.

'We're the ones in yellow,' he said.

'Fuck off. I know that,' she said.

'So, are you going to tell me about Paula's brilliant new lead?' he said as Spurs gained possession and began to make ground.

'Hasn't she told you all about it herself?'

He grinned. 'No, we both understand the chain of command too well.'

'You ganged up on me,' she said. He could tell the storm was over.

'Be grateful we care enough to want to save you from falling on your arse. Like he just did.' He pointed at a Spurs player apparently tripping over a blade of grass.

As they watched, the commentary was drowned out by a tremendous roaring rumble. Smoke drifted across the screen, then a storm of debris began to rain down on one side of the pitch. Carol and Tony stared at the screen, dumbstruck. Then the commentator's voice, hysterical, shouting, 'Oh my God, oh my God, there's a hole . . . I can't hear. Oh my God, there are body parts . . . I think there's been a bomb. A bomb, here at Victoria Park. Oh Jesus Christ . . .'

Now the director had got his act together. The scene

changed from the pitch to what had been the Vestey Stand. In the centre of the middle tier, nothing could be seen except a billowing grey cloud of dust. In the rows of seats below the corporate boxes, people were stampeding for the aisles. The shot changed to a close-up of one of the exits, where some fans were fighting to get out while others were passing children over heads to get them clear. Then they were looking at the stand again, only this time there were flames licking the edges of the dust cloud and black spirals of smoke curling up as the dust cloud moved downwards. And now the people were screaming.

Carol was already on her feet and halfway to the door. 'I'll call you,' she said, opening the door and running. Tony barely noticed her going. He was transfixed by the unfolding of tragedy on the screen before him. Without taking his eyes off the laptop screen, he reached for the remote and turned on the TV. It was almost impossible to comprehend what he was seeing.

Bradfield had joined that most exclusive club. The Twin Towers. Kuta Beach. Madrid. London. A list no city wanted to join. But now Bradfield was among them.

And there would be work to be done.

Tom Cross had served most of his years in the police in the shadow of Irish Republican terrorism. Twelve dead in the M62 coach bombing, two kids blown to bits in Warrington town centre, over two hundred injured and a city centre devastated in Manchester. He and his colleagues had learned vigilance, but they'd also been taught what was expected of them.

So when the bomb went off in Victoria Park stadium, Cross's instincts were to move towards the seat of the explosion. The other 9,346 people in the Vestey Stand did not share his reaction. A floodtide of humanity surged for the aisles and the exits and Cross, sixteen rows below the hospitality boxes, put his head down, grabbed the back of his seat and let it flow over him.

As the press of bodies around him eased, he pulled himself hand over hand to the middle of the row, where there were no people. He started to clamber upwards as fast as he could, wishing he hadn't eaten so much of the delicious lamb stew Jake Andrews had served him for lunch. His stomach felt distended and tender, as if it was swollen to a drum, its contents swilling from side to side like rainwater in a discarded tyre. *Fuck*, he thought as he struggled upwards. Bodies everywhere and he was thinking about the state of his guts.

As Cross grew closer, he could see through the dust and smoke to the hole in the stand. Shattered concrete and twisted metal thrust out into the air, as if a giant fist had punched through from behind. Bodies lay at grotesque angles on the wreckage, most of them clearly dead, many of them lacking limbs. Through the claustrophobic ringing in his ears, he could hear the crackle of flame, the moans of the injured, the PA system begging people to leave in an orderly manner, the sound of distant sirens getting louder. He could smell blood and smoke and shit, taste them on his tongue. Carnage. That's what he was tasting.

The first person still breathing that he came across was a woman, hair and skin turned grey by the dust.

288

Her lower left leg was shattered, blood pulsing from the wound. Cross pulled the belt from her trousers and tied off a tourniquet above her knee. The blood slowed to an ooze. Her eyelids flickered then closed again. He knew the rules about not moving the injured, but if the fire travelled fast, she would be caught up in it. There was no real choice here. Cross slid his arms under the woman and lifted her, grunting with the effort. He stepped over debris, edging sideways till he came to an aisle. He laid her down carefully and went back for more, dimly aware that there were others joining him, some in the fluorescent jackets of the emergency services.

He had no sense of how much time passed. All he knew was the dirt and the blood and the nausea and the sweat pouring down his face and the pain in his guts and the bodies, always the bodies. He worked alone and with others, shifting debris, giving the kiss of life, moving bodies and telling the injured the old familiar lies. 'It's going to be all right. You're going to be fine. It's going to be all right.' It was never going to be all right again, not for any of the poor bastards caught in this shitstorm.

And all the time he was working, he was feeling worse and worse. He put it down to the shock and the exertion. His guts were cramping so much that he had to leave the rescue a couple of times to find a toilet. His bowels emptied in a gusher of liquid both times, leaving him feeling weak and feverish. The third time he tried to return to the bomb site, a paramedic stopped him on the stairs. 'No way, mate,' he said. 'You look terrible.'

Cross sneered. 'You don't look so great yourself,

pal.' He tried to push past, but didn't seem to have the strength. Baffled, he leaned against the wall, sweat pouring from him. He clutched his stomach as another spasm of pain shot through him.

'Here, put this on.' The paramedic handed him an oxygen mask and a portable gas cylinder. Cross obeyed. Shock and exertion, that's what it was. He barely noticed the other man reaching for his arm and taking his pulse. But he did notice that the paramedic looked worried. 'We need to get you to hospital,' he said.

Cross lifted the mask. 'Bollocks. There's people up there with serious injuries. That's who needs to be in hospital.' Again he tried to push past.

'Mate, I'd say you're minutes away from a heart attack. Please. Don't give those bastards the satisfaction of adding another number to the list. Come on, humour me. Let's walk down to the ambulances together.'

As Cross glared at him, his vision seemed to blur and an arrow of burning pain shot from his gut to the fingertips of his left hand. 'Jesus Christ,' he roared, stumbling and clasping his shoulder. The pain fled as swiftly as it had come, leaving him sweating and nauseous. 'OK,' he panted. 'OK.'

Carol made it to A&E in time to catch one of the emergency ambulances being despatched to Victoria Park. As they raced through the streets, siren screaming and blue light strobing, she was on the phone. First to Stacey in the office, telling her to send the rest of the team to meet her at the stadium. Then to John Brandon. He too was in motion, pulled away from a shopping expedition with his wife, who now found herself trying to drive like a police driver without the advantage of lights or siren. 'I'll be there as soon as I can,' he said. 'I know your first instincts are to help preserve life, but I don't want your team involved in the rescue and evacuation. We can't forget this is also a crime scene. Forensic teams are on their way, and your job is to work with them to make sure they can collect and preserve as much as possible.'

'Is it mine?' she asked.

'Only until the Counter Terrorism Command get here from Manchester,' Brandon said. 'They're on their way. They'll be with us within the hour. Then you'll have to step away. But till they get here, yes, the command is yours.'

'Will CTC take over the whole investigation?' Carol asked, snatching at a grab handle as they took a corner on what felt like two wheels.

'In effect, yes. You'll be working to them. I'm sorry, Carol. That's the way it is. They're the specialists.'

Her heart sank. Come tomorrow, she and her detectives would be no more than gofers for those arrogant bastards in CTC who thought being the saviours of mankind gave them the right to walk over anybody and anything in their way. She'd had enough dealings with the Anti-Terrorism Branch and the Special Branch before they'd been amalgamated into the new, bespoke CTC. She knew they thought they were the lords of creation and that people like her and her team were put on this earth to do their grunt work. Bad enough that there were likely dozens dead from a terrorist bomb. Traumatic enough for her team without having to deal with a bunch of outsiders who didn't know the ground and didn't have to take responsibility for their actions. They wouldn't be the ones left to mop up the consequences of shattered relationships among communities and between those communities and the ones left behind to police them.

'Any figures yet?' she asked, knowing it was pointless to complain to Brandon, as powerless in this as her team was.

'At least twenty. There will be more.'

'And the rest of the crowd? Where are we evacuating to?'

'Contingency plans say the school playing fields further down Grayson Street. But I suspect most of them are putting as much distance as possible between themselves and the stadium. It's going to be a nightmare, getting witness statements for this one.'

'We'll do our best. I need to go, we're nearly there,' Carol said, recognizing the swaying view through the windscreen. People were streaming past on either side, forcing the ambulance to slow to walking pace. It was like one of those war movies where an army of refugees were desperately fleeing the enemy.

At last, they made it into the parking area behind the Vestey Stand. Already, the cars parked there were blocked in by police cars and fire engines. The ambulances were parked along the outside edge, ready for a quick getaway. Even as Carol jumped out, one of the other ambulances sped past them, blues and twos.

From the outside, the stadium looked virtually untouched. There was a small hole in the outer skin of the towering stand, but it looked innocuous. The clues to what had happened here were elsewhere.

Hoses from the fire engines and the stadium's hydrants snaked along the ground and in through the turnstiles. Firefighters moved purposefully towards the stand, looking like astronauts in their protective gear. Paramedics hustled to and fro with assorted bits of kit. And in dribs and drabs, the injured, the dying and the dead were brought forth, carried and stretchered by paramedics and police.

Carol could barely take it in. Bradfield looked like Beirut. Or Bangladesh. Or some other faraway place on the news. It looked like the aftermath of a natural disaster, everyone caught on the hop, nobody really knowing what to do but somehow getting done what was essential. People milled around, some purposeful, others less so. And at the heart of it, the injured, the dying and the dead.

She pulled herself together. She had to find out who was in charge, gather her team and do what she could to secure the seat of the explosion. First, she fastened her ID on to the outside of her jacket. Then Carol approached the nearest uniformed cop. He'd just helped an elderly man with blood running down one side of his face into an ambulance and was about to head back to the stand. 'Constable,' she called, running the short distance over to him. He stopped and turned. His face was streaked with dirt and sweat, his uniform trousers filthy. 'DCI Jordan,' she said. 'Major Incident Team. Who's the officer in charge?'

He looked at her with a glazed look. 'Superintendent Black.'

'Where can I find him?'

He shook his head, 'I've no idea. I've been up . . .' he waved his arm towards the stand. 'Match day, he's usually up in the top deck. He's got a cubicle up by the media centre. You want me to show you?'

'Just point me in the general direction,' Carol said. 'You've obviously got more important things to do.'

He nodded. 'You could say that. Take the end staircase all the way up. It's the first one you come to on the left.'

In the mouth of the stairwell, she came up against a young constable who looked completely terrified. 'You can't go up there,' he gabbled. 'Nobody's allowed. It's not safe, it's not been cleared by the dogs. Nobody up there, the super's orders.'

'That's who I'm looking for. Superintendent Black.'

The young lad pointed to where two fire engines stood together in an L-shape. 'He's over there. With the fire chief.'

Carol weaved her way across. People were sitting on the ground, parts of them bleeding. Paramedics moved among them, performing a primitive triage. Some they dealt with, some they sent to ambulances, others they summoned stretchers for. Waves of firefighters passed through, their presence somehow reassuring. It was the 9/11 effect, Carol thought. Since then, firemen with their chiselled, smoke-blackened faces and the deliberate walk imposed by their bulky gear had become iconic.

Among the injured, other fans wandered around in a daze. The police were checking them out, making sure they weren't obviously injured, then encouraging them to leave the stadium area. All around her, faces in shock, eyes blank, lips bitten. She picked her way through the chaos, wondering how the hell she was supposed to treat this as a crime scene.

To her amazement, she recognized one of the casualties. Staggering towards her, the familiar bulk of Tom Cross. She hadn't seen him since he'd left the force seven years before, but he was unmistakable. He was grey faced and filthy, leaning on a paramedic who was clearly struggling under the weight. Cross caught sight of her and shook his head. 'Just catch the fucking bastards,' he said, his voice thick and phlegmy.

'Is he OK?' she asked the paramedic.

'If we can get him to hospital in time. He's been a proper hero, but he's taken a bit too much out of himself,' the man said.

'Let me help,' Carol said, trying to get Cross to lean on her.

'Never mind me,' he snarled. 'Go and do your job. You can buy me a drink when it's all over.'

'Good luck,' she called after him.

When she finally reached the makeshift command post, she was already feeling overwhelmed by the task ahead of them all. She found Black and a senior fire officer poring over an architect's drawing of the stand. 'We've got the fire under control,' she heard the fireman say. 'Apart from the furnishings in the boxes, there's not much that's combustible.'

'Something to be grateful for.' Black looked round as Carol cleared her throat. 'Can I help you?' he said, his voice irritable.

'DCI Jordan, Major Incident Team.'

'You've come to the right place,' the fireman said. 'It doesn't get much more major than this.'

'It's my job to work the crime scene,' Carol said.

'I thought CTC were on their way,' Black said, frowning. 'Surely that's up to them?'

'Until they get here, it's mine,' she said briskly. This wasn't the time to get into a protocol wrangle. 'Do we know what we're looking at here?'

The fire chief pointed to a small room on the plan. 'This is where we think it came from. My lads tell me it looks like there are human remains in there. So, the presumption is suicide bomber. We also think it was probably TATP, like the London tube bombings. It has a particularly distinctive signature.'

'That's all speculation, obviously. Until forensics and the bomb guys have been in there,' Black added.

'Where are forensics?'

'Waiting for the all-clear to go in.'

'Is the Bomb Squad here?' Carol asked.

'On their way. We've got a couple of explosives dogs going through the stands now,' Black said.

'OK. Get one of the dogs to clear the bomb locus, please.' She smiled up at the fireman. 'I'm going to need some protective gear for me and my team. And we'll need someone to show us the way. Can you help us out?'

'I wouldn't recommend it. It's not exactly safe,' he said.

'All the more reason for us to get what we can while we can,' she said. 'The gear?'

He looked her up and down. 'It's going to be a bit big on you, but you're welcome to what we've got. Where's the rest of your team?'

'Give me a minute.' Carol stepped to one side, aware that Black was pissed off with her assumption of control over the crime scene. She got her phone out and called Kevin. 'Bring me up to speed,' she said.

'I'm five minutes away. I've got Paula and Sam

with me. Chris is on her way separately, Stacey's back at the office. She's already calling in as much CCTV footage of the stadium approaches as she can get.'

She told him where to meet her, asked him to brief Chris, then called the forensics team. 'Be ready to roll in ten minutes,' she said. 'We're going in.'

The closer they approached to the site of the explosion, the warmer it became. Carol could feel the sweat plastering her hair to her head under the bulk of the oversized fire helmet she was wearing. The fire officer picked his way along the debris-strewn corridor. Behind Carol came a skeleton forensics crew, followed by her own team.

He stopped abruptly a dozen feet from the edge of a jagged crater in the floor. 'There you go,' he said. 'That's what used to be the electrical junction room for the corporate hospitality boxes and the media centre.'

Not much remained. The walls had been pulverized, the cables shredded and the pipework that had been buried in concrete had been transformed into shrapnel. The force of the bomb had punched outwards and upwards. The walls above had peeled back like the segments of an orange and she could see daylight through the gap. As Carol stared at the destruction, she realized that the red shreds and patches scattered at random over the remains of the room were human flesh and blood. Not much turned her stomach these days, but this was a sight that made her gag. She swallowed hard. 'Can we get round to the other side?' she asked.

The fireman nodded. 'From the other end.'

'OK.' She turned to the forensics team. 'I want half of you to start from the other side. We want as much trace evidence as we can get, but I don't want anybody taking risks. We'll do as much as we can, then we'll get the experts to build us some sort of platform so we can access the rest. It looks as if we've got the remains of a suicide bomber here, but let's get as much material as possible so we can be sure whether there was one or more of them.'

The white-suited technicians set about their business. Cameras flashed, tweezers gripped, bags were filled and labelled. Carol moved back to her team. 'I want you to backtrack through the stand. We don't know how he got in, but there must be security cameras. Paula, Sam – figure out where the access points are and start checking the footage. Kevin, stay here with the SOCOs, take a look at the scene and see what you can come up with. Chris, with me.'

She headed back the way they'd come, Chris at her side. 'Punters don't get into service corridors,' she said. 'Somebody brought him in. We need to find the security staff and whoever was on duty in the corporate hospitality reception. He didn't just walk in off the street with a rucksack bomb. Let's see what we can dig up before CTC turn up.'

It took them twenty minutes to track down the people they were looking for. The crisis evacuation plan provided a safe haven for stadium staff in the assembly hall of Grayson Street Primary. But nobody had keys for the school. At first, it had looked as if the staff were going to melt into the afternoon, but an enterprising turnstile manager had insisted they stay together and shepherded them quarter of a mile down the road to the Chinese restaurant where he liked to eat lunch. The owner had welcomed them with open arms and an avalanche of free dim sum. The only problem was that nobody knew where they were. Finally, Carol had managed to get a number for one of the hospitality receptionists and tracked them down.

It took another twenty minutes to get the bare bones of what had happened. Carol left Chris taking more detailed statements and she headed back to the stadium, making a couple of quick calls on the way. Even in the short time she had been away, things had moved on. The streets around the stadium were much clearer, and were being kept that way by the mounted division. A couple of low loaders were moving cars from the immediate vicinity of the stadium to make way for emergency vehicles. And in the middle of the Vestey Stand car park was the biggest caravan Carol had ever seen. The white trailer looked like a converted cargo container, with two rows of opaque windows along the side. Apart from a strip of black-and-white checks, like a police cap band, there was no identification. A single door in the end of the trailer was flanked by two black-clad officers in riot gear and helmets, semi-automatic pistols held across their bodies. It looked as if the cavalry had arrived. Carol headed for it.

As she approached, both guards shifted, pointing their weapons towards her. *Here we go. Bully boys and borderline sociopaths masquerading as our saviours.* She pointed to her ID. 'Detective Chief Inspector Carol Jordan. Bradfield Metropolitan Police Major Incident Team commander. Here to see whoever is in charge now.'

One of them turned away and muttered into his radio. The other didn't let his hard, flat stare lighten for an instant. Carol stood her ground, reminding herself that this wasn't about her, it was about the injured, the dying and the dead. *Don't get angry. Don't give them an excuse to sideline you even further. This is your patch, you have something to contribute. Don't let them stop you doing your job.*

The one with the radio turned back and stepped closer, checking the photo on her ID against her face. 'A few more grey hairs and a few more wrinkles,' she said. His tough guy expression didn't even twitch. He reached behind him for the door handle, pushed it open and indicated with his gun that she should enter. Biting her lip and refusing to give in to the temptation to shake her head in wonder, Carol did as she was instructed.

She walked into a low-ceilinged entrance hall. A narrow flight of metal stairs led upwards. Two doors faced her, and two more black-clad cops, one at the foot of the stairs, the other between the doors. The one by the stairs stood to one side and said, 'Up top, ma'am.'

Feeling as if she was in a low-budget spy movie, Carol climbed the stairs, a hollow clang at every step. Another vestibule, another guard, who nodded her through another door. She walked into a spartan conference room containing a metal-topped trestle table and eight folding chairs. John Brandon sat in one; three others were occupied by men in black leather jackets over black T-shirts. Two had a pale shadow of stubble on their skulls. The third had a short fuzz of dark hair. At first glance, the only way

300

to tell them apart was the extent to which male-pattern baldness had carved out its territory.

The one in the middle said, 'Thanks for joining us, DCI Jordan. Have a seat.'

'Hello, sir,' Carol said to Brandon as she sat down next to him. She turned to the one facing her. 'And you are?'

He smiled. It did nothing to dispel his carefully cultivated air of menace. 'We don't do names and ranks. Security. You can call me ... David.'

'Security? I'm a DCI. I've worked for NCIS. Who do you think I'm going to tell?'

He shook his head. 'Nothing personal, Carol. I know your record and I've got nothing but respect for you. But we operate along very strict guidelines that are there for our protection. And given the work we do, us being protected means that everybody else is better protected.'

He might work out of Manchester, but his accent said London and the Met. He had that swagger she'd learned to detest when she'd worked there. She'd bet there weren't many women working in CTC. It wasn't a female-friendly environment. All that macho posturing, covering up for the fact that they didn't really have any autonomy. They might like to pretend they ran the game, but the truth was they didn't take a toilet break without the say-so of the dedicated anti-terrorist team of the Crown Prosecution Service. The men in black might deliver the menace, but they were only the message-boys for their masters in Ludgate Hill. And it was clear Brandon had no stomach to stand up to the message-boys or their masters.

'Fine. No names, no pack drill. And if you don't

mind, we'll skip the pep talk about how we're all on the same side and we're all going to work together to nail the bastards who did this. I know the rules. My team and I are at your disposal.'

He breathed heavily through his nose. 'Glad to hear it, Carol. I'm sure your local knowledge is going to be very helpful to us. Of course, we've got intelligence which you haven't about the hothead fundamentalists on your patch. We'll be shaking the trees and seeing who falls out. We'll . . .'

'Round up the usual suspects?' she said sweetly. 'Actually, we might have saved you a bit of time on that already. There's a van parked down in the Grayson Street staff and players' car park. A1 Electricals. Just before three, a young Asian man drove in. He had what looked like authentic paperwork to carry out an emergency electrical repair in the Vestey Stand. One of the security staff took him up to the junction box room and let him in. Less than ten minutes later, the bomb went off. I think it's reasonable to assume our van driver was also our suicide bomber.' She took out her notebook. 'According to the PNC, the van is registered to an Imran Begg, 37 Wilberforce Street, Bradfield.' She closed the notebook. 'It's about five doors down from the Kenton Mosque. You might want to tread carefully when you go knocking.'

'Thank you, Carol. We'll take it from here. If there's anything we need your people for, we'll let you know. Meantime, I know you've got a high-profile murder case to be getting on with, so we won't keep you from that. We've also got our own dedicated forensic team, so we'll be releasing your people back to you once we've collected their evidence.'

302

Carol tried not to show how she was seething inside. 'Where will you be based?' she asked. She knew their practice was to take over a police station and evict its usual inhabitants.

'We were just talking about that,' David said. 'Normally we'd take any suspects back to our dedicated suite in Manchester.'

'However, I suggested David and his team could use Scargill Street for interviews and custody,' Brandon said.

'Good idea,' Carol said. Scargill Street had been taken out of mothballs for the Queer Killer investigation seven years before and had been kept on the back burner ever since, a perpetual Cinderella waiting for the refurb. Letting the CTC loose there would keep them out of the way without creating a pool of homeless officers trying to find perches on everybody else's already overcrowded territory.

'And that's fine as far as it goes, given the scale of this investigation. In Manchester, we're tooled up for specific, targeted raids, not the kind of sweep we're going to end up doing here. But Scargill Street isn't wired up for the latest kit. So we're also going to use your Major Inquiry suite at HQ,' David said.

This time, Carol couldn't hide her dismay. 'So where's my team supposed to work from?' she demanded.

'David's people can use the HOLMES2 office,' Brandon said. 'You're not using that for Robbie Bishop's murder.'

He was right. The Home Office Large Major Enquiry System had been set up as a means of filtering and classifying the volume of information generated either by a series of crimes or a single wide-ranging event. Each force had its own dedicated team of HOLMES2 officers. They were highly trained, skilled officers and Carol didn't hesitate to use them when it was appropriate. But wherever possible she relied on Stacey and her prodigious talents to manage the MIT investigations.

The problem was that now it looked as if there might be linkage between Danny Wade and Robbie, the logical next step was to set up a HOLMES2 analysis of the material produced by both inquiries. But if CTC were in there, that avenue would be closed to them. She knew this was the time to protest, but she couldn't do that without raising something Brandon knew nothing about. And this was not the time to undermine her Chief Constable.

'And it'll be nice and handy when we need you to help us out,' David said cheerily. He pushed his chair back. 'Right, I think we're done here for now.' He stood up.

Carol remained seated. 'Do we have any numbers yet?' she asked.

David looked down at the man on his right, the one with the quarter inch of hair. 'Johnny?'

'Thirty-five confirmed dead so far. Another ten or so critical in hospital. Somewhere in the order of a hundred and sixty injured, ranging from lost limbs to cuts and bruises.'

Now Carol stood up and took a couple of steps towards the door. 'Oh, by the way, I probably should have mentioned: I've got a couple of officers on their way to Imran Begg's address. Obviously, I sent them out before I knew you were here. I'll let you know what they come up with, if you'll give me a number I can reach you on?'

David's face betrayed nothing. 'Thanks for letting me know.' He took a card from the inside pocket of his leather jacket and crossed the room to give it to her. All it said was DAVID and a mobile number. 'I look forward to hearing from you, Carol. But it's time to call off the dogs.'

She walked out with Brandon at her heels. Once they were outside, she rounded on him. 'Do you seriously expect me to ignore this? Not to investigate the biggest crime ever to take place on my ground?'

Brandon refused to meet her eyes. 'It's out of our hands, Carol. *Force majeure.*'

She shook her head. 'A mad world. What about identifying the dead? Talking to their families?'

'Uniform will handle that,' Brandon said. 'Do what you're best at, Carol. Go and find Robbie Bishop's killer. Believe me, you're better out of this shit.' He waved his arm to encompass the stadium and the CTC trailer. He shook his head sorrowfully and walked away.

'We'll see about that,' Carol muttered. John Brandon seemed to have forgotten the crucial element of what made her the copper she was. Like Sam Evans, she was a maverick. But what motivated her, what had always motivated her, was not self-interest but a passion for justice. Something David and Johnny still had a lot to learn about. 'The lesson starts here,' she muttered.

The architects of the Kenton Mosque had made no attempt to have their building blend in with the surrounding area. A grid of red-brick terraces dating back to the turn of the twentieth century surrounded the off-white walls and gilt-topped minarets. 'It never ceases to amaze me that they got planning permission for that,' Kevin said as they drove into Wilberforce Street. 'How do you think they pulled it off?'

Paula rolled her eyes. 'How do you think, Kevin? The planning committee know they'd be heading straight for a shitstorm if they said no.'

'Careful, Paula. You're sounding a tad racist there,' Kevin said, teasing her. He'd worked with enough racist cops to recognize one who wasn't.

'It's not race, it's religion I have a problem with. Doesn't matter if it's Ulster Protestants, Liverpool Catholics or Bradfield Muslims. I hate loudmouthed clerics who play the bigot card every time anyone says no to them. They create a climate of censorship and fear and I despise them for it. I tell you, I've never been more proud to be gay than when Parliament passed that bill outlawing discrimination on the grounds of sexuality. Who knew there was a single issue that could unite the evangelical Christians, the Catholics, the Muslims and the Jews? My small contribution to ecumenism. There's a space up ahead on the right,' she added.

Kevin squeezed into the parking space and they walked back past half a dozen houses, aware that they were an object of curiosity, dislike or anxiety to everyone who clocked them. In this part of Kenton, the part that hadn't been gentrified by the invading army of hospital workers and students, they were the exotics. They stopped outside number 37, neatly painted, anonymous, net curtains at the windows.

The door was opened by a small, slight woman in shalwar kameez, a dupata covering her head. She looked horrified to see them. 'What is it? Who are you?' she said before either of them could say a word.

'I'm Detective Sergeant Matthews and this is Detective Constable McIntyre.'

Her hands flew to her face. 'I knew it. I knew something bad would happen if he went there, I knew it.' She moaned and turned away, calling, 'Parvez, come here at once, it is the police, something has happened to Imran.'

Kevin and Paula exchanged looks. What was going on?

A tall stooped man in traditional dress appeared behind the woman. 'I am Parvez Khan. Imran is my son. Who are you?'

Kevin explained again who they were. 'We wanted to talk to Imran Begg,' he said.

The man frowned and looked down at the woman. 'You said something has happened to Imran? What has happened?' He looked at Kevin. 'What has happened to our son?'

Kevin shook his head. 'I think there's been a misunderstanding. We just want to talk to Imran. About his van.'

'About his van? What is this about his van? He doesn't have his van with him. You're not here because he's had an accident?' the man asked, obviously perplexed.

Kevin didn't want to be the one to say 'bomb'. So he persisted. 'Where is Imran?'

'He is in Ibiza,' the woman said. 'He is on holiday. It was a gift from his cousin Yousef. Yousef took him to the airport on Thursday morning. He called us when he got there, just to let us know he was safe. He's not coming back till tomorrow. So if his van has been in an accident, it is not Imran's fault.' Her bewilderment was obviously not an act.

'Who's got his van?' Kevin said, trying to cut through the confusion.

'His cousin Yousef. They went to the airport in Imran's van,' the man said. 'Yousef is supposed to pick him up tomorrow in the van.'

'And where can we find Yousef?' Kevin asked.

'Downton Vale. One four seven Vale Avenue. But what has happened? Has there been an accident?' Mr Khan looked from one to the other. 'What has happened?'

Kevin shook his head. 'I'm afraid I can't say.' He flashed a quick, tired smile. 'Be grateful your boy is out of the country. Thanks for your help.'

As they turned to walk away, a white Transit van screamed round the corner and raced down the street towards them. Kevin stopped and looked over his shoulder at the frightened faces of Imran Begg's parents. 'I'm really sorry,' he said. 'Come on, Paula, time we were somewhere else.'

As the black-clad armed police officers piled out of the van, they hurried back to the car. They were almost there when a voice yelled, 'Oi. You two.'

Kevin grabbed the car door, but Paula stopped him. 'They're armed, Kevin. Armed and hyped.'

He grunted something incomprehensible and turned round. One of the interchangeable men in black was a few feet away from him, Heckler and Koch at the ready. The others had disappeared into

Parvez Khan's house. 'Who the fuck are you?' he demanded.

'DS Matthews, DC McIntyre. Bradfield Police Major Incident Team. And who the fuck are you?'

'That's irrelevant. We're CTC. This is our game now.'

Kevin took a step forward. 'I want some ID,' he said. 'Something to prove you're not just some private army.'

The man in black just laughed. 'Don't push your luck.' He turned on his heel and sauntered away.

Kevin stared after him. 'Can you believe that? Can you fucking believe that?'

'Only too easily,' Paula sighed. 'Are we off to Downton Vale, then?'

'Oh, I think so. Better not tell the DCI, though. If that lot are anything to go by, it'll be easier all round if we leave her out of the loop for now.'

It didn't matter how many drills you did, you were never prepared for the real thing, Dr Elinor Blessing thought. A&E was a chaos of voices and bodies, the walking wounded and the triage teams, harassed nurses and stressed doctors trying to cope with whatever they were going to have to deal with next. Elinor had dealt with the only two chest trauma cases fairly swiftly. Neither was life-threatening and she had them admitted to Mr Denby's ward as soon as they were stable. As she leaned against the wall in a quiet corner, writing up their charts, a flustered nurse caught sight of her and came over.

'Doctor, I've got a man who came in on one of the Victoria Park ambulances, but I can't make sense of his symptoms,' he said.

Elinor, who was close enough to her training to feel reasonably confident with medical emergencies outside her speciality, pushed herself upright and followed him to a cubicle. 'What's the story?'

'Paramedics brought him in. He'd been helping to rescue the injured, but he was on the point of collapse. They reckoned he might be about to arrest,' the nurse said. 'His pulse is all over the place. First it's up around 140, then it's down to 50. Sometimes it's regular, then it's arrhythmic. He's been sick three times, bloody vomit. And his hands and feet are freezing.'

Elinor glanced at the chart for his name, and looked at the big man on the bed. He was conscious, but clearly in distress. 'When did you start feeling ill, Mr Cross?' she asked.

Before he could answer his body was seized with an uncontrollable tremor. It was over in seconds, but it was enough to convince Elinor Blessing that this was no normal cardiac ailment. 'Start of the match. Before the bomb. My guts were griping,' he managed to force out.

She reached out and touched his hand. In spite of the warmth in the hospital, his hands were like ice. His pale gooseberry eyes stared up at her, fear and pleading evident on his face. 'Have you had any diarrhoea?'

He gave a faint nod. 'Came out of me like water,' he said. 'Two, three times.'

Elinor ran through the mental checklist. Nausea. Diarrhoea. Erratic heart rate. Central nervous system problems. Bizarre and unlikely though it seemed, this looked like her second poisoning case in a week. And both connected to Bradfield Victoria. She gave herself a mental shake. Sometimes coincidence was exactly

310

what it was, no more, no less. And sometimes poisoning was more to do with ignoring food hygiene than criminality. It wasn't yet against the law to eat something past its sell-by date. 'What did you have to eat at lunchtime?' she asked.

'Lamb kebabs. Rice with a fancy sauce with herbs.' He was having trouble speaking. As if his mouth wasn't quite working properly.

'In a restaurant?'

'No. He cooked it. Jake . . .' Cross frowned. What was the name? He couldn't grasp it. It felt too far away, just out of reach.

'Can you remember how long ago that was?' Elinor asked.

'Dinner time. One o'clock, half past?'

Three hours ago. Well past the magic sixty minutes where washing out his stomach was a worthwhile option. 'OK, we're going to try to make you a bit more comfortable,' she said.

She took the nurse to one side. 'I'm not sure but I think he's got some sort of cardiac glycoside poisoning. Digoxin or something.'

The nurse stared at her, panic widening his eyes. 'He came in from Victoria Park. Are you saying the terrorists used some sort of chemical weapon?'

'No, I'm not saying that,' she said impatiently. 'Symptoms this serious don't start that fast. He was already poisoned before he got to the football. I need five minutes to check out the differentials just in case I'm wrong and the treatments just in case I'm right. Meanwhile, I need you to administer oxygen and set up an IV and a pulse oximeter. We need an ECG and we also need constant cardiac monitoring. Can you get that started? I'll be back in five.'

Leaving the stunned nurse behind her, Elinor headed for the nurses' station and a web-enabled PC. It didn't take long for her to dismiss the differentials. The treatment was straightforward too. The administration of Fab fragments was the standard antidote to cardiac glycoside poisoning. She printed out the treatment sheet and headed back to the cubicle where she'd left Tom Cross.

He was, she thought, getting worse. His expression was bemused, his pulse more thready. 'I've phoned down to the pharmacy. They've got thirty vials of Fab fragments in stock. I'm going down myself to pick them up and sign for them. It'll take too long if we send a porter. Get the ECG under way ASAP, and if he goes into cardiac distress, go with the lidocaine.'

The nurse nodded. 'Leave it with me.' He shook his head. 'Hardly seems real, does it? You get a bomb, you get some guy acting like a hero and the next thing, he's lying here poisoned. You couldn't make it up, could you?'

'Let's see if we can give him a happy ending, at least,' Elinor said, already on her way. Somehow, she didn't think this was the week for happy endings.

As soon as they turned out of Wilberforce Street, Paula slapped the magnetic blue light on top of the car. 'Go for it, McQueen,' she said.

'How long do you think we've got?' Kevin asked.

'Depends how traumatized Imran's mum and dad are by the Imperial Storm Troopers. I tell you, they scare the living shit out of me. But you can bet your bottom dollar there's another busload of them waiting for another address to invade. So let's work on the basis that we have no time to waste. Shouldn't you be taking Downton Road?' she said, snatching at the passenger grab handle as Kevin threw the car round a corner and into another grid of back streets.

'It'll be choked this time on a Saturday. All the shopping traffic from the Quadrant Centre. We'll make better time this way.'

When it came to traffic, Paula knew to trust Kevin. Once, he'd been a Detective Inspector but he'd blotted his copybook so dramatically he'd almost been kicked out of the force. His path to redemption had included a six-month stint in traffic, a job for which he had been so spectacularly over-qualified they'd been glad to see the back of him. But it had left him with a useful working knowledge of the city's traffic patterns and the sort of short cuts that only taxi drivers appreciate. So she shut up and held tight.

They made it to Vale Avenue in record time. Kevin gave a satisfied sigh when he pulled up outside cousin Yousef's address. 'I enjoyed that,' he said. 'Got those bastards out of my system.'

Paula pried her fingers from the grab handle. 'I'm glad it was good for you. So, what's our line here?'

Kevin shrugged. 'Be straight with them. Was Yousef driving the van? Where is Yousef now? Can we look at Yousef's room? Be helpful because we are the nice guys and you may need some friends. The next wave won't ask.'

Paula snorted as she got out of the car. 'The next lot won't even wipe their boots.' She looked up the steep drive at the brick semi perched on the side of the hill. It didn't exactly say, 'We've made it', but it was certainly a few rungs further up the ladder than the Beggs' house. An elderly Toyota Corolla and a four-year-old Nissan Patrol sat on the drive. 'Somebody's home,' she said.

The door was answered by a young man in his mid-twenties dressed in sports trousers and a V-necked cotton sweater. His haircut was razor sharp, his gold chains a hairsbreadth away from bling. He had the faintly insolent cock of the head that Paula had seen on too many men of his age, regardless of ethnicity. 'Yeah?' he said.

They held out their ID and Kevin introduced them. 'And you are?'

'Sanjar Aziz. What's all this about? You want to talk to Raj about the bomb or what?' He seemed surprisingly cool.

'Raj?' Paula said.

'Yeah, my little bro. He was at the game, innit? Gave his name to one of your lot and came home because he knew our mum would be going mental as soon as she heard about it. You wanna come in?'

They stepped into the hallway. Laminate floor, a couple of rugs Paula wouldn't have minded having in her own house. The air smelled of lilies, the fragrance coming from a large vase of stargazers on the windowsill. 'Actually, Raj isn't the reason we're here,' Kevin said.

Sanjar stopped in his tracks and swung round. 'Do what?' Now there was a hostile edge to his stare. 'What's all this about, copper?'

'We're here about Yousef.'

Sanjar frowned. 'Yousef? What do you mean,

Yousef?' He sounded agitated. 'You must have it wrong. Yousef is Mr Law Abiding. He doesn't even talk on his phone while he's driving. Whatever anybody's said he's done, they're way wrong.'

Kevin took a deep breath. Nobody ever thought their family members could do any wrong. At least, not when they were talking to the police. 'Is there somewhere we can sit down and talk?' he said.

'What do you mean, sit down and talk? What is going on here?' At the sound of Sanjar's raised voice, a door opened. A teenage face appeared, scared and hollow-eyed. Sanjar caught the movement. 'Shut the door, Raj. Lie down like Mama told you. She'll be back from the shop soon, she'll kill you if you're wandering about.' He flapped his hands, shooing the boy back inside. Once the door was closed again, he led them into the kitchen. A small table with barely enough room for four chairs sat against one wall, cream units lining the other three. The room smelled faintly of spices, warm and bitter at one and the same time. Sanjar gestured to the table. 'Sit down, then.' He threw himself into the furthest chair with ill grace. 'So. What's this about Yousef?' he demanded.

'Where's your mum and dad?' Paula asked.

Sanjar shrugged impatiently. 'My mum went down the shops to get some stuff for this soothing drink she wants to make for Raj. And Saturday afternoon, my dad'll be down the mosque, drinking tea and arguing about the Koran.' His face showed the perennial pitying contempt of child for parent. 'He's the devout one in this house.'

'OK. When did Yousef go out?' Paula asked.

'After dinner. Mam wanted one of us to drop Raj

315

off at the football. I had to go over to Wakefield and Yousef said he was going to meet someone in Brighouse about a new contract.' He shifted in his seat. Paula wondered if he was hiding something.

'New contract?' Kevin interrupted.

'The family firm. First Fabrics. We're in the rag trade. We deal both ends – with the fabric importers and with the middlemen who buy finished articles for the retail trade. I don't know anything about who he was meeting in Brighouse, it was news to me. So, did something happen over there? Did he get in a ruck with somebody?'

'Do you know what he was driving?' Kevin asked.

'He was driving our cousin Imran's van: A1 Electricals. See, Yousef's van needed some work doing, and Imran was off to Ibiza for a few days, so it made sense to borrow his wheels. Save on a rental, right? Look, for the last time, is one of you going to tell me what all this is about?'

Kevin's eyes slid round to Paula's. She could see he really didn't know how to say this. 'Sanjar,' she said, 'can you think of any reason why Yousef would have been at Victoria Park this afternoon?'

He looked at her as if she was crazy. 'Yousef? No, you've got it wrong. Raj was at the game.' He gave a nervous little laugh. 'I don't know how, but there's been a mix-up. Raj gave his name to a cop, I don't know how it's ended up coming back as Yousef. Yousef didn't give a toss about football.'

'What was Yousef wearing when he went out?' Paula asked.

'Wearing? Shit, I don't know.' Sanjar shook his head and twisted his face into a thoughtful expression. 'No, wait. He had black trousers and a shirt on at dinner. A plain white shirt. And when he was going off, I saw him putting Imran's overalls on. He said the clutch kept slipping and if he had to get out and mess around with it, he didn't want his shirt getting all mucky. He likes to make a good impression, my brother.'

'You see, here's the thing,' Paula said gently. 'Obviously you know what happened this afternoon, because of Raj.'

Sanjar nodded slowly, a new look of caution on his face. He wasn't stupid. 'You're telling me Yousef's dead,' he said. 'You're telling me he was at the football? And now he's dead.' His face begged to be contradicted. He didn't want to believe what he thought they were telling him.

'Not quite,' Paula said.

Kevin, conscious of the time slipping by, said, 'A man wearing A1 Electricals overalls and driving your cousin's A1 Electricals van was responsible for delivering and setting off the bomb in Victoria Park. Yes, we think Yousef's dead, but not because he got caught by chance. We think your brother was a suicide bomber.'

Sanjar skidded backwards on his chair, only saved from falling by his closeness to the kitchen cupboards. 'No,' he shouted, stumbling to his feet, 'No fucking way.'

'That's how it looks,' Paula said. 'I'm sorry.'

'Sorry?' Sanjar looked deranged. 'Sorry? Fucking sorry? Don't give me sorry.' He waved his hands at them. 'You are so wrong. My brother's not a fucking terrorist. He's ... he's ... he's just not like that.' He punched the wall. 'This is so fucked. So totally fucked.

317

He's going to walk in that door and laugh at you, man. No way. Just, no way.'

Paula put a hand on his arm and he jerked away as if he'd been contaminated. 'You need to get yourself together,' she said. 'We are the nice guys. Very soon, the Counter Terrorism Command team are going to be here and they are going to tear your house and your lives apart. I know what we've told you is a terrible shock, but you have to be strong, for Raj and for your parents. Now, you and me are going to sit down and make a list of all the people Yousef knew and hung out with. And my colleague is going to go upstairs and search Yousef's room. Which one is it?'

Sanjar blinked hard, as if he was trying to orientate himself in a world turned upside down. 'Straight ahead at the top of the stairs. He shares with Raj. Yousef's bed's the one on the left.' He felt behind him for the chair and slumped into it as Kevin left the room. 'I don't believe it,' he mumbled. 'There's got to be some mistake.' He looked up at Paula, his dark eyes red-rimmed. 'There could be a mistake, right?'

'It's always possible. Tell you what, let me take a DNA sample from you, that'll speed things up.' She took a buccal swab kit from her bag and popped the lid. 'Open wide.' Before he could think twice about it, she swabbed the inside of his cheeks and sealed the tube shut. She opened her notebook and patted his hand. 'Come on, Sanjar. Help us here. Everybody you can think of that Yousef knew.'

Sanjar reached into his pocket and took out a pack of cigarettes. Paula knew by instinct that his mother didn't allow smoking in the house. It was a measure of how distraught he was that he was even

318

contemplating it. But if he went for it, so would she. Without a second thought. 'OK,' he sighed. 'But these other people that are coming?'

'The Counter Terrorism Command?'

'Yeah. Are they going to like, arrest me and my family?'

'I won't lie to you,' Paula said. 'They might. The best way you can avoid that is to be totally honest. Never mind holding back anything you think they don't need to know. Because they will find out, believe me. And if they find out you are not telling them the whole truth, then it will be very hard on you. Now, let's have these names.'

Carol sat in her office and seethed. The most challenging investigation of her career, and she was effectively sidelined. Already her HQ building was crawling with the CTC personnel. According to Brandon, there were two hundred and fifty of them either there or on their way. They already had dedicated lines set up between the HOLMES suite and Ludgate Circus. When she'd gone through to find out what they wanted from her team, she'd been told her services were not required, though they wouldn't mind having Stacey Chen on a free transfer for the duration.

She'd gathered the tatters of her dignity around her and withdrawn. Back in the MIT office, Stacey was already co-ordinating the transfer of digital CCTV footage around the stadium. 'They want you next door,' Carol said.

Stacey sniffed. 'Is it a request or an order?'

'At this point, it's a request. That could change, though.'

Stacey glanced up from the screen she was working. 'I'll stay here, then. I take it we're not just walking away?'

Carol shook her head. 'We'll keep our fingers in the pie. It's our patch. And we do still have Robbie Bishop's murder to solve. Do you want a brew?'

'Earl Grey, please.' Stacey was already immersed in her screen again.

Carol leaned against the wall, waiting for the kettle to boil. Chris Devine barrelled through the door looking thoroughly pissed off. 'Fucking CTC bastards,' she said to Stacey, who gestured with her head towards Carol. 'Sorry, guv,' she muttered, throwing her jacket over the nearest chair.

'No need. You want a brew?'

'I could use a large Scotch,' Chris grumbled. 'Failing that, a mug of builder's tea would hit the spot.'

'What happened?'

'I was just wrapping up my interviews with the hospitality reception crew when half a dozen of them came barging in. You can hear them coming a corridor length away.'

'It's the boots,' Carol said, pouring water on teabags. 'That and the swish of their musclebound thighs rubbing together. So in they come, and as soon as they see me, it's "on your bike, love," like I was a journalist or something. I was out of there before you could say jackbooted fascists. And before they'd let me come back here, they made me sit down and type up my interview product. Like I was going to sneak off and not let them look at my homework.' She shook her head. 'I thought I was leaving them SO12 arseholes behind when I moved up here.'

320

Carol handed over the teas. 'We have to co-operate,' she said. 'Which is not to say we can't also plough our own furrow.'

'Speaking of which, where's the rest of the crew?'

'Paula and Kevin are out there following up on the A1 Electricals van, see what they can get ahead of the CTC. People have a way of clamming up when the men in black kick the doors down,' Carol said. 'I'm not sure about Sam. He was checking out CCTV in the Vestey Stand last time I saw him.'

'He'll be off following some red-hot lead he doesn't want to share with the rest of us poor imbeciles,' Chris said dryly.

'He's his own worst enemy,' Stacey said without looking up. 'He does it for all the right reasons.'

Chris and Carol shared a look. Neither could remember Stacey ever commenting on any of her colleagues. Her complete refusal to gossip was legendary. 'Later,' Chris mouthed conspiratorially at Carol. She slurped a mouthful of tea and breathed deeply. 'I tell you, I never want to see the likes of that again. I still can't get my head round the carnage. Thirty-five dead, they're saying. I never thought I'd see that in Bradfield.'

'It's amazing it wasn't more,' Carol said. 'If he'd planted it at the same spot on the opposite stand where there were just seats instead of corporate boxes, there would have been hundreds dead.' She closed her eyes momentarily. 'It's too horrible to contemplate.'

'There would have been more if the crowd hadn't behaved so well. I expected more crush injuries. I tell you, I know it's a cliché, but it is things like this that

321

bring out the best in people. Did you see that woman on Grayson Street, set up a trestle table outside her house, making cups of tea for people? Spirit of the Blitz an' all that.'

'And sometimes it's the unlikeliest people who end up being heroes,' Carol said. 'I saw a bloke this afternoon – one of the paramedics was taking him to an ambulance, he'd taken too much out of himself getting people out of the wreckage. And I knew this bloke. He used to be one of us till he got drummed out of the Brownies for planting evidence in a murder inquiry. He's the last person I would have had down for helping anybody other than number one. So I suppose we've all got it in us to do the decent thing.' She smiled wryly. 'Except maybe the men in black.'

Right on cue, one of the foot soldiers stuck his head round the door. 'You got a DCI Jordan anywhere round here?'

'That would be me, officer. How can I help you?'

'You're wanted down Scargill Street. Some spot of bother with one of your lads?' He began to retreat but Carol stopped him with a look that would have corroded tungsten.

'Who wants me?'

'Whoever's in charge. Look, I'm just the messenger, all right?' He breathed heavily and cast his eyes upwards. 'You already know all I know.'

'I'll finish my bloody tea,' Carol muttered. But the defiance was only skin deep. Within five minutes, she was out the door, leaving Stacey and Chris to wonder what the hell Sam Evans had done this time.

They didn't have much time for speculation. Not long after Carol's departure, Paula and Kevin burst in, looking pleased with themselves. Kevin, who was walking like a man with a bad back, made straight for Stacey, then opened his jacket and took out a laptop. 'There you go,' he said. 'The bomber's laptop.'

Stacey raised her eyebrows. 'Where did you get that?'

'From the bomber's bedroom.'

'Alleged bomber,' Paula cut in. 'Yousef Aziz. He was certainly driving the van and wearing the overalls earlier today.'

Chris came over and prodded the laptop with her finger. 'I don't think we're supposed to have this.'

'No, and I don't think we'll be hanging on to it for long, so I need to get as much off it as I can,' Stacey said, reaching for it.

'How did you get that away from the men in black?' Chris said.

'Speed,' Paula said. 'We were in and out before they got there.' She explained their progress from Imran Begg to Yousef Aziz. 'I suspect the CTC guys freaked them out so comprehensively it took them a while to give up Aziz and his address. They're so bloody scary, it's counter-productive when you're dealing with decent law-abiding people. They just freeze up. Which worked to our advantage. We got a good twenty minutes with Aziz's brother Sanjar, and the CTC were just turning into the street as we were driving out of it.'

'Nice work,' Chris said. 'So how's it looking? The usual? Young bloke gets his head turned by the mad mullahs and the Al-Quaeda quartermasters fix him up with the necessary?'

Paula sat down on the desk next to Chris. 'I don't

know. His brother was adamant that Aziz wasn't into that stuff. According to Sanjar, Yousef was dead set against fundamentalism.'

'We can't judge Yousef on what his brother says,' Kevin said. 'Look at the London bombers. Their friends and families acted like they were gobsmacked. OK, I didn't find a bomb-making manual in the bedroom, but I didn't get that long in there, and some of the newspapers and books were in script I couldn't read. We'll have a better idea when the CTC have stripped the house back to the bricks and gone through every piece of paper.'

'They'll know,' Chris corrected him cynically. 'Who knows what they'll decide to tell us.'

'You don't need them,' Stacey said absently. 'You've got his laptop and you've got me.'

'Go, Stacey,' Kevin said, punching the air. 'Where's the DCI, by the way?'

'Down Scargill Street,' Chris said.

'Of her own free will?'

'Kind of. I think Sam's dropped a bollock. One of the men in black came in and said there was a problem with one of her lads. And since you're sitting here, chances are it's not you.'

Paula raised her eyebrows. 'Oh shit. Poor old Sam. What do you think is worse? Pissing off the Imperial Storm Troopers or having to be rescued by the chief on the warpath?'

Carol had never seen anything like it. Scargill Street had been transformed into a citadel under siege. Armed police guarded every exit and a police helicopter hovered above, its spotlight pinning her shadow to the ground as she approached. It took a full three minutes for the guard on the back door to get her entry clearance, and when she walked into the familiar hallway, another armed officer was waiting to escort her. 'I thought it was supposed to be secret, where you hold your terrorist suspects?' she said conversationally as they marched through deserted corridors towards the custody suite.

'It is a secret. We don't tell the media.'

'You've got a city-centre police station better guarded than Buckingham Palace and you think people won't notice?'

'Doesn't matter, does it?' he said, taking the turn that Carol knew would bring them to the cells. 'They're not allowed to print it.'

Give me strength. Carol closed her eyes momentarily. 'I thought it was somebody staging an attack that you were worried about.'

'We're not worried,' he said, in a tone that said the conversation was over. He knocked on the door that led to the custody area. A moment passed, then they were buzzed in. The guard opened the door for her and stood back. 'There you go,' he said. 'Someone will come and get you.' He slammed the door behind her.

The familiar area was empty apart from the custody sergeant sitting behind the desk, his paperwork in front of him. To her surprise, Carol recognized him from the first investigation she'd ever worked for Bradfield Police. She walked over, saying, 'It's Sergeant Wood, isn't it?'

'That's right, ma'am. I'm surprised you remembered. It must be, what...? Seven years?'

'Something like that. I didn't expect to see one of ours working the desk.'

'It's the one concession they made to the notion that somebody has to guard the guards,' Wood said. 'I'm supposed to make sure nobody's human rights get breached.' He gave a hollow laugh. 'Like I could stop them doing anything they wanted behind closed doors.' Before Carol could reply, a loud buzzer sounded. Wood waved her urgently to one side. 'Against the wall, please, ma'am. For your own good. Now you get to see the grunts in action.'

Three corridors radiated off from the custody area like the tines of a trident. The clatter of heavy boots on hard flooring came first, then four of them with semi-automatics at port arms came running round the corner at the far end of the corridor. All in black riot gear, all with shaved heads, all terrifying. They stopped outside a cell door and began chanting, 'Stand up, stand up, stand up.' The noise seemed to go on for a very long time, though it could not have been more than half a minute. Carol could feel the adrenalin coursing through her, the fearsome sound reverberating inside her chest, and she was one of the empowered. How much worse must it be for anyone under arrest?

The lead grunt threw the door open so hard it slammed against the wall. Three of them disappeared inside while the fourth filled the doorway. Carol could hear more shouting. 'On your feet. Against the wall. Face the wall. Spread your arms. Spread your legs. Stand still, you fucker.' On and on, an endless barrage of commands. At last, the door man moved away and two of his colleagues backed out of the cell. The third

326

person out was a young Asian man, eyes wide, jaw set. He was trying to look through his guards, but they kept thwarting him by thrusting their faces towards his.

Once in the corridor, he was forced against the wall. One man behind him, one to the side, one in front. The fourth man ranged ahead of them, shouting, 'Clear!' every time he passed a doorway. They escorted the prisoner down the hallway, moving at a speed that made him take tiny little steps.

When the lead officer emerged in the custody area, he did a double take and stumbled when he saw Carol. 'Identify yourself,' he barked at her, swinging round and shouting, 'Hold right there,' back down the corridor.

Carol rolled her eyes. 'Well, obviously, I'm a cop.' She took out her ID and gave him name and rank. She jerked a head at Wood. 'He knows who I am.'

'Thank you, ma'am,' he barked in military tones. 'All clear,' he shouted. Carol watched while the prisoner was led into the interview corridor and hustled into one of the rooms there. The grunts took up post outside the room.

'Jesus,' Carol said, exhaling.

'Something else, isn't it? Don't get me wrong, I hate those bastard bombers as much as the next one, but I wonder what price we're paying when we fight them like this,' Wood said. 'Before this afternoon, I was as gung-ho as anybody else. But what I've seen today . . . This special training they've had. I think they come out with three key words – intimidation, intimidation, intimidation. Anybody that gets dragged in and put through this and they've done nowt –

well, it's a recruiting sergeant for the mad mullahs, isn't it?'

'I'm losing count of how many times I've had to take a deep breath today,' Carol said. 'Do you know who I'm supposed to see, by the way? There's things I need to be doing. Thirty-five people died this after-noon. I don't see how it serves their families to have me kicking my heels down here.'

'Didn't they tell you?' Wood said, resignation on his face.

'No, they didn't. I was just told that one of my lads was in a spot of bother.'

Wood shook his head. 'Rings no bells with me. Hang on a minute.' He picked up a phone. 'I've got DCI Jordan here ... Well, I think you should make time ... With respect, we've all got a lot on our plates this afternoon ...' He looked at the phone in disgust and put it down. 'Give them a minute,' he said, parodying their tough tones.

A couple of minutes passed, then the man Carol knew only as Johnny came through the door that led to the main part of the station. 'DCI Jordan. If you'd come with me, please.'

'Where? And why?' Carol asked, her temper hanging by a thread.

Johnny glanced at Wood. 'I'll explain everything in a minute, if you'd just come with me.'

Carol sketched a wave to Wood. 'If I'm not back in half an hour, Sergeant, call Mr Brandon.'

'There's no need to be so bolshie, you know,' Johnny said plaintively as they climbed the stairs to the main part of the station. 'We really are all on the same side.'

'That's what worries me,' Carol said. 'Now, why the hell am I here?'

Johnny led her into a small office and waved her to a chair. He picked up another chair, turned it round and straddled it, his muscular arms folded across the back. 'I'd really like for us to build some bridges here. It doesn't help your team or mine if we're at odds.'

Carol shrugged. 'So talk to me. Don't act as if my team is part of the problem. Don't patronize us. For a start, you could try treating me like a ranking officer by telling me why I'm here.'

'Point taken. Your boy Sam?'

'See what I mean? "Your boy Sam." He's Detective Constable Evans. Yes?'

Johnny inclined his head. 'DC Evans was at the stadium. What was he supposed to be doing?'

'Are you interviewing me?' Carol said, not even trying to keep the incredulity out of her voice.

Johnny ran a hand over his shaven head, his expression perplexed. 'Look,' he said, sounding exasperated. 'We got off on the wrong foot. You don't like us trampling all over your ground, and I totally understand that. I am not interrogating you, I'm just trying to clarify something before it turns into a situation for all of us.'

'That's not how it feels.'

'No. I realize that. We're not very good at manners. We're not supposed to be. They knock the etiquette out of us when they train us for CTC. I'm sorry. I know we come off as arseholes, but that's how we need to be, doing what we do. We're not stupid, though. We didn't get our ranks because of our size.' He spread his hands in a gesture of frankness. 'One of our teams found your DC in a quiet corner of the stadium with a young Asian male dressed in overalls. He was clearly questioning him. When our guys appeared, the witness, suspect, whatever, clammed up. And your boy refused to share the product of his interview. So we brought them back here. Since when neither of them has said a bloody word. Apart from their names. Oh, and the Asian wants a lawyer. So, I thought to myself, what's the best way to resolve this? And I thought of you.'

'You thought of me how? As somebody you could bully? Somebody you could intimidate?'

Johnny gave a harsh sigh. 'No. I thought of you as somebody who had impressed me with her smarts. Somebody who had a rep in the Met ...'

'What do you mean, a rep in the Met?' Carol demanded defensively.

Johnny looked disbelieving. 'A rep as a bloody good cop,' he said. 'What do you think? People I respect think you're the dog's bollocks. So I thought you were the one who could persuade DC Evans to co-operate with this investigation.'

'Where is he?'

Johnny considered for a long moment. 'Come on, I'll take you to him.'

She followed him back down the hall to another interview room. Sam Evans was sitting on a chair tipped back against the wall, hands clasped behind his head in an attitude of relaxation. When Carol walked in, he jerked forward and stood up. 'Sorry you got dragged into this,' he said.

Carol turned to Johnny. 'Could you leave us, please?'

Johnny bowed his head and retreated. Sam watched him go, shaking his head with ill-disguised contempt. 'What have they said I've done?'

'They say they found you interviewing a young Asian male wearing overalls at Victoria Park. That the pair of you clammed up and refused to say anything. That you won't hand over the product of your interview.' Carol leaned against the wall, her arms folded across her chest.

Sam gave an incredulous little laugh. 'That's one spin you could put on it. Try it from another angle. For a start, he's wearing overalls because he's a cleaner at the stadium. Nothing suspicious about that, is there? For another thing, he's clearly not a suspect. His name is Vijay Gupta. He's a Hindu, not a Muslim. So it seems to me that the CTC guys are getting their knickers in a twist over somebody who is in no sense a potential suspect. I don't have any product to hand over, ma'am. We'd barely started talking.'

Carol didn't know whether to believe him. He was, she knew, the perfect dissembler. What mattered was getting him out of there. Then she could find out whether he was telling the truth. 'Give me a minute,' she said.

She went back outside, where Johnny was waiting. 'There's nothing to tell. The man he had just begun questioning isn't even a Muslim. Now, if you're sincere about building bridges, you shouldn't stop me leaving here right now, with my officer. And I suggest you let Mr Gupta go home, since the only thing he's done to warrant your suspicion is to talk to a police officer.' She turned round, opened the door and said, 'DC Evans? Time we were on our way.'

Head high, Carol led the way through familiar corridors to the back entrance of Scargill Street. Nobody tried to stop them. Once they were in the car and out of the car park, Sam said, 'Working on the principle that we were being recorded, I wasn't strictly accurate in there, ma'am.'

Carol flashed a quick glance at his rueful face and sighed. 'That's what I was afraid of, Sam. That funny smell? It's bridges burning.'

Carol's plans to follow up Sam's disclosure were thwarted by the unexpected presence of John Brandon in her squad room, forbidding in his dress uniform, cap under his arm. Her heart sank. Had her latest run-in with CTC made it back ahead of her? He looked as serious as she'd ever seen him. She'd barely made it through the door when he spoke. 'DCI Jordan, I was looking for you. I need a word.' He gestured towards her office and she led the way in.

'Carol, I have some difficult news,' he said, settling into one of the visitors' chairs and tossing his cap carelessly on to the other.

'Sir?'

'You remember Tom Cross? Ex-Detective . . .'

She nodded, caught off-balance by the direction of the conversation. 'I saw him this afternoon at Victoria Park. A paramedic was helping him to an ambulance. He'd apparently been helping the injured, but he'd taken too much out of himself.' Understanding dawned. 'He didn't make it,' she said, surprised at the stab of sorrow she felt.

'No, he didn't make it. His heart gave out.'

'That's tragic,' Carol said. 'Who'd have thought that

helping other people would be the death of him? Did he have heart problems?'

Brandon shook his head. 'No. And it would appear that it wasn't helping with the rescue attempts that killed him.' He looked troubled; Carol suddenly saw how he had aged in the past few years and it gave her a disturbing glimpse of her own mortality.

'What do you mean, sir?'

'One of the doctors on the civil emergency team down at Bradfield Cross is Elinor Blessing.'

Carol nodded. 'She's the one who spotted the ricin poisoning.'

'Exactly. And she says herself that's probably the only reason poison occurred to her in this case. But occur to her it did. Sadly, before they could get enough of the antidote into his system, his heart failed. They tried to keep him going till they could finish the treatment, but it didn't work out.'

Shocked, Carol clutched at a straw. 'You sure she's not just seeing poison everywhere because of Robbie?'

'I suppose it's possible. But she says this wasn't ricin. She thinks it was another plant derivative, though. Foxgloves or something. The bottom line is that she says she can't write this up as natural causes or accident.'

'So, murder, then?' Carol said.

'It looks that way. At least to Dr Blessing it does. I want your team on this. He was one of us, no matter what happened at the end of his career. You should look at possible links to Robbie Bishop too. Maybe ask Tony what he thinks, if he's up to it.' Brandon picked at a piece of lint on his black trousers. 'I know it's a bit of an irony, given what Tom thought about Tony and his ilk. But we throw everything at this. Leave his widow till tomorrow, but somebody should talk to the doctor this evening. She should be in A&E till late.' He stood up and retrieved his cap.

'We'll do our best,' Carol said. 'But there were another thirty-five murders in Bradfield today. We're trying to give them our best attention too.'

Brandon turned back, his face stony. 'Leave them to CTC. Concentrate on Tom Cross.'

'With respect, sir . . .'

'That's an order, Chief Inspector. I'll expect a preliminary report on Monday.' He marched out of the room, erect as if on parade.

'That is just so wrong,' Carol muttered under her breath. 'So bloody wrong.' She leaned back in her chair and sat for five minutes staring at the ceiling. Then she jumped to her feet and stood in the doorway. 'Everybody – in here, now,' she called.

They jammed themselves in, Kevin and Chris claiming the chairs on the grounds of seniority. 'Sorry about this,' Carol said. 'But I don't want anybody barging in on us. Sam, keep an eye on the main door. OK. Here's how it is. I know you are all as angry and upset as I am about the attack on Victoria Park this afternoon. It was a horrific experience for everyone concerned. But it's our job to get beyond our emotional response and to do what's necessary.' She pushed her hands through her shaggy blonde hair and jiggled her head. 'And I believe you're all as determined to do that as I am.

'Only problem is, we've been told not to investigate the thirty-five murders that happened in our force area this afternoon. Or at least, not unless we're invited to carry out certain tasks on behalf of the CTC. Now, I don't know about you, but that's just not good enough for me. It's my intention to pursue such lines of inquiry as come our way. We have a unique perspective here – this is our patch and we know it. We'll pass on outcomes to CTC, but in the first instance, what comes to us stays with us. It's probably not going to do our careers any good, but I'm not in this for the sake of the glory. If there's any one of you who isn't happy about that, say so now. I won't hold it against you, and there's plenty of other work to be going on with.' She looked around expectantly. Nobody moved.

'OK. In that case, we're in this together. Now . . .' She saw Stacey raise one finger. 'Stacey?'

'We've already got Yousef Aziz's laptop,' she said. 'Kevin and Paula brought it back from his house.'

Carol frowned. 'Who's Yousef Aziz?'

'The bomber,' Kevin said. He brought her up to speed on what he and Paula had uncovered. 'We didn't want to phone you when you were with CTC,' he added apologetically.

'Not a problem. Great work, guys. How are you doing with it, Stacey?'

'He tried to cover his tracks, but it's all over his hard disk. Recipes for TATP, how to build a bomb, how to make a detonator. Deleted emails inquiring about the availability of chemicals. I'm copying it all right now, before we hand it over to CTC. What's interesting . . .' she tailed off, unsure of her ground when she wasn't talking about her speciality.

'Yes?' Carol said. 'What's interesting is . . .?'

'Well, it's a bit of a dog that didn't bark,' Stacey said. 'Apart from the deleted emails about the chemicals, there are no emails at all on this laptop. Nothing to indicate any co-conspirators. It's clean. Either there's another computer somewhere, or they communicated face to face and via texts, or he did this by himself.'

'There must be a computer at work. It's a family firm, he'll have had access,' Chris said.

'Too late,' Stacey said. 'CTC have already got that.'

'How do you know that?' Chris said.

'News footage on Sky. They just showed the men in black raiding First Fabrics and walking out with armfuls of hardware,' Stacey said. 'That's the advantage of having two screens.'

'Thanks, Stacey. That's given us something to think about,' Carol said. 'And we do have something else which we think we have to ourselves at this point. Sam?'

Sam squared his shoulders, ready to strut a little. 'I got a lovely break at Victoria Park. When Chris texted us to say the suspect was a young Asian man wearing overalls and a baseball cap, I was walking along the back of the stand when what do I see but an Asian male wearing overalls and a baseball cap. So I get alongside him double quick. Turns out he's not even Muslim. His name's Vijay Gupta and he's a cleaner at the ground. I run the bomber's description past him and when I get to the A1 Electricals van, I see him reacting. He doesn't want to talk about it, but when I push him, he says he saw a van like that on Thursday evening. He and his brother were visiting a cousin who lives in a bedsit in Colton and he noticed the van because it was parked round the back, out of the way, where him and his cousin usually park so they don't piss off the residents, and he'd never seen it there before.' Sam couldn't keep the self-satisfied grin off his face.

'You did get an address before they huckled you off to Scargill Street?' Kevin said stiffly.

'Oh yeah, I got an address.' Sam reached for a piece of paper and a marker pen off Carol's desk. He wrote something down, then displayed it for all to see. 'You could say I got an address.'

'No, Sam, you didn't get an address. We got an anonymous phone tip,' Carol said firmly. 'Things are already difficult enough with CTC without us going out of our way to make things worse. We got a phone tip and we decided to check it out before we wasted CTC's time with it. That's the line. Now, before we all get stuck into that, there are a couple of other matters. Paula, I know it feels like a lifetime ago, but did you get any further with tracking down Jack Anderson?'

Paula looked at Stacey, who shook her head. 'No, chief. No progress.'

'And I got nowhere with Robbie's parents. They'd never heard the name. So we've got no active leads to pursue on Robbie?' They all exchanged glances, disappointment obvious. 'I'd prefer it if that wasn't the case, but it does mean we're not being derelict by looking at other things. And there is one very big other thing that has just landed in our laps. Seven years ago, a detective superintendent left Bradfield Police under something of a cloud,' Carol said, an

337

image of her old boss as he had been slipping unwanted into her mind.

'Popeye Cross,' Kevin said.

Carol inclined her head towards him. 'That's right. Well, Tom Cross redeemed himself this afternoon. He was one of the heroes who dragged the injured to safety after the bomb. He ended up being taken to hospital himself. He died there earlier this evening. But not because of anything he did in the wake of the bombing. According to the doctor who treated him, he was poisoned.'

'Poisoned?' Paula interrupted. 'Like Robbie? With ricin?'

'No, not with ricin. Though the doctor who treated Tom Cross is the same one who diagnosed the ricin in Robbie,' Carol said.

'Sounds like she's either one smart cookie or else Munchausen's by Proxy,' Chris said. Carol thought she was only half-joking.

'Well, that's what we're going to have to figure out. Paula, I want you to go down to Bradfield Cross A&E and talk to Dr Blessing.'

Paula's face said it all. They were chasing the big game, she was consigned to the small fry. 'But, chief ...'

'Paula, you're the best interviewer we have. Besides, you know her already. I need you to do this because we need everything we can get from her. What poison it was. When it was likely to have been administered. Make arrangements for samples to go to toxicology, and get the results from any lab work they did at Bradfield Cross. Stacey, get what you can from Aziz's hard drive, then be very polite and hand it in to the CTC people in the HOLMES suite. The rest of you, with me. It's time to do what we're paid for.'

'It's a bit freaky, this Tom Cross murder,' Kevin said as Chris eased the car through the heavy traffic towards Yousef Aziz's address.

'What? Because you knew the geezer?'

'Well yeah, that. But the poison thing. If Danny Wade and Robbie Bishop are connected, that's two guys who went to Harriestown High and ended up poisoned, right?'

'Right. But I don't think where they went to school is a big deal.'

'No? Would it surprise you if I told you that Tom Cross is another former pupil of Harriestown High?' Kevin was drumming his fingers on his knees. 'Another one who started off with nothing and ended up loaded. He won the pools, you know.'

'I didn't know that,' Chris said. 'You're right, it is a bit freaky. But I think that's all it is.'

Kevin shook his head. 'No. Three's the charm. It's more than just a bizarre coincidence.'

Chris swore at a white van cutting in front of her. 'How can it be? You think somebody's killing people from your old school because they've made a bob or two? I tell you, even Tony Hill would balk at that one.'

'You can't argue with the facts.'

'We don't know hardly any of the facts,' Chris pointed out. 'But if you think you're on the right track, you'd better watch your back,' she added, a tease in her voice.

339

'What do you mean? I'm skint, me,' Kevin said.

'Yeah, but you drive a rich man's car,' she said, slowing for the final turn before their destination.

'It's not a rich man's car. You could have it for sixteen grand,' Kevin said. 'Anyway, it's not me I'm worried about. There's other rich bastards around who went to the Double Aitch. Maybe we should be warning them.'

Chris shook her head, amused. 'Do me a favour? Make sure I'm in the room when you run it past Jordan.' She pulled up on double yellow lines outside their target address. 'OK, here we are.' She got out of the car but Kevin didn't move. Chris leaned back into the car. 'Come on, Kev. Brood on your own time. We've got Imperial Storm Troopers to piss off.'

He scratched his head and opened the door. 'For once, I wish Tony Hill was around,' he said as he followed Chris up the drive. 'Poison, the Double Aitch and money. Times three. He'd make a case.'

It didn't take long to find out which bedsit had belonged to Yousef Aziz. Two knocked doors and they had the answer. For form's sake, Carol knocked and shouted, 'Police, open up,' before Sam and Kevin shoulder-charged the door. Checking that they were all gloved up, Carol led the way into the comfort-less room. The bitter tang of chemicals hung in the air, making her eyes water and her sinuses prickle.

There wasn't much to occupy the four of them. A fridge that contained nothing but labelled containers of chemicals; a draining board with rinsed glass apparatus; a torn packet of rocket engines with two still inside the clear plastic; and a small sports holdall.

'Should we get the bomb guys up here to check out the holdall?' Kevin asked, his face tight with nerves.

Her first instinct was to say, *No, to hell with it.* But when she examined that gut reaction, she couldn't find a rationale for it. And without a rationale, she couldn't take that level of risk with their lives. For a moment, she dithered, hating herself for it. She wanted to inspire her team, not give them grounds for worry. 'Give me a minute,' she said, stepping out on to the landing. She pulled out her phone and called Tony's hospital room. He answered on the first ring. 'Carol,' he said before she spoke. It surprised her because the hospital phones had no called ID feature. Then she understood that he didn't expect calls from anyone else.

'Hi,' she said.

'Are you OK?'

'I'm fine. But I need your help. Imagine we're in the bedsit the bomber used to build his device. There's no evidence of anybody else being involved. There's a holdall sitting by the door. Is it likely to be booby-trapped?'

'No,' he said decisively.

'Why? I mean, that was my gut reaction, but why?'

'It's another gesture of contempt. Look, here we are, right in the midst of you. This is how we work, this is who we are. We want to show you just how easy this is. Go ahead, Carol. Open the bag.'

She let out a sigh of relief. 'Thanks.'

'And if I'm wrong, and you do get blown to kingdom come, I'll buy you dinner.'

She could hear the smile in his voice. 'I'll talk to you later.'

'Come round when you're done. It doesn't matter how late it is, just come.'

'I will.' She closed the phone and walked back in. The other three were clustered round the draining board reading a list of instructions on the wall.

'Organized little shit,' Chris said.

'But still no sign of any accomplices,' Sam noted.

'We're opening the bag,' Carol said. 'Well, I'm opening it. Out on the landing, you three.'

'Don't be daft,' Chris said. 'If it's safe enough for you, it's safe enough for all of us, right, guys?' Both men looked uncertain, but they made no move for the door. 'Come on, the Al-Quaeda lot don't booby-trap their bomb factories, they want us to see how clever they are.' So saying, she grabbed the bag, swung it on to the narrow bed and unzipped it.

It was a moment of profound bathos. Nothing could have been further from what they expected. A pair of jeans, a pair of chinos. A pair of blue Converse shoes. Five T-shirts. Two striped Ralph Lauren shirts. A lightweight fleece hoodie. Four pairs of boxers, four pairs of black sports socks. 'Looks as if he was planning on coming back here,' Carol said, puzzled. 'What kind of suicide bomber packs for his trip to paradise?'

Chris had her hand inside the bag, fumbling with a zip. 'There's more,' she said, reaching in. A state-of-the-art mobile WAP phone, a digital camera, an EU passport, a driving licence and a folded sheet of paper. Chris handed the paper to Carol who unfolded it.

'It's an e-ticket. For this evening's flight to Toronto,' she said. 'Booked through hopefully.co.uk.'

Chris reached for her phone. 'Christ, I hope Stacey's

still got his machine.' She dialled and said, 'Stace? It's Chris. You still got Aziz's laptop? … Great. He's got a flight booked through hopefully.co.uk. I need you to … yeah, that's it. Call me back.' She ended the call. 'She's going to see whether he saved his ID and password on the computer. If he did, then she can access his booking history, see what else comes up.'

Kevin was studying the passport and the driving licence. 'This is very odd,' he said. 'Not only does it look like he was planning to come back, it also looks like he didn't expect to be a suspect. He's using his own passport and his own driving licence, as if he doesn't expect anybody in Canada to be looking for him. It doesn't make sense.'

'Maybe it was his own little fantasy,' Sam said. 'What got him through it.'

Carol picked up the mobile phone and bagged it. 'This goes to Stacey. The rest of it, put it back together again the way you found it, Chris. Time to come clean.' She took out her phone and the card she'd been given earlier and keyed in the unfamiliar number. When it was answered, she said, 'David? This is Carol Jordan. I think we've found your bomb factory.' She tossed the bagged phone to Sam and made the 'shoo' gesture with her free hand. 'An anonymous tip. Didn't want to bother you with it until we were sure it panned out.' She winked at Chris and Kevin. 'No, we haven't touched a thing. You never know what might be booby-trapped … No, I'll have my officers wait here for you.' She gave him the address and ended the call. 'When the CTC get here, you're free to go.' She looked at her watch.

'It's been a long day. We'll reconvene at eight tomorrow.'

Walking across the cracked tarmac to her car, Carol felt every minute of that long day. Her muscles ached and her body craved a drink. There were plenty of bottles at home, stacked in the rack, waiting for her. But she had one more call to make before she could choose one of those. Maybe she could stop at an off-licence, pick out a decent red, something good to share. He'd like that. And it gave her all the excuse she needed to slip into the comforting embrace of alcohol. Anything to take her mind away from those twisted and torn bodies. When she closed her eyes, she did not want to revisit the injured, the dying and the dead.

The waiting area of A&E at Bradfield Cross had nothing to recommend it as a place to spend a Saturday night. People wandered around with plastic cups of tea, bottles of water and cans of fizzy drinks, looking dazed and miserable. The chairs were full of bewildered and exhausted relatives of the injured, their children sleeping or grizzling. Journalists kept sneaking in and drifted from person to person, trying to get some quotes before they were spotted and ordered out. The department had been closed to routine casualties, which provoked frequent loud arguments with the security guards, battles which threatened to spill over from the verbal to the physical at any moment. When Paula arrived, a pair of drunks with bloody faces had been remonstrating with the security guards. She had walked straight up to them, face to face and toe to toe with the noisier one. 'Fuck off now or spend the night in the cells,' she snarled. 'Don't you know what happened here today? Take your scratches somewhere else.'

The drunk thought about it for a millisecond then, seeing something implacable in her face, he backed off. 'Fucking dyke pig bitch,' he shouted once he was far enough away.

The security guards looked almost impressed. 'If we could threaten them like that, we'd have no trouble of a night,' one said, holding the door open for her.

'You obviously need more dyke pig bitches to teach you how to do it,' she muttered as she waded through the sea of miserable humanity to the desk. She looked up at the clock. Ten past ten. Her interview with Jana Jankowicz felt like half a lifetime away. A receptionist with cornrows and nails that could have been stripped off and used as luges for small children gave her a cool, weary look. 'I'm looking for Dr Blessing,' she said, producing her ID.

The receptionist sniffed. 'I'll see what I can do. Take a seat,' she added automatically.

Paula wanted to laugh and to cry simultaneously. 'I'll just wait here, if it's all right with you.' She leaned against the counter and closed her eyes, trying to shut out the discordant background noises.

A touch on her arm made her start back to full consciousness. Elinor Blessing was looking at her with a faint smile. 'Sorry, I didn't mean to startle you. I thought only junior doctors could actually sleep standing up.'

Paula cracked a smile. 'Welcome to my world,' she said. 'Thanks for seeing me. I know you're run off your feet today.'

'It's eased up now,' Elinor said, leading Paula back into the main wing of the hospital. 'We've pretty much done all we can down here. It's just that we've still got some patients who really need to be admitted, only we've not got beds for them here. You've saved me from having to call round to try and find somewhere for them to go.'

They ended up in a doctors' coffee room on the third floor. It reminded Paula of every similar room she'd ever been in. The same battered chairs past their best, rickety tables marked with rings, unmatching mugs and hectoring notices about washing up, stealing biscuits and putting rubbish in bins. Elinor got a couple of mugs of coffee from a machine and plonked one in front of Paula. 'That should keep you awake till some time next week. It's junior-doctor strength.'

'Thanks.' Paula didn't know why this woman was being so nice to her, but she wasn't about to fight it. She took a sip of coffee and found no grounds to disagree with Elinor's assessment of the brew. 'So, Tom Cross. You think he was poisoned?' Paula took out her notebook.

Elinor shook her head. 'When I spoke to someone earlier, that's what I thought. Now I've had some of the labs back, I don't think so. I know so.'

'OK. And what did your tests tell you?'

Elinor fiddled with her mug. 'Most doctors, the only poisoning they'll ever see is when people take deliberate or accidental overdoses. We're not trained to look for it. Not really. So it's very weird for me to see two cases of deliberate poisoning in the same week. At first, I thought I was imagining things. But

I wasn't. Tom Cross was deliberately poisoned with a cardiac glycoside.'

'Can you spell that for me?' Paula gave Elinor her best pathetic shrug. 'And then can you tell me what it is?'

Elinor took the notebook from her and wrote it down. 'A cardiac glycoside is a naturally occurring compound, generally found in plants. It acts primarily on the heart, either beneficially or not, depending on the glycoside in question and on how much you absorb. An example would be foxgloves, which are the source of digoxin. It's used as a heart medicine, but the wrong dose will kill you.' She handed back the notebook with a smile.

'So is that what killed Tom Cross? Foxgloves?'

'No. What killed him was oleander.'

'Oleander?'

'You've probably seen it on holiday abroad. It's a bushy shrub with narrow leaves and the flowers are pink or white. It's pretty common and it's very poisonous. I looked it up earlier. There's a story that some of Napoleon's soldiers used oleander twigs to kebab their meat with and by morning they were dead. There is an antidote, but often patients die before they can absorb enough of it to make a difference. And to be honest, when you consider Tom Cross's age and weight, his heart probably wasn't in great shape to start with. He didn't have much of a chance. I'm sorry. I know he used to be a police officer.'

'I never knew him when he was in the job,' Paula said. 'But my boss did. So, Dr Blessing ...'

'Elinor. It's Elinor, please.'

Was she flirting? Paula was too tired to work it out. Or, to be honest, to care. Tonight, all she wanted were the facts, so she could go home and sleep. The coffee wasn't working, apparently. She stifled a yawn. 'So, Elinor, have you got any idea when this poison would have been administered? And how?'

'It acts quite quickly. He said he'd had stomach cramps and a couple of incidents of diarrhoea at the football match. While he was still lucid, he said he'd started feeling bad after lunch. He'd had lamb kebabs with rice and a sauce with herbs, he said. You've got two possible sources of oleandrin right there. The lamb could have been marinated with oleander leaves, or sap. Then the twigs could have been used to kebab the lamb. Like the Napoleonic story.' She shook her head. 'Horrible. So insidious a way to kill someone. Such a breach of trust.'

'Did he say where he'd had lunch?'

'He said someone had cooked it for him. So I imagine it was at their house.' Elinor rubbed the bridge of her nose as she struggled to remember what Tom Cross had said. 'Was it Jack . . .? No, not Jack. Jake. That was it. Jake.'

Suddenly Paula was awake, her mind racing with connections. 'You're sure it was Jake and not Jack?'

Elinor looked uncertain, catching a corner of her lower lip with her teeth. 'I'm pretty sure it was Jake. But I could be mistaken.'

Harriestown High, Paula thought. Jack Anderson. Robbie Bishop, Danny Wade and now maybe Tom Cross. Was that the link? Was that what drew them together? They couldn't have known each other at school, not given the disparity in ages. But maybe there was some former pupil organization they all belonged to. Some charity event at the school that had brought them together. Some occasion where they'd all witnessed something they shouldn't have? 'You've been very helpful,' she said softly.

'Really?'

'You have no idea,' Paula said. Now she was wide awake. She knew there would be no sleep for her until she'd found out where Tom Cross had gone to school. She wasn't sure where to look for that information at half past ten on a Saturday night, but she knew a woman who would.

Tony drifted slowly up into consciousness. In the space of a week, he'd grown so accustomed to the comings and goings of the nursing staff that the presence of another person in his room was no longer enough to wake him up. It took something more. Something like the suck and slither and pop of a cork leaving a bottle, followed by the soft glug of liquid into plastic. 'Carol,' he groaned as he put the pieces together. In the dim city light that seeped through the thin curtains, he could just make out her shape in the chair next to the bed. He fumbled for the bed control and eased himself upwards.

'Shall I put the light on?' she asked.

'Pull the curtain back, let a bit more light in from outside.'

She uncurled from the chair and did as he'd suggested. On her way back, she poured him a glass. He sniffed appreciatively. 'Lovely, lovely shiraz,' he said. 'Funny, I don't think I would have listed decent wine among the things I would miss most if I was on a desert island. Just shows me how wrong I can be.' He took another sip, felt himself rising inexorably into consciousness. 'This must have been a terrible day for you,' he said.

'You have no idea,' she said. 'I've seen things today I don't think I'll ever forget. Horrible injuries. Body parts strewn over a football stand. Blood and brains splattered on walls.' She took a long swallow of her wine. 'You think you've seen it all. You think there can't be anything worse than the crime scenes you've already processed. And then this. Thirty-five dead in the bombing, plus one.'

'The one being the bomber?'

'No, the one being Tom Cross.'

He nearly slopped the wine from his cup in his surprise. 'Popeye Cross? I don't understand. He died in the bombing?' His old nemesis's name was the last one he'd expected to hear in connection with the Bradfield bombing.

'No. The bombing apparently brought out the hero in him. He just got stuck right in. They say he saved lives out there. No, what did for him was poison. He'd been poisoned before he even got to the match.'

'Poisoned? How? What with?'

'I don't know the details yet. Paula's somewhere in the hospital getting the information from the doctor who picked up on it. A stroke of luck, really. Because of the bombing she got drafted into A&E, and because of Robbie Bishop, she was particularly receptive to the idea of poisoning.'

'That makes three,' he said. 'And all from round here. Looks like you've got a serial poisoner on your patch.'

Carol glared at him. 'Different poisons, different set-ups. Different delivery systems.'

'Signature,' Tony said. 'Murder at a distance. Targeted administration. Time lag between ingestion and death. These are linked, Carol. You don't get that many deliberate poisonings these days. They've been replaced by guns and divorce. Very Victorian, poisonings. Nasty, insidious, destructive of communities and families. But not very twenty-first century. Admit it, Carol, you've got a serial.'

'I'll wait for the evidence,' she said stubbornly. 'Meanwhile, Tom Cross's death is the one murder I'm actually allowed to investigate.' The anger was coming off her in waves. He could almost taste her fury, a dark bitterness laid over the jammy fruit of the wine.

Tony struggled to make sense of Carol's words. 'What do you mean, the only one you're allowed to investigate?'

'They've taken the bombing away from us,' she said. 'This new Counter Terrorism Command. The misbegotten marriage of Special Branch and the Anti-Terrorism Branch. The northern arm is based in Manchester. Only now, they're in Bradfield with their jackboots and their "no names, no pack drill". Literally. They won't give you their real names, they don't wear any numbers. They say it's to prevent reprisals. I say it's to prevent any comeback. Paula calls them the Imperial Storm Troopers, and she's not far off the mark. They're scary, Tony. Very scary. I saw them in action in Scargill Street, and I tell you, I was ashamed to be a copper.'

'And they've assumed operational command?' he said, imagining what that must be like for someone

351

with as much pride in herself and her team as Carol had.

'Totally. We're supposed to be at their beck and call if they want us to do anything.' Carol gave a harsh laugh. 'It's like being in a police state, and the freaky thing is, I'm supposed to be one of them.'

'And are you doing what you're supposed to do?' Tony asked, trying to keep his tone neutral.

'What do you think?' She didn't wait for an answer. 'Let them do their thing, their rounding up of the usual suspects, their harassment of anybody who happens to be young, male and Muslim. And we'll do what we're best at.'

Tony knew what she wanted, what she *needed* was for him to sympathize, to take her side against those she perceived as the bad guys. To take her part, right or wrong. The trouble was he thought she was wrong. And if there was any value in their relationship, he believed it was rooted in honesty. Some might call it emotional unavailability, and there was likely some truth in that too. But he couldn't lie to Carol, not with any degree of conviction. Nor she to him, he thought. There were times when it was hard to hear the truth; harder still to deliver it. But in the long run, he was convinced they'd both looked back on those moments with an acceptance that they were more closely bound by having survived them. Tony took a deep breath and jumped off the high diving board. 'And what you're best at is not investigating and cracking terrorist cells.'

There was a moment of complete silence in the room. 'Are you saying you agree with what's happening here?' He didn't have to see Carol to picture her indignation.

352

'I think policing potential and actual terrorists is a very specific kind of policing,' he said, trying to tell the truth as he saw it without fuelling her anger. 'And I think it should be done by specialists. People who are trained to understand the mindset, people who can walk away from their lives and go deep undercover to infiltrate, people who are prepared to climb inside the terrorists' heads and try to work out where they're going to take their campaigns next.' He scratched his head. 'I don't think it's the same skill set as you and your team possess.'

'Are you saying it's right to take this outrage away from us? That we shouldn't police our own city?' Carol demanded. He could hear the certainty of betrayal in her voice. She finished her wine and poured another cupful.

'I'm saying there should be something like the CTC to work with you. Just because they've executed it so badly doesn't mean the idea's a bad one,' Tony said gently. 'This is not about you, Carol. It's not a criticism of you or your people. It's not saying you're crap or incompetent or any of those things. It's an acknowledgement of the fact that terrorism is different. And it needs a different approach.'

'A judgement that doesn't apply to you, I suppose. I bet you think you're just as well equipped to profile terrorists as you are serial killers?' Carol said sarcastically.

Tony felt himself in a lose-lose situation. There was no reply that would persuade Carol to back off at this point. He might as well carry on with the truth. It was often the most efficient response. 'I do think I have some useful insights, yes.'

'Of course you do. The great doctor.'

Stung at last, Tony said, 'OK. Try this for size. This bombing doesn't profile like terrorism.'

That stunned her into silence, he thought. But not for long. 'What's that supposed to mean?' Carol said with a note of deliberation rather than the hostility he'd half-expected.

'Think about it. What is terrorism for?'

Almost without pause, Carol said, 'It's an attempt to force social or political change by violent means.'

'And how does it aim to do that?'

'I don't know . . . By making the population so afraid that they put pressure on the politicians? I think that's what IRA terrorism was about.' Carol leaned forward in her chair, eager and engaged now.

'Exactly. It aims to create a climate of fear and mistrust. It aims to attack the areas of life where people need to feel safe. So, public transport. Retail. People need to travel, they need to shop. Right away, we can see that a football stadium, crowded though it may be, isn't in the same category. Nobody is compelled to go to the football in order to survive.' He grinned. 'Some fans might think they feel that way, but they know deep down their lives won't fall to bits in the way they would if they stopped going to work or to the shops.'

'I take your point. But what if they decided a lower-level target was a better option because the primary targets are just too hard for them now?'

'That would be a valid argument if it was true, but it's not, and you know it. You can't police every train, every tube, every bus, every shopping mall or super-market. There's plenty of soft targets there. So the

354

first support for my argument against this profiling as terrorism is the macro target.'

Carol reached for the wine again, 'You've got more than one support?'

'You know me, Carol. I like to be well armed against the likes of you. Line of support number two – the micro target. The thing about terrorism is that, for it to work, it has to strike at the lives of ordinary people. The sort of terrorists we're seeing now do not go for the spectacular assassination. They learned that from the IRA. High-profile murders like Lord Mountbatten and Airey Neave make a big splash, sure. But people are angered and outraged by them, they're not terrorized. Ask your average person in the street to name the top Irish terrorist events of the troubles, and they'll say Omagh, Warrington, Manchester, Birmingham, Guildford, the Baltic Exchange. What they remember are the events that made them feel personally threatened.' He paused to take a drink.

'So what you're saying is that the corporate hospitality boxes were the wrong target?' Carol said.

She'd always been quick. It was one of the things he liked most about her. 'Exactly,' Tony said. 'Going for the fat cats, that's the sort of thing an anti-globalization terrorist would do. But not the Islamic fundamentalist. He wants maximum bucks for his bangs. An Al-Quaeda type of attack would have placed the bomb lower down, in among the punters. Or in one of the other stands.'

'Maybe this was the only place they could be sure of getting into? Aziz posed as an electrician, maybe this was the only electrical junction room right under the stands?'

Tony shook his head. 'Now you're really reaching. I'm betting the utility layouts are pretty much the same on all four stands. The stadium's only a few years old, it's not like it's a thing of shreds and patches like the old ground was. There's bound to be other similar spots that would have taken out more of the hoi polloi. No, this was a deliberate choice, and that's the second reason I'm dubious about this being terrorism.'

'It's a bit thin, Tony. Or do you have something else?' He could hear the edge of scepticism in Carol's voice.

'Given how far out of the loop I am, I think you should be impressed with this much. If you're determined to follow your own lines of inquiry rather than just do what CTC asks you to, there's maybe something there for you to chew on.' And at least it might keep her out of direct conflict with CTC, he thought. 'And when you know more about Aziz and his accomplices, it might even make sense.' Tony leaned back, his energy spent.

'Actually, we've already come up against something that's a bit odd,' Carol said. 'If you're not too tired?'

His interest quickened in spite of his weariness. 'I'm OK. What do you have?'

'It's kind of weird. We got to the bomb factory ahead of CTC. And that holdall I called you about – it was packed with clean clothes, his passport, driving licence and an e-ticket for this evening's flight to Toronto. As if he was expecting to come back. Not just to come back to the bedsit, but to get away afterwards without being suspected. Which is absolutely not what suicide bombers do.'

356

There wasn't much in the field of human behaviour that made Tony stop in his tracks. But what Carol had to say left him fumbling for a response. 'No, they don't,' he said at last.

'Sam had this theory that it was some form of talisman,' Carol said.

'Doesn't work,' Tony muttered, his mind ranging across his experience to try to make sense of what he'd heard. 'The only thing that I can think of is that he wasn't a suicide bomber.' He looked at Carol, her face a dim outline in the near-dark. 'And if he wasn't a suicide bomber, then the chances are this wasn't a terrorist attack.'

Sunday

Carol woke up with the low mutter of TV news in her ears. Her mouth tasted of stale wine and a needle of pain shot down her stiff neck as she tried to move. For a moment she couldn't think where she was. Then she remembered. Carol coughed and opened her eyes. Tony was watching the TV news footage of the bombing. The newsreader was talking about the dead, their individual photographs appearing on the screen behind him. Happy, smiling faces, oblivious to their mortality. People whose death had punched holes through the lives of the living.

'Did you get much sleep?' Tony asked, glancing across at her.

'Apparently,' Carol said. They'd talked in circles through the rest of the bottle of wine, most of which she'd drunk. When she'd made a move to leave, he'd pointed out that she'd had too much wine to even think about driving. Both knew that the chances of getting a taxi in the small hours of Sunday morning in central Bradfield were low to vanishing. So he'd given her a blanket and she'd stretched out in the chair. She'd expected to doze restlessly, but to her surprise she'd woken feeling rested and alert. She cleared her throat and looked at her watch. Quarter to seven. Time enough to go home, feed Nelson, shower and change and get back in time for her morning conference.

'Good. What are your plans for today?' He turned the volume down on the TV.

'Briefing with the team at eight, then I'm going to talk to Tom Cross's widow.' She pulled a face. 'That'll be fun, given how he always blamed me for his fall from grace.' She stood up, trying to shake the creases from her trousers, not wanting to think about the state of her make-up or her hair.

'You'll be fine. There's got to be a link there somewhere.'

Carol stopped midway through combing her hair with her fingers, struck by the sort of thought thrown up by the subconscious during sleep. 'What if your crazy idea about this not being terrorism is right and this is all part of a vendetta against Bradfield Victoria?'

Tony smiled. 'What? Alex Ferguson's scared of what'll happen when Manchester United come to Victoria Park next month?'

'Very funny. Better not make jokes like that around CTC. It's a well-known fact that you have to have your sense of humour surgically removed when you join them.'

'I know that. I do watch *Spooks*.'

Carol was surprised. 'You do? I don't.'

'You should. They do.'

'I don't think so.' She struggled with the thought of David and Johnny doing anything as domestic as watching TV.

Tony nodded vigorously. 'They do, you know. That's how they find out how far they can go.'

'You're trying to tell me that MI5 and CTC make their operational decisions based on a TV series?' Carol tapped the side of her head with her forefinger. 'Too many drugs, Tony.'

'That's exactly what I'm telling you,' he said earnestly. 'Because they have people working for them who understand the psychology of sanction.'

'The psychology of sanction?' Carol's repetition was laced with disbelief.

'This is how it works. When they're watching a show like *Spooks*, even sophisticated viewers suspend enough disbelief for the drama to work. And once that disbelief has been suspended, even a little, the viewer is conditioned to believe the real world is just like that. So it gives permission to those mad bastards in Five to push just that little bit further at the edges of the envelope.' Tony spoke quickly, his hands gesturing.

Carol looked dubious. 'You're saying that what they see on the TV makes the punters accept more extreme behaviour from law enforcement?'

'Yes. To greater and lesser degrees, depending on their credulity, obviously.' He registered Carol's scepticism. 'OK, here's an example. I don't think there's ever been an accredited case of an MI5 agent having their face shoved into a deep-fat fryer. But once you've shown that on a show with as much credibility as *Spooks*, even if it's the bad guys who are doing it, you've created a constituency of opinion who will say, when an MI5 agent actually does shove someone's face into a deep-fat fryer, "Well, he had to do it, didn't he? Or they'd have done it to him." The psychology of sanction.'

'If you're right, then why does anyone protest against torture? Why don't we all just go, "Oh well, we've seen how well it works in the movies, let's just go along with it"?' Carol leaned on her fists on the edge of his bed as she spoke, her tumbled blonde hair falling into her eyes.

'Carol, you might not have noticed, but there's a significant number of people out there who do say just that. Look at the opposition in the US when the Senate decided to outlaw torture just the other year. People believe in its efficacy precisely because they've seen it in the movies. And some of those believers are in positions of power. The reason we don't all fall for it is that we're not all equally credulous. Some of us are much more critical of what we see and read than others. But you *can* fool some of the people all of the time. And when spooks and cops go bad, that's what they rely on.'

She frowned. 'You scare me sometimes, you know that?'

She could see the pain in his face. She didn't think it was anything to do with his knee. 'Yes, I know that. But I don't think that's necessarily a bad thing. In my experience, when something scares you, it makes you all the more determined to beat it.'

Carol turned away, as usual made uncomfortable by his praise. 'So you don't think this is some kind of concerted action against the Vics?'

'No. Because Danny Wade doesn't fit.'

Carol sighed in exasperation. 'Bloody Danny Wade. You and Paula between you, you could argue the hind leg off a donkey.'

Tony smiled. 'I've never understood that expression.

Why would anyone want to argue the hind leg off a donkey? And why a donkey, as opposed to a pig or an armadillo?' He held up his hands to protect himself as Carol batted at him with a folded newspaper she'd snatched up. 'OK, OK. But you know we're right about Danny being connected.'

'Whatever,' she sighed, tossing the paper back on his table. 'What I do know is that I'm going to need more than your psychological theories about targets to persuade anybody that this is not terrorism.' She headed for the door. 'I'll try and swing by later. Good luck with the physio.'

'Thanks. Oh, and, Carol? Somebody really should find out where Tom Cross went to school.'

Within minutes of Carol's departure, the physiotherapist arrived, greeting Tony with a knowing wink. 'Helping the police with their inquiries, were you?' she said archly, handing him his elbow crutches. 'I hope she hasn't worn you out.'

'DCI Jordan was running things at Victoria Park yesterday,' he said in a tone that discouraged discussion. 'I work with the police. She came round to run some things past me. And she was so exhausted she fell asleep in the chair.' Tony knew he was being petty, but he couldn't help himself. Whenever Carol was in the picture, he became over-sensitive to any personal references. It didn't matter if it was his mother or a physiotherapist he was never going to see again after he left the hospital. He was always driven to set the record straight. Well, straight in technical terms, at least. The emotional context beneath the surface was nobody's business but his.

Half an hour later, he was back in his room, tired but not exhausted as he'd been on previous days. 'You're doing incredibly well. You might want to get dressed today,' the physio said. 'See what it feels like to spend a bit of time in the chair, a bit of time moving around. Walk up and down the hall every hour or so.'

He turned the TV volume back up, keeping half an eye on it while he battled with his clothes. The news all revolved around the explosion at Victoria Park. Everything from football experts talking about the impact on the game; structural engineers speculating on the cost and the time involved in rebuilding the Vestey Stand; Martin Flanagan expressing his anger that Robbie Bishop's farewell should have been so desecrated; friends and family of the dead talking about their loved ones; and Yousef Aziz's brother Sanjar protesting that his brother was no fundamentalist. As Sanjar spoke against the backdrop of CTC officers removing cartons of stuff from his family home, Tony stopped wrestling with his sock and directed all of his attention to the TV.

He did not subscribe to the view that it was possible to tell the mind's construction in the face, but years of watching people lie to him and to themselves had given him a reference library of expression and gesture that he could draw on to make his judgements about a person's truthfulness. What he saw in Sanjar Aziz was a blazing conviction that, whatever had motivated his brother to blow a hole in Victoria Park stadium, it had not been religious fundamentalism. The CTC were stripping his home to the bricks and he wasn't protesting about that. What was clearly driving him to distraction was having to repeat again and again what he knew to be true – his brother was not a militant Muslim. The TV interviewer wasn't particularly interested in exploring alternative explanations for the bombing, however. All he wanted was for Sanjar to prostrate himself in apology. It was clear that wasn't going to happen.

Tony's attention drifted as the reporter returned them to the studio for yet another heavy-handed analysis of the consequences of the bombing for Bradfield Victoria's season. Fan though he was, it exasperated him that this was even on the news agenda when thirty-five people were dead. What he really wanted to know was what Sanjar Aziz had to say beyond his denials. Tony had seen his frustration and couldn't help wondering what lay behind it.

He struggled with his sock again, but failed to get it on. 'Bugger,' he said, reaching for the nurse call button. To hell with independence. He wanted to hear what Sanjar Aziz had to say, and he didn't care if it cost him his independence. It was time to get off his backside and do something useful.

Carol gave her team the once over. Already they all looked as if they'd had insufficient sleep and too much coffee. Any murder inquiry provoked a kind of intensity that drove physical needs to the margins. If it went on too long, people fell apart. And so did their personal lives. She'd seen it happen too often. But there didn't seem to be any easy way to avoid it. Officers felt impelled to work at this pitch because of the unique nature of the crime and what it meant to them as human beings. It wasn't about emotional involvement, she thought. It was about confronting one's own mortality. Working a murder case as hard as was humanly possible was a kind of sacrifice to the gods, a symbolic way of protecting themselves and their loved ones.

They all paid close attention as Paula reported her conversation with Elinor Blessing, making a point of the mention of the mysterious Jake or Jack. When she reached the end of her notes, Paula looked up and said, 'I got to thinking. Our three poison victims, they all originate from Bradfield. We know Robbie Bishop and Danny Wade both grew up in Harriestown and went to school there. I wondered if that was a connection worth pursuing. So after I left the hospital, I came back here and logged on to Best Days. Tom Cross wasn't a member, but there are a couple of dozen people his age who are. They've got a section called "Photographs and Memories", and that's where I found this.'

She produced a print-out and handed it round. 'Someone called Sandy Hall posted this. "Does anybody else remember the time Tom Cross locked Weasel Russell in the chemistry supply cupboard then fed laughing gas through the keyhole? Funny to think he ended up a senior policeman." And Eddie Brant replies, "I saw Tom Cross a few months ago at a rugby club dinner. I'd have known him anywhere. He's still larger than life, full of stories. He's retired now. He had a big win on the pools a few years back so he's very comfortably off, he said." So I think we can safely say that, like Danny and Robbie, Tom Cross was a former pupil of Harriestown High.'

'You could just have asked me,' Kevin said. 'I went to the Double Aitch too.'

Paula looked surprised. 'I wish I'd known,' she said, 'It would have saved me a bit of time. Anyway, at least we know now that it's a link. I don't know what it means, or if it means anything at all, but it's definitely something they all had in common.'

'There's something else they had in common,' Kevin said. 'They were all rich. Robbie from football, Danny from the lottery and Popeye from the football pools. Some people thought he must be on the take, to afford a house on Dunelm Drive. But he wasn't. He just got lucky.'

'Interesting point, Kevin. And good work, Paula,' Carol said.

'Do you think we should be warning former pupils of Harriestown High who have gone on to make a mint?' Chris said.

Carol looked startled. 'I don't think we've got nearly enough to be setting the cat among the pigeons like that. Can you imagine the panic that would set in if we did that? No, we need to have a much clearer idea of what's going on here. I'm going to see Mrs Cross this morning. Let's see what comes out of that. Paula, can you speak to Mr and Mrs Bishop, see if Robbie knew Tom Cross? And Sam, the same thing with Danny's family. Kevin, the phone records have just come in for Aziz's mobile. I want you to pursue that. Also, since you've got the connections, get hold of the head teacher at Harriestown High and see if the school had fostered some connection between the three of them. Like you said, they were all rich. Maybe the school had been hitting them up for donations?

Maybe the head had invited them over for drinks? Check it out. And Chris, I want you to take the phone over to CTC. Apologize profusely for us getting our wires crossed and thinking we'd told them about the phone. Smile a lot. See what they've got. And guys? I want you all to keep an open mind on the bombing. I spoke to Tony last night and he has one or two ideas that seemed pretty off the wall to me. But he's been right before in unlikely circumstances, so let's make sure we don't jump to conclusions based on preconceptions and prejudice. Let the evidence do the work. And speaking of evidence, how are you getting on, Stacey?'

'Some interesting bits and pieces . . . Chris asked me to check out hopefully.co.uk to see if Aziz had saved his login details on the laptop. We got lucky. The login was on the machine. But he'd booked nothing else.' Stacey paused. She did like to keep them dangling, Carol thought, noticing the expressions of her team. And how they hated it. 'However,' Stacey continued, 'I was able to dredge up a list of things on the site he'd been looking at. And what attracted the Bradfield bomber were rental cottages in Northern Ontario. I have a list.'

'He was planning to escape to a cottage in Canada?' Kevin expressed the incredulity Carol thought they were probably all feeling. 'Canada?'

'He was thinking about it, at least,' Stacey said.

'You wouldn't think Canada would be the destination of choice of an Islamic fundamentalist fugitive, would you?' Chris said.

'They're very tolerant, the Canadians,' Paula said.

'Not that tolerant. But they do have a significant

population from the sub-continent,' Carol said. 'OK. Kevin, you take care of the cottages. You probably won't be able to do much before tomorrow, but make whatever start you can. Chris, when you get back from CTC, take over the mobile numbers from Kevin.' She smiled at them. 'You're all doing really well. I know we've got a lot on our plates, but let's show them what we're made of. Make sure everything you get comes across my desk.' She stood up, signalling the end of the meeting. 'Good luck. God knows, we need it.'

Tony couldn't help feeling sorry for the residents of Vale Avenue. Their normally quiet suburban boulevard, with its grassy central reservation and its flowering cherries lining the verge, was under siege. Now the eyes of the world were on a street where normally the most provocative event was a dog owner allowing their pet to foul the pavement. TV vans, radio cars and reporters' vehicles were scattered along either side of the road. Police and forensic vans formed a tight cluster round 147. Sitting in the back of the black hack – the cab he'd ordered because it had enough room for his leg – Tony wondered again at the public's capacity for every last drop of so-called news coverage.

As well as those who had more or less legitimate reasons for being there, there were the ghouls and gawpers. Probably some of the same people who had contributed to Robbie Bishop's shrine. People whose lives were so limited they needed the validation of being somehow part of a public event. It was easy to despise them, Tony thought. But he felt they did perform a function, acting as a kind of Greek chorus, commenting in their unconsidered way on the events of the day. Paxman might interview the great and the good, inviting their incisive insights, but the people on the pavement also had something to say.

'Drive right up to the police cordon,' Tony said to the driver, who did as he was asked, crawling through the knots of people, using his horn to clear a path. When he had got as far as he could, Tony struggled upright and shoved a twenty through the gap in the window. 'Wait for me, please.' He opened the door, then manoeuvred his crutches on to the ground. It was ungainly and painful, but he managed to struggle out on to the road. Armed officers stood at intervals across the drive and along the hedge of 147. On the pavement, Sanjar Aziz was giving another interview. He was tiring. His shoulders were starting to droop, his stance was more defensive than before. But the passion in his face was still alive. The lights went off, the interviewer gave perfunctory thanks and turned away. A look of dejection spread across Sanjar's face.

Tony swung himself over on his crutches. Sanjar looked him up and down, clearly unimpressed. 'You want an interview?'

Tony shook his head. 'No. I want to talk to you.'

Sanjar screwed his face up, incomprehending. 'Yeah, right. Talk, interview, same thing, innit?' He was looking over Tony's shoulder, impatient for somebody else to talk to, somebody who would listen to what he had to say, not get into a verbal fencing match with him.

Tony gritted his teeth. It was amazing how much effort it took just to stand upright, never mind standing upright and talking. 'No, it's not the same. The interviewers want you to say what they want to hear. I want to hear what you have to say. The thing that they're not letting you talk about.'

Now he had Sanjar's attention. 'Who are you?' he demanded, his good-looking face twisted into wounded aggression.

'My name's Tony Hill. Dr Tony Hill. I'd show you my ID if I could,' he said, giving his crutches a frustrated glance. 'I'm a psychologist. I often work with Bradfield Police. Not this lot,' he added, nodding towards the impassive riot-clad guards with a trace of contempt. 'I think you've got things to say about your brother that nobody wants to hear. I think that's frustrating you beyond belief.'

'What's it got to do with you?' Sanjar snapped. 'I don't need no shrink, all due respect. I just want this lot –' he gestured expansively at the media and police '– to understand why they're wrong about my brother.'

'They're not going to understand,' Tony said. 'Because it doesn't fit what they need to believe. But I do want to understand. I don't think your brother was a terrorist, Sanjar.'

Suddenly he had a hundred per cent of Sanjar Aziz's attention. 'You saying it wasn't Yousef that did this?'

'No, I think it's pretty clear that he did it. But I don't think he did it for the reasons everybody is assuming. I think you can maybe help me understand why this happened.' Tony gestured with his head towards the waiting taxi. 'We can go somewhere and talk about it.'

Sanjar looked up at his home, where a white-suited forensic technician had just emerged with another plastic bag. He turned back to Tony, who felt he was being appraised. 'OK,' he said. 'I'll talk to you.'

Dorothy Cross poured coffee from a silver pot into bone china cups decorated with roses whose exact shade of pink was picked up in the several patterns that adorned the walls. Two different wallpapers, one above and one below the dado rail, the curtains, the carpets, the loveseat, the two sofas and the scatter cushions each had a different pattern but they were united by toning shades of pink and burgundy. Carol felt as if she'd been sucked into one of those medical dramas where the camera journeys through internal organs. It wasn't a pleasant sensation.

Dorothy stopped pouring and gave the two cups a critical look. Then she added a teaspoonful more coffee to one of them. Satisfied, she passed it to Carol. She pushed the silver milk jug and sugar bowl towards her then looked up with the desperate little smile of someone who is trying to keep herself from exploding into fragments. 'It's cream,' she said. 'Not milk. Tom likes cream in his coffee. Liked.' She frowned. 'Liked. I have to keep remembering. Liked, not likes.' Her chin quivered.

'I'm so sorry,' Carol said.

The look Dorothy flashed her was sharp as a shard of glass. 'Are you? Are you really? I thought the two of you never got on.'

Fuck. What happened to British reticence? 'It's true we didn't see eye to eye sometimes. But you don't have to be friends with someone to appreciate their worth.'

Carol could feel herself slithering around on a shiny surface of hypocrisy. 'He was very popular with his junior officers. I'm sure you know that. And his actions yesterday . . . Mrs Cross, he was heroic. I hope you've been told that already.'

'It doesn't make any odds to me, DCI Jordan. What matters to me is that I've lost him.' It took both hands for her to raise her cup to her lips. It was strange to see such a big, solid woman reduced to fragility. But Carol could see the signs of her unravelling. Her shampoo-and-set hair was strangely asymmetrical, her lipstick line a little smudged. 'He filled this house with his personality, and he filled my life the same way. We met when we were only seventeen, you know. I don't think either of us has seriously looked at anybody else since. I feel like I've lost half of myself. What it's like is that whenever one of you forgets some detail from the past, the other remembers it. What am I going to do without him?' Her eyes were bright with tears, her breath catching in her throat.

'I can't imagine,' Carol said.

'It makes no sense, you know.' She kept touching her wedding ring with the tip of her right index finger. Again, she flashed Carol that incisive look. 'I'm not stupid. I know there must have been plenty wanted him dead at one time or another. People he'd arrested, people he'd got across. But why now? Why seven years after he left the force? I'm sorry, I just don't believe anybody stays angry for that long. And the sort of people he put away? They're not poisoners. If one of them was going to come after them, it would have been a shotgun on the doorstep.'

'I couldn't agree with you more. I'll be honest with you, Mrs Cross. We think this might be part of a wider investigation, but I can't tell you what that is right now.' Carol took a sip of the excellent coffee. 'I know you'll appreciate how it is.'

Dorothy looked pained, as if she didn't like the idea of her husband's death not being a unique event. 'I want whoever did this to be caught and punished, DCI Jordan. I'm not bothered about any other investigation you're dealing with.'

'I understand that. And Tom's death is our number one priority.'

Dorothy reared up in her seat, considerable bosom heaving, and looked down her nose at Carol. 'You expect me to believe that? With thirty-five dead at Victoria Park?'

Carol put her cup down and looked Dorothy straight in the eye. 'They've taken that away from us. That's up to Counter Terrorism Command. We're concentrating on Tom's death and I have to tell you that, when it comes to investigating murder, my team has no equal.'

Dorothy subsided slightly. But being Tom Cross's wife for the best part of forty years had left its mark. 'They'd never have dared take the Bradfield bombing off my Tom. He'd have given John Brandon what for,' she said, making it plain what she thought of Carol and Brandon both.

Carol told herself she was dealing with a grief-stricken widow. It wasn't the time to debate Tom Cross's views on policing. 'I was hoping you could help me with Tom's movements yesterday,' she said.

Dorothy stood up. 'I knew you'd want to know

about it, so I looked it out for you. I'll be right back.' She bustled out of the room. Carol couldn't help thinking that if there were to be a biopic of Tom Cross's life, you'd have to cast Patricia Routledge as his wife.

Dorothy came back with a sheet of paper and handed it to Carol. While she poured more coffee, Carol read a letter from the head teacher of Harriestown High, asking Tom Cross to act as security consultant for a fundraiser. At the bottom of the letter, Cross had jotted the name Jake Andrews next to a phone number and the name of a restaurant. Beneath that, in a different pen but in the same hand, he'd written Saturday's date, the name of a pub in Temple Fields, and '1 p.m.'.

'Do you know who Jake Andrews is?' Carol said.

'He was organizing the fundraiser. Tom said it was going to be at Pannal Castle. Him and Jake had lunch a couple of weeks back in that fancy French place round the back of The Maltings. They were meeting in the Campion Locks pub yesterday then going on to Jake's flat for lunch. Do you think that's when it happened?' Dorothy said. 'Is Jake dead as well? Were you investigating him?'

'This is the first time I've heard his name. Do you know his address?'

Dorothy shook her head. 'According to Tom, they were meeting in the Campion Locks because Jake's flat is hard to find. He told Tom it would be easier if they met in the pub then walked round to his place.'

Carol tried not to let her disappointment show. This case was full of frustrations. Every time they had something approaching a lead, it frittered out. 'Is there anything else Tom said about Jake Andrews?'

Dorothy thought for a moment, stroking her chin in a peculiar gesture that reminded Carol of a man caressing a beard. Finally, she shook her head. 'He said he seemed to know what he was about. That's all. Is that when it happened?'

'We don't know yet. Before he met Jake – was there anyone else Tom was seeing?'

Dorothy shook her head. 'He didn't have time. His taxi came at half past twelve. Just right to get to the far side of Temple Fields.'

Carol couldn't argue with that. 'Had he had any threats? Did he ever speak of having enemies?'

'Not specifically.' She stroked her non-existent beard again. 'Like I said, the people who had it in for Tom wouldn't do anything subtle. He knew there were places he shouldn't go in Bradfield. Places where he'd put too many of the locals away. But he didn't live in fear of his life, DCI Jordan.' There was a catch in her voice. 'He lived his life to the full. His boat, his golf, his garden . . .' She had to stop for a moment, hand on her bosom, eyes shut. When she gathered herself together again, she leaned forward, close enough for Carol to see every line on her face. 'You catch whoever did this. You catch them and you put them away.'

It felt strange being back inside his house. No wonder people spoke of becoming institutionalized. A week away and Tony felt as if his capabilities had been compromised. He led Sanjar into the living room and collapsed into his armchair with a surge of relief.

'Sorry,' he said. 'As you can see, I'm not in a position to be very hospitable. This is the first time I've been home in a week. There won't be any milk, but if you want some black tea or coffee, you're very welcome to help yourself. There might even be some fizzy mineral water in the fridge.'

'What happened to you?' It was the first thing Sanjar had said to him since they'd left Vale Avenue. He hadn't spoken in the cab, which Tony had been grateful for. He hadn't anticipated how much energy the physical activity would take. But the twenty-minute cab ride had allowed him to recoup some of his resources.

'I think the technical term is a mad axeman,' Tony said. 'One of our patients at Bradfield Moor had an episode. He managed to get out of his room and get his hands on a fire axe.'

Sanjar pointed at him. 'You're the bloke who saved them nurses. You were on the news.'

'I was?'

'Just on the local news. And they didn't have no pictures of you. Just pictures of the mental case that went for you guys. You did good.'

Tony fiddled with the arm of his chair, embarrassed. 'I didn't do good enough. Somebody died.'

'Yeah, well. I know what that feels like.'

'There's not really been any space for you to grieve, has there?'

Sanjar stared at the fireplace and sighed. 'My parents are really fucked up,' he said. 'They can't take it in. Their son. Not just that he's dead, but that he took all those people with him. How can that be? I mean, I'm his brother. Same genes. Same upbringing.

376

And I can't get my head round it. How can they? Their lives are destroyed, and they've lost a son.' He swallowed hard.

'I'm sorry.'

Sanjar looked suspiciously at him. 'What are you sorry for? My brother was a killer, right? We deserve all the shit we get. We deserve to spend the night in police cells. We deserve to have our home ripped to bits.'

The pain and anger were obvious. Tony had carved a career out of his capacity for empathy and imagination. He would have done almost anything to avoid being in the terrible place where Sanjar was. 'No, you don't. I'm sorry that you're hurting. I'm sorry that your parents are suffering,' he said.

Sanjar looked away. 'Thanks. OK, I'm here. What did you want to know about my brother?'

'What do you want to tell me?'

'What he was really like. Nobody wants to hear what my brother Yousef was really like. And the first thing you need to know is that I loved him. Now me, I couldn't love a terrorist. I hate those people and so did Yousef. He wasn't a fundamentalist. He was barely a Muslim. My dad, he's really devout. And he gets so pissed off with me and Yousef because we're, like, not. Both of us, we'd find excuses not to go to the mosque. When we were kids, as soon as we were old enough, we quit going to the madrassa. But here's the thing,' he carried on, taking over the question Tony was trying to ask. 'Even if we had been devout, even if we had been down the mosque every day, we wouldn't have heard no radical shit. The Imam in the Kenton Mosque? He's totally not into that shit. He's the kind that talks about how we're all sons of Abraham and we have to learn to live together. There's no secret gangs meeting behind closed doors plotting how to blow people up.' He ran out of steam as suddenly as he'd found it.

'I believe you,' Tony said, almost relishing the expression of bemused surprise on Sanjar's face.

'You do?'

'Like I said earlier, I don't think your brother was a terrorist. Which raises a question that interests me very much. Why would Yousef take a bomb into Victoria Park and blow a hole in the Vestey Stand?' Tony deliberately didn't mention the dead. Not that either of them was going to be forgetting the dead any time soon. But there was no need to drag them into the foreground. The last thing Tony wanted was to put Sanjar even more on the defensive.

Sanjar's mouth twitched then set in a straight line. Time stretched out before he eventually said, 'I don't know. It makes no sense to me.'

'I know this is going to sound kind of crazy,' Tony said. 'But is there any way he might have been paid to do it?'

Sanjar jumped to his feet and took a step towards Tony, hands bunched into fists. 'What the fuck? You saying my brother was a hit man or something? Fuck. You're as fucked in the head as those bastards saying he was some kind of fanatic.'

'Sanjar, you don't have to act like you're defending the honour of the family. There's only you and me here. I have to ask because there's some evidence that suggests that maybe Yousef thought he was going to survive yesterday afternoon. That he was going to be able to leave the country afterwards. Now, that's not the mindset of a suicide bomber. So I have to try and think of another explanation. OK? That's all I'm doing.'

Sanjar paced, agitated. 'You've got it wrong, man. Yousef, he was a gentle guy. He was the last man on the planet to be a hit man.' He smacked his fist into the palm of his hand. 'He'd never been to no training camp. He'd never been to Pakistan or Afghanistan. Fuck, we've never even been to the bloody Lake District or the Dales.' He clapped his hands to his chest. 'We're peaceful, me and Yousef.'

'He killed those people, Sanjar. There's no getting away from that.'

'And it doesn't make any sense,' Sanjar moaned. 'I don't know how to get you to understand.' He suddenly stopped, staring at the console table where Tony's former laptop had been retired. 'You got wireless? Can I turn your computer on? There's something I want to show you.'

'Go ahead.'

Sanjar waited for the machine to boot then navigated his way to a blog called DoorMAT – the portal for Muslims Against Terrorism. Meanwhile, Tony managed to get to his feet and cross the room. He leaned against the arm of the sofa and looked at the screen. At the login screen, Sanjar typed in an email address. 'Look,' he said. 'Yousef's address. Not mine.' At the password prompt, he typed 'Transit350'. He looked back at Tony. 'We always use our vehicles for our passwords. That way you don't forget.' Once accepted on to the site, Sanjay clicked the mouse a few times and up popped a listing of Yousef's posts to the blog. Sanjay clicked at random.

OK, Salman31, I haven't lived in a city where the BNP have seats on the council. But I know if I did, I would be making protests that got better headlines than the rabble on the streets in Burnley. The BNP thugs act like savages, it's what people expect from chavs with shaved heads. Nobody thinks any worse of them, but we do the same, and suddenly we got no reputation, we should know better, ect, ect. We have to be better than them, we have to be.

'You go through his posts, that's what they're like. That doesn't sound much like a hit man, does it?'

'No,' Tony said, thinking how much he wanted to spend some time with Yousef's posts when his brother wasn't looking over his shoulder. 'You make your point very well. So has anything changed recently? Has Yousef changed? Has there been anything different about him lately? New friends? New routines? New girlfriend?'

Sanjar's brow furrowed in concentration. 'He's been a bit up and down the last six months or so,' he said slowly. 'Off his food, not sleeping. Up, like a geezer with a new lady, then down like she'd dumped him. Then up again. I didn't see him with anybody, though. We'd go out together, clubbing or just for a meal with friends, and he wasn't hanging with any of the girls in particular. I never saw him with a girl, not lately. He'd been working pretty hard too, nailing down some new contracts. A lot of meetings and shit. So he didn't really have time for a new girl, innit?'

'And he never said anything?'

Sanjar shook his head. 'No. Not a thing.' He looked

at his watch. 'Look, I gotta go. I promised my dad I would be back.' He stood up and stretched a hand out to Tony. 'I appreciate you listening. But I don't think this is ever going to make sense.'

Tony searched his pockets till he finally unearthed a business card. 'This is who I am. Call me if you want to talk.'

Sanjar pocketed it with the nearest Tony had seen to a proper smile. 'No disrespect, like, but I don't think I'm gonna need a shrink.'

'I'm not a shrink. Not the way you're thinking of it. I don't have people lying on couches telling me about their miserable childhoods. I get too bored too easily. What I do is find practical uses for psychology. Often, I don't know what they are till I get there. I like trying to fix what's broken, Sanjar.'

The younger man smiled and reached for the pen and notepad beside the computer. He scribbled something and dropped it back on the table. 'My mobile, innit? Call me if you want to talk. I'll see myself out.'

Tony watched him go, feeling quite deeply disturbed. As Sanjar had said, same genes, same upbringing. If Yousef Aziz had been anything like his brother, Tony couldn't imagine how he'd ended up blowing thirty-five people to kingdom come. He desperately wanted to read those blog contributions. But first, he'd better get back to hospital before they called the cops. Carol would really love that.

Kevin reckoned that Nigel Foster would never have made head teacher of the Double Aitch in his day. The man who had ruled the roost back then had the build of a prop forward and a voice like a foghorn. Foster was tall, already slightly stooped at forty-something. His polo shirt and jeans hung baggy on his thin frame. His head and neck had the defleshed look of a wasted old man. But his expression was lively, his eyes bright and watchful. He'd suggested meeting at his home, but Kevin had wanted to see the Double Aitch up close and personal. Foster had protested that it was too much hassle to disarm the building security, so they'd compromised. They'd settled on the rickety wooden stand that overlooked the football pitch. A swell of nostalgia surged through Kevin. He'd had some of his finest hours on that turf. He could still remember some of the plays. 'I loved playing here,' he said. 'Not many schools had a proper spectator stand like this. You could almost believe you were doing it for real.'

'It's due for demolition, I'm afraid,' Foster said in a pleasant tenor voice with traces of a Welsh accent. 'Health and Safety. It would cost too much to fire-proof it the way they want it.'

Kevin's face twisted into a cynical sneer. 'We molly-coddle them these days.'

'We've developed a culture of blame and litigation,' Foster said. 'But I mustn't waste your time. How can I help you with your investigation, Sergeant?'

It was, Kevin thought, a subtle rebuke for taking up the headmaster's valuable Sunday. 'Three men have died recently from a variety of poisons. We think the cases may be connected, and one of the links between them is that they are all former pupils.'

A quick flash of surprise crossed Foster's face. 'I knew about Robbie Bishop, of course. But there have been others?'

'You might have missed the story, with all the news coverage of the bomb. But another man died yesterday, nothing to do with the explosion. Ex-Detective Super-intendent Tom Cross.'

Foster frowned. 'He died? I read something about him being one of the heroes of the hour.'

'His death didn't make the early editions. But he died from poisoning too, similar to Robbie. And a third man, Danny Wade. Also a former pupil. Also poisoned.'

'That's shocking. Terrible.' Foster's expression was troubled, like a priest who's losing his faith.

'The thing is, they were all rich men. And we won-dered if you'd maybe brought them together for some fund-raising project? With them all being alumni . . .' Kevin paused expectantly.

Foster shook his head rapidly. 'No. Nothing of the sort.' He gave a bitter little laugh. 'It's a good idea, but it never occurred to me. No, I've never met any of them. And as far as I know, none of them had any connection with FODA.'

'FODA?'

'Friends of the Double Aitch. It's an alumni organ-ization that organizes reunions and raises money. I'm surprised you've not been approached to join.'

Kevin gave him a flat, level stare. 'Apart from the footie, it would be fair to say that these were not the best days of my life.' Without taking his eyes off Foster, he pulled out his notebook. 'We believe Tom Cross was lured to his death by someone purporting to be you,' he said.

Foster literally flinched, as if Kevin had slapped him. 'Me?' he yelped.

Kevin glanced at the notes he'd taken from the conversation he'd had with Carol Jordan only minutes before meeting Foster. 'A letter on what appears to be the school's headed notepaper was sent to Cross, apparently from you, asking for his help arranging security at a charity fundraiser for the school.' Kevin showed the phone number to Foster. 'Is this the school number?'

Foster shook his head. 'No. Nothing like it. I don't recognize it.'

'It connects to an answering machine that says it's Harriestown High. According to Superintendent Cross's widow, her husband left a message on the machine and someone claiming to be you called him back.'

Foster, agitated and twitchy, said, 'No. This is all wrong. Nothing remotely like this ever happened.'

'It's all right, sir. We're not treating you as a suspect. We think you've been impersonated. But I need to run these things past you.' He almost wanted to pat Foster on the knee in a bid to calm his twittering.

Foster sucked his lips in and made a visible effort to pull himself together. 'OK. I'm sorry, it's just a little shaking to be told you're implicated in a murder inquiry.'

'I appreciate that. The fundraiser was supposed to be at Pannal Castle?'

'No, this is mad. I don't know Lord Pannal or anybody connected to him. I mean, it would be wonderful to do an event there, but no. Nothing has ever been suggested, never mind planned.'

Kevin continued without a pause. 'Now, again according to Mrs Cross, the person claiming to be you told her husband to liaise with the event organizer, a man called Jake Andrews. Have you ever worked with anyone by that name? Jake Andrews?'

Foster breathed out heavily. 'No. That name means nothing to me.'

Kevin, watching him carefully, saw nothing to indicate the man was lying. 'I need you to check the school records,' he said.

Foster nodded, his Adam's apple bouncing up and down. 'We've been computerized for a few years now, but all the old stuff is still on paper. I'll call the school secretary. She knows where to find it. If there's any record of this man, we'll find it.'

'Thanks. Sooner the better, really. We may want to come back and talk to some of your longer-serving staff members,' Kevin said, getting to his feet. 'One last thing – where were you yesterday lunchtime? Around one o'clock?'

'Me?' Foster seemed unsure whether to be angry or upset.

'You.'

'I was birdwatching at Martin Mere in Lancashire with a group of friends,' he said, standing on his dignity. 'We arrived around noon and stayed till sunset. I can supply you with names.'

Kevin fished out a card with his email address. 'Send them there. I look forward to hearing from you.' He gave the pitch a last lingering look, then walked away, a smile twitching the corners of his mouth. It wasn't often life presented him with the chance to make a teacher miserable in the course of duty. It was petty, he knew, but he'd enjoyed taking a small revenge on behalf of his sixteen-year-old self.

The Campion Locks had started life as a boatmen's drinking house back when the canals of the north of

England had shifted coal and wool back and forth across the Pennines. It was set back from the canal, near the basin where three major waterways came together. When it had been built, Temple Fields was a literal name for the area. Now, instead of animals grazing outside the pub, the Sunday-morning crowd grazed on bruschetta and bagels, calming their scrambled stomachs with eggs and smoked salmon.

As they approached, Chris checked out the eclectic mix of customers. She nudged Paula in the ribs and said, 'Now this is a bit of all right. Jordan should send us places like this more often. We fit right in here, doll. I'll have to bring Sinead down here one of these Sundays, remind her what young love feels like.'

'You're lucky you've got someone to remind,' Paula said. 'I've got to the point where sex feels like a past-life experience.'

'You need to get out more. Find some gorgeous girl who'll bring a smile to your chops.' Chris steered a path through the drinkers milling around on the paved area beyond the tables, waiting for seats to be vacated.

'That is so going to happen in this job,' Paula said. 'Every time I get a night off, all I want to do is sleep.'

They walked through the doors. It was almost as thronged inside, but much noisier because of the slate floors and low ceiling. 'Speaking of which . . .' Chris said. 'How are you sleeping these days?'

'Better,' Paula said curtly, head down as she rooted in her bag for the photo of Jack Anderson.

'Glad to hear it.' Chris turned and gave Paula's

elbow a squeeze. 'For what it's worth, doll, I think you're doing brilliant.'

They made it to the bar, where three bar staff and a waitress struggled to keep pace with orders for drinks and food. Chris flashed her warrant card at one of the barmen who laughed out loud and said, 'You've got to be kidding. Come back in an hour when the rush has died down.'

Normally, her eagerness to get the job done would have made her remonstrate with the barman. But the sun was shining and they'd both seen too much unpleasantness in the past twenty-four hours. So much death had reminded Chris that there were times when it was important to pause and smell the flowers. So she smiled. 'In that case, we'll have two pints of lager shandy.'

Nursing their drinks, they found a stretch of wall facing the canal and sat companionably in the sunshine, talking in circles about the poisonings and the bombing. Gradually the crowds began to thin as people finished their drinks and headed off to make the most of the sunshine. 'If we were on the TV, this would be the point where one of us had a penetrating insight that solved the whole case,' Chris said, staring placidly out over the canal, where a brightly painted holiday rental narrow boat was negotiating the first of the three locks leading into the basin.

'If we were on the TV, you'd never have bought the drinks,' Paula pointed out. 'That would have been my job as the trusty but stupid sidekick.'

'Damn, I knew I was doing something wrong.' Reluctantly, Chris pushed herself upright. 'Better get some work done, hadn't we?'

There were no longer jostling crowds at the bar waiting for service. The barman saw them approach and came round the end of the bar to greet them. He looked like a student eking out his grant, his long black fringe and his wispy goatee supposedly marking him out as artistic and sensitive. He needed all the help he could get on that score, given his burly frame and budding beer gut. 'What can I do for you, ladies?' he said, a Welsh accent now apparent. 'Sorry about earlier, but it gets mobbed on a Sunday lunchtime, and we can't afford to let up. We've got this deal: if you don't get your food within twenty minutes of ordering it, you don't pay for it.' He pulled a wry face. 'And it comes out of our wages.' He led them to a recently vacated table in the far corner and sat down. 'I'm Will Stevens,' he said. 'I work weekends.'

They introduced themselves and Chris said, 'Were you on yesterday lunchtime?'

Stevens nodded, twisting a chunk of his fringe round his finger. 'Yeah. It's not quite so crazy on a Saturday. What's all this about, then?'

Paula spread a selection of photos on the table. 'Do you recognize any of these men as having been in here yesterday?'

He pointed straight at the photo of Jack Anderson. 'Him.' Light dawned on his face. 'He was drinking with that bloke that died after the bombing yesterday. What was his name . . . it'll come to me, we were watching it this morning when we were setting up, and I went, "He was in here yesterday, I served him." Cross, that was it. Sounds like he was a real hero yesterday.' He paused. 'Didn't they say something about him being a copper before he retired?'

'That's right. So, he met this man –' she pointed to the photo of Anderson '– in here? Lunchtime?'

'That's right. Cross, he was here first. He had a pint of something, I don't remember what. Then this younger bloke, he arrived. They acted like they knew each other. He had a glass of house red. I wasn't really paying attention to them, we were too busy. Next time I looked, they were gone.' He tapped the photo of Jake. 'I've seen him in here before. He'll meet people in here, they'll have one drink, then they'll all go off together. Always the same routine. He never eats in here. I think it's just a handy place to meet up with people. He probably lives local.'

'I don't suppose you know his name?'

Stevens nodded, his smile as smug as the party child who's won Pass the Parcel. 'I do. It's Jake.'

'You're sure it's Jake? Not Jack?' Paula asked.

'Jake. That's what your Mr Cross called him. Definitely Jake.'

'And they didn't eat here?'

He shook his head. 'No way. Just the one drink, then they were offski.'

Chris stood up. 'Thanks, Mr Stevens. You've been very helpful.'

He looked up at them, beaming. 'Is there a reward, then?'

There was a camaraderie among geeks that transcended other differences. Carol may have formally assigned Chris Devine to liaise with the CTC, but Stacey had already built her own connections. One of the many things beloved of geeks is back doors into other people's systems, and Stacey had an admirable collection. When it came to swap-shop time, she always had something to trade. It didn't hurt either that, in geek terms, she was the Mona Lisa.

She'd bonded over Aziz's laptop with the CTC's main geek, a rotund twenty-something with a skanky ponytail and an inadequate concept of personal hygiene. What Gerry lacked in personal charm, he made up for in his knowledge of systems and his willingness to deal. In exchange for a back door into a confidential social security database, he'd given her HM Customs and Revenue, probably the only major government access she didn't already have. They were both well aware that what they were doing was illegal, but each was confident of their ability to stay out of jail. They were, after all, the only people in their organizations qualified to catch themselves.

Stacey hadn't expected to need the new access quite so soon. But when Carol told her to start looking for a Jake Andrews living in central Bradfield, and Chris called to confirm that Jake Andrews and Jack Anderson were one and the same, she was pleased at the chance to play with her new toy.

What she was not pleased about was that Jake Andrews was as much an invisible man as Jack Anderson. At least there had been trace evidence of Anderson until three years before. But Jake Andrews, resident of Bradfield, had left not even a smudge on the official records. The violence of her reaction surprised Stacey herself. She'd been so sure she would be able to provide the crucial information with her unique systems access. But cyberspace had let her down. Some small-time killer had evaded her electronic spider's web.

As pissed off as she'd ever been, Stacey marched into Carol's office. Her boss looked up from the pile of witness statements CTC had asked her team to check. 'Any luck?' Carol asked.

'He's not on any of the records I can access. No phone. No mobile phone. No council tax. No National Insurance or tax ID. No TV licence. No car registered in his name. No passport or driving licence. No credit history. Mr Nobody, that's who he is.' She knew she sounded like a small child but she didn't care.

Carol leaned back in her chair, linking her hands behind her head in a stretch. 'I didn't really expect you to find anything,' she said. 'But we had to look. If he went to all the trouble of killing off Jack Anderson, I didn't think he'd be so obvious as to step straight into another documented ID. What's your take on it?'

'I think there's a third ID,' Stacey said. 'He'll have all his official stuff under that ID. He'll use Jack Anderson when he's luring people who might have known him at school, and Jake Andrews for anything else. And ID number three is the one that has left traces.'

'And that's the one we know nothing about,' Carol sighed, getting up and walking round her desk.

'I think it's a fair bet he's used the same initials,' Stacey said. 'It's classic scammer behaviour. Strange but true.'

'That's not much use, is it? It's not going to take us anywhere. It's about as much use as Chris and Paula's barman, the one who wanted a reward for overhearing a first name.'

391

Stacey shook her head. 'Actually, it's not useless. I have some pretty sophisticated search software. I built it myself. It might just get us somewhere.'

Carol looked faintly worried. It was a look Stacey was used to from her boss. 'I sometimes think you really shouldn't tell me all the things you can do, Stacey. OK, get cracking. Do what you can. We need to find this guy.' She stepped out into the squad room behind Stacey. 'Paula,' she called. 'I've got a job for you.'

The nurse bustled in with Tony's chart and his medication, still emanating an aura of deep disapproval. 'Oh good, you're still here,' she said.

He looked up from the laptop screen. 'And there was me thinking this was a hospital, not a prison.'

'You're here for a reason,' the nurse said. 'Look at the oedema in that leg. You're not supposed to go gallivanting when the mood takes you.'

'The physio said I should get dressed and move around today,' he said, obediently taking the pills and swallowing them with a glass of water.

'She didn't say you should leave the building,' the nurse said severely, sticking a thermometer in his mouth and taking his pulse. 'Please don't disappear again, Tony. We were worried. We were afraid you'd fallen somewhere you couldn't attract attention.' She whipped the thermometer out. 'You're lucky you're not in a worse state.'

'Can I go off the ward if I tell you where I am?' he said meekly. Not that he had any plans to move; his energy levels were too depleted for another adventure like this morning's.

'As long as you don't leave the building,' the nurse said sternly. 'You're very lucky we don't have matrons these days. My auntie was one, you know. She'd have strung you up by your naughty bits.' She was halfway to the door when she paused. 'Oh, I nearly forgot. Your mum stopped by earlier. She wasn't very pleased either.'

Tony felt a weight come down on him. 'Did she say when she'd be back?'

'She said she'd try and come by later this afternoon. Make sure you're here, now.'

Left to himself, Tony made a fist and punched the mattress. He really didn't want the distraction his mother would bring in her wake. He was operating well below his normal level and he needed all the acuity he could summon to focus on the bombing and the poisonings. In spite of the promise he'd made to the nurse, he thought he might be making another bid for freedom that afternoon.

But for now, he could restore his energy levels by lying here, doing nothing more strenuous than reading. He'd gone back to the blog Sanjar had taken him to. Reading through all Yousef Aziz's posts had been fascinating. Here was a young man, intelligent but not articulate enough always to express himself clearly. Quite a few of his posts were made in response to people who had misunderstood a previous point because he hadn't managed entirely to say what he meant.

The overall picture Tony formed was of someone who was frustrated at the inability of people to coexist peacefully. Aziz respected other people's views; why couldn't everyone see that was the sensible way to live? Why did some people seem to have such a big investment in conflict?

On his first pass through the posts, nothing struck Tony. But when he re-read the earlier posts with the later ones still fresh in his mind, he sensed something different. He went back and forth a few times, almost at random. He was right. There was something going on there. Something that chimed with what Sanjar had told him. Now he was definitely going to have to make a break for it.

It took more than a major bomb attack to stop premiership football. So Paula discovered when she turned up on Steve Mottishead's doorstep to talk about the old school mate whose photo he'd sent to the police. 'I'm watching the game,' he said petulantly. 'It's Chelsea v Arsenal. I told you all I know about Jack Anderson when I spoke to you before.'

'We can talk while you watch, can't we?' Paula smiled sweetly.

'I suppose,' he said, grudgingly holding the door open and letting her in. Steve Mottishead's house was a former council property on the edge of Downton. The rooms were on the small side, but the house butted on to the golf course that formed the natural boundary between Moortop and Downton so the views from the through lounge he led her into were spectacular.

Paula was the only one interested in the view, however. Sprawled on the sofa in front of a vast TV were two other men who were definitely brothers under the skin. All three wore England shirts, track-suit bottoms and big fat trainers. Each clutched a can of Stella Artois and the air was thick with cigarette smoke. *This sporting life*, Paula thought, picking her way across extended legs to the far end of the room where there was a rickety dining table and four spindly chairs.

'I'll need binoculars to see the game from here,' Mottishead complained, scratching his belly as he sat on a chair Paula would have sworn couldn't take his weight. He plonked his can on the table and took his cigarettes from his pocket. 'I don't suppose you're allowed to have a beer while you're working?' He lit up, making Paula long for one herself. But she tried not to smoke during interviews, even when the punter did. She worried it could make her look weak and dependent.

'Thanks, but no thanks. I'm surprised the game's on after yesterday,' Paula said.

'It's football, love,' one of the others said. 'Spirit of the Blitz. What made this country great. Two minutes' silence then the show must go on. No fucking Paki bomber's going to put a stop to our national game.'

'He doesn't mean it like that,' Mottishead said. 'It's just that we're all upset about what happened yesterday. We were there, like.'

'Yeah, we were,' his mouthy mate said. 'So why aren't you out there finding that bastard bomber's mates instead of bothering Stevie?'

'Because I'm too busy trying to find who killed Robbie Bishop,' Paula said. 'I'd have thought you'd approve of that.' Her aggressor harrumphed and pointedly settled back into his game. Paula turned back to Mottishead. 'I appreciate what you told us before. And it was very helpful. But what I want you to tell me is what Jack Anderson was like. Not the facts of his life, but his personality. What sort of lad he was.'

Mottishead scratched his stubbly head and grinned. 'He was up for anything, Jack. After his dad died, it was like he went off his head a bit. Like he had to get everything crammed in before he died. He was shocking with the lasses – if they wouldn't shag him, he dropped them like a hot potato. And if they did shag him, he'd get bored in a few weeks and dump them anyway. I heard tell he was into all sorts – threesomes, bondage . . . you name it, he'd have a crack at it. And if he liked it, he'd do it again. Drink, fags, drugs – he had to be the first to try everything that was going the rounds. It was like the brakes came off when his dad died, and they never went back on again.'

He sounded like a prince, Paula thought. Lucky for him their paths had never crossed. 'Didn't anybody try to get him to calm down? His mum? Teachers?'

Mottishead pushed his lips out and shook his head. 'His mum was in a world of her own half the time. Looking back, I think she was popping Valium like Smarties. And the teachers weren't interested in owt that happened outside the classroom. Jack was too smart to let his schoolwork go down the drain. He knew getting some qualifications was the only sure way to get out of Bradfield. And he wanted out.'

'Did he ever talk about how he was going to get out? Did he have a career in mind?'

'He never said what he was going to do for a living. He always said how he was going stratospheric. He was going to leave the likes of us behind and go all the way to the top.' His forehead creased with the effort of memory. 'One time, I remember, we were having a General Studies class and we were talking about ambition. And the teacher was going on about how that Tory bloke, what's his name, Tarzan they called him . . .'

'Michael Heseltine?'

'That's the one. Well, apparently when he was a lad, he wrote down a list of what he was planning for his future. Top of the list was Prime Minister. Well, he never made that but he got bloody close, and he did all the other things on the list. The teacher's going on about this, and about setting goals. And we're all thinking, "Get a job, get a girlfriend, get a season ticket for Victoria Park." But not Jack. He's writing down stuff like, "Get a Ferrari. Own a house on Dunelm Drive. Make a million by the time I'm thirty." We all laughed at him, but he was serious.'

'Sounds pretty ambitious,' Paula said.

'That was Jack.' Mottishead turned serious. 'If you're thinking Jack killed Robbie Bishop, I won't be the one on the telly going, "I can't believe it." The road that Jack was on all those years ago? Murder would just be another taboo to walk all over. And he'd make a bloody good job of it. You'd have your work cut out to catch him, never mind to put him away.'

Paula felt herself shiver. 'This team he used to do the pub quiz with? The Funhouse? Did they all work together?'

'No, they'd got together because they all play those online games. You know, I'll be a wizard and you be a dwarf and we'll have a fight? Anyhow, they'd worked out they all lived local and they decided to get together for the pub quiz. Nice blokes, but a right bunch of anoraks apart from Jack. He didn't really fit in with them. Mind you, he never really fitted in anywhere. For all his antics, he never really had proper mates. Just people to do the mad stuff with.'

'And you've no idea where he is now?'

'Not a Scooby. Sorry. I asked around after I spoke to you the other day, but nobody's seen hide nor hair of him for years.'

'I don't understand that,' Paula said. 'We believe he's got a flat in Temple Fields. We think he was in Amatis the night Robbie was poisoned. He must be out and about. I can't believe nobody's seen him around.'

Mottishead took a swig from his can. 'Maybe that's because he doesn't live there. A lot of those fancy flats in the city centre, they're just crash pads for rich sods that live some other place. Maybe Jack made it after all. Maybe he just comes to town when he's got somebody to kill.'

Hands and shoulders aching from the crutches, Tony made his way down the third-floor corridor. He didn't remember it being this far from the lift to the MIT squad room. But then the hospital corridor also seemed to have stretched since that morning.

He'd lied to the nurse. He'd said he was going down to the café on the ground floor to do some reading accompanied by decent coffee, and not to expect him back for a while. The truth was he worked best when he could talk and listen to the team face to face. He wanted to show Carol Yousef Aziz's blog posts, because he didn't think he could convince her without showing her what he meant. And as much as these things, he wanted to avoid another destructive encounter with his mother.

He was disappointed when he walked in to find the only person around was Stacey. Not that he had anything against Stacey. It was impossible not to respect her abilities. He knew from past experience how vital her skills had been to the team's success. There were people walking around Bradfield who wouldn't be if it hadn't been for Stacey's intimate understanding of silicon and cyberspace. It was just that she'd never quite mastered human communication. He always felt awkward around her, perhaps because he could understand how his own social skills might have been that stunted if he hadn't worked so hard at passing for human.

Tony swung across the room, smiling as Stacey looked up. Her eyes widened and she jumped to her feet, placing a second chair behind her desk. He sat down gratefully, unslinging his computer bag from across his body. 'We didn't know you were coming in.' He knew it wasn't meant to be an accusation, but it sounded like one.

'I was getting stir crazy,' he said. 'And besides, this is where I belong at a time like this.'

'It's good to have you back,' she said with all the animation of a talking doll. 'How's your knee?'

'Incredibly uncomfortable. Sometimes very painful. But at least I can get around with this leg brace and the crutches. But I need to take my mind off my leg, which is why I'm here. Do you know if DCI Jordan's due back?'

'She's in a meeting with the Chief Constable,' Stacey

said, already staring at the screen, far more interested in that than in him. 'She went off about twenty minutes ago. She didn't say when she'll be back.'

'OK, I'll wait. I need to talk to her about Yousef Aziz.'

Stacey sneaked a quick glance at him. 'You're working on the bombing?'

'And the other stuff. What are you on?'

Stacey gave him a little smile, like a cartoon cat who's just done something horrible to the dog. 'I'd rather not say how, but I've got all the data from the First Fabrics computer.'

'First Fabrics?'

'Yousef Aziz's family textile business. I've printed out all the correspondence and sent Sam off to find a quiet corner to read it in. He's better at picking up the human interface stuff than I am,' she said.

'Did you just take the piss out of yourself?' Tony said.

She flicked a quick glance his way, a twinkle in her eye. 'I may be a cyborg, but I still have a sense of humour.'

Tony acknowledged her response with a mock salute. 'So what are you looking at?'

'The financials.'

'And?'

'It's stupendously dull, for the most part. They buy textiles from half a dozen different sources, they sell on finished garments to a couple of middlemen.'

'Middlemen? I don't understand.'

Stacey took her hand off the mouse. 'Rag trade 101. The end user is the retailer. They have suppliers who are in effect the wholesalers. The retailer tells the wholesaler what they want to buy and what price they're prepared to pay for it. The wholesaler goes to the middleman and tells him what the order is. The middleman parcels out the order to the manufacturers. Who may not be in this country. Or, who might be illegal sweatshops. Some legit manufacturers, like First Fabrics, also do their own samples, which they pass up the line to try and get orders for.'

'It seems . . . over-complicated?'

'You'd think so, wouldn't you? But apparently that's the way it works. And every step of the way, there are profits to be taken. You buy a shirt in a shop for twenty-five quid, the chances are the manufacturer didn't get more than fifty pee. So the machinists have to make a lot of shirts so their bosses can stay in business.'

'Aren't you glad you've got a skill that earns more than sewing shirts?' Tony said, sighing.

'You bet. Anyway, like I said, that's what First Fabrics does. Buy cloth, make clothes. Sell clothes to one of two middlemen. At least, that's what they did until about six months ago.'

Tony's attention quickened. Anything relating to Yousef Aziz six months previously interested him. 'What happened then?'

'This company appears in the accounts. B&R, they're called. They're paying more per item than the middlemen. From what I can figure out, the price B&R are paying First Fabrics is roughly half way between what a middleman would pay and what a wholesaler would pay the middleman.'

'And this started six months ago?'

Stacey clicked with her mouse and brought up a new screen. She swung her monitor round towards Tony. 'There.' She pointed to a ledger entry. 'First time they show up.'

'So who are B&R?' he asked.

Stacey tutted. 'I don't have access to Companies House database, and they don't issue detailed information like directors and company officers on a Sunday. All I have is a registered address, which is an accountant's office in north Manchester, and the nature of the business.'

'Which is?'

'Garment wholesaler.'

'So for some reason, six months ago, First Fabrics discovered the joy of cutting out the middleman?'

'That's about the size of it, yes.'

He could sense her impatience to continue with her work. 'That's really interesting. Now I need to make a phone call.' He pushed off with his good leg and the wheeled chair scooted a few feet away. He swung round so his back was to Stacey, then dialled the number Sanjar Aziz had given him. The phone was answered on the third ring. But not by Sanjar.

'Hello,' said the voice. Deep, Mancunian and cautious.

'Is this Sanjar Aziz's number?' Tony said, equally cautious.

'Who's calling?'

'This is Dr Tony Hill. Who am I talking to?'

'Mr Aziz is not available right now. Can I take a message?'

'No message,' Tony said and ended the call. He was about to ask Stacey how to find out whether Sanjar

402

Aziz had been arrested when Kevin walked in with a sheaf of papers.

'Hiya, Tony,' he said, looking genuinely pleased to see him. He perched on a desk opposite and ran through the usual questions about the mad axeman and the knee. 'You here to give us a hand?'

'I hope so,' Tony said. 'I need to talk to Carol. And you? What are you working on?'

'This and that. I went to see the Double Aitch's headmaster. All three of the poison victims went there, but the head says he's never met any of them and he didn't set up the trap that reeled Popeye in. For what it's worth, I think he was telling the truth.'

'Wait a minute. What trap?'

Kevin outlined what Cross's widow had told Carol. 'He's not leaving much to chance, is he?' he concluded.

Tony looked thoughtful. 'No,' he said. But his mind was racing. *Sophisticated, elaborate. You've lined up your targets in advance. You take risks, but they're carefully calculated in advance and you do everything you can to minimize their effects. You like connection with your victims but you don't need to see them die. I think you've planned this whole campaign out in advance, beginning to end, and you're methodically working your way through it. And I don't understand what's in it for you. What's the pay-off here?* He sighed. 'None of which takes us much further forward. So, what are you up to now?'

'Aziz's mobile. We got the call records this morning and I've been shut in a cupboard checking out all the numbers.'

'Anything interesting?'

Kevin shook his head. 'Mostly business and family. A few mates, but we already had their names. There's

403

only one thing that looks a bit dodgy.' He pointed out a number to Tony. 'It's a pay-as-you-go phone bought with a false name and address. Those fucking phone shops would sell a phone to Osama bin Laden if he walked in with the cash. They're supposed to ask for ID, but do they buggery. Anyway, as you can see, there's a lot of calls and SMS traffic between the two phones. Unfortunately, Aziz erased all the texts. I tried ringing it, but nobody's home.'

'When did these calls start?' Tony asked.

'Dunno. Aziz only got this phone six months ago. The calls are there more or less from the beginning.'

Again, the magic six months. Before Tony could say more, the door swung open and Carol walked in, speaking over her shoulder to someone in the corridor. When she turned and spotted him, she shook her head in obvious despair.

'What are you doing here?' she said. 'Did they discharge you already?'

'Not as such,' he said. 'I wanted to talk to you, and I wanted to avoid my mother. You know?'

'Will you excuse us, Kevin? Unless you have something that won't wait?' Kevin backed off and headed for his own desk. Carol pushed his chair further away from Stacey and pulled up another next to him.

'Are you crazy?' she said. 'They keep you in hospital for a reason, you know.'

'You sound like the nurses.'

'Well, maybe they're right, did you consider that?'

He rubbed his jaw. 'I need to be working, Carol. It's all I know. I don't do smelling the flowers.' He saw the spark of understanding in her eyes. She'd once spent three months trying not to do her job. It

404

hadn't healed her. It had nearly finished her. Nobody knew that better than him. He pointed to his computer bag on Stacey's desk. 'I have something I want you to look at. I think I'm seeing something, but I'm not sure if it's just that I want to see it.'

Carol fetched the laptop and waited while Tony opened the file he'd made of Yousef Aziz's blog posts. 'Where did you get this?' Carol asked.

'Sanjar Aziz showed it to me,' he said, distracted by the screen.

'When did you talk to Sanjar Aziz?'

'This morning. There, have a look at that.'

Carol put a hand on his arm. 'You know the CTC have brought him in for questioning?'

He stared at the keyboard, head bowed. 'That's what I was afraid of.' He squeezed the bridge of his nose. 'He's no more a terrorist than his brother was.'

'Yes, well, there's a lot of people round here who wouldn't agree with your assessment,' Carol said. 'His brother did blow up a football stadium, Tony. It's not unreasonable of them to bring him in.'

'Why didn't they do it yesterday?'

'They were trying not to inflame the Muslim community. His brother was dead, his parents and his younger brother were in distress, he wasn't going anywhere.'

'So why now? They've got a funeral to arrange. When's that going to be? Tomorrow? Are they going to let him out in time to bury his brother?' His voice was rising and Carol put her hand on his arm again.

'Did Aziz tell you anything useful?'

Tony told her what had passed between them and what he thought he had seen in Aziz's blog posts. 'I think I can see a shift in his position. He starts off talking about how we should all learn to live together in respect. His tone is more despairing than angry. It's like, I can see this, why can't our leaders, why can't everybody else? But gradually, it changes. By the end, he sounds much more angry. Like he's taking it personally that there are these cultural and religious conflicts that mess up people's lives. Look, I'll show you what I mean.' He started moving back and forth between posts, pointing out examples of what he meant. After they'd gone through a dozen or more, he looked anxiously at Carol's face. His confidence, he realized, was nearly as messed up as his leg. 'What do you think?'

'I don't know. I see what you're getting at, I'm just not sure if it's significant. I'm not even sure where we're going with this. Because if Yousef Aziz wasn't a terrorist, then there's not a terrorist cell and we're all wasting our time.'

'CTC are, but not necessarily you,' Tony said. 'There could be something else going on. Maybe he was hired to deliver the bomb but something went wrong. Maybe he was blackmailed into it, his family threatened. It may not have been terrorism, but that doesn't mean there aren't other people out there involved in this. We should be looking at victims, Carol. That's where we always start. Who died? Who were they? Who gained from their death? I need victim information, Carol. That's what I need right now.' He was so fired up he didn't register the new arrivals.

'And who's this, Carol?' the shaven-headed man in the black leather jacket said.

406

Tony frowned, cocking his head back to take in the newcomer's full height and breadth. 'I'm Tony Hill,' he said. 'Dr Tony Hill. And you are?'

'That's none of your business, really,' he said. Then, to Carol, 'What is he doing here? There's nothing for your tame profiler to do on this one.'

Carol turned to Tony. 'This is David. He's with CTC, as you've no doubt worked out for yourself. I'm told they don't do manners.' She stood and faced up to David. 'He's not working on this one. He's working on another one. It may have escaped your notice, but we've got a poisoner on our patch. That's what Dr Hill is helping us with.'

'Let's hope it doesn't involve getting anywhere in a hurry,' David said. 'Mind you, from what I've heard of your exploits, it's probably just as well you can't get around. Carol, say goodbye. We need you next door.' He turned on his heel and walked out.

'Christ,' Carol exploded. 'What is it with those people?'

'He almost certainly has a small penis,' Tony said. 'And he's most likely read the briefing paper I did for the Home Office on what CTC should consist of.' He smiled sadly. 'If they'd listened, it wouldn't be run by people like him.' He winked at her and was relieved to hear her snort of laughter.

'Come on, I'll walk you to the lift,' she said.

'You're sending me away?' he said.

'Yes, but not because of that twat. Because you should be in bed. You look like shit. I'll try to come and see you later.' She helped him to his feet and walked ahead of him so she could open the door. They moved slowly down the hall, Tony conscious that his energy was dwindling fast. 'By the way,' she said. 'You asked me where Tom Cross went to school. Paula had already checked it out. Harriestown High. So there's your link, I guess.'

'Yes, Kevin told me. That's one link,' he said, leaning against the wall by the lifts.

'There's more?'

'Luck, Carol. They were all lucky.'

Carol looked incredulous. 'Lucky? They were all poisoned. They died horrible deaths. How is that lucky?'

The lift arrived and Tony staggered in. 'The luck came first. And I think it might be what got them killed.'

It was late and Carol was tired of CTC's antics by the time she made it to the hospital. The night nurse tried to say something to her as she shot past, but she was in no mood for conversation. She knocked softly on Tony's door and opened it quietly, hoping not to disturb him if he was sleeping. If he was out cold, she'd just leave the bundle of print-outs relating to the stadium bomb victims and go.

There was a pool of light over his bed table, and Carol could see Tony's hand holding a pen, resting on top of some papers. He was groggy from drugs and sleep, his head lolling on his shoulder. But his were not the only hands on the table. Holding the papers still, guiding his hand to the right place was a perfectly manicured claw with scarlet talons.

'Good evening, Mrs Hill,' Carol said loudly.

She tried to snatch away the papers, but Carol was too quick for her. 'What the hell do you think you're doing?' Vanessa demanded. 'This is none of your business.'

Carol snapped on the overhead light. Tony blinked furiously as he came round. 'Carol?' he said. She was too busy scrutinizing the papers Vanessa had been trying to get him to sign. Vanessa herself was lunging at Carol, edging round the bed all the while, desperate to get her hands on the papers.

'I should remind you that I'm a police officer, Mrs Hill,' Carol said in the tone of voice she normally reserved for the more contemptible of the criminals she dealt with. 'Tony? What do you think these papers are? The ones your mother is trying to get you to sign?'

He rubbed his eyes and struggled to sit up. 'It's to do with my grandmother's house. I half-own it. I need to sign the papers so we can sell it.'

'Your grandmother's house?' Carol wanted to double-check before she delivered what she suspected would be a bombshell.

'Yes.'

'He doesn't know what he's saying,' Vanessa protested.

'I do so,' he said, stroppy as an over-tired toddler. 'You've been on at me to sign them ever since you tracked me down in here.'

'And was your grandmother called Edmund Arthur Blythe?' Carol said, feigning an innocence that was calculated to infuriate Vanessa.

'How dare you,' she hissed at Carol.

'What?' Tony said. 'Who's Edmund Arthur Blythe?'

Vanessa lunged at Carol again and she straight-armed her away without a moment's compunction.

Vanessa staggered back, hitting the wall. She stood there for a moment, face stricken, hands to her mouth. Then she slid down the wall like a drunk and huddled on the floor. 'No,' she moaned. 'No.'

Carol stepped over to the bed and said, 'Someone who thought he was your father.'

Monday

Tony didn't want to think about Edmund Arthur Blythe. He'd asked the nurse for something stronger than usual to make sure he slept, because he didn't want to lie awake thinking about Edmund Arthur Blythe. Tony Blythe. That would have been his name if Vanessa had married him. He wondered if he would ever know why that hadn't happened. With a different woman, he'd either have been able to make a reasonable guess or he'd have been able to ask. But he couldn't ask his mother. And guessing was pointless because there were so many possibilities. Maybe he'd been married to somebody else. Maybe he'd taken fright at the idea of being married to Vanessa. Maybe she'd never told him she was pregnant. Or maybe she'd told him to bugger off, she'd be better off on her own. For forty-three years Vanessa had kept his identity and the circumstances of their relationship secret. He didn't think she was suddenly going to feel the need to change that any time soon.

Before Carol had thrown her out last night, Vanessa had claimed her only motive was to protect Tony from the trauma of discovering his father was dead.

411

'Protecting him to the tune of a few hundred thousand pounds,' Carol had pointed out coolly.

Because of the drugs, it had taken him a little while to get his head round what Vanessa had tried to get him to sign. The papers were nothing to do with his grandmother's house. They were a formal renunciation of his claim on the estate of his late father in favour of his mother. An estate which, according to Carol, amounted to a house in Worcester, fifty-odd thousand in savings and a boat. 'She's a criminal, Tony,' Carol had said. 'That was attempted fraud.'

'I know,' he'd said. 'But it's all right.'

'How can you be so understanding?' Carol said, frustrated.

'Because I understand,' Tony said simply. 'What do you want me to do? Bring charges against my mother? I don't think so. Can you imagine how much damage she could do to the pair of us under cover of court privilege?' It had taken Carol about two seconds to understand the force of what he was saying.

'Let's forget it, then,' she'd said. 'But if she dares to show her face again, don't sign anything.' And she'd gone, taking the papers with her for safe-keeping and leaving a stack of information about the victims. He'd been glad of it. It took his mind off Edmund Arthur Blythe.

And that was why, at seven o'clock sharp on Monday morning, he had filed his request for company information on B&R at the Companies House website. While he waited for them to send the fruits of their search, he began to work his way through the list of Yousef Aziz's victims.

It was a devastating catalogue. Eight colleagues from

412

an insurance company, celebrating the birth of a child; a primary head teacher and his wife, the guests of executives from the company who had donated his school's computers; three musicians from a local band who'd just released their first CD; a motivational guru and his two teenage sons, along with the CEO of the mountain bike manufacturing company who had invited them; three men who had been friends since childhood, part of a group of successful businessmen who had a season ticket for the box they occupied. The heartbreaking list went on – the youngest, the seven-year-old son of an MP: the oldest, a seventy-four-year-old retired car dealer.

At first glance, there was no obvious candidate for assassination. But then, nobody had done any serious background work on the victims because nobody was seriously considering an alternative explanation to terrorism. He couldn't understand why Carol wasn't more enthusiastic. They'd worked so closely together for so long, her first instinct should be to trust him. But it was as if she was using his accident as an excuse for dismissing his professional opinion. If she didn't want to take on CTC, fair enough. He could understand that. What he couldn't understand was why she wasn't saying that to him, to explain why she was so lukewarm about his ideas. All these years they'd worked together, all the intimacy that went with bouncing ideas back and forth, all the support they'd shown each other. Sure, Carol had seen off his mother. But what had happened to their professional relationship?

His laptop gave the discreet click that told him a new email had arrived. Eagerly, he opened it. There, laid out before him, was the company information relating to B&R. The company secretary was the accountant whose address Stacey already had. The two directors were Rachel and Benjamin Diamond. With an address in Bradfield. Tony drew his breath in sharply and reached for the victim details.

Hastily, he riffled through the sheets. At last, he pulled one page free. His pulse was racing and he could feel the fizz and pop of adrenaline shooting through him. He'd remembered right. No matter what Carol thought, his brain was working just fine. He knew exactly where he'd seen that name already that morning. He spread the paper out on his laptop, devouring the words. This was beyond coincidence. Carol was going to have to listen to him now.

Carol barely recognized the HOLMES suite, so thoroughly had CTC colonized the space. Their information boards broke the room up into segments, their computers and peripherals covered every desk. The air was pungent with male sweat and cigarette smoke. Clearly, the building's smoking ban did not apply to the chosen of the gods. As she walked in the door, she felt the atmosphere shift. It had been the same every time she'd entered what had been her own territory. A moment of immobility, like dogs scenting strangers; the stillness before the hackles rise. They didn't like having her here, they wanted her to be afraid of them and their masculinity. She wondered, as she always did, how many of them knew her own history, knew about the rape, knew John Brandon had brought her back from the brink. She wouldn't mind betting that, even if they knew about the assault, they wouldn't have heard about the betrayal that had gone hand in hand with what had happened to her. Because the betrayal made men like them look bad.

'I'm here for the meeting,' she said to the grunt nearest the door.

Stony faced, he logged off from his terminal and walked her to the far end of the room, where David and Johnny had set up camp behind baffle screens. Before she'd even sat down, David leaned forward, elbows on knees, and said, 'We're not having a very good time here, Carol. We've rounded up everyone in your fair city that we had any intel on. And it seems like nobody knew our friend Yousef. His brother is a complete waste of time. He's about as politicized as a toilet seat. As are the so-called mates of our suicide bomber.' He jumped up and started pacing, pulling a cigarette packet from his jacket as he prowled.

'This is a non-smoking building,' Carol said.

'What are you going to do? Arrest me?' David sneered.

'I thought I might just pour the water over your head.' Carol pointed to the jug on the table. Her smile could have slit a sack from top to bottom.

David tossed the cigarette on the table in frustration. 'I can't be arsed arguing with you,' he said. It wasn't a bad attempt at face-saving, but Carol knew she'd scored a small victory. Doubtless she'd pay for it down the line, but right now it felt worth it.

'We wondered if you had any intel we've not been given,' Johnny said. 'Not necessarily about Yousef, but about Islamic militancy generally.'

Carol shook her head. 'We leave that to you. Anything we get, it comes to us incidentally, in the course of other stuff. And we pass it on routinely. We're not holding back any terrorist-related intel.'

'So what are you holding back?' Johnny said, pouncing on her careful words. 'Come on, Carol. We're not stupid. Lines are for reading between.'

She was saved by the arrival of the third member of their cabal. The one who hadn't even bothered to give her an alias. He cocked an inquiring glance at Carol.

'It's all right,' David said.

'Forensics,' the third man said, tossing a folder on the table. 'On the bomb. They got lucky. The configuration of the room meant the mechanism stayed relatively intact. Totally what you'd expect. Except for one thing. They say there were two trigger mechanisms. One to be set manually, the other to be activated remotely.'

'What does that mean?' Carol said.

David picked up the folder and skimmed the sheet of paper inside. 'They don't know. It's not something we've seen before. We'll have to run it past the cousins and see if they've any experience of it.'

'You mean the Americans?' Carol said. David nodded. 'Why don't you just say so?' She rolled her eyes. *Boys and their toys.* 'So, with all your experience, would you hazard a guess as to what this means?'

The third man dropped into a chair as if he was punishing it for offending him. 'No,' he said. 'We don't do guessing. We do inference and deduction. Me, I think he was going to set the manual timer and get clear. Then if it didn't go off, he could use his mobile to trigger the device remotely.'

David gave him the look priests normally reserve

416

for heretics. 'Are you saying you don't think this was meant to be a suicide bomb?'

'I'm looking at the evidence and trying to make sense of it,' he said. 'Doesn't mean he's not a terrorist. Fucking Provos managed to create mayhem without blowing themselves up. Makes sense. You go to all the bother of training somebody to do this shit, you might as well get more than one mission out of them.'

It did make a kind of sense, Carol thought. 'Funnily enough, we'd been wondering something similar,' she said.

All three heads swivelled towards her. 'You what?' David sounded indignant.

'In fact, we were wondering whether it was even terrorism,' she said. 'Dr Hill suggested Yousef might be a gun for hire, as it were.'

The third man exploded in laughter. 'You are a fucking tonic,' he said. 'I love it. I mean, you need a hit man. Who're you gonna call? A clothes factory manager. Stands to reason.' He slapped his thigh. 'Plus, who's going to kill thirty-five people for one hit? That's not how gangsters work, sweetheart.' He laughed again. 'Priceless.'

'That'll do,' Johnny said, his voice soft and his eyes dangerous. He turned to Carol. 'Bottom line? Yousef Aziz was a Muslim. There's a significant tranche of Muslims who hate us. They want to blow us to kingdom come and impose Sharia law on what's left. They don't want peaceful coexistence, they want to destroy us. That's enough, surely? That's all that's going on here, Carol.'

'Hit man,' the third man repeated. 'I love it.'

Carol stood up. 'There's just no point talking to

417

you, is there? You live in your own little bubble. If you need a comedy break, you know where to find us.'

She marched out of the room, head high. When Tony had called her just before the meeting, she'd wondered if he was losing it. Seeing ghosts in the natural coincidences of life. Now, she really wished he could be right. She'd like nothing more than to ram an alternative, correct conclusion down their arrogant throats.

Trouble was, she lived in the real world. The one where wishes tended not to come true.

Tony rang Sanjar Aziz, hoping the CTC had decided he was harmless. Otherwise he was going to have to track down the rest of the family to see if they could shed any light on B&R. He didn't want to face Rachel Diamond without some preparation. This time, Sanjar answered his own phone. 'Yeah?' he said, sounding harassed. Tony felt a surge of relief.

'It's Tony Hill, Sanjar. I was sorry to hear they'd pulled you in.'

'Bound to happen sooner or later, innit? At least they let me go in time to make it to Yousef's funeral.' He sounded surprisingly calm for someone who had just spent the night in the cells rather than supporting his grieving family.

'That's today, is it?'

'This afternoon,' he said. 'It's going to be pretty weird. Apparently there's not much left to bury.' Tony could hear him breathing heavily. Sanjar gave a weak laugh. 'I dunno how we're going to work out how to get him facing Mecca.'

'I'm sorry. Are you doing OK?'

'What do you think? My mum's devastated, my dad won't open his mouth and my little brother's heart-broken and terrified at the thought of going back to school.' He sighed. 'Sorry, you didn't deserve that. So, what did you want? Why are you calling me?'

'I need to ask you a couple of questions. To do with work.'

'Work? You mean First Fabrics?'

'Yeah. What can you tell me about a company called B&R?'

'B&R? They were Yousef's big idea for how we could change the way we did business.'

'What do you mean?'

'Margins have got so fucking tight, man. So we needed to cut out the middleman to increase our profits. B&R's a wholesaler, they sell direct to the retail trade. They've got some pretty good accounts. They're a great match for us.'

'So this was Yousef's idea?' Tony asked.

'Well, it was something we'd talked about before, but he actually managed to get it off the ground. See, the trouble with cutting out the middleman is that he's the one who commissions the work from you. He tells you what to make, in effect. Even if it's your own design that's been pitched to the store on your behalf, he's the man. You piss off the middleman and suddenly he's not calling you with orders.'

'So how did Yousef get round it?'

'We increased production. B&R only sell designs from us that are exclusive to them. So the middleman doesn't see any change in the level of commitment

419

he's getting from us. We're not rocking his boat, so he's not trying to take us down. And we have a new profit centre.' Sanjar sounded jaded, as if he couldn't care less whether First Fabrics made a profit.

'So Yousef just went out and sorted it with B&R?' Tony asked.

'He'd like you to think he did, but it was more of an accident than that. Yousef had gone to see Demis Youkalis, one of our middlemen. To let you know, guys like Demis treat guys like us as if we're dumb fucks who've been put on the planet to mess up his day. Just because the Cypriots got off the plane five minutes before we did. Anyway, Demis wasn't there. He hadn't been there for so long he'd missed his previous appointment, which was with the guy from B&R.'

'Was that Benjamin Diamond?'

'No idea, mate. Yousef just said, "the guy from B&R". They got talking, and the B&R guy said how much he liked our stuff, and what a pity we were both putting money in Demis's pocket when he basically does fuck all for it. So they talk a bit more, then they go to a café and try to figure out a different way of doing business. Which is how we ended up where we are, doing business direct with B&R.'

'Who did Yousef deal with at B&R?'

'No idea. He used to have regular meetings with them, going through new designs and product ranges, but that was his job. I don't know who his contact was. It's not like we would see them socially, know what I mean?'

'No,' Tony said. It was a lie but he wanted to hear if Sanjar knew who B&R were. 'What do you mean?'

420

'They're Jewish, man. It's not a problem when it comes to doing business, their money's as good as anybody else's. But we're not going to be their friends, you catch my drift?'

'I understand,' Tony said. He glanced at his watch. In ten minutes, Paula would be waiting downstairs. 'You do know that Benjamin Diamond from B&R died in the bombing on Saturday?'

A long silence. 'No way,' Sanjar eventually said.

'I'm afraid so. Are you sure Yousef never mentioned him by name?'

'No, he always just said "the B&R guy". I'm pretty sure he never mentioned a name. So maybe it wasn't this Diamond geezer that he dealt with?'

'It's possible. It just seemed like an odd coincidence,' Tony said mildly.

'Shit like that, it happens. You get coincidences all the time, right?'

'We don't really believe in them in my line of work. I need to go now, Sanjar. I hope you get to bury your brother with dignity.'

'We're trying to keep where we're doing it a secret,' he said gloomily. 'The last thing we want is any trouble kicking off.'

'Good luck.' He ended the call and eased himself off the bed and on to his crutches. He'd had a very uncomfortable encounter with Mrs Chakrabarti that morning. The nurses had reported his absences and the contretemps between Carol and his mother. The surgeon had not been impressed.

'You work in a hospital, Dr Hill,' she'd said severely. 'You should understand that patients have the best chance of getting better if they actually follow the directives of those taking care of them. I was thinking we might discharge you today or tomorrow, but frankly, the way you've been behaving, I'm afraid to do that in case you have a relapse.' Then she'd twinkled a smile at him. 'I don't want you playing football before the end of the week.'

She'd told him not to go out. But he didn't have a choice. Somebody had to pursue the line of inquiry, and Carol had made it plain when he'd called her that it wasn't high on her list of priorities.

'I'll go by myself, then,' he'd told her.

'I don't think that's one of your better ideas,' Carol said.

'What? You think I'll say something I shouldn't?'

'No, I think you'll fall over your crutches and that poor bereaved woman will have to pick you off the floor. I'll send Paula, she can chaperone you.'

'I bet she'll be really thrilled.'

And so it had been agreed that Paula would pick him up outside the Outpatients Department. He didn't want to pass the nurses' station, so he decided to take the emergency stairs near his room.

One flight nearly killed him. He was bathed in sweat, his good leg was aching and his broken knee felt as if it was on fire. He wobbled along to the lift and managed to make it to their rendezvous without discovery. Paula was leaning on her car, parked in the ambulance-only zone.

'You look like you've run a half marathon,' she said, nose wrinkling in distaste.

'It's the jogging pants. They're all I can get over my leg brace.' Shaking her head in amusement, Paula opened the door and he let himself drop back into the seat, then swung his legs round and in. 'Just as well Carol didn't send Kevin in his Ferrari,' he gasped as he tried to make himself comfortable.

'We'd have had to get a crane to get you in and out of that,' Paula said, getting in the driver's side.

'Quite. So, what have you been up to?'

She brought him up to speed with their inquiries into Jack Anderson and his aliases. 'He sounds a bit of an oddball,' she added. 'Apparently, when he was at school, he had this list of goals. Like Michael Heseltine's "I'm going to be Prime Minister" list.'

Until then, nothing Paula had said had piqued Tony's curiosity. But this was different. 'Do we know what was on his list?'

'According to Steve Mottishead, it was stuff like, get a Ferrari, get a house on Dunelm Drive, make a million by age thirty. Not the kind of thing that most people aspire to.'

Her words triggered a chain reaction in Tony's brain. He gazed at Paula in appalled wonder. 'Paula, Tom Cross lived on Dunelm Drive. Danny Wade won the lottery; he was a millionaire by age thirty. He's killing people who went to his school who have achieved his goals.'

Paula took her foot off the accelerator in surprise. The jolt as the gears protested made Tony yelp. 'That's crazy,' she said. 'Even for you, that's pretty wild. You're saying he's killing people out of envy? Because they've got what he wanted?'

Tony's hands made incoherent shapes in the air. 'There's more to it than that . . . It's something to do with having his dreams taken away from him, so he's taking their lives from them. But in essence, yes. His goal list is also his murder list. I bet you that "playing for Bradfield Victoria" or at the very least, "playing premiership football" was on that list too.'

'You really think that's it?' Paula sounded incredulous.

'It makes sense.'

'That's your idea of sense?'

'Paula, in the world I work in, that's not just sense, it's celestial logic.' He fell silent, holding up a finger to hush her when she tried to speak. He rubbed his eyelids with finger and thumb then turned in his seat to face her. 'Kevin went to the Double Aitch,' he said slowly.

'Kevin? You don't think –'

'He drives a Ferrari. He's Bradfield born, bred and buttered.' Tony was already struggling to get his phone out of the pocket of his waxed jacket.

'What are you doing?' Paula asked.

'I'm warning him.' The phone was free and clear, Tony's index finger poised to strike.

'You can't go off on one like that. You've got no evidence,' Paula protested.

'I've got about as much as I usually have when I draw up a profile,' Tony said. 'You lot are generally happy enough to act on that.'

Paula bit her lip. 'Shouldn't you talk to the chief first? See if she thinks there's anything to it?'

'Paula, I'm not asking Kevin to do anything operational. How would you feel if I didn't say anything and . . .' His voice trailed off. He knew exactly how she would feel. He'd listened to her enough to know the answer.

'Phone him,' she snapped. 'You're right, damn it. You've been the only one who's had a fucking clue on this case. Do it.'

Tony dialled the number and waited. No ring tone, just a straight transfer to voicemail. 'Shit, his phone's off . . . Kevin, this is Tony. This is going to sound crazy, and I'll explain it all later. I want you to avoid eating or drinking anything that could have been tampered with. Things in tins and bottles and vacuum packs are fine as long as the seals are intact. Or if you're cooking with fresh ingredients, probably. Because I think there's a chance you might be next on the poisoner's list. I can't go into it now, Paula and I are about to interview someone about Saturday. But . . .' He heard a beep in his ear, indicating his time was up. 'Voicemail,' he said. 'I hope he picks it up.'

Paula turned into a driveway. The house, he knew, must have cost the thick end of a couple of million, given its location, its acreage and its size. It was a beautifully proportioned manor house in mellow Victorian brick. Long herbaceous borders flanked the drive. Water features sparkled in the middle distance. It reeked of opulence and good taste.

Paula whistled. 'Makes you wonder how all those crappy clothes get into the shops. Benjamin Diamond must have used up all his taste on the house.'

'It's very choice,' Tony said. 'But I don't suppose any of it makes much difference to his widow right now.'

Paula looked chastened. She pulled up by a row of garages which had obviously started their working lives as stables. 'Do you need a hand?' she asked.

'I think it's better if I just struggle,' Tony said, doing just that. Everything hurt today. Mrs Chakrabarti was right. He was in hospital for a reason. Unfortunately, killers never took things like that into consideration.

Rachel Diamond answered the door, introducing herself before Paula had the chance to speak. She wore a charcoal silk shirt tucked into a black skirt that swirled and flowed as she walked. Tony didn't know much about clothes, but he felt pretty sure Rachel's mourning outfit didn't come from any of the chain stores B&R supplied. She ushered them into a large sitting room with a deep pentagonal bay window on one corner, giving on to a vista of shrubbery and trees. In a gap between foliage, there was a turquoise sliver of swimming pool. The room itself was furnished and decorated in a toned-down contemporary version of Victorian domestic style. It had the slightly scuffed air of a room that was used rather than displayed. A touch of vivid colour came from half a dozen bright, warm paintings of desert landscapes.

Rachel fussed over Tony, bringing him a couple of footstools and various cushions so they could establish the most comfortable position for his leg. She knelt by his feet, shifting and adjusting things till he was comfortable. Her dark hair was glossy and thick, but he could see some tiny flecks of silver at the roots. Then she looked up and he had the chance to look at her properly for the first time, free from the distraction of managing leg and crutches.

She had good skin, creamy and faintly olive tinted. He knew she was thirty-four, but if he hadn't known, he would have placed her in her late twenties. Her well-shaped brows followed the high arch of her eye sockets perfectly, drawing attention to almond-shaped hazel eyes rimmed with red and sporting a fan of faint lines at the corners. Plump cheeks, a nose like the inverted prow of a ship, a lean-lipped mouth bracketed by a pair of lines that gave the impression she smiled a lot. She was striking rather than beautiful, but she looked combatively intelligent and good fun. 'How's that?' she said.

'As comfortable as it's been in a week,' Tony said. 'Thank you.'

Rachel got to her feet and curled her legs under her in a squashy chintz armchair. Paula was off to one side, happy to look like part of the furniture until she felt the need to make a contribution.

Now there was nothing practical to occupy her, Rachel looked sad and lost. She folded her arms across her chest as if she was hugging herself. The room was warm, but she gave a little shiver. 'I'm not really clear why you wanted to see me,' she said. 'That's probably me. Nothing's really making much sense right now.'

'I wouldn't expect it to,' Tony said gently. 'And I'm sorry to intrude at a time when the last thing you want is strangers in your living room.'

Rachel relaxed slightly, her shoulders dropping and her arms loosening. 'It fills some of the time,' she said. 'Nobody talks about that, do they? They all talk about the grief and the tears and the despair, but they don't talk about the emptiness of your hours, the way the time stretches out.' She gave a bitter little laugh. 'I even thought about going into the office, just for something to do. But Lev's home from school, I need to be here for him.' She sighed. 'Lev's my little boy.

427

He's only six. He doesn't understand dead. He doesn't grasp that it's permanent. He thinks Daddy's going to be like Aslan, coming back to life, and everything as it was before.'

Her grief, he thought, was almost tangible. It seemed to flow from her in waves, lapping around him as it filled the room. 'There are some things I need to ask you,' he said.

Rachel pressed her hands together as if in prayer, elbows on the chair arm, cheek against the back of one hand. 'Ask what you like. But I don't see how it can help you do whatever it is you do.'

There was no way to come at this question delicately. 'Mrs Diamond, did you know Yousef Aziz?'

She looked startled, as if this was a name she never expected to hear in this house. 'The bomber?' She gagged, as if she was going to be sick.

'Yes,' Tony said.

'How would I know some fundamentalist Islamic suicide bomber?' Each word spilled out as if it took a huge effort. 'We are Jewish. We go to temple, not to the mosque.' She sat up convulsively, her hands jerking in irregular, spastic movements.

'His family's garment business traded with B&R,' Paula said, her voice as gentle as Tony's. 'You are a director of B&R, Mrs Diamond.'

She looked hunted, an animal at bay. 'I work in the office. Benjamin, he did all the ... He was the one with the ... I never heard this name before he blew up my husband.'

'Is there anybody else at work he might have mentioned Aziz to?' Paula asked.

'There's only us. It's not a labour-intensive business,

our part of it. We did it together. No secretaries, no sales team.' She smiled, a sad, wistful affair.

'Are you sure? It's been in all the papers, Rachel,' Tony said. 'His name. The family firm, First Fabrics. You didn't recognize it?'

Rachel was rocking in her chair, her eyes flickering from one to the other. 'I recognize the name. I see it in the B&R accounts. But I haven't been reading the papers. Why would I want to read about this thing? Why would I want to read about how my husband died? You think I've been poring over the news-papers?'

'Of course not,' Tony said, trying to soothe her agitation. 'I just thought you might have noticed it. But the thing is, B&R has been dealing directly with First Fabrics. Cutting out the middleman. So I'm thinking that Benjamin must have known Yousef Aziz. They must have spoken on the phone. They must have met. You see, it's very unusual for there to be any relationship between a bomber and his victims.'

'Relationship?' Rachel made it sound as if she'd never heard the word before. 'What do you mean, "relationship"? What are you suggesting about my husband?'

'Nothing beyond the fact that they knew each other,' Tony said hastily. This was not going well. 'Generally, you see, one of the things that makes it possible for a bomber to carry out his mission is that he can depersonalize his victims. They're not real people, they're the enemy, they're corrupt, whatever. If they have any personal connection to the poten-tial victims, it makes it much harder for them to do what they've set their heart on. That's why I'm curious to know how well Benjamin knew his killer.' He spread his hands, beseeching. 'That's all, Rachel.'

'How do you know that this, this piece of . . . this bomber had any idea Benjamin was going to be there? Why would he research which individuals he might kill? He just wanted to make his filthy, stupid point.' She gave a deep, shuddering sigh. 'This is just a horrible coincidence.'

She might be right, Tony thought. Sometimes a cigar is just a cigar. Or it would be if the target had profiled right. He clung on to his theory, unwilling to concede that he was wrong when it came to understanding the patterns of human behaviour. 'It's possible,' he said.

She shuddered again, covering her face with her hands. She looked up at him piteously. 'We paid them money. We have their . . . In our warehouse, we have things their hands have touched. It disgusts me. What kind of people are they, to do a thing like this to us?'

'I'm sorry,' Tony said. 'So very sorry. But I have to be sure. Your husband never spoke about who he dealt with at First Fabrics? He never discussed his meetings with them?'

'You're welcome to look at his diary. It's at the office. But this is all I know. Benjamin was supposed to meet with a Greek Cypriot we buy from, but the man had been delayed. While he was waiting, he met someone from a company whose work we'd bought before, via the middleman. We liked their work, it was good quality, reliable. Which is more than you can say for a lot of them.' It was an acid little aside. 'Benjamin told me they'd got talking and they'd ended up doing a deal on some exclusive designs that First Fabrics had worked up themselves. It was an arrangement that worked for both of us. And it was working out.'

'There was no question of you pulling out of the arrangement? No bad feeling for any reason?' Paula came in with the detective's question.

Rachel pushed her hair back from her face, looking suddenly weary. 'Nothing like that, no. If anything, we were happy to do more business with them. Because of the way we'd set it up, there was a better profit margin for us. Detective, there was no possible business reason for this person to attack Benjamin. As I said before, it can only be some horrible coincidence.'

Before either of them could press further, the door opened and a small boy came in. Slender and dark, he looked as if he still had to grow into his features. He shuffled from foot to foot, fiddling with the fringe on a throw. 'Mum, I need you to come and help me with my Lego,' he said, ignoring the strangers in his house.

'In a minute, darling.' She turned back to Tony. 'This is our son, Lev.' She stood up. 'I think we're finished here. There's truly nothing more I can help you with. Please, let me show you out.'

They followed her to the door, Tony struggling to keep up. Lev walked with them. 'Do you know my dad?' he said abruptly to Tony.

'No,' he said. 'Do you look like him?'

Lev eyed him curiously. 'I will one day,' he said. 'But I'm still too little. I just look like me now.'

'And a very handsome me you are too,' Tony said.

'What did you do to your leg? Did somebody blow you up too? Somebody blew up my dad.'

'No, nobody blew me up,' Tony said. 'A man hit me with an axe.'

'Wow,' Lev said. 'That's pretty cool. Did it hurt?'

431

'It still does.' He'd almost caught up with Paula and Rachel. 'But it's getting better.'

Lev reached up and grabbed his hand. 'Then will you kill the man who hit you with the axe?'

Tony shook his head. 'No. What I'll do is try to help him not to do it again. I'm a kind of doctor, Lev. I try to make people feel better inside. If you feel bad inside, there are people like me you can talk to. Don't be afraid to ask. Your mum will help you find the right one, won't you, Rachel?'

Rachel swallowed hard, her eyes brimming. 'Of course I will. Say goodbye now, Lev.'

Somehow, they got out without anybody cracking up. 'Fuck,' Paula said as they walked back to the car. 'That was no fun at all. And no use at all either. She's got a point, you know. Why would Aziz have any idea that Diamond was in that precise part of the stand? And even if he did, according to what Mrs Diamond said, there's not a shred of motive.'

'So it seems,' Tony said. 'And I could be totally wrong.' He dragged himself a few steps nearer the car. 'On the other hand, I might just be right. And I'd have thought you lot would have been gagging to take my side on this one.'

'Why?' Paula stopped and waited for him.

'Because, if I am right, then CTC will have to piss off home with their tails between their legs.'

Paula grinned, her eyes dancing. 'When you put it like that . . . Let's see if we can find some evidence, Dr Hill.'

Kevin smiled at the phone. 'That's right. Aziz. Yousef Aziz. The rental would probably start from the

beginning of this week ... Yes, I'll hold.' He twid-
dled his pen between his fingers, trying to move it
from one side of his hand to the other without dropping it. The voice on the other end spoke to him.
'OK, fine, thanks for trying.' He crossed another
name off the list and prepared to dial another holiday
home rental in Northern Ontario. Of the sites Yousef
Aziz had visited, he'd now managed to contact eight
out of seventeen. None of them had rented a property to Yousef Aziz. None of them remembered
speaking to him or receiving an email from him.

Just as he was about to dial the next number, Carol
stopped at his desk. She held out a box of cakes.
'There you go, Kevin, help yourself. I thought we all
needed a bit of sugar to get us through the afternoon.'

He looked at the cakes, wondering. 'Can I ask where
you got them from?' he asked.

'The baker's shop in the precinct,' Carol said. 'The
one we usually get our cakes from. Why?'

Kevin looked embarrassed. 'It's just that ... Well,
Tony left me a voicemail and told me not to eat
anything that could have been tampered with.'

'He did what?' Carol's annoyance was unmistakable beneath the incredulity. 'Did he say why he
thought that?'

Kevin shook his head. 'He said he'd talk to me
later. But I've not heard from him since.'

'I sent Paula out with him. Have you seen her?'

'She said she was going to hit the bricks in Temple
Fields this afternoon with our pictures of Jack
Anderson, see if she could get any leads. I've not
spoken to her since she went out this morning.'

Carol took a deep breath. He could see she was simmering. 'And what are you doing?'

'Following up on the rental places that Aziz looked at on his computer.'

'OK. You stick with that.' Carol walked back to her own office and closed the door behind her. She called Paula's mobile. When the call connected, she said, 'Paula, were you with Tony when he called Kevin this morning?'

'Yes, I was.' Paula sounded cautious.

'Can you tell me why he took it upon himself to warn one of my officers about being poisoned without telling me?'

A short pause, then Paula said, 'He knew you were in a meeting and he thought it was urgent.'

'And why does he think someone might want to poison Kevin?'

'The short answer is, because Kevin went to Harriestown High and he drives a Ferrari.'

Carol gently massaged her closed eyelids and wished the newborn pain in her head would go as quickly as it had arrived. 'And does the long answer make any more sense than that?' she said.

'When I interviewed Steve Mottishead yesterday, he said Anderson had made a wish list when he was at school. Like Michael Heseltine wanting to be Prime Minister?'

'Go on.'

'He remembered a few things off the list. Having a house on Dunelm Drive. Making a million by thirty. Driving a Ferrari. When I told Tony about the list, he reckoned that was what connected the victims, as well as being former pupils of Harriestown High. And

434

then he remembered Kevin's car. So he made the call.'

'And you didn't think that was a little sudden? A little quick off the mark?'

A long silence. 'We both thought, better safe than sorry, Chief.'

Don Merrick's name hung in the silence between them. 'Thanks, Paula. I'll speak to Tony. Do you happen to know where he is?'

'I dropped him back at the hospital. He was pretty knackered.'

'Did you get anything from Mrs Diamond?' Carol asked.

'Nothing that takes us any further forward. She made the point that Aziz couldn't have known her husband was going to be at the match, so it must have been coincidence.'

'Not necessarily. As I understand it, that was a season ticket box, hired by the same bunch of guys for years now. It's possible Benjamin Diamond mentioned it in passing in one of their meetings. In my experience of men and football, it's exactly the kind of thing they like to drop in passing. I think we need to talk to Diamond's secretary.'

'He doesn't have one. According to Rachel, the two of them ran the whole operation between them. She mostly did the office stuff, he mostly did the customer contact.'

'OK. Good luck with your photo trawl. I'll speak to you later.' She put the phone down and pressed her fists against her temples. What was he playing at? She was used to Tony flying off at tangents, but he generally ran things past her. After his last

435

encounter with a killer, she thought he'd finally learned the lesson of thinking before he acted. Obviously, she'd been mistaken. She reached for the phone, girding her loins for the usual complicated encounter. Why couldn't her life be simple for once?

She was cursed with the granting of her wish. No fractious conversation with Tony. His mobile was switched off and he wasn't answering the phone in his hospital room. Bloody man. Bloody, bloody man.

The bloody man in question had been roused from a deep sleep by the phone next to his bed. Tony didn't care who it was, he wasn't ready for speech yet. That was one of the few joys of being stuck in hospital with a fucked-up knee. In the usual run of things, he had to answer his phone. He had patients who might have urgent needs. He had contracts with several police forces across Europe who might also have pressing requirements. But for now, he was officially out of action and he could ignore the phone. Someone else could take responsibility.

Except of course that he was bound to Carol and her team. Bound in a way that went far beyond the contractual. He probably should have answered the phone. But the meeting with Rachel Diamond had left him drained. He'd come back and taken his drugs, eaten his lunch and fallen straight into a thick, heavy sleep that had left him feeling stupid and inarticulate. Not the best time to talk to police officers if you wanted to convince them you were right about something.

He hoped Kevin had taken him seriously. Certainly what Paula had told him about Steve Mottishead's recollections was the most chilling thing he'd heard about Stalky the poisoner. The Harriestown High connection was already established in his head. But Jack Anderson's list, conforming as closely as it did to two of the apparently unconnected victims, had set Tony's antennae quivering. The mentality that drew up such a list with serious intent was ruthless. Predictably, such a person would pursue their goals relentlessly. But if they lacked empathy, if they had sociopathic or psychopathic tendencies, how they would go about dealing with the thwarting of those goals was entirely unpredictable.

He remembered one patient who had proudly told him how she had deliberately split up the marriage of her business partner. Not for any sexual or emotional reason, but because her partner's wife was less than whole-hearted about the business. 'I had to do it,' his patient had explained in the most matter-of-fact way. 'As long as he stayed married to Maria, he was never going to give the business his full commitment. And I needed that from him. So she had to go.' If Jack Anderson had been deprived of his dreams, what would he rationalize as a reasonable response?

It seemed that he'd chosen murder. His victims were men who had come from a similar background to his own. They'd attended the same school. In theory, they'd had the same opportunities as him. And they'd demonstrated his dreams weren't so crazy, because they'd each realized one of his goals. But for whatever reason, Anderson had decided he wasn't going to be able to achieve the ambitious targets he'd set himself. Some people would have reconciled themselves to that, acknowledging that their adolescent dreams had only been castles in the air. Others would have grown bitter, turned to drink, taken out their frustrations in ways that were mostly self-destructive. Jack Anderson had decided to kill the achievers. That way, they could no longer reproach him for his failure.

That's why there was no sexual element to the murders, why they were committed at arm's length. They were about desire, it was true. But not sexual desire.

And why poison? OK, it was perfect if you got no kick out of watching your victims die, and you wanted to avoid suspicion by being a long way away when it happened. That meant you couldn't go the route of most killers, who opted for methods that were, in essence, unskilled. Guns, knives, blunt instruments. But still, why choose something so arcane, something that felt as though it had come from an Agatha Christie novel?

He had to fathom this out. There had to be a reason. Murderers generally chose to kill using what was to hand, or what they had experience of. What if the poisons were chosen not because they were arcane but because they were close at hand? Carol had already questioned Rhys Butler, a man with access to pharmacological drugs. That had made a kind of sense.

But Anderson wasn't using prescription drugs. These were all derived from plants. Ricin from the castor oil plant, atropine from belladonna, oleandrin from oleander. Not your everyday garden plants, but nothing wildly exotic either. Who would have a garden with plants like that, though? You'd have to be some sort of specialist. Something was tickling at the back of his mind. Something about gardens and poison. He sat up and woke the laptop. Once he was back online, he Googled 'poison garden'. The first thing that came up was the Poison Garden at Alnwick Castle in Northumberland, a cornucopia of deadly plants, open to the public under strict supervision.

But as Tony discovered when he explored further, this was by no means a new idea. It had been directly inspired by the Medici family, who built a garden near Padua to find better ways to poison their enemies, and by the monks of Soutra Hospital near Edinburgh, who used soporific sponges with exactly the right amount of opium, henbane and hemlock to anaesthetize a body for between two and three days – just as long as it takes to amputate a limb and for the body to come out of shock and go into a natural state of healing. There had been other, private poison gardens through the ages, and Tony found various speculative references to them in newsgroups and blogs.

What if Jack Anderson had access to one of these? What if poison was, for him, the weapon of opportunity? He glanced at the phone. Now would be a good time for it to ring.

Instead, Mrs Chakrabarti entered hot on the heels of a perfunctory knock. 'I hear you went walkabout again,' she said without preamble.

'I came back,' Tony said. 'You all tell me I need to be up and about.'

'I think it's time you went home,' she said. 'Frankly, we can make better use of your bed, and you're so bloody determined, you're going to make a great recovery in spite of us. You'll have lots of visits back here for physio. If you think it's been tough so far, wait till you have to start moving the joint again.' She smiled cheerily. 'You'll be crying for your mother.'

'I don't think so,' he said wryly.

Mrs Chakrabarti laughed. 'I see your point. Maybe not. But you'll certainly be crying. So, tomorrow morning, provided my SHO thinks you're safe to be let out, you can go home. Do you have someone who can help you with shopping and cooking and so forth?'

'I think so.'

'You think so? What does that mean, Dr Hill?'

'There is someone, but I think she's a bit annoyed with me right now. I'll just have to hope for pity. Failing that, takeaways that deliver.'

'Try to behave yourself for the rest of the day, Dr Hill. It's been an interesting experience, having you as a patient.'

Tony smiled. 'I'll take that as a compliment.'

Another knock at the door, another take-charge woman. Carol swept into the room, her mouth open to begin her tirade, stopped short by the sight of Mrs Chakrabarti. 'Oh, I'm so sorry,' she said hastily.

'I was just going,' the surgeon said. She turned to Tony. 'This would be the someone?'

'Yes,' he said, nailing his smile firmly to the mast.

'Better devote some energy to getting on her good side, then.' She nodded to Carol and left.

'I suspect that might take more energy than I have right now,' Tony said, correctly identifying Carol's mood.

She gripped the bottom rail of his bed. He could see the knuckles whitening. 'What do you think you're playing at, Tony? You have one of my best detectives running round the countryside conducting interviews that are going nowhere on something that technically isn't even our case. You have another of my detectives frightened to eat a cream cake in case the Bradfield Poisoner knows his cake preference and has taken a job at the precinct bakery. And you can't even keep me in the loop. I hear about the poison stuff from Kevin. I hear you got nowhere with Rachel Diamond from Paula. You know, I've stood up for you I don't know how many times –'

'That's not been such a hardship, as it turns out,' he interrupted, too tired and in too much pain to bear the brunt of Carol's frustrations with the system that was oppressing her right now. 'My track record for getting it right is pretty good. And you know it. Hitching your wagon to my star hasn't exactly earned you the "loser" label.'

She glared at him, clearly shocked as well as angry. 'You're saying my success is down to you?'

'That's not what I said, Carol. Look, I know you want to take a pop at CTC, but your hands are tied. So you come round here and take it out on me. Well, I'm sorry. I haven't got the resources to act as your punch bag right now. I'm trying to help you, but if you'd rather I cut you out of the process, fine. I'll deal with John Brandon instead.'

She literally stepped back, as if he'd slapped her. 'I can't believe you just said that.' She looked on the verge of throwing something at him.

Tony screwed his face up and shook his head. 'Neither can I. Maybe we shouldn't be talking to each other right now. You're wound up, and I'm fucked up.'

His words didn't seem to have had much of a conciliatory effect. 'That is just so typical of you,' she shouted. 'You can't even have a proper bloody row.'

'I don't like fighting,' he said. 'It makes me hurt inside. Like I'm a kid again. In the cupboard, in the dark. If the grown-ups are fighting, it must be my fault. That's why I don't do rows.' He blinked hard, to keep the tears at bay. She was the only person in the world who could make him feel so exposed. It didn't always feel like a good thing. 'Carol, I'm going home tomorrow. I can't manage without you. Not in any sense. So can we stop this now? I can't do it.'

His words stopped her in her tracks. 'Home? Tomorrow?'

He nodded. 'I don't need you to do much. I can get the supermarket to deliver a stack of ready meals ...'

Carol tipped her head back, closed her eyes and sighed. 'You are impossible,' she said, all the anger dissipated.

'I'm sorry. I didn't mean to tread on your toes. I just wanted to help and not be in your way.' The jagged edges of the argument still filled the air, but the atmosphere between them had altered to something more like its normal state.

She sat down. 'So now I'm here, fill me in on what you're thinking. What can we do about Aziz now Rachel Diamond has closed down that avenue?'

'I don't know that it's closed,' he said. 'I just need to work out another approach.'

'Let me know when you do. I want to be there this time,' she said firmly. 'Oh, and here's something I didn't get the chance to tell you.' She explained about the forensic team's discovery of the two timers. 'CTC think that it signals a new move, to more IRA-style terrorism, where the bombers live to fight another day. Me, I think it moves us closer to your idea of a hit man. Belt and braces. "If my timer doesn't go off, I'll be able to set it off remotely with my mobile." That sort of thing.'

Tony felt the vague shape of something forming in the back of his mind. 'That sort of thing,' he said softly. 'Yes.' He gave her a quick, clear smile. 'We're moving further and further from any credible assertion of terrorism,' he said.

'We just need some incontrovertible evidence. I'm stuck in the middle of two cases where the evidence is intangible.'

Tony made an impatient movement with his hand. 'When you find Jack Anderson, you'll find your evidence. I think he's connected to a poison garden.'

'What is a poison garden?'

'They've got one at Alnwick Castle,' he said. 'That's a public one, where anybody can go and see all these killer plants. But there are stories and rumours of private ones. Individuals who specialize in growing deadly species of plants that have been seeing people off for as long as there have been people. Hemlock, that killed Socrates. Strychnine, that women used to kill off their husbands in the Middle Ages. Ricin, that killed Georgi Markov in the seventies. You can grow these plants in your back garden if you know your stuff. Wherever risk-averse Jack Anderson is hiding himself and hatching his careful plots, I think you're going to find a poison garden.'

Carol rolled her eyes. 'Every time we work together, there comes a point where you trot out some brilliant bloody insight that makes me go, "And how the *fuck* am I supposed to make use of that?"'

'And what makes you really crazy is that once you work out how to use it, it turns out to be irritatingly useful,' he said. 'It's what they pay me for.'

'What? To be irritating?'

'To be useful in a way that nobody else is expected to be. Go home now, and sleep on it. Chances are you'll have figured it out by morning.'

'You think?'

'I know. The subconscious is a grafter. Does its best work when we're asleep. Anyway, you're going to need all the rest you can get so you can fetch me cups of coffee after a hard day's crimefighting.'

Carol snorted. 'Get yourself a thermos and a bit of string.' She got to her feet. 'I'll see you tomorrow.' She kissed the top of his head. 'And don't interfere with my staff without talking to me first. OK?'

He smiled, pleased that they'd got past the anger. 'I promise.' And when he said it, he meant it.

Tuesday

He'd been wrong, Carol thought as she made for the shower, mug of coffee in hand, cat muttering at her ankles. The answer had not been there when she woke up. Possibly because Tony hadn't factored a bottle of pinot grigio into the equation. She'd gone back to the office after her hospital visit, for all the good it had done her. Nothing that was happening there was calculated to improve her mood. Kevin had drawn a blank with the Canadians. Sam had found nothing suspicious in Yousef Aziz's emails. Paula hadn't found anyone in Temple Fields who recognized Jack Anderson apart from a woman who'd been at school with him and hadn't seen him since they'd gone out together for three weeks when they were sixteen. Chris had been getting nowhere with Tom Cross's phone records. And Stacey had found nothing of interest on any of the several hard drives she'd been fiddling with. All told, her team had spent the day racing up dead-end streets. By the time she got home, she was ready for the cul-de-sac of another wine bottle.

She turned the shower on and finished the coffee while she waited for the hot water to come through.

She hung her dressing gown on the door and stepped into the extra-wide cubicle the builders had squeezed into a forgotten corner of the cellar when they'd done the conversion. She loved this flat, in spite or because of the fact that it occupied Tony's basement. But the time was drawing near when she'd have to accept that she really was back in Bradfield for good. To convince herself that her return from London wasn't temporary, she reckoned she'd probably have to get a proper place of her own.

Not that she wanted to abandon her proximity to him. That was what she'd wanted, wasn't it? Some way of bringing them closer? Except that occupying the same building hadn't actually drawn them any closer, either emotionally or physically. Perhaps it was time to get some distance again, to see if that would force them to confront what lay between them.

Or maybe it was just too late.

The water cascaded over her, an external current that seemed to encourage an internal flow of thought. A poison garden would require space. Space and privacy. You didn't want the neighbourhood kids smelling flowers or scrunching leaves or picking berries if you were cultivating poisonous plants.

It would take money too. She didn't imagine these were generally to be found in the local garden centre. They'd have to come from specialist growers. They might even have to be imported, in which case there would be records. Somewhere, there would be Jack Anderson's other alias.

And with that thought came the flash of memory. Pannal Castle. Where Tom Cross was supposed to be arranging the security for a fundraiser. The school knew nothing about it, according to Kevin, so the connection had to be via the killer. It was a risk, using the name of a venue if you didn't know enough about it. And Tony had called him risk-averse, a careful plotter.

Barely taking time to rinse the shampoo from her hair, Carol hustled out of the shower. Wrapping a towel around her, she headed for the phone in the living room. Her control room gave her the number for the nearest police station to Pannal Castle, which came under the jurisdiction of the neighbouring force. Carol rang the number for Kirkby Pannal police office and waited impatiently for four rings. As soon as it was answered, she spoke. 'This is Detective Chief Inspector Carol Jordan from Bradfield Police. To whom am I speaking ...? Good morning, Constable Brearley. I need the private number for Pannal Castle . . . Yes, I know it's ex-directory. That's why I'm calling you . . . No, I'm calling from home . . . Yes, I'll hold.' Carol drummed her fingers on the arm of the chair. The boy on the other end of the line didn't seem to grasp that checking with BMP that there really was a DCI Jordan meant that he was actually speaking to DCI Jordan. Still, she wasn't about to waste time putting him right.

A couple of minutes later, he came back on the line and dutifully gave her the number. 'Thank you,' she said, ending the call and immediately calling Pannal Castle.

'Hello?' The voice on the other end sounded posh and cross. Carol introduced herself and apologized for calling so early. 'No matter,' the voice said. 'Always happy to help the police. This is Lord Pannal speaking.'

Carol took a deep breath. 'This may seem a slightly

strange question, Lord Pannal. But do you happen to have a poison garden?'

By half past nine, Tony was a free man. The nurse who had spent most time taking care of him walked him down to his taxi. 'Don't do too much,' she cautioned him. 'I mean it. You'll pay for it later if you do.'

His house had never felt more of a home than it did today. Nothing was convenient as it had been in the hospital. But it was his little world. His books. His furniture. His bed, his duvet, his pillows.

He hadn't been sitting in his favourite armchair for five minutes when he had his brainwave. If Rachel Diamond hadn't been watching TV and reading the papers, it was possible she hadn't seen a picture of Yousef Aziz. She may have seen her husband in his company without even realizing it. He needed to make sure. He needed to see her reaction to a photo of her husband's killer.

He fished his phone out of his pocket and called Carol's number. She answered, sounding breathless. 'Not now, Tony,' she said. 'I'm right in the middle of something. I'll call you in an hour or two.' And she was gone. An hour or two? In two hours, he would be out of energy. He would want to be upstairs, horizontal under the duvet, sleeping in the warm embrace of his own bed.

Well, she couldn't say he hadn't tried. He'd have preferred to have had someone with him, if only to make the drive more congenial. But Carol had made it plain she didn't want him suborning her people. He'd just have to go it alone.

While he was waiting for the taxi, he called Stacey and had her email him the best head-shot they had of Aziz. Then he realized his printers were upstairs. So he had the taxi wait while he dragged himself upstairs, printed out the photo, and winced his way back down again. 'You look knackered,' the cabbie said, insisting on helping him aboard.

'I feel it,' Tony said. He put his head back on the seat and was out for the count by the time they reached the end of the street. He woke with a start when the cabbie shook his shoulder twenty minutes later.

'We're here, mate,' he said.

'Can you wait?' Tony said. 'I shouldn't be long.'

He went through the rigmarole of getting out of the taxi, smoothing down the hair that the cabbie pointed out was sticking up, and walking up to the front door. The bell was answered by a woman in her early sixties. She looked like a Jewish version of Germaine Greer and actually had a pencil sticking out of her unruly steel grey hair. She peered at him over little oblong glasses. 'Yes?' she said, looking puzzled.

'I was looking for Rachel,' Tony said.

'Rachel? I'm sorry, you've had a wasted journey. She's gone into the office. I'm her mother, Esther Weissman. And you are?'

Before Tony could introduce himself, Lev appeared at his grandmother's side. 'I know you. You came yesterday with the policewoman.' He looked up at his grandmother. 'A man hit him with an axe.'

'How very unfortunate,' Mrs Weissman said. Lev slipped past her and craned his head to the side so he could see the photo Tony was holding against his crutch.

449

'Why have you got a picture of Mummy's friend?' he asked.

Startled, Tony balanced himself on the arm supports and held the photo right way up. 'This is Mummy's friend?'

'We met him in the park one time. He bought me an ice cream.'

Mrs Weissman was trying to see the photo. Realizing that he was holding the equivalent of a rucksack full of TATP, Tony moved so she couldn't see it. 'What have you got there?' she demanded.

'Just someone from the thing on Saturday,' he said, trying to suggest this was something not to be discussed in front of a child. 'A question of identity. I hoped Rachel might be able to help. I'm with the police. It's all right, I'll catch her at the office.' He was trying to back away, keep the photo out of sight and not fall over Lev. It was a major achievement just staying upright.

For a terrible moment, he was afraid Mrs Weissman was going to grab the photo from his hands. But the manners of polite society prevailed and she managed to stop herself. 'I'll be off, then,' he said, swinging himself round and making for the cab as fast as he could.

'I didn't catch your name,' Mrs Weissman called after him.

Childish though it would have been, he wanted to shout, *Nemesis*. Instead, he settled for, 'Hill. Dr Tony Hill.' Rachel would doubtless figure it out soon enough. As the taxi pulled away, he called the MIT squad room. It was Paula who picked up. 'I need your help,' he said.

'I can't,' she said. 'The chief gave me a bit of a lecture about how I don't work for you.'

'Paula, this is vital. I tried to call Carol, but she was too busy to speak to me. Look, I went out to Rachel Diamond's house, to see if she might recognize a photo of Aziz. Given that she said she's not been following the media, I thought it was possible she'd seen him without knowing it. Only, she wasn't there.'

'And?' Paula sounded exasperated.

'And Lev saw the picture and went, "Why have you got a picture of Mummy's friend?"'

For a long moment, Paula said nothing. Then she breathed, 'Oh my God.'

'Yeah. They met in the park. Aziz bought the kid an ice cream, which will be why he remembers him so clearly.'

'Oh my God. You need to talk to the chief.'

'I told you. Whatever she's doing, she's too busy to take my call.'

'She's gone to Pannal Castle with Chris,' Paula said absently. 'What do you want me to do?'

'Rachel's supposed to be at her office. Call to make sure she's there, and then stake the place out till I can talk to Carol. I'm sure her mother's already on the phone to her, telling her about the strange man who came to the house with a photo. We don't want her to take off.'

'We've got no evidence,' Paula said. 'There's no way you're going to get the kid to testify against her.'

'True. But I have one or two ideas about that. Please, Paula. I'll take the flak. If there is any. But we need to not let her out of our sight.'

'She knows me.'

'What about Kevin?'

'He's not here. Personal time, he said. I'm not sure when he'll be back.'

'We'll just have to –'

'I'll take Sam with me,' Paula said. 'Talk to you later.'

Tony leaned back on the cushions. And for the second time that morning, everything drifted away.

Kevin stood at the window, admiring the view across the rooftops of Temple Fields. He wasn't accustomed to this perspective on an area he knew so well. It looked remarkably innocent from this height, he thought. Impossible to see what misdemeanours the matchstick figures below were up to. He'd known the top ten floors of the Hart Tower were residential, but this was the first time he'd had the chance to experience the panorama. He turned back to his host. 'You're lucky, living with a view like this,' he said.

Justin Adams pushed his dark-framed glasses up his nose and swept the fringe of his long dark hair across his forehead. 'It's not actually mine,' he said. 'It belongs to a photographer I do quite a bit of work with. He lets me use it when I'm working up here. My base is in London.' He grinned, smile white against a couple of days' stubble. 'Nothing like as grand as this.' He walked across the room towards the kitchen area. 'I can, however, offer you something to drink. We've got beer, vodka, gin, wine ...' He raised his eyebrows in a query.

'Thanks, but I'm due in at work later. I don't want to walk in smelling of drink.' Kevin settled himself in a squashy tweed armchair the colour of winter bracken.

'Yeah, I suppose that doesn't go down too well in your line of work. What about a soft drink? I'm having an orange juice.' He took a carton out of the fridge and ripped the plastic seal free. 'You fancy a glass?'

Sealed, and he's drinking it too, Kevin thought, then mentally called himself a paranoid wuss. This interview had been arranged long before the poisoner had taken a victim. He'd seen Justin Adams's byline in motoring magazines for years. 'Yeah, go on,' he said, watching as Adams poured two tall glasses, adding a couple of cubes of ice from a tray he took from the freezer. Both glasses were in clear sight the whole time, from pour to delivery. Kevin waited till Adams had taken a hearty swig, then he swallowed a couple of mouthfuls. It was delicious; sweet, tangy and bright.

Adams placed a small recording device on the coffee table that stretched between them. 'You don't mind if I record this, do you?'

Kevin waved an expansive hand in the direction of the machine. 'Be my guest,' he said. 'It'll be funny doing a recording that doesn't begin with the date and time and a list of who's in the room.'

Adams's smile barely made it across his mouth. 'Not the kind of recording I expect I'll ever make,' he said.

Kevin laughed. 'Depends how fast you drive those cars you write about.'

Adams leaned forward and pressed a silver button. 'Tell me about the first time you remember seeing a Ferrari.'

List 3

1. Danny Wade

2. Robbie Bishop

3. Tom Cross

4. Kevin Matthews

5. Niall and Declan McCullogh

6. Deepak

Pannal Castle had stood on its present site since the Wars of the Roses. A ruin by the mid-nineteenth century, it had been rebuilt by the 14th Baron. Although from the outside it looked like a substantial medieval pile, indoors it had central heating and modern plumbing, as well as a layout that conformed to modern rather than ancient needs.

Probably the best thing about it was its range of astonishing views, a gift appreciated only by the few, since Pannal Castle remained resolutely closed to the public. Wool, coal mining and, more recently, the Red Rose Fine Arts and Craft Village had allowed successive lords Pannal to hang on to their castle and lands without having to resort to day-trippers.

Lord Pannal himself had actually worked for a living. For a dozen years, he'd been a relatively undistinguished documentary film maker, which now fitted him to be a member of all sorts of boards and committees. He was, as far as Carol knew, a decent enough bloke in spite of having once had Tony Blair up to Pannal to open the new gallery at the craft village.

As they drove up the gentle rise of the private road

that led to the castle, Chris looked around. 'This must have been spot on as a defensive position way back when,' she commented. 'You'd have a hard job creeping up on them.'

'I expect that's why it's still here,' Carol said.

'That and the poison garden, eh? If you don't get them with the cannonballs, get them with the soup.'

'No wonder English food got such a bad name.'

'So what's actually here?'

'Lord Pannal got interested in poison gardens when he was making a documentary about the Medicis a dozen years ago, so he decided to make one of his own.'

'And they say TV isn't educational. So what's he got there?'

'I don't know the full list, but he's got the ones we're interested in. Castor oil plant, belladonna, oleander. He says his poison garden is surrounded by eight-foot railings with razor wire along the top, which makes casual burglary unlikely. But he does have a deputy estate manager called John Anson.'

'JA. I like it. I like it very much.'

A short man in a tweed cap and a Barbour jacket was waiting for them as they drove across the massive wooden drawbridge and into the courtyard. Three black Labradors mobbed them in leisurely fashion as they got out of the car. 'Benson, Hedges, Silkie, come away,' the man called, letting Carol and Chris come to him as the dogs slumped to the ground at his feet. 'Lord Pannal,' he said, holding out a hand as they approached. His pink face, blue eyes and bristling moustache gave him a bizarrely charming resemblance to a new piglet. 'I'm a bit slow on the uptake first

456

thing in the morning. After our call, it dawned on me. That footballer, and the chap who saved all those people after the bombing – they were poisoned.' He bit his lower lip. 'Awful thing. Terrible if the poisons came from Pannal. Did you want to look at the garden?'

'I think we'll leave the garden for now.' Carol nodded to Chris, who took half a dozen photos from a folder and spread them across the bonnet of her car. 'Lord Pannal, would you mind looking at these and telling me if you recognize anyone?'

He craned his head forward, like a big pink turtle emerging from its shell. He studied the pictures carefully then extended a plump finger. 'That's John Anson. Works for me. Deputy estate manager.' He looked away, blinking crossly. 'This is awfully hard to credit. Hard-working chap. Been with us a couple of years, very obliging.'

'Do his responsibilities include the poison garden?' Carol asked.

'Comes under his remit. Not in a hands-on sort of way – that's up to the gardeners. But it's within his area, yes.' He spoke in abrupt little jerks, clearly upset, though he would have been mortified had anyone offered him sympathy or support. A Scotch might have been acceptable, but Carol wasn't even sure that would do.

'Do you know where we can find him now?' Chris said, scooping up the pictures.

'In Bradfield.' He bit his lip. 'He's interviewing prospective tenants for a vacant unit in the craft village.'

'Where exactly in Bradfield?' Carol asked gently.

'I've got a bolthole there. We use it for business as well as a pied à terre in the city. In the Hart Tower.'

Chris and Carol exchanged a telling look. 'On the edge of Temple Fields,' Carol said. 'We'll need the address.'

Tony gave the smile all he had. 'The thing is, I'm not supposed to ask you to do anything. Carol says, perfectly reasonably, that you don't work for me, you work for her. Me, I think we're all working for the cause of justice, but I'm not going to argue with her.'

'Not the mood she's been in this past week,' Stacey agreed, not even glancing up from her screen. 'Interesting that the boy ID'd the photo. No doubt in your mind?'

Tony shrugged. 'No doubt in the kid's mind. That's what matters here. He was absolutely positive. Mummy's friend who bought him an ice cream.'

'That makes sense of everything that raised a question mark for us. What you said about it not profiling right for terrorism – well, that follows if it wasn't terrorism. The two timers – Aziz thought he was getting away, but Rachel Diamond's plan was different. She wanted him to die.'

'But she didn't want him to know that,' Tony said thoughtfully. 'If I were you, I'd be contacting airlines to see if Rachel Diamond and her son Lev are booked on a flight to Canada any time soon. And I'd be checking whether any of those rental cottages Kevin was checking out had a booking in her name.'

Stacey frowned. 'You think she was planning to join him?'

Tony shook his head. 'I think she wanted him to think she was planning to join him.'

Stacey gave him a look of respect. 'Oh, that's very clever,' she said. 'Very evil, but very clever.' Her fingers were already flying. 'I think I might also make some phone calls to Canada.'

'Don't mind me, I'll just read the paper,' Tony said, sitting back and relaxing.

The journey from Pannal back to Bradfield took significantly less time than getting there, but still it felt interminable. 'Come on,' Chris urged the traffic in front of her every time she had to slow.

'I can't believe nobody in the office had a list of the prospective tenants,' Carol said for the third or fourth time. 'You'd think there would be more than one copy of something like that.'

'Yeah, we could have got Stacey on to it. Maybe figured out which one was his next victim. Move, you twat,' Chris shouted at the dawdling people carrier in front of her.

'Unless ...' Carol's voice tailed off as another possibility dawned on her.

'Unless what?' Chris sounded impatient as she rounded the dawdler.

'Unless there isn't a list at all. Maybe that was just an excuse he made up for Lord Pannal to cover his back. Maybe his next victim has got nothing to do with the craft village at all.'

Chris stamped on the brakes and blasted the horn. A startled SUV driver swerved out of her way as she powered through. 'It doesn't really matter at this point, does it? All that counts is getting to them before

Jack or Jake or John or whoever fills them full of some untreatable poison.'

As they hit the outskirts of the city, Chris tried to work out the best way to the Hart Tower. 'I wish we had Kevin with us,' she said. 'Nobody knows the back doubles like him.'

'You're doing just fine,' Carol said. But she wasn't at all sure she was telling the truth.

'Beautiful dream come true. Beautiful dreamer.' Kevin frowned. Had he just repeated himself? Every time he thought he'd said all there was to be said about his lovely car, he remembered something else he wanted to say. Then, when he said it, he felt as if he'd said it before. More than once.

He shifted in his chair, which seemed to have become treacherously slippery. His limbs weren't doing what he wanted them to do; more than once he'd had to grab at the arm of the chair with its interesting texture to stop himself slithering to the floor. Where there was a really beautiful rug with colours like jewels that he wanted to embrace.

A strange blob kept crossing his field of vision. Pink with bristles, topped with thick brown fur like a bear. The fur was different, somehow. Before it had been like a flowing horse's mane, but suddenly the mane had exploded into the air in a great spiral of silky strands. He had watched it whirl through the air in slow motion before it landed on the wooden floor.

Kevin turned his heavy head, heavy heady heavy head to look at it again. Like a pompom that somebody had steamrollered flat. Beautiful. Everything, really, was beautiful.

The next thing he knew was the blob was in front of him, making a noise. It all felt very sudden, as if he'd fallen asleep and woken in a different place. But no, he was in the same chair. At least, he thought he'd been in this chair once before. A long, long time ago.

And suddenly, he wasn't. He was on his feet. Hands in his hands, leading him. Too hard. Too very strangely hard. Kevin collapsed to his knees and fell forward, My, how smooth the beautiful rug was. He kissed the rug and felt a giggle well up in his throat. As he laughed, he began to roll, aware of the hands on his body. A hundred hands, a million hands, a Brazilian hands, rolling him.

He felt he could roll across the planet for ever. And ever. And ever.

Gaining access to the building was easy. Lord Pannal had been desperate to help, as if, by hiring a bad apple, he had somehow been responsible for what had happened. So he'd given them the spare swipe card that would let them into the underground garage, the lift and the apartment itself, provided they had the right PIN code, which he'd also given them.

Everything worked perfectly till they got to the door of the apartment, where the LED display told them the PIN was incorrect. Carol tried it a couple of times before admitting defeat. 'I bet he changes the PIN when he arrives and changes it back when he leaves,' she said. 'Bastard.'

'What do we do now?'

'Hasn't Stacey got one of those gadgets you plug in that reads PIN codes?'

Chris snorted. 'I think that was in a movie, guv.

But even if she did, we haven't got time for that sort of malarkey. What about building security? D'you think they'll have some sort of override card, like a master key?'

'Go and find out,' Carol said. 'I'll wait here.'

It was a long eight minutes before Chris returned with an erect elderly man in the uniform of the Corps of Commissionaires. He looked sniffily at Carol from under the peak of his cap. 'I'm going to need to see photo ID,' he said.

'Staff Sergeant Malory is in charge of security,' Chris said, doing her level best to be ingratiating.

Silently, Carol produced her warrant card and her Bradfield Police HQ building pass. Malory scrutinized it carefully, tilting it against the light to make sure the holograph was authentic. 'Shouldn't you have a warrant?' He gave her a stern look.

Carol bit her tongue. 'Section Eighteen of the Police and Criminal Evidence Act,' she ground out between her teeth. 'I don't need a warrant if I have grounds to suspect that I can prevent a serious criminal offence from taking place. Which I have. And which I am not going to share with you, Mr Malory.'

Behind his back, Chris rolled her eyes and mimed hanging herself. But contrary to her expectation, Malory folded. 'That's fine by me, ma'am,' he said, swiping the card and tapping the number pad with a flourish.

A subdued buzz, and the door swung open at the pressure of fingertips. Signalling Chris to follow silently, Carol crept down the short hallway. She could see nothing through the open doorway at the far end, but she could hear the grunts and groans of exertion from the far side of the threshold. She had a moment to decide. Creep or rush?

With a quick flick of her hand to beckon Chris forward, Carol leapt through the doorway. She took it in like a snapshot. Kevin on his back on the floor, legs bent, trousers undone, arms above his head, ginger hair askew and a silly smile on his face. Beyond him on the floor, like a discarded soft toy, a wig resembling a starburst of hair. Bending over him, trying to roll him, was the man in the photograph. The man who had come a very long way from the starting point of Jack Anderson. His short hair was plastered to his head with sweat and he hadn't shaved for a couple of days, but there was no question of identity here.

Chris streaked past Carol and made for Anderson. But he was quicker than either of them expected. He jumped to his feet and used Chris's momentum against her, straight-arming her in the face and twisting her over to his left so she'd have to trample Kevin or stumble over him. Blood blossomed across her face as she windmilled her arms, trying to stay upright.

Anderson kept going, shoulder-charging Carol. She snatched desperately at him, managing to grab his shirt as he passed. Buttons flew off as he wrestled away from her, shedding the shirt like a snake its skin, leaving her staggering backwards, away from him.

Then he was gone, past them both and racing for the door. 'Fuck,' Carol screamed in frustration as he disappeared.

She had forgotten Staff Sergeant Malory.

Tony was still working his way through the features section when Carol and Chris limped into the squad

463

room. 'Result,' Carol said. 'We've got Anderson, or Andrews or Anson, whatever you want to call him.' Then she saw Tony. 'You were right,' she said. 'The subconscious. It's a great tool. We got there just in time to save his next victim. Anderson had got him off his face, but we're pretty sure he hadn't delivered the poison yet.'

'Tell me?' Tony felt faintly sick.

'You were right to warn Kevin. You just didn't know who you should be warning him against,' Carol said.

'Is he OK?' Tony demanded.

'The medics seem to think he'll be just fine. He's still high as a kite but he's not showing any symptoms of anything other than rohypnol or GHB or something like that.'

'So, do we have any idea what happened?'

'Anderson set up their encounter weeks ago, long before he killed Danny Wade.'

'How do you know that? I mean, if Kevin's still off his face?'

'Because I'm the one they have to ask for time off, and Kevin booked this morning off at least a month ago. Anderson was impersonating a freelance motoring journalist who wanted to write about Kevin and his car.'

'I knew he was planning ahead. But this is gob-smacking. Is he talking?' Tony asked.

'Doh,' said Chris through a red-stained cloth she was holding to her nose. 'Dot a word.'

'He doesn't want a lawyer, refuses to speak. He won't even admit to being Anderson.' Carol slumped into a chair and turned to Tony. 'We found a pessary and a bottle of anti-retroviral drugs in his jacket. We've got witnesses that can put him alongside the victims and we've got access to the poison garden. But I would like a confession. Any bright ideas?'

'Let me talk to him.'

'You know that's not how it works,' Carol said.

'We've done it before.'

'But not with the eyes of the world on us the way they will be for Robbie Bishop's killer.'

'He's not talking, Carol. What have you got to lose?'

She looked away, struggling with her need to do this by the book versus her need to get a confession. She knew her team was watching her, willing her to do what was necessary to get this boxed off and put away. They needed a proper result, not a partial one. 'OK,' she sighed. 'But only if we do it under caution and he agrees to have the tapes running.'

'Deal,' Tony said.

He pushed himself on to his crutches and began to move towards the door. 'Where is Paula?' Carol said. 'And Sam? I could do with them out at Kirkby Pannal with the forensics crew searching Anderson's cottage.'

Stacey and Tony exchanged a look. They both knew answering Carol's question might well demolish Tony's chances of getting to talk to Jack Anderson. 'Off on some lead about Aziz,' Stacey said.

Tony hid his amazement. Stacey didn't dig people out of holes. Then he remembered who was out on the street with Paula and it began to make a kind of sense. He gave her a quick nod when Carol's eyes were elsewhere, then headed for the custody suite.

News of a major arrest always spreads fast in a police station. By the time Tony and Carol emerged from the MIT squad room, people were standing in door-ways, calling out congratulations, applauding as they passed. Even the doorway to the CTC's base was crowded with men in black offering taciturn support. As they waited in the hallway, the lift disgorged David and Johnny. 'Nice one,' David said, passing Tony and Carol on their way into the lift.

'I hear he's not talking, though,' Johnny added. 'Let's hope the lads in the white suits come up with something solid for you.'

The doors closed before Carol could answer. Tony said, 'You'll be glad to get them out of your hair.'

Carol snorted. 'That's not going to happen any time soon.'

'Ah. Well, the thing is –' The lift stopped and two civilian staff got on. Not the time to tell her about Rachel Diamond.

Walking from the lift to the custody suite didn't offer much of an opportunity either, given how much concentration it took. And besides, he wanted to get his head straight before he confronted Stalky at last. Sufficient unto the day, he thought. At the custody desk, a technician fitted the tiny earpiece that would allow Carol to communicate with him, then they were off again down the hallway.

Carol stopped before one of the interview room doors. 'As soon as I hear anything from the CSIs searching his cottage I'll let you know. Good luck.' She held the door open for him.

The time it took to get across the room gave Tony the opportunity to take a look at Jack Anderson. Seated, it was hard to gauge his height, but judging by his frame, Tony thought he was probably a little under six feet. He was twenty-six, the same age as Robbie Bishop, and he looked in good shape. Designer stubble, well barbered, no visible tattoos, a single diamond stud earring. He was wearing the jacket to his suit over his bare chest. On him, it looked like a fashion statement. And he was handsome, even with the swollen lump on his jaw where Malory had felled him. He looked good on his photograph, but in the flesh he was even more attractive. It was easy to see that he'd had no trouble attracting girls. The young Robert Redford, only with dark hair and better skin, Tony thought. And cool as Paul Newman at any age.

Anderson's face didn't show a flicker of expression as Tony struggled across the room and into a chair. 'I'm Tony Hill,' he said as soon as he was settled. 'I work with the police. I'm a profiler.'

One corner of his mouth twitched in a crooked smile. 'Like *Cracker*, only skinny.'

Tony suppressed a smile. Once the silence was broken, it was that much harder to go back there. 'No problems with drink or gambling either,' Tony said cheerfully. 'You've been advised of your rights?' Anderson nodded. 'You don't want a lawyer?' He shook his head. 'And you know that this interview is being recorded?'

'It makes no odds, since I don't plan to say anything of consequence.' Anderson leaned back in his chair and folded his arms across his chest. 'To embarrass myself by quoting Billy Joel, "I am an innocent man."'

Tony nodded. 'I think at one level you genuinely believe that. But I also think you know that's going to be hard to sustain in practical terms. The police already have some evidence, and there's going to be a lot more. However justified you believe your killings may have been, the hard truth is that in a day or two you're going to be charged with three murders. And that would be because you killed three men.'

Anderson said nothing. His face had returned to its former immobility.

'I'm going to call you Jack,' Tony said. 'I know that whatever happened three years ago makes you feel Jack is dead, but he's the one I know most about, so Jack it's going to be. I think of that boy Jack, and my heart goes out to him. Lots of kids grow up without dads. I'm one of them, so I understand a bit about what that means. But my dad wasn't killed. I always had the possibility of him coming back into my life, no matter how remote a chance that was. But you didn't, did you? Your dad was gone for ever. No hope to hang on to for you. And worse than that, he died a hero. A soldier's death, dying for queen and country. That's far too much for a teenager to live up to.

'And then there's all the things he lost, dying when he did. All the things he never saw, never did. The internet. iPods. Digital cameras. Cheap air fares. Google. You growing up. I suppose that's why you got so greedy for experience. Women. Drink. Drugs. Men. Snorting, shooting up, shagging, getting shit-faced. All of it, there to be grabbed –'

'What do you mean, men? I'm not a poof.' His arms had unfolded, his hands gripping the side of his chair.

Bingo. The anti-retrovirals had been the clue, but even so, Tony hadn't expected a crack in the armour so early. 'I never said you were.' Tony's voice remained calm and relaxed. Hypnotic, almost. 'I was talking about the desire for experience. I thought you wanted to experience everything? To feel it for yourself. Fearless and receptive to everything, every sensation. To take everything the world had to offer and grab it, to miss out on nothing. Am I wrong, then?'

'Your words, not mine, Doctor.' Anderson was doing his best to be the tough guy, but Tony could sense the anger and anguish underneath. All that pain, and nowhere to put it.

'But I'm right. We both know that,' he said. 'I'm not a poof either, if that helps. It doesn't mean I've not thought about what it would be like. I mean, when you've gone through every other experience, you do have to wonder. Would it be more of the same or would it be different?' Time for a shift of tempo. 'Then when your mum died – that was one experience you didn't want to have. Didn't want her to kill herself, didn't want to know about that kind of despair. Didn't want her to die, did you? How hard it must have been for her, hanging on till she thought you were sorted, and then going for it. For that one experience that nobody gets to share. She did what she could and then she clocked off. Left you to it. I'd guess if there was anything you'd missed out on before that, you went for it after she took herself off.'

Anderson shifted in his seat. 'Have I got to listen to this amateur psychology all day?' he burst out.

'Nothing amateur about it, Jack. I get paid for this. So, what else was on the list? Play premiership foot-ball. Buy a house on Dunelm Drive. Make a million by the time you hit thirty. Drive a Ferrari.' Tony could see it working. Every sentence provoked a tiny flutter

469

of reaction. Time to step up the pressure. 'How am I doing, Jack? How many more on the list? How many more were you planning to poison? Poison their lives like he poisoned yours?'

He drew in a ragged breath. 'You're talking bollocks. What does that mean? Poisoned lives? You think whoever killed these guys was using murder as a metaphor? How can you trivialize death like that? You're sicker than the killers you're supposed to be hunting.'

Tony shrugged. 'You're not the first to suggest that. But the bottom line is that I'm not a killer. You are. And the only reason you interest me or anybody else right now is because we want to know why. I think I know why, but it would be good to hear I'm right.'

'You're so full of shit,' Anderson said. 'People like you, thinking you know what drives people – you don't have a clue.'

'Smokescreen, Jack. It might put some people off, but not me. I'm not interested in your attempts to set up a diversion. Let's get back to what this is really about. Your attempts to extract revenge for having your dreams stolen from you by the man who poisoned your life.'

'I am not a poof,' Anderson said, more loudly this time.

'Who said anything about a poof?' Tony said, all innocence, hands spread. 'I was asking about your little list. About what else was on it. Three down. How many more to go? I know there's at least one. Kevin, the Ferrari guy. Did you really think they'd sit back and let you take another one of theirs? You got Tom Cross, because we weren't looking in the right place.' Tony leaned forward, getting in his face, still calm but inescapable. 'But no way were you getting Kevin Matthews.'

For the first time, Anderson looked shaken, his face startled and alert. 'I do a bit of freelance journalism. I was interviewing him.'

'How long did it take you to find a journalist with the right initials? Or was it seeing the real Justin Adams's by-line that gave you the idea of how to get to Kevin?' Tony cocked his head and appraised Anderson. 'I'm curious, you know. Are you relieved that we've stopped you? Or are you pissed off because you didn't get to finish what you started? Just out of curiosity, what was your endgame? Were you going to do the list and then stop? Live out whatever life you've got left? Or were you going to bottle it like your mother did?'

A muscle bunched in Anderson's jaw. 'I told you. It was an interview. I do some freelance journalism, OK? Then he started to freak out. I have no idea why. You should be asking where he was before he arrived at my place. Whatever he took, he must have taken it there. I don't know what you're on about. Poison, gay sex? That's not my world.'

Tony was about to speak, but Carol's voice in his ear made him pause. 'Tony, I've just had a message from the CSIs. They've found his list, taped underneath the keyboard of his computer. The two you don't have are, "Make a chart CD" and "Date a top model". You got that?'

He nodded. 'Oh yes it is, Jack. Kevin and his Ferrari. Also on your little list. So who was going to be next? Which of Bradfield's charting artistes were you going to take down? Or were you going for the guy with the model girlfriend? Let me think, who do we have from Bradfield who's got a top catwalk chick? That would have to be Deepak, wouldn't it? Our home-grown fashion designer. Was he on the list too?'

Anderson's eyebrows had drawn closer, creating a shallow vertical crease between them. Anxiety, that's what Tony was going for now. Make him anxious. Make him uneasy. Shift the ground beneath his feet. And then offer him comfort.

'They're very upset about Kevin, you know? He's popular around here. What was it going to be this time? Monksbane? Foxglove? Strychnine? I tell you, you hit on an elegant idea there. Poison. Poison their lives the way he poisoned yours.' And suddenly, he knew. The repetition, designed to unsettle Anderson, had opened the door for Tony. It was a leap, he knew. But it was a leap that made perfect sense.

He folded his hands together on the table and let the pity he felt flow out. 'Just one time. That's all it took. You wanted to taste everything, wanted to know everything. But it wasn't like all the other times when you pushed the boundaries and had fun, was it? You hated it. Because you're right. You're not a poof. You thought it would be OK, but you hated it. Hated it so much it made you hate yourself. That's when you stopped being Jack, wasn't it? Jack was ruined, fucked up. So you left Jack behind. You knew that being dead meant saying goodbye to the past, so you did. Jack became John and sometimes Jake. You still had your dreams, though. Still had the list. Still believed you could make the climb.'

Anderson gripped his chair more tightly, his

shoulder muscles bunched and taut. He shook his head violently, as if he were trying to shake off something sticky and disgusting.

Tony spoke softly now. 'And then you found out. Just one time, that's all it took. That infection in the blood, poisoning you. Killing you. It doesn't matter that these days you can take the drugs and live longer. Who wants to live longer without their dreams? What's the point in existing? You had the world at your feet, you were going to be somebody. And one bad night took it all away.'

The silence between them stretched out, tight and dramatic. Anderson looked as if something was going to snap inside him. Tony decided to try and make it.

His tone was silky, sweet. 'So you decided if you couldn't have your dreams, then the men who had walked the same path as you weren't going to have them either. You could have been them, but you weren't, so they weren't going to be allowed to be them either.' Then his voice changed abruptly. Harsh and loud, Tony said, 'Well, here's the news, Jack. You don't get to take away anybody else's dreams. You're going to jail, where they'll take good care of you and make sure every day you have left is filled with misery. You're going to live long and prosper behind bars. Where everybody else inside with you will know all the juicy details from your trial.'

Anderson jumped up and lunged for Tony, who swung one of his crutches hard through the air, smacking it into Anderson's ribs and catching him off balance enough to make him fall to the floor. 'You see? They're not rushing in to help me, are they?' Tony said. 'That's because they know you're not up to giving me a proper beating. You don't like violence. Chris Devine just got unlucky in the heat of the moment. If you'd had to think about it, you'd never have hit her. That's another reason why you chose the poison. So you could kill at arm's length.' He shook his head. 'I started out feeling sympathy for you, Jack. Now, I just feel pity.'

Anderson scrambled to his feet and slunk back to his chair. 'I don't want your pity.'

'So earn my respect. Tell me how it was. If I'm wrong, tell me now. I'll take it back.'

Anderson slumped in the chair, defeated. 'I'm not going to talk about it. Whatever evidence they find, I'm not going to talk about it. I'll plead guilty. But I'm not going to talk about the stuff you were saying. There won't be any trial to taint me. It'll always be a mystery, why I did it.' His eyes blazed anger. 'I killed them. That's what you need me to say, right? I did what I had to do. I killed them.'

After they took Anderson away, Tony found he really didn't want to move. Drained and in pain, he was unwilling to do anything that might make either of those states worse. So he sat there. The custody sergeant brought him a cup of coffee that must have come from his private stash because it tasted of something. Other than that, they left him in peace. He drank most of the coffee, then let the last inch cool so he could use it to swallow some codeine. What kind of a job was it where the high point of success meant feeling so shit?

He wasn't certain how much time had passed when Carol came back. She sat down opposite him and reached across the table to put her hand over his. 'Kevin's doing fine. He's going to be all right. And we've charged Anderson,' she said. 'If the CSIs come through, we'll be home and dry. We can tie him to Tom Cross for sure, and there's circumstantial evidence with Danny Wade. And the attempt on Kevin. And if he sticks to the guilty plea, we'll get Robbie as well.'

'He'll change his mind as soon as a brief gets to work on him,' Tony said. It was the way of the world. Whoever ended up representing him would see the potential for headlines as well as the need for justice to be seen to be done. 'Let's just pray it's not Bronwen Scott.'

'Is there anything else you'd like to talk to me about?' Carol said, taking her hand back.

His eyelids flickered with tiredness. 'Oh,' he said slowly. 'Now you come to mention it . . .'

'Tony,' John Brandon's voice boomed from the doorway. 'Congratulations. Fresh out of hospital and you're doing our job for us. Well done.' He shook Tony's hand and pulled up a chair. 'Now, Carol tells me we have something of a delicate situation on our hands. It might be helpful to have your input here. Carol?'

'It seems we have an alternative scenario for Saturday's bombing,' she said. 'Tony and DC McIntyre went to see Rachel Diamond yesterday. The widow of Benjamin Diamond, one of the stadium bomb victims. It had emerged that Mr Diamond's company had links to Yousef Aziz's family business. Tony had already raised doubts with me about whether this might be something other than a straightforward terrorist outrage, so when he asked if he could talk to Mrs Diamond about any possible connection between her husband and Yousef Aziz, I thought it would be worth pursuing. Tony?'

'Rachel Diamond claimed she hadn't been following the media coverage, and it occurred to me afterwards she might not have seen a photo of Aziz, and so she might not have realized something she'd seen and written off as completely innocent was in fact something quite different. So I went back to her house today with a photo of Aziz. She wasn't there, but her son Lev was. He caught sight of the photo of Aziz and said, "Why have you got a photo of Mummy's friend?" I didn't press him in any way, I know the rules about juvenile witnesses. And he said that they'd met Aziz in the park and he'd bought him an ice cream. It dawned on me that there was a different explanation from either of the ones we'd been considering.'

Brandon looked worried. 'CTC are not going to like this,' he said.

'Tough,' Carol said. She hadn't forgiven Brandon for what she still saw as spinelessness in the face of the enemy. 'Tony?'

'Yousef Aziz wasn't a terrorist. He wasn't a hit man either. He was a lover. He was snarled up in ... forgive me for sounding like a bad tabloid headline, but there's no other way to describe it than forbidden love. The son of a devout Muslim falls in love with a married Jewish woman. It's not going to play well at home, is it? They're both going to be cast out of their families and the businesses they've worked so hard to build.

'I think Rachel was the brains behind it.' He shook his head. 'Actually, having spent some time with

476

Rachel, I have a creepy suspicion that she went after Aziz with the sole intention of setting up what finally happened – killing two birds with one stone. But I'm getting ahead of myself.' Brandon looked as if he wanted to be anywhere but with them. Undaunted, Tony carried on.

'They're having an affair. Aziz is head over heels in love, he'd do anything for her. And Rachel hits on a great idea. They fake a terrorist bombing. They'll get rid of Benjamin without anyone suspecting the motive. Aziz also gets to strike a blow against the system that oppresses his people, because the people they're blowing up are the rich bastards who despise the likes of him and his family.

'What Aziz thinks is going to happen is this. He's going to set the manual timer, get out of there before it blows, drive to the airport and be gone before anybody even starts to look for him. He's going to go to Canada, which is a clever choice, because there are quite a lot of Asians there. Rachel is supposedly going to join him there –'

'I hate to interrupt,' Carol said, 'but I have some information on that front. Stacey has traced a booking on a flight to Toronto next Friday for Rachel Diamond and her son Lev. And we've found a holiday rental company who leased a cottage for a month, starting on Saturday, to Rachel Diamond. Yousef Aziz had previously viewed the cottage on his computer. Both flight and cottage were paid for on her personal credit card. So Tony's right. Whether she was planning to join Aziz or not, she had the bookings to demonstrate her intent.'

'It's very thin,' Brandon said.

'There's more to be found,' Carol said. 'We'll be able to trace the call to the remote-control timer. If she used her landline, it'll be on her phone records. If she used a mobile, we'll be able to find what mast it went through. I'm betting Stacey will be able to find some evidence on one of the Diamonds' several computers. We'll be talking to all the Diamonds' friends. There must be someone who knew the marriage was in trouble. There always is. And now we know what we're looking for, we'll find witnesses who saw them together. And Tony will give evidence of what Lev said.'

'Hearsay,' Brandon said.

'Actually, sir, I think this comes under one of the exceptions to the hearsay rule,' Carol said politely.

Brandon shook his head. 'I don't like it, Carol. You think a jury's going to buy the idea of a Jewish woman setting up her Muslim lover to kill himself and thirty-five other people, just to get rid of her husband? Why didn't she just divorce him, like the rest of us do?'

'Because she's greedy,' Tony said. *And I know all about greedy women.*

'I want to arrest her, sir,' Carol said. 'On thirty-six counts of murder. Because if we don't, as soon as her mother tells her what Lev said to Tony, she'll be on the next plane out of here. And if you think what we've got is thin for an arrest, it won't even get to first base on an extradition warrant.'

Brandon groaned, 'I don't like this, Carol. It feels like a fishing expedition.' There was a knock at the door. 'Come in,' Brandon shouted.

Stacey walked in looking very pleased with herself.

'I thought you'd want to see this,' she said, laying the folder she carried on the table.

'What's this?' Brandon asked.

'The CSIs who turned over Aziz's flat found a receipt for a Coke and a cake at the City Art Gallery on Friday morning. So we took the initiative and seized the CCTV footage from the café and the gallery. We've got the whole thing upstairs, but I thought you'd like to see the edited highlights now.'

Brandon flipped the file open and they all stared at the contents. The first photo showed Yousef Aziz sitting at a table reading the paper, Coke and cake in front of him. In the next shot, Rachel Diamond was approaching from behind carrying a newspaper. The next shot showed her putting the paper on the table in front of Yousef. In the final shot, she was beyond him, no longer carrying the paper. 'Three points of contact between them,' Carol said. 'I say it's definitely time to go fishing.' Brandon still looked dubious, but he nodded his assent.

'Look on the bright side, John,' said Tony. 'This way you get to tell CTC to piss off.'

Three months later

A bright Sunday afternoon, a classic Northern England landscape of high moors and long valleys. A scarlet Ferrari convertible, top down, drifted along a single-track road that wound uphill to a high plateau. 'Where are we going?' Tony asked Carol. 'And why are we going there in Kevin's car?'

'It really doesn't matter how many times you ask, I'm not going to tell you till we get there.'

'I hate surprises,' he grumbled.

'You'll appreciate it,' Carol said. 'So stop whining.'

A couple of miles on, the road flattened out. On the moor, shooting blinds stuck out of the bracken and cotton grass like gun turrets on a ship. A track cut off to the right and Carol pulled up. She reached into the back seat and grabbed a backpack. 'Come on,' she said. 'This is it.'

Tony looked around at the blank landscape. 'This is what?'

'Follow me.' She set off down the track, then turned round to wait for him. The limp was still noticeable. She wondered if it would ever disappear completely. They were talking about replacing the joint, she knew. But he wasn't keen on the idea of more surgery. Not even at the hands of the redoubtable Mrs Chakrabarti.

'I still can't walk far, you know,' he said, catching up with her.

'We're not going far.' About half a mile down the track, the hill dropped away abruptly, providing a spectacular view of the valley below and, at its head, a fine castle. 'This'll do nicely,' Carol said. She opened the backpack and took out a lightweight groundsheet. They sat down next to each other and she produced two pairs of binoculars, a half bottle of champagne and two glasses. She glanced at her watch. 'Perfect timing.'

'Are you going to tell me what is going on?'

'Use your eyes.' She handed him a pair of binoculars. 'Look up the valley, towards the castle.' As she spoke, a wisp of smoke twisted into the sky. Then there was a sudden whoosh of flame and a swathe of greenery turned scarlet and yellow and black with fire and smoke.

'Is that what I think it is?' Tony asked, gazing at the spectacle through his binoculars.

'Lord Pannal's poison garden,' Carol said. 'He's been wanting to do it since the day we arrested Jack Anderson. But we needed to be sure the prosecution and the defence had done all the research they needed. They both signed off on it on Friday, so His Lordship's finally got his way.'

'I see now why you borrowed the Ferrari.' Tony lowered the glasses. 'Is Anderson still pleading guilty?'

Carol nodded, twisting the champagne cork with

her thumbs. With a soft pop, it flew out and she poured it. 'His brief has tried everything to get him to change his mind, but he's smart enough to understand that, if he sticks with guilty, almost nothing will come out in court about the reasons why he went off the rails the way he did. And of course, since the toxicology guys found the pessary in his pocket was loaded with strychnine, it would be hard to argue that he was just an innocent bystander.'

'No kidding. Did you ever find out how he administered the roofies?'

'Ice cubes. One side of the tray was laced with rohypnol. The other side was clear.' She gave a little snort of laughter. 'The side with the drugs had a big "R" written on it in magic marker, to keep him straight.'

Tony sipped his drink. 'I wondered at the time if he was going to cheat us.'

'Cheat us? How?'

'The cyanide capsule in the shirt button. Or whatever. I wouldn't have been surprised.'

He stared out over the valley. 'Anything new on Rachel Diamond?'

'She's still protesting her innocence. But we have witnesses to the fact that the Diamonds' marriage was shaky. And the stuff Stacey managed to get off her office computer coupled with the handover in the gallery café is going to nail her. You did a brilliant job, figuring that out.'

He shook his head. 'It was a very strange time for me. The pain, the drugs, the weirdness of the cases. And my mother.' *And the fact that we hardly stopped fighting from start to finish.*

'Has she been in touch?'

'No. She probably won't be, until the next time she wants something from me.'

Carol leaned into him. 'Are you still thinking about trying to find out more about your father?'

He sighed. Sometimes he wished she wouldn't pick at his scabs. He knew she did it out of concern and affection, but that didn't mean it didn't hurt. When his father had been unknown, he'd been able, like Jack Anderson, to inhabit his dreams. Now there was a flesh-and-blood reality to investigate, he wasn't sure he wanted that part of his inheritance. 'I never thanked you properly for sorting Vanessa out,' he said.

'It's all right. I know it's complicated for you.'

He looked down at her, hair gleaming in the sun, long legs stretched out in front of her. Anyone observing them would presume them to be a long-standing couple, out for a Sunday-afternoon walk, comfortable with each other. The truth, like most things in his life, was far more intricate and less attractive. He gave a wry smile. 'It's just that sometimes I wish you'd never stopped me signing,' he said.

She pulled away and looked at him, shocked and hurt. 'You wish I'd just stood by and let your mother rip you off?'

'No, that's not it,' he said, struggling to find the words. 'We spend so much of our lives, you and me, figuring out the answers to mysteries. We've got so into the habit of it that we can't leave anything alone. We've always got to take the wheels off and see how it works. And increasingly, I find myself wishing for a bit of inscrutability and vagueness. Being and doing instead of thinking and analyzing.'

'You're not talking about your father now.'

'No,' he said, lying back and looking at the sky. 'I'm not.'